THE
RAGGED
EDGE
OF
NIGHT

ALSO BY OLIVIA HAWKER

Writing as Libbie Hawker

Tidewater
Baptism for the Dead

THE RAGGED EDGE OF NIGHT

OLIVIA HAWKER

LAKE UNION
PUBLISHING

Text copyright © 2018 by Libbie Hawker
All rights reserved.

Published by Lake Union Publishing, Seattle

www.apub.com

Amazon, the Amazon logo, and Lake Union Publishing are trademarks of Amazon.com, Inc., or its affiliates.

ISBN-13: 9781503900905 (hardcover)
ISBN-10: 1503900908 (hardcover)
ISBN-13: 9781503902121 (paperback)
ISBN-10: 1503902129 (paperback)

Cover design by Rex Bonomelli

Printed in the United States of America

First Edition

In memory of our Opa, *Josef Anton Starzmann,*
1904 to 1988.
And for my husband, Paul; my mother-in-law, Rita;
and Aunt Angie, with love.

AUTHOR'S NOTE

In this work, the Nationalsozialistische Deutsche Arbeiterpartei (the National Socialist German Workers' Party), has been abbreviated as "NSDAP" or referred to as "the Party" or "the Nazi Party." The Schutzstaffel (a paramilitary organization under the NSDAP) is usually abbreviated to "SS." Certain factual elements, including the timing of some events, have been altered for the sake of storytelling.

PART 1

FATHERLAND

SEPTEMBER 1942

1

The train picks up speed as it leaves Stuttgart. He grew up here, amid long shady streets footed in ancient cobblestones and gardens bright-spotted with afternoon light, but it is no longer the place Anton knew when he was young. Stuttgart is slowly falling, its gray innards exposed, blocks of cement cracked like bones, and the bowels of shops and houses ripped open, spilling into the streets. Dust, like ash, hazes the air. How many bombs have fallen on the city of his childhood? He lost count long ago. It is not the place he knew as a boy, but no place in Germany is the same.

He presses his forehead against the window and looks back. The wire rims of his spectacles tick against the glass. In the train's wake, he can just make out, if he strains hard to see it, the long black line of the track. Straight, perfectly straight, like the road to Riga, crossed by a whirl of cold gray cement dust, bomb dust, dancing this way and that, as if anyone has reason to dance.

He cannot help but feel some affinity for all this gray. It hasn't been a year since he put away his friar's habit; gray still suits him, still offers mute comfort, even when he finds it in the corpse of a city. There was a time, those first weeks dressed in an ordinary man's clothes, trousers and shirt, when he told himself that this would not be forever. *When the war ends,* he told himself, *the Catholic orders will be free to practice again. I will be a friar again, and everything will be restored, will go back to the way it was.* That is a story he no longer believes, a tale he cannot tell himself. Someone has remade this world—this place we, the people of Germany, once called home. What passed has passed, and gone is gone. He wears trousers every day now.

Anton straightens in his seat. The newspaper in his lap, neatly folded, rattles its few dry pages together. He lays his hand upon it, palm down, like a friend's hand falling on your shoulder or a priest's quiet blessing.

The last small houses at the edge of Stuttgart fall away. The scar of the city lies behind; here the earth's flesh is whole and blooming—fields of barley ripening, browning in the late-summer sun, and cattle in their pastures, standing belly-deep in green ponds or arrested in their slow progress to the milking shed by the rapid perspective of the passing train. Color and life, sudden and everywhere, lift the pall of silence from the train car. Conversation picks up—tentative, low. Who does not speak quietly in public these days?

In the seat behind him, a woman says, "I wonder if the White Rose will come here, to Stuttgart."

Her companion, a man: "Hush."

"I only wondered," the woman says. "I didn't say—"

"Hush all the same."

You know it isn't safe to speak of resistance. Not in a place like this, the narrow confines of a train, where anyone may hear and no one can hide. In this country, dissenters emerge like ants from every dark crevice. They are small and scuttling, but before they are crushed, they will bite the descending heel and leave a painful sting. The White Rose is not the only party of resistance. The Social Democrats—the Sopade—may have been banned when Hitler seized power, but despite the imprisonment and murder of their leaders, despite their dissemination by exile, they have not left us entirely. The Freie Arbeiter Union have not forgotten the part they played in the November Revolution. Their pamphlets have been outlawed—merely to possess one could mean death—but still they are printed, still they are read. Catholics and Protestants, who refuse to see eye to eye on matters of doctrine, have joined hands in this cause. It seems that every week Anton hears of another speech given by some brave Father in a public square, another treatise written by a preacher or a Jesuit or a doomed, earnest nun exhorting the German people to listen to reason, to heed the cold, choking voice of their own hearts.

Resistance is everywhere, but the White Rose is, perhaps, the most poignant incarnation. It is a children's movement—or, at least, Anton can't help but think of them as children. Half his age and braver than lions, braver than he ever was. The young students of Munich have taken to the streets with pamphlets and paint. Since June, they have covered brick walls with their slogans, imploring their fellow Germans to resist: *"Widerstand!"* They have covered the streets with their leaflets—God alone knows who prints those subversive and deadly things. In the three months since these children have risen to their feet, Anton's mood has grown darker and his sleep more restless. How long can resisters hold out? Once Hitler turns his flat, cold stare on Munich, the White Rose will wither and fade. The Führer will pluck those tender petals one by one and grind them underfoot. Anton could almost accept it, if these were grown men and women. But the founders of the White Rose and the students who follow them—they are too young, too precious. The whole of their lives lies ahead. Or should lie ahead, if God had more power in Germany than Hitler.

There was a time when children sang before church, *Dear God, keep me pious, so I will go to Heaven.* Now we chant in pubs and on the streets, at dinner parties and in our sleep: *Lord God, keep me quiet, so I don't end up in Dachau.*

After a pause, the woman on the train says, "I thank God we've been spared the worst of it here. There's much more damage in Berlin."

"A funny thing, to thank God," says the man beside her.

"What do you mean by that?"

Silent, listening, Anton watches the countryside pass by. A hedgerow of sunflowers splits a mown field. He remembers playing among the sunflowers as a boy—their dry-smelling stalks like a palisade, the whisper of their leaves. Yellow light that came down, filtered through the petals. His sister made a playhouse among the sunflowers: *Anton, you must be the father of my house, and tell my little children: if you don't wash up for supper, Mother will be cross!*

"I mean," says the man, "there isn't any sense in bringing God into the war. What has He to do with any of this? Don't tell me you think anything the Führer has done is part of God's plan."

The woman does not speak. Nor does Anton. The sound of his sister's voice vanishes from memory.

At length, the woman says, "You talk as if you don't believe in God at all." She sounds as if she might cry.

Her companion is quick to answer, quick to defend. "It's only this: I've never seen God. Why should I credit Him for a blessing, or leave Him any blame? Men are quite capable of destroying the world on their own, as we can plainly see. They don't need any help from above."

Before he can stop himself, before he can think, Anton turns in his seat. "I have never seen Hitler, either—not in the flesh—yet I believe in him."

The couple are young. They stare at him, faces blank with shock. Moment by moment, they go pale, then paler still. The woman lifts a hand to cover her mouth. Her neat dark hair is rolled and pinned above her smooth, pretty brow, but fear mars her beauty. The man's eyes widen with panic and then a black flash that says, *I will fight; you won't take us easily.* An instant later, grim acceptance settles over his features. His mouth turns down, steel-hard and calm. Anton can see the fellow bracing himself, reconciling with whatever must come next. What he said about the Führer . . . what his companion said about the White Rose, that wistful tone in her voice, the tentative hope upwelling. One never knows, these days, who listens and reports, and who listens and agrees.

6

Lord bless me, I have frightened them out of their wits. Anton smiles. It is a friendly, calming smile, so wide it seems too large for his narrow face. Straightaway, without sound reason, that smile puts the young couple at ease. He can do that without thinking: put a person at ease, convince them all is well, there is nothing to fear, life and the Lord are good. It's one of his gifts. He uses it liberally, whenever occasion demands. If God gives you a gift, are you not obligated to employ it? *Lord, grant me the strength to use what poor talents You have given me, wisely and well. And whatever I do, let me do it for Your true purpose and not the whim of any man.*

The young fellow crosses his arms, sighs, and settles back in his seat. He won't look at Anton now but studies the passing landscape with a frown. All the same, Anton can see relief flooding his body. His cheeks color more with every rapid beat of his heart. The woman giggles. She kisses her fingertips to Anton. He has taken her part in the argument; that's as good as a win. Anton offers an apologetic shrug—*sorry for startling you*—and turns again, determined this time to mind his own business.

He never has seen Hitler, not face-to-face. But how could he fail to believe? The proof is ever-present; memory, knit red into his marrow, will never let him rest.

The land, the world, tracks backward through time. From the hard, colorless age of Stuttgart—a place that is all stiff joints and stubborn resistance against the Tommies—the Württemberg countryside flourishes into soft green youth. Beyond farm and pasture, dark reaches of woodland extend along ridges never touched by a plow, as if the Black Forest, too, is making its way consciously east, leaving ruin and desolation behind. To the south, the Swabian Jura rises and falls, waves of varicolored blue, mountain crests lost in a glow of low-hanging, mist-white cloud. Stuttgart looked like this once, when Anton was a child. He thinks of the children—the living ones, the ones in whom hope still resides—and he slips his hand down into the pocket of his jacket, where his rosary hides. He prays Hail Mary, pinching every pale bead. The beads, like years lost, lives lost, impress themselves in his flesh. *Heilige Maria, Mutter Gottes, bitte für uns Sünder jetzt und in der Stunde unseres Todes.*

The train jolts over some rough stretch of track. The newspaper shivers and slides across his lap, threatening to fall to the floor. With his free hand, he stills it. It would seem almost a sacrilege for that paper to land among the tramping feet, the mud and dust. It's this newspaper that brought him clarity, renewed ambition, and strength of will when he'd thought all hope gone for good. Lulled by the rocking of the car, he dozes, rosary in one hand, purpose in the other, until the train slows in a hiss of steam and the conductor calls the stop at Neckar and Unterboihingen.

When he steps from the train, he bats away a cloud of steam that reeks of coal and heat and settles his hat in place. The sun is bright this afternoon; it raises a glare from the white stucco station and the houses beyond. Unterboihingen is a village from a fairy tale, all brick and white plaster, high-peaked roofs, dark beams of ancient wood crossed below steep-angled eaves. This is the old, the original, Germany, unaltered since the days before there were states or Deutsches Reich, before there existed any Axis of power.

A young man in a smart station uniform approaches and stands ready beside the compartment. "Any bags, *mein Herr?*"

"Oh—yes," Anton says, rather hesitant. "A few, I'm afraid."

The attendant raises the baggage-hold door.

"This trunk here." Anton points; the attendant retrieves the old chest with its creaking leather handles and age-worn straps. "And that one, with the ropes tying the lid shut."

"Heavy," the young man notes.

"This one here, and that one in the back."

The attendant stifles his annoyance as he crawls on hands and knees into the belly of the compartment. He drags the heavy trunk out and lets it fall hard onto the platform. Anton slips him a few coins for his trouble. Then the attendant raps a signal on the car door, and the train coughs, groans, and crawls away.

Anton waits beside his baggage. Eastward, the train diminishes. When it has gone, taking the stink of its hot breath, the natural scent of Unterboihingen flows in around him like a flood: dry grass; slow water in the ditches; the sharp, rustic bite of animal dung. In the distance, cattle low to the hollow accompaniment of their collar bells. The music carries, as sound is apt to do on a still summer day, broken and intermittent, comfortable across a long stretch of hazy afternoon.

A handful of boys tumbles onto the tracks, scuffling and laughing together, forelocks sticking to sweaty brows. They are thirteen, fourteen, playing in the last summer of their youth. They search between the sleepers for bits of flattened tin. In a year or two, three at most, they will be old enough for the Wehrmacht. They will be pressed into service, channeled to the Eastern Front via Hitler Youth. Serving the country, as if this country can find no better use for its children than to catch bullets in some Russian field.

"You must be Herr Starzmann." The thick voice belongs to a stout man with a little dark mustache not unlike the Führer's and a bald pate shining through patchy hair. He emerges rather languidly from the station's shaded porch. Perhaps all things move slowly in a town like Unterboihingen—men, cattle, the bleak thoughts that follow you everywhere. The stout man extends his hand; Anton shakes it. "Bruno Franke. Pleased to meet you."

"My new landlord." Anton offers one of his winning smiles; Herr Franke takes little notice. "I'm very glad you found the room to board me, Herr Franke. This is such a small village. If you hadn't had that room available, I would have found myself bedding down in a pigsty come nightfall."

"It's not an especially large room," Franke says with a withering look at the four travel trunks. "You might prefer the pigsty."

9

"God willing, I won't need to board for more than a week." Unconsciously, he pats the newspaper, tucked tight beneath his arm.

"I've brought my truck. There's room for your things, but I'm afraid I can't help you load them up. My knees aren't what they used to be."

"And my back leaves something to be desired. A Wehrmacht injury. We two old fellows, eh?"

Herr Franke shrugs and turns back toward the station.

Something darts among the railroad tracks. The sudden motion among Unterboihingen's wheat-dry laziness catches Anton's eye. One of the boys has bent to retrieve a bit of something from the gravel, hot and black with coal dust. He holds it up; the little treasure he has found winks in the sunlight, and he crows to his friends.

"A moment," Anton calls to Herr Franke. He steps down from the platform and approaches the boys. "My friends"—smiling—"how would you like to earn a little money?"

They abandon their hunt for mangled bits of tin. They flock around him, eyes bright and eager.

"I've got four big trunks to load on a truck, and then they must be carried up the stairs to my boarding room. Who will help me?" Five boys; he calculates quickly what money he has, what he can safely spare. "Twenty reichspfennig to everyone who helps."

The boys cheer. Twenty reichspfennig will buy you a nut bar or even a bit of chocolate, if you know where to find it. He only prays the boys won't spend their money on the sticker books the government has placed in every toy store and candy shop from Munich to Cologne. Each page has frames, and titles, but no portraits. The object, you see, is for children to hunt down and trade for the sticker cards that will complete their album. What better way to make a child love the Führer and his pack of demons than to make those vile creatures the center of a harmless game?

The boys follow Anton like pups, jostling and yipping, cuffing one another in good-natured excitement. In no time, they have carried all four trunks from the platform and lifted them to the bed of Franke's truck.

Franke is already waiting at the wheel, staring out rather peevishly above the sign painted on the truck's door: "Franke's Fine Furniture."

Anton grins at his new landlord. "If it's all the same to you, I'll ride in the back with the boys."

"Suit yourself." Franke starts the engine.

Anton climbs up to the truck's bed. For a moment, he feels happy and energetic, as he must have felt when he was thirteen, fourteen, but that was so long ago. Like the boys, he sits on the lid of a trunk. He takes the promised coins from his pocket, passes them around, and the children hush themselves, turning the reichspfennig over in their dirt-blackened fingers. There is a sort of magic in those coins, the bright metallic gleam of something unexpected: an adult who has kept his word to children.

"I have this, too." As the truck makes its way along the dirt roads of Unterboihingen, Anton retrieves a packet of waxed paper from his knapsack. He opens it carefully, revealing amber chunks of hard honey candy. "Take as many as you'd like."

The boys make quick work of the candy. "These aren't like the honey drops we have here," one says. "Where did you get them?"

"Prussia."

They look at Anton with greater reverence now, all wide eyes and cheeks flushed with awe.

"Are you a soldier, *mein Herr*?"

"I was," he says. "But my back, you know. It's a minor complaint, but still—that's why I couldn't manage the trunks myself."

"How was your back hurt?" They nudge each other, elbows to ribs, fidgeting in anticipation of his answer. Who is greater, what fellow is more a man, than the soldier with his guns and his grenades? What man is better than one who fights to defend the Fatherland?

He can think of a thousand better men. But it wouldn't serve to teach these children any better if he were to scold them or cast shadows on their boyish fantasies. He didn't stand fifteen years at the head of a classroom for nothing. He knows how to hand along a lesson, and how to make it stick.

Offhandedly, he says, "Jumped out of an airplane, going into Riga."

Two of the boys shout together, *"Prima!"* Another cries, "Cool!" It's a Tommy word, the sort of thing a Brit or an Australian would say—a puppet of the International Jewry, to quote Goebbels. The boys goggle at their friend for a moment, stunned by his audacity. Then they dole out his punishment: a hard slug on the arm, one from each. The offender takes his licks with red-faced meekness.

Anton laughs gently as the boy rubs his smarting arm. He finds one last piece of candy in his pocket and passes it to the lad; all is forgiven. But laughter feels foreign to him now. When he looks back on his Wehrmacht days, it is not to find joy or pride in heroism. The Fatherland holds no claim on Anton's heart; it deserves none of his loyalty. The Führer took Anton and held him under duress. Hitler and those poor, damned souls who follow him ripped away the friar's habit and replaced it with a soldier's uniform. The injustice of it still takes his breath away whenever he allows himself to think of it—as does every outrage, every numberless affront, that has followed. And yet, Anton was lucky. He only marched, and fired his rifle in the direction of men he never intended to hit. There was no crueler service to which he could be compelled, no more heartrending work the Party could force upon him. A friar has no wife, no children—no love that may be weaponized. There is no tender, hallowed gun to press against his temple. The only life he stands to lose is his own, and so he is as good as worthless, impervious to the Führer's tactics.

But he did see Riga burned. He smelled the thick black smoke, heavy in the hot July air. He had gone to Latvia under the banner of liberation. He could have borne the loss of the friar's life, if his company had freed those people from Soviet oppression. But the Reich had intended no such thing after all. The Latvians who welcomed German intervention fell at once under a new brand of despotism, almost before their cheers had died on their lips.

My back, you know. A hard landing in a black field, on a warm but windy summer night. Rolling in the lines of his parachute, the tumbling world a thunder in his ears. The Franciscan novitiate did not instruct its men in the art of paratrooping. A minor complaint. His back was hurt in the jump, but even so, he could have marched for miles more, days more, years without end. But he decided in Riga, under flags of smoke, with the screams of hopeless women in his ears: never again would he lend his back or his legs, nor his hands nor his heart, to any purpose that served Adolf Hitler.

He lied to evade further service in the Wehrmacht. A damaged back. To lie is a sin, but God also commanded: *Du sollst nicht töten*—thou shalt not kill. The Lord will be his judge—a God he has never seen, but in Whom, nonetheless, he believes.

2

Herr Franke had not been lying when he said the room was small. There is barely space to fit the four trunks, let alone Anton. A narrow bed stands opposite the door; above it is a small window with a heavy curtain, dark blue, pulled aside to admit a peaceful golden light. A washstand, a round mirror above it, a porcelain pot beneath the bed. Pinned to the drapery, a note in precise handwriting: *Achtung! Halten Sie den Vorhang bei Dunkelheit geschlossen.* Keep the curtain closed after dark.

Once the boys have gone, clattering down the staircase—at least the boarding room has a private stair—Anton stands in the middle of his new home, hands on hips, head ducked to avoid the sharp, treacherous slope of the ceiling. Below, he can hear Franke going about his business in the furniture shop, thumping and scraping, cursing at a child or a dog.

He checks his pocket watch, the one his father gave him when, at age eighteen, he ceased to be Josef Anton Starzmann. He donned the gray robe of his order and became Bruder Nazarius instead. Never had he imagined that he would take up his old name again. Never could he have foreseen this—the Catholic orders disbanded by a fanatical government. The complacent ones went wherever the NS ordered them: nuns and monks, Fathers and friars, forced back into the lay world, the dull world beyond their cloisters. Those who did not comply met a different fate. Often he has asked himself: *Was it cowardice, to abandon*

Bruder Nazarius so easily, to become Anton again? Should I have fought and died for my faith? For many months, he believed he was a coward, until he heard the voice of God calling. After so many months of black silence, the thunder of certainty came again. He understood that the Lord had preserved him for a new work and was giving him a chance at redemption. God woke him from a long slumber, raised him up like Lazarus. It was not his lot to fight and die—not yet. There is still work to do, in God's name.

The afternoon light flashes on the watch face, running a golden circle around its rim. Time is short. He returns the watch to his pocket, where it settles among the beads of his rosary. With a brisk energy, he sets about making himself presentable.

He opens one trunk, the smallest. Even though he knows what he will find beneath its lid—he is braced for the sight—still the curves of brass strike him with a jolt of pain. Like the other three, this trunk is filled with the musical instruments he has kept for seven months. They are his relics, the last reminders of what was lost. Like bones in an ossuary they lie, silent yet voluble in memory. Their bells hold the echoes of remembered lives, and in the reflections bent and distorted around their smooth curves, he can see the expressionless faces of his children.

A bundle of clothing lies tucked in one corner of the trunk, pushed down deep, below the circle of a French horn. He extracts it; the bundle is tied with a cheerful blue ribbon. That's the work of his sister, Anita, who had lived as Sister Bernadette until the Führer tore up his own Reichskonkordat and spat in the eye of the Holy See. After their respective orders were destroyed, Anton and Anita both stumbled back to their mother's house on the edge of Stuttgart, stunned and bereft, neither knowing what to do next. When he'd met Anita at the station, she had stepped off the train in a green dress, sober in color yet fashionably cut, and her shoes had been of patent leather with smart, clicking heels. Her hair was pinned and rolled just like the girl's, the one back on that last train, who had kissed her fingers to Anton. He hadn't seen Anita's hair since she had donned her habit at age sixteen. It was no longer the golden yellow he remembered from childhood, bright as falling water. It had darkened to soft, pale brown, like the velvet of a mouse's pelt, and there were strands of white caught up in her curls, catching the light and glittering. They were both getting older now, but Anita was still as lovely as she'd ever been. He had thought, *How pretty my sister is in laywoman's clothes.* Shame had struck him, cold and hard, immediately after. What kind of man finds a nun agreeable when she has been stripped of her sisterhood?

Anita had faced up to their new reality with her usual pluck and game. "I was a bride of Christ," she said that day, laughing ruefully and taking her little brother's arm, "but I suppose He has annulled our union."

"You shouldn't joke that way," Nazarius said—Anton said.

"Don't worry." She winked at him, spirited, unsisterly. He could see it still, could feel his own hesitant amusement. He remembered the way she had tilted her head toward him, her strangely uncovered head with its ash-colored curls. "Lord Christ and I, we'll make it up, as soon as all this mess with the Führer is sorted."

Anton unties the blue ribbon. The sober cloth of his friar's habit unrolls across his bed. Anita has ironed and folded his best suit, wrapped it in the habit, but he sets the suit aside and runs his hands over the coarse gray wool. The knotted cord that was his belt is there, too, coiled neatly upon itself, a sleeping serpent dreaming of lost Eden. He can all but feel the cord's weight swinging from his waist. The habit still smells of the school, St. Josefsheim, Kirchenstraße. Wood polish and chalk dust, apples from the orchard, the pipe Brother Nazarius smoked each evening when the children were tucked in their beds. He can smell sweet myrrh from a swinging censer and the sweeter hands of the little ones, sticky from the candy he brought from town twice a week if they were good. They were always good.

Perhaps he'd been too naïve then, a fresh young friar brimming over with earnest desire to heal the world and the unshaken belief that he could do it, too. From his hands would the mercy of Christ extend and pour out into the world like blood from His sacred wounds. And then, this unexpected resurrection: Anton pulled up from the very grave into which they had thrown Bruder Nazarius. This is not the life he pictured when he first donned his habit. But this is not the sort of life anyone dreams of. Even Hitler, he thinks, must be surprised that he ever got so far—that it has all been so simple to take, to destroy. In his moments of despair—and there are many—Anton wonders whether God Himself ever dreamed it could come to this.

He unfolds the suit. Anita, bless her, pressed it perfectly, and scented it with lavender and cedar to keep the moths away. He closes the blue curtain, leaving the note pinned in place. A trace of yellow light filters around the curtain's edge. He dresses carefully by that dim glow, rolls the old suit in the friar's habit, and tucks the bundle away among the silent horns. Clumsy hands struggle to recall the necktie knots his father taught him when he was a boy. It has been almost a year since the order was disbanded; that should be enough time for a man to learn his knots again. He frowns into the little round mirror on the wall, talking himself through the motions. Cross over and tuck behind, pinch the top as you pull down. When he has combed his hair and adjusted the angle of his glasses on the bridge of his long, thin nose, he is surprised to see Brother Nazarius looking back at him, despite the suit and tie. Perhaps the old identity is not as dead as he first thought. Did not Saint Francis say, *The world is my cloister, my body is my cell, and my soul is the hermit within?*

There is work to be done here, in this small village of Unterboihingen—good work and true. After many dark months of silence, of distance, the Lord has spoken. He has called the friar who is no longer a friar; He has awakened Anton to his appointed task. Father of the fatherless and protector of widows is God in His holy habitation.

17

3

He knows her at once when he sees her, though they have never met before. Elisabeth is as prim and hard as her handwriting, her manner every bit as guarded as the letters made her seem. She is sitting on the edge of an iron chair at a small table outside a bakery. The immaculate light of afternoon, golden and low, falls on her like a halo. In that perfect glow, she is neat and composed—rigidly so, not a pleat or button out of place. Her dress is of a blue so deep it is almost char gray, the neckline high and unadorned. Her brown hair is dull but arranged in faultless symmetry, framing and emphasizing a round, unsmiling face. There is a sense of order about her, a stoic control he can all but feel from across the street. A hard determination to hold all things together in a world that, day by day, falls ever more apart.

When she notices Anton—crossing the dirt road from the direction of Franke's Fine Furniture—she seems to recognize him, too. The woman's eyes lock with his; she lifts her teacup but doesn't drink. She watches him without the least betrayal of thought or emotion as he comes, smiling, toward her. Midway across the street, he sees himself in a wrenching flash, as if through a woman's eyes—an inversion of perspective, a lurch back through time into a mind-set he hasn't adopted since he took his vows to the order. He had been youthful then, and when men are young, they believe themselves the handsomest things in God's creation. Now, thirty-eight years old and with such foolish convictions long behind him, he is rather shaken by the realization that he falls somewhat short of attractive. Very tall, with the blondest hair and bluest eyes the Führer could desire—his coloring is a rebuke to him now, a daily reminder that he was deemed worthy of life while others more deserving were judged unfit. His face is as narrow as his body. His eyes sit too closely together, an effect somewhat mitigated by his round glasses, though the glasses also draw attention to the nose on which they perch. Large and curved, it is far too strong for such a thin, delicate face. But his eyes . . . will she be put off by them? Anita used to say, teasing, *Shall I jab my finger between your eyes, little Anton, and pop them farther apart?* When he swallows this sudden, unexpected fear, his prominent Adam's apple presses uncomfortably against the knot of his tie. At least he has that kind, disarming smile at his ready disposal. It is some small consolation.

When he reaches her table—shuffles up somehow, though this storm of misgiving drags at him, shackled to his ankle—Anton doffs his hat. "Good afternoon, *meine Dame*. Would you happen to be Elisabeth Hansjosten?"

She blinks once. "I am Elisabeth Hansjosten Herter." Her voice is lovely, smooth and rich, even if she uses it like a sword. She reaches out to shake hands before Anton does. "You are Josef Starzmann?"

"Yes—but please, call me Anton."

She gestures to the other wrought-iron chair. Numb, with heart pounding, he sits.

"Thank you again for answering my advertisement." She picks up her teacup, shifts it absently from one hand to the other, and sets it down again. He has never seen a woman look more self-possessed, yet the cup gives away her secret anxiety—the way it moves from hand to hand, and its undiminished fullness.

He brings out another smile, doing his best to put Elisabeth at ease. "Make no mention of it. I brought the very paper along, in fact." He produces it from beneath his jacket and lays it on the table between them—the Catholic periodical *Esprit*, which he has carried all this way from Stuttgart. It is markedly thinner than in years past—paper rationing, to say nothing of the suppression of the Catholic voice—but at least it is neatly folded. "Just in case I didn't find you here and had to prove I was not a madman to all the ladies I pestered. 'Pardon me, are you Elisabeth? Are you Elisabeth?'" He laughs.

Her stern mouth yields no ground to the joke. "Why would you not find me here?"

He stops laughing. He's almost grateful for the excuse. "Never mind." He tries yet another smile. His charm will work on her sooner or later. He's determined that it will. "I am glad you agreed to meet me."

"It is I who am glad," she says, sounding more businesslike than grateful. "You came a long way."

"The train ride was pleasant. This is a beautiful village. Lovely countryside. Of course, you said as much in the two or three letters we exchanged, but I had no way of knowing just how beautiful this place was until I saw it for myself."

"And you have found somewhere to stay?" *In case I decide against you after all*, her brusque manner says.

"Yes. Herr Franke has let me a room above his shop."

Now, at last, her expression softens—only for a moment, with the slightest lift of one corner of her mouth. It's a very marginal smile, and there is something sickly in her amusement. But it provides a fleeting glimpse inside her armor, and the small relinquishment of tension puts Anton at ease. "Bruno Franke?" she says. "Bruno Möbelbauer. That's what the children call him." The name means "furniture maker." An appealingly simple epithet.

"Your children. Tell me something about them, please. You've mentioned them in your letters, of course, but I would love to know more." He has already made up his mind to love these fatherless *Lieblinge*, despite knowing almost nothing about their characters.

Most women brighten when they talk about children—theirs or anyone else's. Elisabeth does not. She lists their attributes flatly, as if reading from a bill of lading. "Albert, the eleven-year-old, is bright and inquisitive, always very thoughtful and kind. Paul is my boy of nine. He is very sweet, and helps me without being asked, but he often gets into trouble, being so young and not very thoughtful. Maria is six, as I have told you. I suppose I did not tell you that she is as full of mischief as the Lord ever permitted a girl to be." Not a hint of fondness, though she must love her children beyond all reason. Only love could have led her to take out that advertisement. This is a woman pushed beyond gladness, almost beyond hope. She has reached the end of her wits and her strength. Everything has worn her down—the war, the bombings, the long stretch of unrelieved hardship. And the stories we all hear, of removals from the internment camps to darker places. The places of extermination—Chełmno and Treblinka, Sobibór and Auschwitz-Birkenau. As if, merciful Jesus, the Einsatzgruppen were not shame enough for our people to bear.

Elisabeth needs his help. These children need his help—Albert and Paul and little Maria. Anton has never turned his back on a child in need, except when the guns of the Schutzstaffel forced him to do it. Except when the Schutzstaffel goaded him into unforgivable cowardice.

"Their father," Anton says gently. "Was it the war . . . ?"

Elisabeth's face goes blank as a wiped slate. She sits up straighter, shoulders square, hands precisely folded on the tabletop. "No, not the war. It was blood poisoning that took him."

"I'm sorry to hear it." He waits, inviting her to say more, but she only watches him, silent and firm. It's clear she will not speak another word on the subject of Herr Herter, the first husband. Anton must be content with her silence.

"Do you have any questions for me?"

"Yes," Elisabeth says. Now that they have broached the uncomfortable fact of her widowhood, she lifts the teacup again. This time she drinks, a long, thirsty draft; the tea has gone cool enough to take it in all at once. "In your letter, you said you were a brother of the Franciscans."

"I was."

"And you left the order because . . . ?"

He smiles. "It was not my choice to leave."

"Of course." She blushes, and the coloring of her cheeks seems to strip away years and hardship, revealing a bright yet delicate portrait of the girl she once was. She is like the soft white core of wood exposed by a carver's knife—hard outer layers stripped away, scars and weather-beaten crags gone for the moment. Inside, a tenderness, yielding and sweet. She says, "I am sorry, *mein Herr*. I should have been more thoughtful."

He laughs lightly. The sound lifts her brows, and perhaps her spirit. "You are no trouble to me, Elisabeth. If we are to be married, we must get comfortable with one another. We must speak freely."

"If. Yes." She picks up the paper, opens it to the advertisement section. Anton watches as she reads the notice she placed three weeks ago. It's a plea for mercy and relief, sent out in a moment of surpassing desperation to a world too tortured to care. She blushes again, as if for the first time she sees her plight through another person's eyes—Anton's, and those of all the other men who chanced to read her notice but were not moved to respond.

As for Anton, he has read Elisabeth's advertisement so many times, he can recite it like holy scripture.

Good churchgoing woman, widowed, mother of three. In need of a humble, patient man, willing to be a father to my children. Interest in legitimate marriage only. I have no money, so those who think to profit need not reply. Must be willing to relocate to Unterboihingen, Württemberg, as health will not permit us to move elsewhere.

She sets the paper down and looks at him—stares at him, assessing his fitness for the role, guessing at his motives. The moment stretches, silent but for a sudden clash of pans from somewhere inside the bakery and in the distance the low, repetitive clucks of a yard full of hens. Elisabeth is perfectly still, clear-eyed and considering. She is asking herself every question she can think to pose; Anton can all but hear her thoughts. *Have I done something foolish? Have I set in motion something I can never stop? He is a stranger to me; what kind of mother trusts the lives of her children to unknown hands? But Mother Mary, I am left with little choice.*

When she speaks, she asks a question Anton did not anticipate. "Will I be condemned for this, I wonder?"

"Condemned? I don't understand."

She lowers her eyes and turns the teacup on its saucer. "This is a kind of whoredom, wouldn't you say?"

Startled, he finds he can barely hold back a laugh. "Certainly, I would not say it. Your advertisement specified that you sought a legitimate marriage. God does not consider marriage a sin, *meine Dame*."

"He might consider this marriage a sin."

Her voice is so low, Anton hardly catches the words. He thinks perhaps he was not intended to hear them. Gently, he says, "What do you mean?"

Resolute, Elisabeth straightens. She lifts her face and meets Anton's eye with a frank, unwavering stare. "I made no secret that I am only seeking a husband for his money."

"Times are hard, Elisabeth. We all must do what we must do."

"But this? Does it not go too far, to offer . . . what a wife has to give . . . for money's sake? And anyhow, I still—" She breaks off and casts her eyes down again, but Anton can see the sudden shimmer of dampness on her lashes.

"You still love your first husband," he guesses.

Elisabeth doesn't shrink from his words. She only nods, calm and stoic. "Yes. So I wonder, is it a sin—is it harlotry—to marry under false pretense?"

Anton smiles, relieved or amused—or both. He sees at once how to set her mind at ease, and it's only now, in finding the solution to Elisabeth's turmoil, that he can identify the vague, formless fear that has clung to him from his first correspondence with the widow. Hitler may have torn away the friar's robes, but Brother Nazarius still lives in Anton's heart. From age eighteen, he has lived under a vow of chastity. Perhaps if he had left the order of his own accord, he might find it easier to imagine doing what husbands and wives do. He might picture himself leading any number of women into every conceivable variety of harlotry and whoredom. But this was never his choice, and he is not so eager to abandon his old Franciscan ways.

"You need not fear," he says quickly. "In truth, I . . . I can't engage in . . ." He clears his throat, uncertain what to say.

Elisabeth's brows lift again. She watches him, waiting and silent, but curiosity has replaced her shame.

Anton tries again. "I'm unable to father children." It's technically true. If he has no appetite for the act—if he is still a friar in his heart, bound by his vows—then it hardly counts as a lie. "I was injured in the Wehrmacht. You understand." Let her believe the injury was severe enough to render him incapable, if she chooses to believe it. It will make no difference; she'll never learn otherwise. Elisabeth needs a protector and partner, not a lover. Anton needs redemption for his sins. Each of them can give what the other seeks; there's no need to complicate this arrangement with the things ordinary husbands and wives take for granted.

"I see." Elisabeth's businesslike manner has returned. Some of the color has come back to her cheeks, too. The prospect of sharing home and bed with an impotent ex-soldier seems appealing.

"That's why I've sought out just this sort of arrangement," Anton says. "A widow, a good woman with several children of her own—she wouldn't expect more from me, now, would she? A girl who had never married and never known the joys of motherhood—she wouldn't care to take on a husband with my . . . limitations."

"But if you are"—her cheeks color again as she searches for the most delicate word—"incapable, then why marry at all?"

"Surely there's more to gain from marriage than *that*." He laughs lightly. "I'm seeking what all men seek: purpose. I want to be useful—do some good before the Lord calls me home."

Elisabeth nods. She seems to understand. Under her breath, she says, "The saints know, there is an imbalance of good and evil just now." Then she straightens suddenly and fixes Anton with a hard stare. "In one of your letters, you mentioned you're not a member of the Party."

He offers a small bow of acquiescence, hand to heart.

"Have you ever been? Might you be in the future?"

He says quietly, "The NSDAP stripped me of my place in this world. They disbanded my order, closed my school—and did more, besides. I will never be loyal to the Party. If that troubles you—"

"It doesn't trouble me," Elisabeth says at once. She smiles, then—the first smile she has shown. It is small, self-conscious, and restrained, but it suits her round face beautifully.

"It seems we see eye to eye, where political matters are concerned."

"It seems we do."

"I'm no expert on marriage, but I believe that gives us some small advantage—a chance for success."

"If you are content to be . . . well, shall we say, a companion—"

"I am quite content. So long as I may be useful." *So long as I may find forgiveness. A chance to do right—to protect those who cannot protect themselves, as I should have done when God first gave me the opportunity.*

"Then I . . . I am . . ." Elisabeth breathes deep, presses a hand to her stomach as if she seeks to quell a bout of nausea. She is not ready to say it, not yet. She can't release the past as easily as that. Who among us can? What has gone before drags behind. As we move through our lives, our workaday habits, we trail our ghostly wakes.

He gives her the courtesy of time and silence to order her thoughts, to set her heart upon the path. He feigns interest in the men across the street, walking slowly past a fabric shop (long closed, painted sign peeling), with their coats slung over shoulders and their armpits darkened by sweat. Anton can't help squinting as he watches the men pass, as if by narrowing his eyes he might see through flesh and bone, past the unassuming façade we all must show in the open, into their hearts and spirits. Who are these men, really? For that matter, who is Elisabeth? Even in quiet Unterboihingen, you can't be too confident, too careful. No place is free of disease. Hitler has breathed his hatred over the whole of Germany; there is no telling who is festering inside, who has succumbed to the black fever.

From the side of his gaze, even as he watches the men, Anton still sees Elisabeth. She seems to occupy the whole world. Her presence is looming, dominating—commanding in the urgency of her need. He has fixed his attention to the pale roundness of her face, the meticulous part of her hair, a straight line of scalp pinked by the sun. Or she has taken his attention and now holds it, a mild surprise to him. How long has it been since he looked at a woman this way? Twenty years? Even as a friar, he was still a man; to appreciate what God has made is no sin. But there was no possibility of romance in those days. No woman left Brother Nazarius sleepless—such longings would have been impractical—and if visions of feminine beauty haunted his thoughts when he ought to have been concentrating on his rosary or the Stations of the Cross, they did so no more often than memories of a rose garden or an especially moving line of music. Twenty years of celibacy have left him unprepared to confront his own heart. Elisabeth is attractive, in her way. Somewhat younger than he. She is no great beauty, though if her eyes were not so desolate and her mouth not so hard, she might come close. But outward beauty indicates nothing of real value—not to God and not to Anton. Little though he knows her, he can't help but admire her courage, her fortitude, the great towering force of her faith. He is willing to make this marriage work, provided she is also willing. Provided God forgives him for the lie—the second one he has told today. He can find the redemption he needs with this hard-eyed woman. He feels certain of that. And he can do her good, too; yoked together, they might find it easier to toil in the traces of life.

Still, Elisabeth hesitates. Her hand lies beside the empty teacup, and she is clenching her fingers hard, pressing her neatly filed nails into the skin of her thumb until the color drains away and whitens beneath the pressure.

"You don't have to decide now," Anton says.

"I might as well make up my mind. You've come all this way to meet me." Another pause. She looks down into the teacup, thoughtful or shy. "But you should meet the children first. If they don't take to you, there would be no point in going forward."

The thought shakes him for a moment—facing children again—but he pushes the fear away. This, after all, is why he has come to Unterboihingen. "I want very much to meet the children. I was a teacher, when I was still a Franciscan—I believe I told you as much, in our letters. Children are dear to me, and I flatter myself in thinking I've got a certain useful way with them."

Inside the bakery, he buys a box of *Hausfreunde*. Side by side, walking slowly, Anton and Elisabeth cross the town of Unterboihingen, talking and nibbling the butter cookies as they go. One drop at a time, Elisabeth thaws. They say the path to a man's heart runs through his stomach, but it's every bit as true for a woman. She licks the chocolate topping from her *Hausfreunde* slowly, making the moment last.

"I haven't tasted chocolate for so long."

"Neither have I."

"I feel I'm eating it too fast, and yet I want to pop the whole thing in my mouth in one bite. Who can say when we'll have another chance to enjoy chocolate? It's almost a miracle that our bakery had any today. The supplies have been unreliable for years, here in Unterboihingen, ever since the war began—supplies of everything, not only sweets."

"I imagine chocolate is easier to find in Berlin just now, but not by much."

She takes a sparing bite. "You paid far too much for these."

"Maybe," Anton says, laughing. "But it was worth it, don't you think? Anyway, the children will appreciate a little treat."

She examines her cookie for a moment, critical and stern—the same expression she wore outside the bakery, assessing the stranger Herr Starzmann. "The apricot marmalade in the middle . . . it isn't the same. The bakery used to make it a different way, when we first moved to the village."

"They've made the marmalade with honey, I assume," Anton says. "Ran out of white stamps for their sugar rations."

"I'm sure you're right. At least there are plenty of beehives in Unterboihingen, out there in the fields. We may run out of coal by wintertime, but we'll never suffer from bitter tea."

He likes her voice. It is mellow and confident; rich yet restrained chords of subtle humor play against a predictable melody of staunch sensibility. When he can hear the music in a person's soul, he can understand them. Music has been his mother tongue ever since, as a boy of ten, he taught himself to play the church organ. Pumping the great bellows with his feet on a Friday night, hands mashing clumsily on the yellowed ivory keys, while the priest swept the cobwebs from the corners of the nave and shouted, "Well done, Anton! Make a joyful noise unto the Lord, all ye lands!" His parents had had no money for lessons, but God opens every way for an earnest heart.

"It seems this little village has done well," he says. "As well as can be expected, in times like these. Compared to the cities I've seen—Stuttgart, Munich."

"Yes." A brief, disbelieving laugh. "I always liked city life, and I thought it a great hardship—almost a curse—to be stuck here in Unterboihingen. But Paul has bad lungs, you see; he can't take the city air. Ever since the war began, I've come to see country life as a blessing. I never imagined I could."

The dubious miracles devised by war.

She says, "There is something beautiful about this village, the community we've made. Something Godly. In the city, we would struggle more—never enough to eat, and the bombs—constant danger. My children would go hungry. There aren't enough stamps in all of Germany to keep Albert's belly full, not enough rations to feed a growing boy. But here, we have cows and goats for milk, and plenty of eggs. Fields full of potatoes and onions. And whatever we can't raise ourselves, we trade for. Everyone here raises a little more than his family needs, bakes a little more bread, kills an extra hen. We trade our humble excesses to one another. That way, no one suffers."

"I can see what you mean," he says. Godly. Surely this is the way the Lord intended mankind to live: neighbor loving neighbor, each brother safely kept.

"Strange, to think we tend to one another here, while the rest of the world . . ."

Her words trail away. She has forgotten the half-eaten cookie in her hand. Strange, that love can grow at all in a world shaded out, strangled by vines of hate. Reluctantly, Anton allows himself to consider the numbers. Fifty-four thousand dead, last month alone—and that is only the tally of German soldiers. Unfeeling figures, cold and stark, so emotionless a man could almost be forgiven for taking them in blandly with his morning tea and toast, like a report on the health of stocks he doesn't own. There is no count of civilian deaths—not that he can trust. Certainly, no admission of what goes on in the concentration camps, as if, by convenient omission, the Party can hide its sins from citizens and from God. There is little word from the press on enemy casualties, though when headlines crow, *Blitzkrieg! 5,500 tons dropped on London; British brought to their knees!*, one can infer.

But the British were not subdued, were they? And now, with their fleet bombed last December in Pearl Harbor, even the circumspect Americans have been goaded to fight. You hear the news in Munich. A man pulls his hat lower, sheltering beneath its brim. He says, *They never meant to bombard London in the first place. There's not a damned thing that fool of a Führer can get right.* You hear the news in Stuttgart, passed from mouth to ear beside the ruins of a church where smoke and dust still rise like incense to Heaven. The Reich suppresses and contorts the truth. The Reich lies outright, and what are we to do about it? The papers, like whipped dogs, piss themselves and cringe. Reporters sit up and beg. When the Master snaps his fingers, he wants a show of loyalty. But what can we expect? Any press not controlled by the Party disappeared by '34. Editors and journalists, declared racially impure, were made enemies of the state. If they didn't see what was coming and flee to France or Canada, then they met their ends in Dachau, knees knocking together in the predawn snow. Truth cannot feed your children. Integrity doesn't keep a man warm.

They pass a farmhouse. Barred and speckled hens scratch in the yard, cackling now and then as they fight over grubs. Elisabeth watches the birds until the farmhouse lies behind them. Then she turns again to face the road ahead. "Until this spring," she says, "I worked at the ration center. There were fifty or so women who worked with me; they came from every village along the Neckar, and each of us was responsible for packing the weekly ration boxes with our particular type of food. One lady cut salted pork to the right size, another put the pork into the boxes. Another put in the butter, another the cheese, and the marmalade, the flour, the sugar, and so on. Eggs were my duty. Each of us was expected to waste a certain amount of food every day. You can't help it, sometimes; even the most careful person will drop a bit of cheese or a jar of preserves every now and then. I never dropped a single egg, though; I simply wouldn't allow myself to do it. Those eggs were too precious. But I marked them down on my sheet, every day—the ones they expected me to drop, the eggs they allowed me to waste. When no one was looking, I slipped the extra eggs into my skirt pockets."

"For your children?" Anton guesses.

The look she gives him then is almost enough to wither. "Mother of mercy, no. I hope you don't think me selfish, Herr Starzmann. At the end of the day, before the drivers came to load the boxes on their delivery trucks, I hid the extra eggs among the neediest families' rations. The ones with little children and dead fathers, or sick babies, or mothers who had grown too sad to go on as they should, as we all must."

Abruptly, she looks down at her feet and will say no more. He wonders at her sudden silence, but a moment later, he finds the reason in her reddened cheek and the narrowing of those determined eyes. She has told him too much—this stranger, this man she has known for only an hour but whom she will marry, if God is willing. She has let him inside her heart. It's not a mistake she'll be quick to make again.

Elisabeth leads him down a rutted lane. Hollyhocks lean across rank ditches, proffering spikes of faded flowers, the last kindness of summer. Beyond the hollyhocks stands an ancient orchard, gnarled branches heavy with golden fruit, and amid the trees, a white stucco farmhouse, its first floor made of brick.

"This is your home?" Anton says, pleasantly surprised.

"No," she answers, apologetically. "Frau Hertz lives there—my landlady. She lets the old house in back—the original farmhouse, at least a hundred years old—and that's where we live, the children and I."

He can see the old house now through the glossy foliage of the apple trees. Age and tradition are evident in its simple utility. A gabled roof, undersized windows, the wood darkened by years, almost to black. The house stands high above the earth, raised up on thick wooden piers. A stone-and-mortar wall surrounds the first floor; blue daylight and a slant of umber shadow share the space between the top of the wall and the bottom of the house.

Elisabeth leads him under the crisp, sweet branches of the apples. Calf-high grass whisks the hem of her skirt, and when she bends her neck to avoid a low-hanging branch, the movement is unconsciously graceful. The air around her is spiced with sun and dampness and the richness of ripe fruit. They approach the old house. Something heavy stirs in the shade among the house's piers, and into the sigh of breeze comes a slow, rhythmic grinding—the sound of animals at rest, animals chewing. He looks over the stone wall into cool blackness. Two white goats look back at him; they bleat in hope. The family's dairy cow, soft-eyed and pale, reclines at her ease.

Elisabeth, embarrassed by the rusticity, knocks grass seeds from her skirt with an impatient fist. "You see what I mean, why I thought it a curse to live here, once. This is the way peasants lived, isn't it? In the olden days. It seems too ridiculous for us now. This is the twentieth century, not the Dark Ages. But it's not as filthy as it seems. The muck from the animals runs down the slope of the floor and into the *Misthaufen*, there."

A trench runs around the inner perimeter, lidded by a rudimentary screen of narrow planks. At the house's north corner, where the *Misthaufen* has its outflow, flowering weeds grow up in tangled profusion. There is a smell, of course—but somehow, it's not unpleasant. The dung trough and the animals, the thick greenness of weedy growth—together they smell of times long ago, of centuries past. The olden days, as Elisabeth has said. The smell raises in him a throb of *Sehnsucht*, the pleasant pain of longing for an era he has never known. There was a time when we were not at war. There was a time when Germans could be proud of who and what we were.

"I like your house."

Elisabeth says briskly, "The animals below are great for heat in the wintertime. I suppose that's why they did it this way, in the days before coal stoves."

"It's an ingenious system."

"We only have to burn our coal on the chilliest nights. That leaves enough left over to trade. God makes every kind of unexpected blessing." A smile; Anton can't say whether it is bitter. Elisabeth cups her hands around her mouth and calls, "Children, I'm home! Come down!"

A moment later, their footsteps clatter down an unseen stairway. That graceless, eager, joyful thunder shakes Anton to his soul. The last time he heard children running for the pure fun of it, he was a teacher at St. Josefsheim, enjoying his pipe in the shade. The boys chased each other around and around, breathless and laughing. A ball rolled slowly in the dust, forgotten, along with the rules of the game young Bruder Matthias had tried to teach the children. "Don't take it personally," Anton told Matthias. "Some of these boys—they understand very little, except for love. But love is all they need."

The children—the living ones—come bounding around the corner of the house. They move with a freedom and gladness that belong to all children by right, but there is something restrained in their smiles. Is it only the war, which subdues us all, or are they still haunted by the loss of their father? As yet, he knows nothing of their grief—how fresh it may be, how long they have suffered.

The little girl, Maria, bears a smear of red marmalade across her cheek, and her yellow hair is tangled. She runs toward her mother, but the eldest boy catches her hand and stops her. He wipes her face with his kerchief while Maria whines and struggles. Albert's face is as serious as his mother's. He bends over his sister with a furrow in his brow. Paul hangs back, kicking pebbles in the grass, watching Anton with equal parts curiosity and caution. His knees are skinned and pink, his short pants too short to keep up with a nine-year-old's coltish growth.

"This is my Albert," Elisabeth says formally, "and Paul, there behind him. And my girl, Maria."

Albert turns Maria around to face her mother and Anton. The girl twists petulantly in her brother's grip until he lets go of her shoulders, but then she spins impulsively, throws her arms around his neck, and rises on her toes to kiss his cheek. Albert's smile is shy but pleased.

"This is Herr Starzmann," Elisabeth tells her children. She hesitates. How to explain? "My . . . my new friend."

Anton sinks to his heels. He opens the box of cookies. "Look what I have here. Do you want some?"

Maria runs to the cookies at once; she takes one in each hand and crunches. In an instant, chocolate replaces the marmalade her brother cleaned away. The boys are slower to react—polite, or wary?—but the sight of *Hausfreunde* brightens their eyes. Paul backs away once he has his cookie, but his grin is wide and unrestrained.

"I'm very glad to meet all of you," Anton says.

"Pleased to meet you, too, Herr Starzmann." Albert offers a hand to shake, well trained by his mother.

"You may call me Anton, if you like."

Albert glances at his mother. Such a quiet intelligence in his eyes, in the tensing of his freckled cheeks. He takes a meditative bite of his cookie, then says, "But you aren't from Unterboihingen, Herr Anton."

"You haven't seen me around, is that it?"

Paul shouts, "We know everybody in Unterboihingen! May I have another cookie? Maria got two."

Anton opens the box again. "You're correct: I am new here. I grew up in Stuttgart, but I worked in Munich for many years, so that city was my home, too, as much as Stuttgart ever was."

"But why have you come here?" Albert says.

Elisabeth tuts quietly. The question is not exactly rude; perhaps she is afraid of how Anton might answer.

He considers carefully before he speaks. "I have come to help people in need. There are so many people in need, just now."

"Because of the war," Albert says, sagely.

"That's exactly it."

Fists on hips, Maria shouts up at Anton, "Let me put on your glasses, Herr!"

"No." Elisabeth grabs her daughter by the hand. There is an air of victory in the moment; it seems Maria is not one to stand still for long.

Albert goes to his mother automatically and takes charge of the little girl. He slides his own hand into Elisabeth's grip, then nods up at her once, as if he has understood from the start what is happening here—what must happen, if they hope to keep on until the war finally ends.

It's not until Albert has approved that Elisabeth faces Anton squarely. "All right." Her voice is low, as if she is afraid the children will hear—afraid of what the younger ones might say, once they understand. "If you are still agreed, I will marry you, Herr Starzmann."

Anton lays his hand gently on Paul's sun-warmed hair as the boy edges closer to the cookie box. Of course he is still agreed.

4

Anton removes his hat as he enters Franke's Fine Furniture. The shop's bell chimes behind him, bouncing on its coiled spring. The interior glows with afternoon light, flooding in at the window, bouncing in all directions from the polished curves of chair backs and table legs. Franke looks up from a sideboard; the rag in his hand is brown with wax, and the room holds the smell of it, mineral warmth mingled with the caustic bite of chemical spirits. Franke's round face is pink, damp, flushed with the effort of his work.

Anton goes to him. He smiles at the half-waxed sideboard, the grape leaves carved along its edge. "Fine work. I carve, a little—or I used to. Haven't tried in a couple of years."

Franke grunts. He turns back to his business, working the deep-brown wax into raw oak with hard, heavy circles.

"I'm paid up through the week," Anton says, "for my room."

"So you are."

"I would like to extend for another week, if I may, but after that time, I'll stop waking on your alarm clock."

Elisabeth has asked for two weeks—fourteen days of prayer and reflection, time to ready her family for the change. It's clear she knows this union will benefit the three small souls who depend entirely on her, but she still seems unable to reconcile herself to the decision. In another time and place—in a gentler, saner world—she might find it easy enough to go on as a widow. In another time and place, God might never have taken her husband away.

"Leaving so soon?" Franke says, still polishing. He hacks a short laugh. "Unterboihingen not to your liking?"

"On the contrary; I intend to stay for a very long time. I'm to be married, you know."

"What?" Franke drops his rag, stares in disbelief. "Married? To whom?"

"Elisabeth Hansjosten Herter."

"The widow?" Franke laughs again. "She's a cold one. Believe me."

"She's not cold; she's only frightened." Surprising, how quick he is to defend her. Are a husband's instincts burgeoning in him already? "Isn't everyone frightened now?"

"No." Franke's gaze darkens. Suddenly Anton can smell his sweat, sharp and acrid like the polish in its dented can. "I'm not. I can't think why I should be—why any loyal German should be."

Remember the man on the train. Ready to fight, rather than submit—relieved Anton wasn't one of *them* after all, a nationalist. We must all be careful what we say. There are a few in Germany—even here, in this idyllic paradise—who love the Führer and rejoice in his power.

"Of course," Anton says, smiling as if he means it, "there's nothing for you and me to fear. We're good, honest men—loyal. But women and children, you know. They're frightened by the Tommies, the bombs."

"The Tommies." Franke looks as if he might spit—would, if he weren't standing in his own shop. "There's nothing to fear from those cowards. Those *Inselaffen* in their cardboard planes." As if Stuttgart doesn't lie gutted, deboned, less than thirty kilometers away.

"Anyway—in two weeks' time." Anton passes the reichsmarks to his landlord. He leaves as fast as propriety will allow, before Franke can prod him into saying more. With his back to the man, Anton makes the sign of the cross, though he doesn't know whether he is blessing

37

himself or Herr Franke. *Forgive the man, Father. Lord, forgive him. He knows not what he does.*

As he steps outside the shop into the dry dirt road, the church bells ring the hour. Anton pauses, hat in hand. The great, mellow roundness of the sound rolls across the land, pasture and field, street and quiet lane. It echoes from a line of low black hills. He has always loved the sound of bells, but these are especially moving. The music seems bigger than Unterboihingen itself—older, an aged-bronze call rich with the memory of countless years. They have sung in times of peace and war. They remember when all the world was peace; every stroke of hammer on dark metal curve resonates with remembered joy. For a minute, as the bells sing, he believes that, somehow, all will be well, and the space inside his chest, the hollowness where fear coils tight in its shadows, quivers with sympathetic hope.

Drawn by the sound, he finds his way to the church. A low sign, carved in dark wood, stands outside: "St. Kolumban." It is an unadorned building, sturdy and square, with plain, dark, arch-topped windows set into plaster walls aged the color of new butter. A single ridge beam runs the length of a red tile roof. Even the buttresses are uncarved, clinging dutifully to the church's shallow wings. The bell tower is massive, square, flat-faced. It reminds him of the obelisks in Egypt; not that he has seen Egypt with his own eyes.

As he stands staring up at the tower—the final peals draw themselves out in a thin, bronze-throated hum—two small figures clamber up from the ditch at his feet: Albert and Paul, their legs streaked with mud.

"Heavens," Anton says, "what has happened to the pair of you?"

Albert says, "Nothing. Mother told us to go play for the rest of the afternoon."

"Do you always play in drainage ditches?"

"They're good fun," says Paul, stamping his feet aimlessly, full of a boy's natural energy. "We play at being soldiers."

"Mother said you were a soldier."

"Only for a very short time, Albert."

The boy thinks hard for a moment, pressing his freckled lips together, squinting into the distance. At length, he says, "My friends call me Al, so you can, too, if you think it's all right to do it."

"I think it would be just fine, as long as it suits you."

"What are we to call you?"

Paul says at once, "I won't call you 'father.'" Then he blushes, alarmed at his own boldness, and hides his face against Al's back.

"I won't require it." Smiling gently. "I promise you that. You can call me Anton, if you like."

"Mother may require it." Al twists, side to side, as if unsure what to do with his confusion, the snarl of feelings inside.

"Then I will speak to her about it. We'll come to an agreement. Would that be all right?"

"Yes, I suppose."

Behind the bell tower, where the roof meets its monolithic face, Anton can make out an untidy pile of sticks and leaves and a few clinging white feathers. The boys pause for a moment in their fidgeting. Something has drawn their gaze to the sky—a shadow passing over grass and road or the whistle of stiff wings cutting through air. A great bird flies lazily overhead: white body, black-tipped wings, trailing red legs knobby at the joint. It carries a long, slender branch in its beak. The stork circles once, twice, then descends to the church roof with an awkward fold of its wings.

"They never stop working on their nests—even at this time of year, when their chicks have grown up and flown away," Anton says to the boys. His future stepsons.

Al says, "Vater Emil told us the nest is good luck."

"He is the priest of this church?"

Al nods. "Storks on a bell tower keep evil away—that's what the father said. But I don't believe it, not entirely."

"Surely the priest would never lie to you." Anton watches the stork again, so the boys will see no glimmer of amusement in his eyes.

"I don't think he lied, exactly. But only the Lord can keep evil away."

Paul cries with sudden indignation, "The Lord made storks and tells them where to fly!"

"That's so," Anton says. "The Lord made all good things."

"Did the Lord make bad things?" Al's question is quiet, almost a whisper.

"What sort of bad things do you mean?"

Paul shouts, "Spiders and poison snakes!"

Al shakes his head, tolerant of his little brother. He says, "I mean, people who hurt others." He is growing up too fast for a boy his age, but that is the way of children raised among suffering. Like seedlings sprouted in a dark corner, they shoot up thin and spindly, grasping and pale. Who can grow strong roots when the very earth is unsafe, when we are starved for light?

"You've heard stories about people who hurt one another?" He prays these boys haven't seen violence with their own eyes, young as they are.

"Yes," Al says. "I don't like the stories. I wish they weren't true, but they are true, aren't they? The boys at school tell me about . . ." He pauses and looks around cautiously. This young boy has learned already that some thoughts are too dangerous to speak aloud. Father of Heaven and creation, why did You make us to live through such times? Why should a child fear to speak truth? "The boys tell me about bad things soldiers do." Pragmatically, he doesn't specify whether German or Tommy soldiers are to blame.

"No, my boy," Anton says. "The Lord does not make men do evil things to one another. But the Lord gave us the right to choose. Whether we do good or evil, it is our own decision and our own responsibility."

Al squints at the stork. He watches as the bird weaves the branch into its lucky nest. "I don't understand why anyone chooses to do evil."

Anton lays his hand on Al's shoulder. The boy is as thin as a bird himself, bony and light. "I don't understand it, either." Then he makes himself smile. "I heard the bells and wanted to come see the church for myself. But I should head back to my room. My shirt needs changing before I have my supper. Would you like to come along?"

"Mother won't mind," Al says, after moral consideration.

They walk back through Unterboihingen. Tall as he is, Anton must shorten his stride to avoid outpacing the boys. It has been some time since he shepherded children anywhere. They bounce and skip and dart about, even Albert; no eleven-year-old can remain a thoughtful little man forever. There is a strange gulf between them—one of Anton's mental making, he has no doubt, but knowing the source makes the divide no less real. *There are so many years that separate us. If I was ever so young and resilient, I can't remember now how it feels.*

"I wanted to tell you," he says at length, grasping for the right words, "I don't intend to replace your real father. In your hearts, I mean. It's all right if you don't ever come to love me the way you love him. I've come to help you boys—and your sister, and your mother. That's all I intend to do—help."

"Why?" Paul says.

He understands the boy's question. Why do you care for us? We are strangers to you. He says, "Because God has commanded us to love one another."

"Are we even meant to love the Jews and Gypsies?"

Al grabs Paul by the collar, as if he means to shake him to silence. But Al only stares around the street, wary and tense.

I may never have been so young, but neither was I ever so frightened as this child.

"Yes," Anton says. "We are all children of God, no matter what anyone else may tell you. But"—with a glance at Al—"it's best to talk about these things where we're sure no one else can hear. Not everyone agrees with us, and sometimes when people disagree, they may become angry."

We are all children of God, made by the same hands—the Jews and Gypsies, the strong and the weak, the whole of mind and those who are fractured. Paul and Al are not so very different from the children he taught at St. Josefsheim. Elisabeth's boys are bright. Few of Anton's students had ever been called bright, but their innocence had been worth much to the Lord—their innate kindness, so much greater than one could find in any whole-minded person, and more generously given. *Did You truly call me here, O merciful God, to play father to one widow's children? Or is this of my own devising?*

He obeys the giver of all laws, but he knows, too, that he acts of his own will, hoping to redeem the irredeemable. Praying he might find, in the shape of these happy, living children, the resurrection of those he did not save, and relief from the burden of his sins. What are his sins? He numbers them in his thoughts—in every thought, in every beat of his heart. Cowardice; weakness; obedience to a regime that crosses the Father of All with every move it makes, every stride across the continent toward dominion.

As they round the corner of the bakery, Maria appears, running, her fists clenched in determination and her knees making her skirt ripple and fly. She collides with Anton's legs and stands there, stunned and wide-eyed. She is making up her mind whether to cry.

"What are you doing here?" Al scolds. "You aren't to go past the lane! And your dress is torn. Mother will be so angry. She has too much work to do already, and you only give her more!"

Maria has decided not to cry. She says to Anton, "Mother is very tired." Reciting a simple fact of the world—the sky is blue; cats have whiskers.

Anton says, "You must go straight home, Maria, or Mother will be worried. When you get home, change into a new dress and give this one to your brothers. They will bring it to me at my room over Franke's shop."

"All right." Maria goes sunnily into the custody of her brothers, as untroubled by the possibility of an angry mother as she is by her torn dress.

That evening, as Anton eats a simple supper of bread and butter and cold tinned beans—as he was used to doing at St. Josefsheim—Al and Paul come stamping up the stairs to his room. Paul holds Maria's green dress balled up in his fist. "Mother was cross anyhow. We told her you said to bring it to you, and she threw up her hands and said, 'Do what your father says!' Are you our father now?"

"I will be, once your mother and I marry." He takes the dress and smooths it over his knee to examine the damage.

"Why are you going to marry her?"

Anton chuckles. "Is there a reason why I shouldn't?"

"No," Paul says, while Al goes pink, flustered by his little brother's unrestrained talk. "I like you for a friend, and I guess I'd like you for a father, too."

Al is quick to correct him. "A stepfather."

"I hope I didn't anger your mother by sending for Maria's dress." He rises from the edge of his bed and opens one of his trunks to search for his small roll-out sewing kit, bound in leather. The glitter of late-day light over smooth brass captures the boys' attention; they both hurry to the trunk and peer down inside.

"Prima," Al whispers.

Anton says, "You can take the instruments out, if you'd like to look at them closer. But better not to try to play. We don't want to disturb Herr Franke downstairs."

"Good that you don't upset Möbelbauer," Al says as he examines a cornet, fascinated by its tubes and turns, its slick, cool surface. The pure-white keys are capped in mother-of-pearl.

"Why is that? Is his temper very bad?"

"Yes. And also, he's our town gauleiter."

Surprise steals Anton's breath, even as he unrolls the sewing kit. He gives every impression of unconcern—doesn't want to upset the children—but there is a painful pressure in his throat. Unterboihingen, of all places, has a gauleiter? They are the Reich's eyes and ears, governors of districts on behalf of the National Socialists—and to a man, every gauleiter is tucked deep in the pockets of Hitler and his highest men.

"Funny," he says casually, testing the point of a needle. "I'd never guess a place like Unterboihingen had any need for a gauleiter."

"We haven't any need," Al says quietly. "That's what some of my friends say—that's what their fathers have told them. No one thinks of us here, in this small village. We aren't important." He relaxes subtly as he speaks, his thin neck bending over the cornet. The boy derives some relief from the simple fact: we here in Unterboihingen count for nothing. Now that he thinks on it, Anton finds it comforting, too. "But Möbelbauer," Al says, "has ambitions."

The boy makes this pronouncement so solemnly that Anton almost laughs, though it's hardly amusing. He can just imagine the schoolboys, with their short pants and skinned knees, whispering hedge to hedge: *Watch out for Möbelbauer. He has ambitions.* Their parents' words, repeated like a charm against warts. But a man with ambition is dangerous in this place and this time. Al and his friends seem to know it.

"Don't you dare repeat that to anyone," Al says to Paul.

Paul looks up, surprised to be addressed. He has been engrossed the whole while in the treasures of Anton's chest—the horns and flutes, the little cymbals muted with pads of felt.

"He hasn't heard me, anyway," Al says. "It's a mercy. Paul can talk and talk, and never shut his mouth."

"You have a big responsibility, looking out for your brother and sister." The green thread in Anton's sewing kit is not the right shade to match Maria's dress, but it's the closest one can hope to find. Textiles do not come readily to hand these days.

Al makes no reply, and so Anton begins to stitch. He watches Al from the corner of his eye as he works. The boy depresses the valves of the cornet, slowly and carefully, one after another. They make a softly hollow sound, a faint, padded sticking and tearing.

After a while, Anton says, "I can see that you do a good job of keeping your family safe. That's honorable work—a man's work."

"You didn't seem worried to hear that our town has a gauleiter."

He hears the boy's unspoken question. *Why aren't you frightened? Are you so loyal to the Party that you have nothing to fear?*

"I've dealt with my share of gauleiters before." His tone is conspiratorial. "And men worse than they, too."

Much worse. But the SS won that encounter, didn't they? The sight of the boys with the instruments in their hands scours Anton with fresh pain. He watched the last children who ever held those instruments loaded onto a gray bus. They all went, trusting and smiling, as was their nature—skipping past the men with guns. Men who herded them into the belly of the hearse. Trusting and smiling, while Brother Nazarius and the rest of the friars quietly pleaded, or placed themselves gently in the way, only to be pushed aside by the muzzle of a Karabiner. *Stand in my way again, and I'll run out the bayonet.* Cold steel pressed hard into Anton's chest.

The needle pricks him, and he pinches his thumb against his fingertip until the bleeding stops.

"You needn't worry," Anton whispers to Al. "Herr Möbelbauer answers to his ambition, but I answer only to God."

Al puffs out his chest. He is pigeon-breasted, like his wiry stepfather. "So do I—only to God."

"You're a good boy. I'll be very proud to be in your family."

He holds up Maria's dress, and Al and Paul both examine the hem. Except for the off-color thread, it is perfectly repaired.

Awestruck, Paul says, "But men don't sew!"

"This one does. When I was a friar, I did all my own sewing. I had to; a friar has no wife to do his mending."

The youngest boy goes wide-eyed. Somehow, in whatever discussion the family has had about Anton and the pending marriage, the fact that he was once a friar has escaped Paul's notice.

"You might learn to sew, Paul," Anton says, "so you can help your mother and Al. Then they won't be so tired all the time. A big, strong boy like you—I imagine you could be a great help to the family. Wouldn't you like that, to help like a grown man?"

"I'll do it, if you'll teach me how."

Anton ruffles his pale hair. "One of these days, we'll have a sewing bee—just we two fellows. It's not as hard as it looks."

Paul stares for a moment at the cornet, still clutched in his big brother's hands. "Will you teach me to play music, too?"

Anton folds the dress carefully and passes it to Paul. "Maybe I will, little man."

5

Beyond the road, in the shadowed confines of the churchyard, wind bends the grass that has grown up, knee-high, between the tombstones. The stones are so old you can no longer read the words carved into their faces. "Sacred to the Memory" and "In His Will Is Our Peace"—lichen has pitted and degraded every surface. If Anton were to touch a stone, run his hand across a face where once a name was written, he would feel granite crumbling to dust. The yard needs cutting, but no one will do it now. It is late. Dusk has settled in, a restless purple half-light below a shy white sickle of moon. The wind tugs at his hat; it rattles the stork's nest like bones against the flat, colorless stone of the bell tower. The breeze pushes Father Emil's robe against his legs. The priest works in near darkness. Across the churchyard, above it, the sloping shoulder of a hill lifts its ancient burden toward the sky: a black vastness of woodland. At the foot of the hill there stands a wall—age uncountable, old beyond knowing—and spilling down the wall, a heavy curtain of ivy. Wind stirs the ivy leaves and reverses them, bottom to top, silver undersides exposed. The priest is cutting back the ivy, clearing the way around a steel door set into the wall, sunk into the hill. He moves with the stiff, sharp gestures of reluctance.

Despite the dim shadows of dusk, Anton can tell the wall and hill and ivy are each too old, too long-established, to be reactions to our present difficulty—the Tommies with their cardboard airplanes. But the door—the door is new. Steel rivets shine, even in this pale disjection of moonlight. Does some cave or tunnel wait back there, dug into the hillside and smelling of ancient earth, lined with blankets and lamp oil and tins of food, a bulwark against British retribution? Out here in the countryside, tunnels run from town to town, a warren of hidden passages through which, in ages gone by, pilgrims or messengers in medieval tunics crept, lit by the sallow fires of smoking torches. Those tunnels would make fine shelters when bombs fall.

By chance, the priest pauses in his work and looks up. He sees Anton standing there, thin and stretched, pale as a specter among the graves. His body makes an involuntary jump; the trimmer falls from his hand into the long grass underfoot. But then with a laugh, charming self-deprecation, he waves in greeting.

Anton crosses the yard and searches for the trimmer in the grass.

"You are the man who has come to marry Elisabeth," says the father. "Herr Starzmann?"

"That's so. You know me already? I've been here only two days."

"Small town, you know." Another laugh, rueful and apologetic. "Our ways must seem strange to a man used to city life. Or if not strange, then too rustic for comfort." He shrugs. "And I saw you at service yesterday, sitting all the way at the back of the nave."

Anton hands him the trimmer. "I'm sorry I didn't introduce myself then. I meant to, but, well . . ."

Elisabeth had been there, each of her children scrubbed to pinkness and dressed in their patched Sunday best. Little Maria had showed the hem of her dress, mended, to anyone who would stop and look. Elisabeth had asked for privacy—two weeks to pray, to think, to contend with her memories. Two weeks to resolve herself and accept what she must do. Anton had given his word: he would leave her entirely alone, unless she sent for him. Courtesy is a small favor to ask, and he is a man who respects grief. He has come to understand it well.

Good-natured and grinning, Anton says, "How much has Unterboihingen said on the subject of Herr Starzmann? Did you know, for example, that I used to be a friar?"

Father Emil did not know. He takes a step back, rests his thumbs in the wide black sash of his robe, a posture of respect and admiration. Anton wishes he had his rope belt swinging from his own waist. It was like an anchor chain, holding him fast during hours of storm. Of late, he has felt unmoored.

"They disbanded your order?" Emil guesses.

"Yes, and shut down my school."

"You were a teacher?"

"I was." He finds he can't hide his joy or pride, any more than he can hide his sadness. He means to say more on the subject, but the words will not come. Pain like a hard hand grips his throat. The loss of the little ones is still too fresh, too near. All those sweet faces stilled forever; the mouths that once opened in ready laughter now hang wide in death, death's ever-triumphant grin. In a gray camp somewhere, behind a gray wall, there is a stack of little bodies piled sixteen high. They were always so quick to laugh. Any common miracle could move them to gladness—a butterfly, a puppet show, rain tapping on a classroom window.

The priest takes Anton's arm in brief, silent consolation. Then he blesses him with a cross. In the presence of the holy sign, Anton feels nothing, except gratitude for the father's concern. He doesn't know when it happened, when he ceased to feel the power of the cross. But it was long before the SS came. He thinks it was, in fact, the night the Reichstag burned.

"When are you and Elisabeth to marry?"

"The second of October."

Emil nods. He tests the weight of the hedge trimmer in his hand, finding its balance, his eyes downcast and thoughtful. "God brought you to her. She is a good woman, devoted to her children and the Lord."

His words imply, *God gives the best to the best. You are her reward for faith, even in the face of misery.*

"I sense that in her," Anton says, "that she is good, though I hardly know her. But I find myself frightened, Father. No, not frightened, exactly. But doubting. You see, I don't know how—" He falters. He goes still. The priest's kindness and patience work their intended spell over Anton, bending him, wind against grass. He opens his heart to the man, spilling out reservations he only half suspected before. "I don't know how to do this the right way. I came to help her, but how can I help? What shall I do? I have never been a husband, or a father."

"Of course you have not."

"I don't know how it's done."

Mildly, Emil says, "I have never been a husband, either, my friend. Nor a father—not the kind you are about to become. But I think it can't be so different from being a man of the cloth. You must be guided by integrity, mercy, and justice. You must let love carry all your decisions, all your words. That is what the Lord asks of us in every role: father, mother, brother, child. Neighbor and friend—nun and friar. That is *all* the Lord asks—that we live by Christ's example."

How can any man claim those qualities now—integrity, mercy, justice? Everything the Reich has done, all the cruelties and death, the burial of our rights in an unmarked grave—none of it has been Anton's will, nor does he approve. Yet he can't help feeling he is to blame. And aren't we all to blame? What has brought us here, if not heedlessness or willful neglect? We have forgotten some crucial lesson our forefathers learned long ago, but ignorance is no excuse; the price must be paid. How did we err, and how did we sin, to allow the Reich so much power? How far back must we go—we, as a people—to undo each small step toward infamy? The first thin roots of this evil twine through history's soil. But where do they start? We cannot look to 1934, when the chancellor Adolf Hitler declared himself Führer. That was only the culmination of a long black line of discord. The kaiser signed the armistice and we became, suddenly, a republic, reeling and disoriented. Was it then that we turned? Or will we find the first track of this bleak progress in 1918, one generative footprint lying stark and crisp in November snow? Must we look further still—to Wilhelm I wrenching power from the states; to 1814, Vienna, a confederation still reeling from Napoleon's blow? We look back—the Thirty Years' War. The Peace of Augsburg, and forty years before, at Martin Luther tapping his tacks into the dark, blank face of an old church door. A third of us dead in 1348, riddled with seeping black boils, and no one to help us, no one to bury us, no one to comfort the dying. Further back still, to Widukind submitting, debasing himself before gold-robed Charlemagne. Baptismal water washes from his hard, Germanic face a war paint made of boar's blood. It drips onto the black fur of his garments and from there to the clean stone floor. It carries away the smell, the feel of his oaken, pagan groves. We have nursed this cancer from our earliest days. How deep into the heart of Germany has the tumor spread? Or did it originate there, in hot red fiber and pumping blood, in the secret pockets of darkness we hide from our neighbors and deny day to day? Whatever the source of our rage, we have carried it too far now. We cannot excise this disease without bleeding our nation dry.

"Your thoughts are dark," Emil says.

"My thoughts are often dark, these past years."

Emil nods. There is no need to specify; we all know. These years since Poland. And before that, the chaos of the summer of 1930, when there was no parliament to check the rise of the National Socialist German Workers' Party. By the time the autumn came, and tempers cooled with the season, Herr Hitler had won the hearts of the people—or enough people, at any rate, for him to plant his boots in the Reichstag, where he stacked kindling for his fire. Desperate hearts are easy to secure. When her children are starving, a woman will believe any vile promise you whisper in her ear. When a man is cornered, he will trust you if you tell him he cannot sin.

"But you are not to blame," the priest says, "for the dark things, for the world's evil."

"I want to believe that's true. There are days when I can't convince myself, though."

"I know." The priest chuckles, but it's a sound without humor. His smile is bleak with disbelief. Look where we found ourselves, reeling, shame-faced Germany, before we even knew we were in danger. "Most days, I can hardly convince myself, either."

"How can I do it?" Anton says. "How can I be a good father to those three little children—how can I be a good husband to that poor widow—when I cannot even . . . ?"

What he cannot do is unspeakable, indescribable. Most of all, it is unforgivable. I can't turn back time. I can't tell where we first went wrong—we, this people, this nation to which I belong. And if I could, I would have no way to stop whatever progress has led us here. I am too weak, too human.

"Come inside."

Anton follows the priest into the church. Its beauty strikes him anew, as it did at Sunday's service. Outside, the building is plain and functional. Inside, St. Kolumban, lit by a few old-fashioned oil lamps, soars with ivory arches lined in dark brick, with white angles that cross and climb and lead the eye up, ever up to Heaven. It is more beautiful than any church in a tiny country village—a place of no consequence—ought to be. This simple act calms him a little, stepping inside the house of God. Together, Anton and Emil dip their fingers in the holy water. They bow as they pass before the altar and sit in the nave's first row. The priest sighs and puts his feet up on the prayer bench in front of them. It's this act of familiarity that makes Anton like the man all the more, wholly and beyond all reason.

"Years ago," Emil says, "when I was newly come to the cloth, I was called upon to perform an exorcism. Ordinarily, I think, the work would have fallen to an older priest—one with more experience. But this was in a very small town, you see—not Unterboihingen, but much the same—and I was the only priest to hand. It was a woman who thought herself possessed. A mother of four. She was perhaps thirty-five years old."

"Thought herself possessed? You don't believe in possession?"

Father Emil makes an evasive gesture, not exactly a shrug. Anton understands. The Bible tells us there are demons, and what sort of Christians would we be if we didn't trust in God's word? But in these times, what terrors can we find in the common threats of Hell? There is an old, old saying: One man is devil to another. Among the Tommies, the words are different, but the meaning is the same: Man is wolf to man. In this world, evil heaps itself on evil, and the spire of unchecked power climbs higher by the day. This is a tower of man's own building. Around its base the wolves circle, greedy and grinning—white, cold eyeteeth bared, numberless as stars.

"I worked with that woman and her family for five days," Emil says, "but none of my prayers had the least effect. She moaned and shook in her bed; she screamed like an animal in a trap. She wept, Anton—wept for hours, but her tears seemed to have no limit. They fell and fell from her eyes—I can see them still, that far, blinded look. The whole of her spirit was concentrated on some terrible affliction I could neither understand nor reach. Whatever had affected her—grief, pain, suffering—perhaps it was, after all, a demon—I couldn't close the door. I had no power to banish it, to make it leave that poor soul in peace."

The priest falls silent. His gaze is fixed on Mother Mary, painted in broad blue strokes behind the pulpit. His foot tips the prayer bench, rocks it gently on stout legs, forward and back.

After a pause, Anton says, "What happened? Did the woman recover?"

"She did." The bench comes to rest again, squarely on its old carved legs, sure of its place. "She seemed to heal herself. To be sure, it was none of my doing. She was simply better on the sixth day. It was like a fever breaking, or a winter storm passing. Her family thanked me and praised me as if I had done it, but I knew the truth. I had played no part, despite my best efforts.

"I went on, Anton—carried on with the business of my life. That is the way of things, isn't it? That's the way we're made, to carry on. But the experience stayed with me for a long time. I was far more shaken by my failure—my helplessness—than I had been by the woman's torment. Her terrible screams, the foul things she'd said in the throes of her anguish—they were nothing beside my fear and my doubt. Time and again, I asked myself, 'Emil, how can you continue to lead a congregation?' I lay awake almost every night, knowing myself to be weak, fallible, and knowing that even with God on my side, I would surely fail again."

At that moment, the bells ring out the hour. The sound fills the chapel, quakes the weary bones of the world. The notes, massive and mellow in every stroke, shake loose the strictures on his heart. He closes his eyes and the purity of their music fills him; a song spills over inside. There is no room left in his heart for doubt or fear. He thinks, *These same bells have rung since long before the Reich existed. And they will ring still, even after it has fallen.*

When the last stroke has sounded, Anton holds his breath, feeling the note's dying hum. It vibrates in his chest, still, long after sound has faded. He exhales slowly, mindful of the silence, its fullness, its suffusion of hope.

"They're beautiful, aren't they?" Father Emil says. "The bells. They've hung in that tower for hundreds of years; imagine the things they have seen, the worlds they have known. When my thoughts are at their darkest, I listen to the bells and I remember that Germany hasn't always been what it is now. Those bells remember it—the way we were before." He casts a sheepish smile in Anton's direction, and the prayer bench begins to rock again. "I know I sound like a fool—perhaps I am one. They are only bells, yet I can't help but think of them as something more. Old friends, that's what they seem to me."

"You're not foolish, Father. I was just thinking much the same thing."

Emil turns on the pew and stares up to St. Kolumban's ceiling as if he can see beyond its layered arches into the night-darkened bell tower. "If I'd had the misfortune to find myself in some other church—one without bells—I think the war would go harder on me. I'd be an unhappier man. But every time I hear them, I hear the past singing, too. I can't help but remember all the people who came before. The ringing mechanisms are automated now, of course, just like a clock—I will show you how the gears work, someday—but long ago, it was the father of this church who made those bells sing. He knew everything that passed in his congregation. Every birth and death, every baptism, every marriage. Every cause for joy and sorrow. I think of them all—generations of people—families, friends, lovers. Theirs was a different world. They didn't fear what we fear now."

"But surely the bells rang in times of fear, too, as in times of happiness. This church would have sounded the alarm, I imagine, whenever fires or floods threatened the village."

"Yes," Emil says, chuckling, "and—who knows?—packs of wolves descending from the hills. Those were simpler times. Floods and fires and wolves can't compare to strafing with English bombers. Yet the dangers those people faced in years gone by were no less terrifying to them. No one still lives who remembers simpler days. But the bells remember—they keep the memories for us, so we will never entirely forget the time when we were all brothers."

Softly, Anton says, "That woman—the exorcism. What did you learn? How did you go on leading your church through so much worry and doubt?"

"I took each day as it came. I still do—what else can any man do? I can't worry about what might happen in the future; I can only tend to my small flock here and now, today, hour by hour, and pray that what I do is what God wills."

"Trust that everything is in God's hands."

Emil makes that strange, evasive movement again—not a shrug, not really, but something akin. He is leaving words unsaid, hanging in the silence where moments before the roll of the bells uplifted. Anton hears the words Emil will not speak aloud. *All is in your own hands, just as much as God's. And whatever your hands may do, do it with all your strength and will.*

"It's getting late. I should finish my work, then rest. Tomorrow is a new day." The priest stands, smiles down, his eyes enigmatic. He offers a hand and pulls Anton to his feet. With a squeeze to Anton's shoulder, he says, "The second of October. Then your new life begins."

6

The bells will ring, even after the Reich has fallen. Everything in me that is sensible, everything that is rational, can't believe it's true. The Reich will never fall; it is too strong now, too deeply rooted, fixed in the routine of life. We have accepted. We have moved along, carried on with the business of our lives, and this is what our lives have become. My days are as long and dark as night; this war will never end. The pillar of evil will stand until the last day comes, until the angel neglects to sound his horn and everything that might have been withers, forgotten on an untended vine. But when, in moments of quiet, in my stillness of despair, I dare to ask what yet may be, the black veil parts and light pours in. It strikes me to blindness with its beauty. It floods my soul with tears.

O God, my Father, why do You do this to me? Can You not content Yourself to leave me in the surety of misery? You have laid bare the frail bones of my grief; You have humbled me before myself and proven to me that I am a coward, unfit for life. Yet I persist. I go on living. I will cling to hope, even knowing, as I do, that hope is worse than futile.

Why this relentless, this secret optimism—this resolve, hard and hot at the base of my spine, and buried none too deep in my breast? The cancer that gnaws at us is too hungry to be sated. And I am one man—one man. Christ Jesus, I always believed You were merciful, but this is a monstrous cruelty, to make me dream of a time when evil may fall. Whatever sins have brought us here still reside in our blood, even to the third and fourth generation.

Yet You said, in your boundless love and wisdom, *Weeping may endure for a night—joy comes with the morning.*

I cannot help but know it. Against all sense, I believe. Somewhere, beyond the ragged edge of night, light bleeds into this world.

PART 2

LET LOVE CARRY ALL YOUR WORDS

OCTOBER–DECEMBER 1942

7

October second. A crisp orange bite to the air. Across the field, where spent stems of oat or wheat lie down over furrows of stubble, there is a drift of woodsmoke, barely visible. Summer's birds have moved on, the better part of them, flown to friendlier places. Anton walks to the church with his new family—today they will be. The boys skip beside him, kicking pebbles into the street. Elisabeth holds herself somewhat apart and keeps Maria's hand in her own. She is stiff-backed, eyes clear and determined, mouth as hard-set as ever. She looks as if she's marching into Riga. She is wearing the blue dress, the one he first saw her in, and she looks like a flagging Madonna—face fallen into acceptance, and behind her resolute stare, a well of love for her children as inexhaustible as her body and spirit are not. She looks weary, beyond even God's capacity to measure.

That morning, in the small room over Herr Franke's shop, Anton stood in a beam of pale sunlight, staring at his thin face in the dim, narrow mirror. Then, he had thought it best to wear his Wehrmacht uniform to the wedding—but now, he can't say why. The uniform, drab and thick with a forced, upright grimness, is the most formal set of clothing he owns. That must be why he chose it over the suit folded in lavender, the one Anita tied with her blue ribbon. But the uniform makes him distinctly uncomfortable, and not only because the jacket and shirt have grown too tight around the waist. Somehow, in this time of ration stamps and deprivation, he has managed to cultivate the beginnings of a paunch. Too much time spent sitting and thinking; too much time spent slowed and hobbled by bleak memory. This uniform is nothing but a reminder of times better forgotten. Was that, perhaps, the point? Was remembrance his purpose—only now realized—when he pulled the old uniform from one of his trunks and brushed specks of dust from the bronze-green wool? This is his hair shirt, his girdle of thorns, like those some monks wore in ages past—an admonition never to get too comfortable, never to forget how the savior suffered. Monks wore hair shirts, but never friars, until the second of October.

When they first met that morning in the lane outside the farm, the boys seemed reluctant. Al was quiet, unusually still, even for that thoughtful child. More than once, from the corner of his eye, Anton saw the boy open his mouth and close it again, blushing, as if wanting to speak but knowing a child has no right. Paul followed Albert's lead, as is the way of younger brothers. But when the boys looked up and saw that Anton was wearing his uniform, their eyes brightened. They wanted stories—soldier's stories. He obliges them with the only one he's got.

"After I left the order"—after it was taken from me—"they scooped me up and put me in the Wehrmacht."

"Why?" says Paul.

Hoping to kill me off, no doubt. I'd given them no sound reason to run me through or shoot me when they came to close St. Josefsheim. What else should they have done with the Catholic menace but send us to the Prussian front? To the boy, he says only, "Someone must fill all those army boots.

"Russia had been in Latvia for a long time by then, and the Latvian people were very unhappy and afraid. So we, Germany, said to them, 'We'll come over and help you.'

"But it would have been a very long walk, indeed, from Germany to Latvia. Instead, they loaded us all onto airplanes—huge ones, as long as two train cars, maybe bigger. We flew over Prussia in the dark of night."

"Like the bombers," Al says.

"A bit like the bombers, yes. But instead of dropping bombs, we dropped soldiers. When they opened the plane's door, the wind was so cold and fast, it stole the breath right out of my lungs. That wind roared louder than the engines. But the commander, he stood beside the door as if he didn't notice that terrible noise, and he counted—*eins, zwei, drei, vier, fünf*—and every five seconds, one of us jumped."

In truth, Anton doesn't know whether he jumped that night or was pushed, whether some flat, hard hand came out of the roaring darkness and tipped him off his feet into the howl and bite of the plummeting sky. Jumping or falling, the end result was the same. The brute force of gravity, the fury of the wind, the scream of the plane's engines, somewhere not far above as he rolled through the air. Stars and an inevitable black density—the ground—spun around him. Now and then he could make out, in slow motion, with a kind of momentous and final clarity, the limbs and bodies of other men, paper cutouts against a barely lit sky. And then, like a miracle, the few minutes of his training came back to him. His mind and spirit decided, *We will survive this.* He felt the downward pull, the frightened, desperate force in the center of his gut, and he oriented around that fear. His limbs spread like the limbs of a falling cat; for a moment, he must have been almost graceful, and the view of the land far below—what little he could see by night—was something close to beautiful, dark and austere. He found that, all along, he had been counting—his mind had sequestered itself in a sheltered corner, far from his panic, and he measured out the seconds with scrupulous care. When the time was right, not a moment before, he pulled the rip cord, and the chute opened above him, spreading and flapping like the wings of an angel.

His landing lacked both grace and composure. A man of thirty-eight never thinks himself old until he's pushed from a plane in the dead of night. The way you land, even with your chute open, it's enough to knock gouts of blood from your nose or batter the soul right out of your body.

The boys cheer at the image, their step-*Vati* a paratrooper. Won't their schoolmates turn sick with envy when they hear? "What did you do next?"

"We cut ourselves free from our parachutes, and we formed up in ranks. We marched until the sun came up—and for a long time after that, too. As it grew lighter, I could see more of the land around me. And you know, the road we walked was perfectly straight and flat. I'd never seen a thing like that road before. I doubt I will again." Immaculately, dismally straight, the road to Riga. "It never curved the least bit, to the right or the left. It never went up or down the smallest hill. That's the way they do their roads, in Prussia. Very strange people."

The boys laugh. Anton does not. Something had unnerved him, then, about the unabated straightness of the road. He hasn't thought of the march in months, but now he finds that the road haunts him, cleaving its hard, dark, unvaried way into his thoughts. We march inexorably toward our destination. There is no curve or gentle slope to relieve us; straight ahead lies the conclusion of our national folly, the terrible work we set in motion at some unknown point in time. Behind, the long, narrow way of our past, paved in hard history and stretching into blackness.

But there is the church, tall and sturdy, pale as the autumn fields. And there is Father Emil, coming out to the yard to meet them with a handful of friends and neighbors. The women and children hold bunches of wild daisies, gathered from the hedgerows and smiling like hope in their hands. The people wave and call out, *"Alles Gute zur Hochzeit!"* We all welcome the excuse for a celebration.

Drawn by their school friends, the children run inside, and Elisabeth and Anton pause for a moment in the churchyard, side by side. Once they enter St. Kolumban, they must approach the altar with solemnity. There will be no time for talk, no last-minute negotiation, no chance to admit regret.

She turns to him. She smiles tentatively; her eyes slide away. "You did a fine job mending Maria's dress."

"I was glad to help."

She looks down at her shoes, scuffed gray at the toes but polished all the same. She blushes, caught in the hot rush of some emotion, some thought she will never share with Anton.

He offers an arm. "Shall we go in?"

When the ceremony is over and the bells ring out brightly, Anton feels as tired as Elisabeth looks, as stunned and committed. They have said the holy words before God; they have taken the sacrament and made their pledge. There is no going backward now. Their road stretches out before them, straight and clear toward eternity.

8

The day has held, fine and brightly blue, one of those early-autumn afternoons when it seems October seeks to impress upon you, with warmth and a sense of contented indolence, how brief the summer really was. Residents of nearby farms have filled the orchard with tables and chairs; Elisabeth and Anton sit in the place of honor, she crowned with a wreath of flowers like a youthful virgin bride. Her small, clean hands are folded neatly on a white tablecloth that someone embroidered long ago with turkey-red threads. The threads are fraying now, and the stitches of some letters have been picked out, leaving only needle holes behind. But Anton can read the words easily enough: *Wer seine Arbeit gut vollbringt, auch manches Andere oft gelingt!* Apply yourself to your work, and success will follow.

With a quiet thrill of discovery, he finds that he likes to watch Elisabeth as she greets each neighbor. She has a charming way with familiar people—a warm clasp of the hand, a kiss on the cheek, and some small compliment for each of them, delivered with a soft, friendly laugh. *You look well today, Herr Egger. You seem to be over your sickness. I'm glad you brought your potato salad, Frau Gerhard. Everyone knows it's the best recipe in Unterboihingen.* With him, Elisabeth is stiff and formal—but it's only her discomfort showing. She doesn't understand how to be his wife any more than he knows how to be a husband. Among the people she knows—those whom, over many years, she has come to trust—Elisabeth is gentle and clement, gracious and kind. He thinks, *Someday we will know each other well, and then we will bring these simple joys to one another: friendship and comfort.* Someday. But only God knows how long it may take.

Frau Hertz, the woman who owns the farm—the one from whom Elisabeth rents the old cottage—comes bustling out from her brick-and-stucco house, carrying a cake perched on the pink pedestal of a footed plate. She talks ceaselessly as she crosses the orchard, though no one is near enough to hear; she moves with quick steps, perfunctory gestures that put one in mind of a nervous hen or a plump, gray-haired *Oma*, sweet and solicitous, easily distracted, smelling of cinnamon and vanilla cream. The Frau's hair is dark, not the least bit grayed, though she is at least twenty years older than Anton. He can see, however, that Frau Hertz used to be plump, and quite recently: loose skin hangs at the front of her neck, the remnant of a double chin melted away by the privation of wartime rations.

As she approaches the table of honor—the bride crowned in her glory, the groom sinking in his chair, uncertain what he ought to say and to whom—Frau Hertz marshals her aimless chatter, reins it and directs it. "A wedding celebration needs a cake," she announces, loud enough for the whole town to hear. "It's not the same without. You, Elisabeth—you wouldn't let us do any of the rest of it, shame on you! But you will have a cake, I insist, I insist!" She sets the cake between them—bride and groom. It's a simple affair, three golden layers spotted with raisins and thin bands of buttercream and marmalade between each. "But it's humble," Frau Hertz says. "Ought to have a prettier cake, but you know we all must conserve. I did the best I could with what I had on hand."

"It's beautiful," Elisabeth says, taking her landlady's hands in thanks.

"There isn't enough for everyone, but you both must have a good, fat slice. For luck."

Frau Hertz cuts hearty slices for Anton and Elisabeth, which she tips onto delicate china plates. She mutters as she works, "Who ever heard of a wedding without the dancing, or the fun?"

"Aren't we all having a good time?" Anton asks. The neighbors are milling about the orchard, and laughter shimmers with the autumn sunlight among golden leaves. Plates are piled high with simple fare: sauerkraut and salads, unleavened bread rolls, slices of liver with onions. This is nothing to turn the head of a Berlin gourmand, but we are all glad for a celebration. Any excuse will do, if we may forget our troubles for an hour.

Quietly, to Anton, Elisabeth says, "I wouldn't allow Frau Hertz, or anybody else, to make a big show of our wedding. She planned to have me kidnapped and hidden—you know that silly game young girls play at their weddings—and then send you out to hunt for me." To her landlady, she says, "Herr Starzmann doesn't want to spend the afternoon tramping around the fields and hedges looking for his wife. And it's ridiculous to think of—me, sitting on a stool in some thicket, being eaten alive by bugs while I wait for him to turn up and rescue me!"

Anton has the briefest of visions, parting a dry hedge with one hand to find Elisabeth there, looking up at him, blanched white and gripping the edges of her seat with hard, impatient hands. Dead branches framing her face, a cross and baffled expression.

"It's the tradition." Frau Hertz is sulking. "And no rice, either."

"It would be criminal to throw rice when so many people go hungry. Besides, Frau, this is my second husband. Those games are all right for girls who have never married before, but for me—"

"It's Herr Starzmann's first wedding. And, *mein Liebste*, a second marriage doesn't mean you can't enjoy yourself. I should know." Frau Hertz leans close and kisses Elisabeth on the cheek. Elisabeth smiles at her friend, though not without a certain tension around her mouth.

When the woman has hurried off to another corner of the orchard, Elisabeth turns to her slice of cake, sighing, shouldering the burden of duty. "We'd best eat it all. Nothing else will please her. She is the dearest thing, but she's more mother hen than landlady."

There is a sudden stillness in the air, a shift in the atmosphere. Anton looks up; what has caught his attention? Then he sees the children gathered under the largest apple tree—not only Albert and Paul and Maria, but their friends, too: half a dozen boys and girls in their church-day finery. They are pressed close together, as if they've just been whispering among themselves. And their eyes are fixed on the cake. He gestures to them: *Come on, then.* They run across, giggling and shrieking with renewed vigor, and the orchard is lively with sound again, sound and laughter.

"Line up," he says, "one at a time." He cuts his slice of cake with the side of his fork, carefully, into equal pieces, enough for each child to enjoy one bite. They moon over their small portions, savoring the sweetness of honey and raisins, their eyes half closed.

"Now you've given away all your cake," Elisabeth says. She splits her slice in two and transfers half to Anton's plate. "Don't tell Frau Hertz what I've done. She'll make me eat another whole piece. For luck."

The children dart away. They organize themselves into a game of *Katz und Maus* without any discussion of the matter, with the instinct for play all young creatures possess. Albert and Paul have bounced back from the morning's reserve. Maria never seemed the least bit troubled by Anton, nor did the proceedings of the ceremony faze her. Thank God, she stayed quiet and behaved herself; Elisabeth had committed the girl to Frau Hertz's keeping for the duration of the wedding, and Frau Hertz may be the only person under Heaven who can extract obedience from that child. It is not Sunday, yet Maria is wearing her best dress—that's all that matters to the girl. Adaptable, as young ones can be, Elisabeth's children have accepted this new reality: they have a stepfather. Anton has a family. He thinks, *I must write to my sister and tell her the news. She will never believe it—not of me.*

He tastes his wedding cake. His first wedding; his only. Simple the cake may be, but the rich sweetness of honey and brandied raisins sings on his tongue. How long has it been since he has eaten anything so delicious? For years, life's sweetness has been dulled and salted by the ash of war, but no longer. He closes his eyes.

"Frau Hertz does know how to bake," Elisabeth says, "even if I think she's foolish to squander her butter and flour on us." Amusement in her tone at Anton's reaction—and warmth, too. They smile at each other over their plates. It's a moment of unexpected connection—an intimacy he never thought to find with his wife. His wife. He blushes—another unsettling surprise—for now he realizes, now it strikes him that he has shared this moment with Elisabeth in front of so many people, virtual strangers. It embarrasses him, for the unexpected intimacy, so sudden and raw, feels almost carnal. He is far beyond his depth; when was the last time he had anything to do with a woman personally, privately? As a friar, there was always the barrier of impossibility between Anton and the women he knew—those he met at the school or in his daily business or going about the streets of Munich. The gray habit and knotted belt had ensured his protection, visible reminders that he was a man apart, not to be considered. And he had never considered any woman, except as one must regard all people, as brothers and sisters in Christ. This military uniform, tight around the waist and growing tighter—it makes him conspicuous. It makes him vulnerable and male. Dizzy, he sees himself as if from far away, watching his movements, his every gesture across the orchard, across the whole of the village. When he stood at the altar with Elisabeth, repeating Father Emil's prompted vows—and later, kneeling in prayer beside his new wife—he felt no emotion worth remarking. Nothing but resolve and comfort in the knowledge that this was what the Lord intended; this was his next calling. But now, beneath the apple trees in the mild October sunshine, with the laughter of neighbors and children all around, the full weight of reality descends upon him and sinks into his chest. The vow he has taken today—it cannot be unsaid.

He longs for the habit, his gray armor. He doesn't know how to be himself in layman's clothes. He never knew who he was in a soldier's uniform, either, and so he doesn't know himself now. The children, playing, dash by. They slip on rotten apples hidden in the grass and go down, shrieking, bob up again, turn and run. They climb up into the trees and lie like cats along the warm branches until their mothers scold them down and tweak their ears for staining their best shirts. How free they are, how unaware of duty or responsibility. They have taken no vows. Sometimes at St. Josefsheim, when his pipe could no longer hold his attention, he would play in the yard with the children. On days when fine weather put an early end to his lessons, he ran with his students in the field behind the school. He can't run as well now—that's the price of aging—but the longing for freedom and the innocence of play is no less powerful. He thinks, *Lord, I have done what you asked. I have gone where you sent me. Now make me good at my work—better than I was at protecting my students from harm.*

Three young men arrive late, shaking hands as they make their way through the orchard. Elisabeth leans close—not close enough to touch, but he is aware of her nearness and the unfelt pressure of contact that will never come, a phantom warmth against his shoulder. She lifts her chin in the direction of the newcomers. "The Kopp brothers. They own that big potato farm; you know the one. Out on the east side of the village." She tells him the children call the Kopp brothers, collectively, Kartoffelbauer—"potato maker." It is their private joke again, their habit of naming every citizen in Unterboihingen after his or her profession.

Kartoffelbauer make their way to the bride and groom. One must look closely to discern their differences—the nose a bit sharper on this brother, the chin stronger on that one, and the third with the first light lines of age traced in the corners of his eyes. They could almost be triplets, with their pale-blond hair and the same tenor note to their voices. In their three strong and youthful, sun-browned bodies, they make one polite, unison bow before the table of honor. They straighten at exactly the same time. Below the table, where Kartoffelbauer cannot see, Anton pinches the skin between his thumb and finger to keep himself from laughing.

"Herr Starzmann," says one of the brothers, "we stopped by Franke's place and loaded up your things."

"How thoughtful! Thank you, my friends."

"We've moved all your chests to the shed outside the house," another says. He jerks his thumb toward Elisabeth's stilt-legged cottage. "We didn't want to go inside without your permission."

"You know you're always welcome," Elisabeth says. "It was so kind of you to think of moving Herr Starzmann's things. I had entirely forgotten to see to it."

"So had I," Anton admits. He shakes the three right hands of Kartoffelbauer.

"Any time you need help," the eldest says, "I hope you'll call on us, *mein Herr.*"

These days, everyone is inclined to band together, even in the cities. Now we look out for our fellow man. We anticipate needs and give small tokens of comfort. We offer the milk of human kindness, free to drink all you will, for every other kind of sustenance is rationed on the stamps, with never enough to satisfy.

The brothers disperse into the crowd, eager to join in the celebration while it lasts. Anton watches them go. He thinks, *If we had taken up this habit of kindness long ago, before we fell into darkness, what suffering might we have spared the world and ourselves?*

The bleakness of his own musing embarrasses him anew; again, he feels his face burn red. A man ought to cultivate happier thoughts on his wedding day. But Anton has never done this before.

9

Dusk comes earlier as autumn takes hold. It steals the light from the world so fast that the wedding celebration has barely broken up, the tables and chairs carried back into Frau Hertz's house and the embroidered white cloth shaken off, folded in a neat square—and then full darkness has come. Anton and Elisabeth herd the sleepy children inside. The stairwell creaks and groans as they climb it together, this new-made family.

Inside, while the children cluster together in the dark, Elisabeth walks with her hands out, slowly and carefully, feeling her way toward light. She keeps a supply of candles in a small cupboard near the improvised kitchen: a porcelain sink, supplied by a hose from the farm's cistern, and a woodstove in the corner, walled on two sides with terra-cotta tiles. A match strikes in the black room—a quick hiss, a crackle of flame, a spot of orange light flowering. The smell of sulfur, acrid and sharp. She nurtures the light with a steady hand cupped behind the candle, a sheltering curve of amber.

"There has never been any electricity in this old house," she says, half apologetic, "so we're used to candlelight. The good news is, we're never troubled by blackouts, since we haven't any electric lights to miss."

The lone candle glows, revealing itself in an old-fashioned holder of plated brass with a dented handle. Behind the candle, behind the cupboard on which it sits, the wall plaster is pitted and cracked. Elisabeth produces from some shadowed corner another candle, whose wick she bends over with her stub of a match. The second flame catches. Then a third, and a fourth. The interior of the old house reveals itself, coming shyly out of hiding. It's the first time Anton has seen the inside of Elisabeth's home—his home, now. Curious, and with a tight lump in his throat, he examines the place. The sitting area, which takes up the better part of the main room, is neat and orderly. Sewing work lies folded in a basket, which is placed precisely next to a chair, with not a thread overhanging its edge. All the books are put away on a shelf below the window, in proper order with spines neatly aligned. There is an old-fashioned sofa against one wall, dark green fading to white on the worn cushions, but not a speck of dust on the upholstery. Everything is as tidy and ordered, as rigid as Elisabeth herself. Children never keep a home so well; their mother must spend every waking hour on housework when she isn't sewing shirts for the few clients who can still afford to pay. This ceaseless cleaning, endless organizing—is it something she does because it is in her nature? Or do those chores distract her from the world, from the things she knows are happening out there beyond the walls of her home?

Even with the candles burning, the house is dark. The curtains are drawn across the windows, which are not large at any rate—thick woolen curtains, made to smother the life out of any wayward flicker of light. Anton goes to the nearest window and pulls a curtain aside by no more than a handsbreadth. He is gripped by an urge to see the stars tonight, as if he might fix in his mind the date and time, the celestial map of the moment when his life changed forever. Chart the planets in their courses.

Elisabeth crosses the room, unhurried but stern. She tugs the curtain from his hand.

Maria says, "We keep the windows covered so they can't find us and drop bombs on us."

"Don't talk of such things," Elisabeth says at once. Lightly, she claps her hands. "You should all three be preparing for bed now. Go on, get to it."

This system of protection is elegant in its simplicity. By night, when the bombs do fall, a village as small as Unterboihingen will be invisible from the air. So long as no one leaves a curtain carelessly open while he reads in bed or finds his way to the toilet, the town will go unnoticed. Stuttgart is far too large for such practical defense, and still too full of life, despite the Tommies' best efforts. Berlin and Munich, too. So this is how the tiny village has escaped destruction while Stuttgart, less than thirty kilometers to the northwest, has borne one terrible bombardment after another.

The children haven't moved. They remain staring at Anton, in awe now of his proximity—of the very fact of a man standing among them. He is a new presence in their household, almost an invader. He stares back, uncertain, resisting the urge to shift from one foot to the other like a hapless boy. Should he say something? Lead them off to their rooms? Where are the children's rooms, exactly?

"You heard me," Elisabeth says. "Off with all of you; get dressed for bed. I'll be in to hear your prayers soon."

"I want the new *Vati* to tuck me in," Maria says.

Hesitant, Anton looks to Elisabeth for approval—perhaps she is not ready for this yet; perhaps in her two weeks of contemplation she has never asked herself, *What will I do, and what will I think, if my children take to their new father too strongly? If they turn to him for comfort—this stranger who I have brought into our orderly home—instead of me?* But Elisabeth nods, untroubled. This is no surprise to her. She answers Maria readily, practiced and calm. "Put on your nightgown and wash your face. When was the last time you brushed your teeth?" Maria shrugs. "Albert, take this candle into her room so she can dress. Then send her into the bathroom; I'll see to it that she cleans her teeth."

75

Maria resists. The dentifrice tastes bad. She doesn't like the way it foams on her toothbrush. She doesn't like her toothbrush; it tickles her mouth. But the boys pull her dutifully toward her room, and Elisabeth vanishes to the back of the house, and in a matter of moments, Anton is left alone in the dim sitting room.

He sinks down on the armchair, slowly, wincing. He is afraid it will creak, make some noise that will betray him—betray what? His inadequacy. His confusion. He looks at the empty, sagging sofa. Looks down at the sewing in the basket. This is how Elisabeth makes her meager pay, altering shirts and trousers. Small wonder she needs another income. That is not to say she's a poor hand. Anton can see little in the dim light of one candle (and that candle across the room), but he can make out enough of the precise, even stitches to tell that her work is excellent, as one would expect from this woman, so conscientious and correct. Who, though, can afford to pay a seamstress? Even in the cities, they have taken to mending and making their own clothes, rather than part with the money. Ragpickers do a brisk business, salvaging useful cloth from blown-apart buildings and God knows what other unthinkable sources. In Munich, the young ladies have made a fashion of it. They sew their own things from whatever they find in the streets or in the knapsacks of the rag boys who come calling, shouting out their wares. One would be thought unstylish now if one were to hire out the work.

From the bathroom, he hears the children locked in mild argument—a nighttime routine as ordinary as breathing. Elisabeth moves among her children in self-contained quiet. She pushes them apart, steps between, and the children settle complacently. Even Maria quits her protests and brushes her teeth. Below the floor, in the cool autumn air, he can hear the animals rustling, easing into sleep. Warmth rises from their bodies, from their home-scented hides. The dim space around him fills with sweet odors of hay and dry dust.

"All right." Elisabeth leans out from the bathroom door. "Maria is done, and she may have her story, if you are willing to tell one."

The little girl is dressed in a voluminous white gown of soft flannel. Bouncing on her toes, skipping through the night with her gold curls flying, she looks like a cherub come down from a stained-glass window. This is all an adventure to her. He follows her into the tiny room that is hers alone. It is scarcely larger than a closet; Anton can't imagine its original purpose, back when the farm was new. A pantry, or a cell for aging cheese? There is a bed stretched from wall to wall, just large enough to hold the six-year-old. Beside the bed, someone has placed a stool with a broken leg, making do for a nightstand. Anton sets the candle on the stool as Maria jumps onto her bed and burrows beneath the covers. He sinks down on the braided rug and folds himself against the wall. He just fits, with his knees pulled up as close to his chin as they will go.

"You look funny." Maria clutches the edges of her blanket and sheet.

He draws the covers up to her chin. "They didn't make this room to fit me."

In the candlelight, he can see that her eyes are red. She cried over the dentifrice after all.

"I want to hear a story," she says.

"Prayers first. Then a story."

She closes her eyes and presses her small hands together in a peak just below her lips. She whispers, "Dear God, thank You for sending us a good new *Vati*. I will try to be nice to him. And please make *Mutti* less sad now, since she has someone to help her." She opens her eyes. "Is that good?"

"It's a very nice prayer. And now you say—"

"Amen."

"Well done, Maria. If I tell you a story tonight, will you be good tomorrow night, and clean up without your mother watching to be sure you do it properly?" This seems the sort of thing a father ought to say to his daughter.

As Maria is in ready agreement, he recites an excellent story, a fairy tale about a funny old witch who lives in a house with chicken legs. Where did he hear it first? St. Josefsheim, from one of the other friars? Or did he pick it up in the Wehrmacht, on the long march to Riga? He can't remember now.

The girl is getting sleepy. Eyelids heavy, she says, "I thought you would tell a Bible story, since you were a monk."

"I was a friar. That's different from a monk. Do you want a Bible story next time?"

"No," she says quickly. "I like friars' stories better."

Before he knows just what he is doing, he is leaning forward to kiss her forehead. The gesture surprises him, but the glad ache in his heart surprises him more—how easily he has come to love these three little souls, how readily he has taken to this new role. Maria isn't troubled by the kiss, nor does she seem surprised. She sinks at once into sleep, her breath steady and slow.

Awkward in the cramped space, he stands and edges close to the room's tiny window. Before he moves the curtain aside, he remembers that he ought to blow out the candle. Out there, in the world beyond this small sanctuary, night deepens over the countryside. Fields and hills ripple one into another, black into dull, dark silver. The autumn stars are pale but numerous, not a single point of light overwhelmed by the distant glow of any city. The western horizon is lightless where Stuttgart ought to be. The city is blacked out tonight—power grid blown or taken out by some earlier offense, inaudible here in our secret village. We are invisible from the sky. Or perhaps in Stuttgart they have only run out of candles. Tonight, with the world black and quiet, no bombs will fall. There is nothing to see, no one to target, and we may sleep without fear.

He pulls the curtain closed, sheltering his small new daughter from harm.

When he reenters the sitting room, Elisabeth is waiting in her chair. A man's shirt is spread across her lap; she's looking down at it with an attentive air that makes him think she half expects the garment to get up and dance. But she isn't sewing—only looking. The boys have gone to bed. Tired as they are from the day's excitement, they may be asleep already.

Elisabeth folds the shirt and lays it carefully on her sewing basket. She rises; half a room apart, they stand together in awkward silence, neither quite looking at the other, neither knowing how to approach the subject of where Anton is to sleep.

At length, she says, "You might come and sleep in my bed, as there is nowhere else but the sofa, and it isn't very comfortable. But you needn't think—"

"I don't think," he says, smiling to put her at ease. "I quite meant what I said—our agreement, you understand. I'll give you some time to change. I'll just step outside and have a moment with my pipe."

Relieved that the matter is settled, easy as that, Elisabeth disappears into her room, the one at the back of the old house. Anton slips out the door and descends the stairs as silently as he can manage.

Once out of doors, he realizes there is not as much starlight as he'd first thought. The night is as dark as the bottom of a well, and beneath his feet, the steep stairway feels rickety and treacherous. By the time he eases down the unfamiliar steps, he has lost all desire to smoke. In the shadows below the house, the animals sigh. With one hand, he feels his way along the stone foundation and finds the little shed where Kartoffelbauer left his things. The door sticks; it scrapes over the old stone threshold. He opens one trunk, then another, groping through them in perfect blackness, searching for his necessities by feel. The world is so lightless, the night so cold, that he is seized all at once by instinctive terror. The hair at the nape of his neck rises, and his spine burns with a ripple of dread. When he was a child, fear of the dark would take him this way, every now and then, sudden and strong.

In those moments, when he froze in the grip of panic, he would often imagine a tiger crouching just where he couldn't see, its body tight and quivering, gape-jawed and hungry. Or sometimes a *Nachzehrer*, a blood drinker, wearing the guise of a long-dead uncle or a cousin Anton never knew, trailing its funerary shroud and chewing on its own bones. Those were a child's fears. Now he dreads something altogether different. The bayonets, the rifles, the gray bus belching smoke from its rotted belly. And in Riga, by the light of a church on fire, women who were once raped by Russian soldiers raped again by their German liberators.

He finds his bundle of clothing, spins to face the darkness, and leaves the lid of the chest to slam shut behind him. He had expected a shadow moving across the old shed's threshold, reaching out one black hand to claim him. But there is nothing beside the open door, nothing over his shoulder but a mire of memory.

When he reenters the cottage with its blessing of candlelight, Elisabeth is still vanished behind her door. He changes into his night-shirt in the empty living room. The candle has burned down to a tiny stub, almost to nothing. He must find out whether his wife has more candles. If she hasn't, it must be he who gets them, he who buys them. That is what husbands do—husbands and fathers. They see to it that no one goes wanting.

In his nightshirt, he stands and waits, listening—for what? The house is silent and still, but the air is dense with another remembrance, ripe and heavy with its own sort of hostility. Anton can all but see him—the first husband, the one who will never buy candles again, nor kiss Maria on her forehead, nor share a slice of cake with Elisabeth. The man is restless, besieged by his own heart, angered by all the things left undone. His shade paces around the room in the dull umber slant of shadows.

To the memory of Herr Herter, Anton whispers, "I only want to be good to Elisabeth, and to your children. God willing, my friend." He hopes it's enough to dissipate the chill in the air.

Anton takes the candle, almost burned away now, and taps on Elisabeth's door. "Come in," she says, her voice thin and emotionless.

He edges carefully into the room. She has placed her candle on the dresser and stands before it—before the square mirror hanging above—tucking her hair into a lace-edged nightcap. She moves away, stepping out of her slippers and placing them side by side just beneath the edge of her bed, and Anton, hesitant, occupies the space she has left. He sets his nearly exhausted candle on the dresser beside her own. The flame thins itself in a pool of oily wax, gathered in the cup of the candlestick. Like the memory of a flame. He imagines Herr Herter, watchful in his grave, gripping one thumb, left eye open.

"Did you close the curtain in Maria's room?"

"I did."

"Thank you." Such a formal thing to say to one's husband.

Elisabeth gets into bed. She is so tidy in her movements, so carefully controlled, that he hardly sees her do it. One moment she is standing; the next, she is flat beneath the white quilt. But why shouldn't she be at ease here? This is her house, her bedroom, her family.

He blows out the remnant of his candle. Then he pinches the wick of Elisabeth's light, too. He climbs into her bed, stomach knotted, shoulders aching. There is a tingle on his thumb where he touched the flame. Through the mattress, he can feel Elisabeth's tension, the stiffness of her back and the quiver of her limbs.

He needn't think, and he doesn't think. He rolls onto his side, confining himself to the edge of the mattress, where he may put his new wife at ease.

10

In the morning, Anton follows the children outside to gather eggs. They are glad to have someone to hold the basket; it frees them up to play around the corners of the chicken coop. They lift rocks and tear apart the woodpile to search for salamanders; they jump across the ditch to the hedge, where brambles still hang a few honey-scented berries in patchy shade, the last of summer's sweetness. Despite their ceaseless movement, their peregrinations about the farmyard, the children are remarkably smart in their work, and the basket fills quickly. Anton settles the handle in the crook of his elbow where the weight is easier to manage.

When Al decides they've collected enough eggs, he leads the way under the apple trees, down the lane with its remnant of hollyhocks toward the village market. The younger children run ahead. They lash tall roadside weeds with sticks, snapping off seed heads and scattering dust in the weak autumn sun. Al remains beside Anton. The boy's gaze shifts and slides along the rutted road. Al has the strained air of having something important to say.

Anton waits for him to speak. Finally, the boy says, "We usually get good trades for our eggs—flour, this time of year. And there will be some vegetables, and maybe some marmalade or apple-peel jelly."

"Your mother has told me how the town makes trades. It seems a very clever system to me."

"Yes, but I wonder . . ." A pause; Al stuffs his hands deep into his pockets, as if reaching for courage down there among the pebbles and marbles he's collected. "I wonder what you'll do to support us. Now that you're our stepfather."

"It does you credit, that you think about such things." What a world we live in, where an eleven-year-old boy must trouble himself with a man's concerns.

Anton has often wondered himself what he ought to do, now that he is the father of a large and hungry family. A friar's staples of bread and tinned beans won't do, except in extremity of want—and anyway, the modest sum of money he has stretched since his discharge from the Wehrmacht can't last forever. *How will you support them, now that you're their stepfather?* The two weeks he spent waiting for the marriage, pacing above Franke's furniture shop, ducking his head to avoid the slope of the ceiling, he asked himself that same question more times than he could count.

"I had thought," Anton says to the boy, "I might be a teacher. I used to teach, in my life before."

"But Unterboihingen has enough teachers already. There are only the two schools, one for the oldest children, one for the little children—and none of them are wanting."

"I see. Perhaps I could teach music, if you think there is interest." Unterboihingen does not appear to have a music teacher. During his strolls through the village, when he walked alone with his thoughts, he detected no signs of lessons—no tempo-less plunking of piano keys, no tortured screech of a violin. "What do you say, Al?"

The boy smiles up at him, shyly, grateful to be consulted like a man. "I think it's a fine idea—worth trying, anyhow." But his lips thin for a moment, and he squints thoughtfully after his brother and sister, who, far ahead on the road, have begun to shout at the neighbor's dog, trying to make it shout back. In Albert's silence, Anton finds the distinct and uncomfortable impression that he is already something of a disappointment to his new family. A proper father would have had work lined up before the wedding—a good job with steady hours, ready and waiting. A proper father wouldn't need to ask his son, *What do you think I should do?*

◆ ◆ ◆

Saturday, market day. The square at the center of the village bustles and boils with activity. Boys and girls have come from every farm, and wives and old men, too, with the last of the harvest's produce to offer up in trade. This system of barter is a quaint tradition, one that would never exist today, in our modern world of automobiles and radio broadcasts, tinned food, and electric lights. It's war that has resurrected these cunning old ways; deprivation keeps the past alive. But if one good thing has come from the war, surely this is it. Throughout the square, people gather, shaking hands and sharing the week's news. They display their squashes and sacks of barley with obvious pride. In an improvised rope pen, seven-month lambs bleat and mill, ready for the slaughter, while two young women look on proudly, shoulders thrown back and fists on hips. Had war never come, those girls might have been secretaries or seamstresses, smartly dressed behind a desk in Munich. Now they are shepherdesses with mud to their knees. The work they do keeps the children of the village strong and healthy, well fed and ready to face the winter.

One of the shepherdesses waves to Al as he enters the market square, and someone else calls, "Who needs eggs? Young Herr Herter has arrived!" Every home in Unterboihingen has its own hens, of course, but Al's birds are special. He has bred them carefully, an assiduous boy, with special attention paid to production and lineage. His eggs have a reputation: the best and biggest in Unterboihingen, big as ducks' eggs, large and rich enough that two for breakfast can fill a grown man's belly right through until suppertime. Anton watches the boy move confidently through the marketplace; he needs no guidance from Anton or any other man. Al has taken the egg basket from Anton's arm. He speaks to each customer in turn, driving his bargains with one hand stretched across the basket's top, protective of his wares. Al holds every egg close, and barters dearly. Only the best squashes will win a trade of half a dozen eggs from young Herr Herter—great, round, ribbed squashes, with skins so darkly green they are almost black and flesh sweet as honey. Al directs the fellow with the squashes to deposit them in Anton's arms. In the shed beside the cottage stair, Al says, the squashes will keep for months, nice and cold through fall and winter. Mother will make a stew with them. She'll keep it simmering on the stove for days at a time; one squash will fill our bellies for a week at least. For three more eggs, Al secures two bunches of beet greens. They aren't Maria's favorite, but Mother says she must eat them all the same. For eight eggs, he wins a real prize: a fat triangle of ripe cheese sealed in yellow wax.

"Not many boys your age would trade for greens instead of candy," Anton tells him.

"They wouldn't?" Al seems surprised.

"How many eggs are left?"

"Ten. I think I can get some honey, if Frau Werner has any left from her beehives. And Kartoffelbauer might have some old potatoes, too."

"I'm afraid you must tuck whatever else you find in your basket. My arms are full."

Smiling, Al nods. He works his way into the crowd with the last of his eggs, leaving Anton alone, an island in a sea of friends and neighbors.

Anton hugs the produce to his chest. He turns slowly, taking in the crowd, trying to pick out anyone he may recognize, hoping he can match names to some. It's long since time he got to know the people of his home village. His eyes slide over faces that may as well be blank and featureless; he knows no one, though surely some of these people attended his wedding. But then, with a jolt of surprise, he spots a single familiar figure in the crowd. Across the square, he finds Elisabeth, her expression more serious than ever before. She is carrying a flat basket by its looped handle. Whatever the basket contains is covered by a checked cloth, tucked neatly in at the edges. She leans close to a tall blonde woman, whispering in her ear. The blonde woman nods, nods again; her eyes are as shadowed as Elisabeth's, her jaw as firmly set. The flat basket changes hands. The blonde woman makes off across the market square, moving quickly, glancing now and then over her shoulder. Elisabeth watches her go.

"Elisabeth!"

When Anton calls out to her, she jumps, guilty and flushed. Her brow furrows when she sees him, a fleeting expression of annoyance, but she quickly smooths it away. She tilts her head—*Come with me*, the gesture seems to say—and threads her way through the crowd before Anton can reach her side.

When he catches up, Elisabeth is beyond the market square, walking slowly and alone down an empty street. The murmur of the crowd and the low, insistent bleating of the lambs thins behind them.

"I didn't expect to find you at the market," Anton says.

She glances at the things in his arms, the tassel of beet greens spilling over the deep ribs of squashes. "Albert chose well."

"Are you sure I didn't choose?" he says, teasing.

Her smile is brief, indulging. "Something tells me you don't know how to market properly. Not yet."

"That's so; I can't deny it. When I was a friar, St. Josefsheim handed me everything I needed—and Wehrmacht food wasn't any good, but I never had to trouble myself how to get it."

"You'll learn, in time." She is distracted, eyes and thoughts far away. They walk on in silence for a moment. Then Elisabeth turns to him suddenly, wringing her hands. "I don't know if I did right, Anton. And I'm dreadfully afraid I've done something terrible—something unforgivable."

"Elisabeth." Should he call her something else? Dear, darling, *meine Liebste*? "Whatever do you mean?"

She draws a breath, then shuts her mouth tightly. He is quick enough to catch the look she gives him from the corner of her eye—searching, wary, untrusting.

"Whatever it is, you can tell me," he says. "I am your husband, after all."

"Yes, but—" She swallows hard. *But you are a stranger to me still. But who really knows whether anyone can be trusted, in this world, in this Germany?* As she hesitates, wrestling with uncertainty, Anton can all but feel her heartbeat, thick and racing, tight in her throat. He's about to say, *I will never betray your secrets,* or perhaps, *Whatever you've done, we can undo it, if need be*—when Elisabeth turns to him again with that same rush of desperation. "It was pork, Anton. In the basket. I told Claudia to pass along word that it's beef. And it was smoked, so I suppose that's all they'll taste. But what if they know the difference?"

He lets out a slow breath, understanding. "Claudia—that blonde woman—she's hiding a family?"

There is no need to specify what kind of family. The better part of the nation's undesirables have already been netted and filtered into camps—the Gypsies, the journalists, the mentally unwell. The men who love men, the women who love women. It's the Jews who have made the most tenacious stand, refusing to leave—or unable to leave, poor souls. The lucky ones, the ones who might have some frail hope of survival, huddle in ghettos or live like rats in darkness, cringing between our walls, in the attics of our homes.

"Not Claudia," Elisabeth says quietly. "I don't know who it is—who in Unterboihingen has opened up their home. Perhaps they aren't in Unterboihingen at all but some other village along the river. It's better if I don't know, of course, for if trouble ever comes here, they'll punish anyone who knew, anyone who didn't report it to the gauleiter."

If trouble ever comes. If the SS come.

"But Claudia knows who."

Her eyes fill with tears. "You won't say anything. Please, Anton—I know we aren't supposed to hide them, but I can't. I can't just go on living as if nothing is wrong, when I know what *they* do, where they send the Jews when they catch them—"

"There, now." Gently, like soothing a frightened child. If his arms weren't full of squashes, he would take her hand. "You have nothing to fear—not from me. I'll never tell a soul, Elisabeth. I promise you that. Certainly, I will never tell that gauleiter."

She nods. She sighs, a long and shuddering sound, releasing the better part of her fear.

"But you gave them pork?" Anton doesn't want to laugh. It isn't exactly funny, and yet there is precious little humor in the world.

"It was all I had." She shakes her head, caught up, too, in an irreverent desire to smile. "A small ham that Frau Hertz and I smoked this spring. I had planned to save it for the winter, but when Claudia told me about that poor family, how badly they need food . . . The ham will keep better than anything else I could have sent, say eggs or potatoes. I could have spared some oats, but I suppose they have no way to cook, hiding in an attic or a cellar."

"You did right," Anton says. "It was good of you. Generous. It's food from your children's plates, but you gave it willingly."

"We'll do all right, with Albert's eggs." She presses her hands to her cheeks, as if trying to cool the heat of embarrassment. "But what if they know it's pork, Anton? What if Claudia forgets to say it's beef or lamb? They'll think I've done it to be cruel—that I'm mocking them with a ham."

"They'll think no such thing. Even if they can tell it's neither beef nor lamb, they will be grateful. They won't turn their noses up, I'm sure."

"If they can tell, and they eat it, anyway, then I've made them break their laws. God's laws."

"God will forgive. Of that, I'm certain." In the worst extremities, God does not resort to pedantry. The creator of all things has more sense than that, or so Anton believes.

"Here, give me those." Elisabeth takes two of the squashes from his arms. "You shouldn't have to carry everything yourself."

"And neither should you. Shall we make our way home?"

"Yes. Albert will bring the little ones home when he's finished with his eggs."

At home, when the squashes and cheese have been installed in the shed, waiting in an orderly row on the shelf over Anton's trunks, Elisabeth stands in the trampled yard in a shaft of late-morning light. The beet greens trail from her hand, tips of dark leaves brushing the earth. She stares up at the cottage, raised on its stilts, her head thrown back so she can see the highest window, and above it, the peak of the roof and the small attic space it conceals.

11

In daylight, there is no need to draw the curtains. Elisabeth has pulled the lengths of heavy wool aside and tied them back with strips of braided rag, and mellow afternoon light floods the cottage, warming every corner, gleaming on the smooth-worn wood of the ancient floor. The old furniture loses its austerity in the wash of sunshine. It looks comfortable and easy now, and even more so when Elisabeth settles on her chair and sorts through her sewing basket, one knee crossed over the other, her dark head bowed over pincushion and thread. The children have gone outside to play.

Anton lingers beside the window. It's a simple pleasure, to bask in the sun; its warmth drives away the dark thoughts that plague him, that have followed him from St. Josefsheim. From the cottage's height, he can see the tops of the apple trees, where a few golden fruits still cling to the uppermost boughs.

"Perhaps I ought to leave the sewing to you," Elisabeth says comfortably. "Maria's dress has held where you patched it. I never thought to find a husband who could sew."

"I'm no tailor, but I learned enough in the order to keep my habit from falling to rags."

"I could teach you to tailor, if you like." She doesn't look up at him, and there is no change to her tone, but Anton takes her meaning readily enough. *What will you do for work?*

"I had thought I might teach," he says, "but Albert tells me there's no need for teachers in Unterboihingen."

"I believe he's correct. The two schools are quite small."

"Naturally. What are you working on?"

Elisabeth lifts her work from the basket—a pair of boy's trousers in gray-brown tweed. "Albert's," she says. "I can let out the cuffs by a few more centimeters, but that's it; I can do no more with these. And he's growing so fast. Of course, Paul can make use of these trousers once Albert outgrows them, but I shall have to patch the knees and the seat by then. They're getting quite worn. I'd rather not send Paul out of the house with patches all across his bottom, but we must make do, I suppose." She sighs and returns to her work. "Patches will do for Paul, but I must make a whole new pair of trousers for Albert soon. I'll need good, thick wool, so they'll last through the next few winters."

"Good wool isn't easy to find just now. I don't suppose the ragpickers find their way to Unterboihingen." Anton tests one of the curtains between his fingers, feeling the weight and drape.

"We don't get rag sellers here, no—and I won't part with my curtains, so don't even suggest it, *Herr*. Only a fool would leave their windows uncovered. The plain truth is, Anton—we need to buy new fabric."

"It's terribly expensive."

She frowns over her stitches. "Of course it is, but there's no getting around it. In a city, I might make do with rags, but there's nothing I can hope to scavenge in this village. I've already begged and traded with the neighbors for their old clothing—anything I might alter to fit the children. But Unterboihingen exhausted its supply of secondhand goods years ago. If we don't purchase a few yards of wool soon, I hate to think how we'll fare next winter."

Now, at last, she does look up, holding Anton's eye with an expression that says, *You're my husband now. What are you going to do about it?*

Sheepish, Anton says, "Albert gave me much the same lecture this morning. I should have thought more carefully about what I could do to support the family."

"Have you anything to sell? Anything valuable?"

"Nothing, I'm afraid. Friars don't live extravagant lives. You say the schools have plenty of teachers, but with my experience, perhaps I might tutor students in the evenings."

"This isn't Munich or Stuttgart. No one has money to spare now for something as frivolous as tutoring."

"Frivolous?" He smiles.

Elisabeth is not smiling. "Tutoring is frivolity, in times like these. No parent would choose history or geometry over food for their child's belly. Or clothes for their child's back," she adds pointedly.

He had hoped to tutor children in music, not geometry, but it's likely that parents have even less use for private music lessons. Now it's his turn to sigh. "You're right. Perhaps I should go down to the church and speak with Father Emil."

A consultation with their priest seems as good a use of his time as anything else Anton can devise. In any case, the father is likely to know best whether Unterboihingen can support a music tutor. It's always the local clergyman who knows the intimate details of every family, every sheep in his fold.

At St. Kolumban, he lets himself into the narthex—the door is never locked—dips his hand in the holy water, and makes the sign of the cross. Emil enters from somewhere beyond the lectern, from an unseen passage behind the pierce-work screen. The priest halts, surprised by the sight of Anton with his fingers still dripping holy water. But Emil recovers quickly and smiles in welcome, his aging face all crags and lines. He is somewhere near the tail end of middle age—just on the brink of being old but still retaining a notable strength, the resolute, upright posture and square shoulders of a man undaunted. Certainly, Father Emil exhibits the enthusiasm of a much younger man.

"Herr Starzmann, my friend." He stretches out his hand and takes Anton by the shoulder. "How do you find married life?"

"It's hard to say. I've only been married for a day."

"But even so."

He shrugs. "I'm doing as well as can be expected of a man like me." A man out of his depth, disoriented and, for the first time in his life, without a clue as to how he should proceed.

Emil laughs good-naturedly. Together they sit, as before, on the frontmost pew.

The priest says, "Do you know what I think? I believe being a father suits you. There's a gladness about you I hadn't noticed before, a certain lightness of the spirit. I can see it in you already."

"I do enjoy the children—very much. They're such good, earnest little people; Albert especially. Maria is contrary, but she doesn't mean to be. She's only young. She'll mellow, with time. And Paul—he makes me smile every minute I'm with him."

"I have always been quite fond of the Herter children. Or are we to call them the Starzmann children now?"

Anton says distractedly, "They can go by whichever name they please. I'll care for them just the same, either way." A pause, and then: "Yes, the children make me feel quite content. I only hope I'll find the same joy in being a husband—but I fear it will be some time before I do." Friars do not live by the same codes as other men, but even so, he knows it's a shameful thing, for a husband and father to admit to such a failing. How can a man be so confounded by his wife?

"Elisabeth is . . . a complicated woman," Emil says carefully. "She has her defenses. But don't we all?"

But will she ever let me in, past the walls she's built around her? And have I any right to expect it? He says only, "Times are hard, you know. I'm worried about the children, and Elisabeth."

"Times are hard, indeed. But that is why God brought you here— to worry over this precious family."

"I need to find some way to provide, Father. That much is clear already. The boys are growing too fast; Elisabeth needs to make new clothes for them both, but we haven't enough money for cloth. You know how expensive it is these days. If we had ragpickers here, like in Munich, we might hope to find good cloth we can afford. But no rag-pickers would bother trekking out here to Unterboihingen."

"And Elisabeth has inquired, I suppose, of other mothers in the village?"

"Yes, but no one has clothing to spare—not that will fit the boys. We're in a bad place, with winter coming. If I had a little income, I would go to the city and find whatever Elisabeth needs. But what are we to do? No one will accept eggs in trade for wool or canvas. It's a *job* I need."

Emil nods thoughtfully, eyes fixed on the altar. He strokes his chin, waiting for Anton to say more.

"I had initially thought I might take up with one of the local schools. But Albert and Elisabeth both set me straight; there are enough teachers already."

"That's so."

"Then I thought I should offer music lessons—but as we agree, these days are difficult for everyone. Who can afford to pay a music tutor?"

Father Emil frowns at the cross, gilded yet small above the altar. His eyes are distant as he searches and sorts through a long corridor of thought. At length, he says, "I think you can expect to make some money by teaching music, Anton. You won't earn a fortune, that's certain—but I believe you will make enough to get by. Even a small income will help stretch the trades young Albert makes at the market—and that, I'm sure, will relieve some of Elisabeth's fears. Tell me, can you play the organ?"

Anton brightens. "I can."

"Well, then." The priest stands, eager and energetic. He gestures to the rood screen behind the podium, to the shadowed space behind it. "Come along and show me."

Together, they climb to the chancel and step behind the screen. There the organ stands, shrouded in shadow, almost as old as St. Kolumban itself. It is all gleam of polished oak casing and smoothness of ivory keys, a forest of slender pipes with angular black throats sharply incised, ready to sing.

Anton shakes his head in wonder. "I had no idea it was here, hiding behind the rood. It's beautiful."

"Beautiful," Emil agrees, "but I haven't heard it played for years. We had a woman who knew how to do it, but she moved away, and no one in this town has taken her place. I'm quite hopeless when it comes to music—it has never been my strength—but even if I did possess some modest skill, I couldn't play while leading the service."

"No, I suppose you couldn't." He can't take his eyes off the instrument.

"Don't be shy," Emil says, giving him an encouraging tap on the shoulder, almost a push toward the bench.

Hesitant with awe, Anton approaches the organ. His pulse leaps, and in his chest, there is a telltale pressure, a poignant yearning, as if he draws near a sacred relic. He brushes the white keys with one hand. They are smooth and cool, worn by uncountable years. Then he touches the black keys, letting his fingers fall into the spaces between. He hardly dares to do more.

Long before he ever touched a cornet or a flute, Anton began by playing the organ. It was so long ago now that it seems more than a lifetime has passed—as if it had happened to another man who lived long before Anton. When he was only a boy, younger than Paul, he came to know the organ's keys and foot pedals. His legs seemed to grow with the express purpose of playing, unlocking for him a greater range of those deep, dark, rumbling bass notes. He grew tall and thin, with arms long enough to rival a stork's wingspan, just so he could reach farther to the left and the right, and find new scales and octaves waiting. Long before he realized he ought to be intimidated by the sheer size and complexity of the instrument, the organ became his friend. It was his first love, the door that opened for him—but how long has it been since he played anything with a keyboard? Months, if not a year. Or more than a year—and that was the old piano in the music room back at St. Josefsheim, the one that never managed to stay in tune.

"I do hope you'll play something," Emil says. "You are most welcome. I would love to hear this old dame sing again. I imagine she needs tuning, or fixing—whatever is done with an organ when it hasn't been touched in years, except to clean the dust off now and then."

Anton takes the bench; it creaks beneath him, an aged and rusty whisper. Tentative, shy, he feels with his feet; the pedals push back against his toes with ready pressure. From this angle, the pipes tower overhead when he cranes back his head to look. They seem tall as St. Kolumban's bell tower, and delicate as the arches of a cathedral. Humbly, conscious of his shortcomings, Anton begins to play. The music fills the church first, occupying the nave with its bright, sudden leap into being. A heartbeat later, it fills him—a simple chord to test the sound, but it shakes his bones like a roar, like a peal of the sweetest thunder. He holds the note. It goes on and on, around him, in him; his heart wells with the sound, with the feel of music, and then, when the glad weight in his chest is more than he can bear, his hands begin to move of their own accord. He reaches for the notes with instinctive confidence and lapses into the first musical thought that comes to him: *"Großer Gott, wir loben dich."*

The organ needs tuning, but still the sound is delicious, palliative. Music eases every pain we don't know we carry. It banishes the fear that is so commonplace now, we have grown inured to its shadow and chill. Anton gives himself over to the simple pleasure of unrestrained worship.

Hark! The loud celestial hymn
Angel choirs above are raising,
Cherubim and seraphim,
In unceasing chorus praising;
Fill the heavens with sweet accord:
Holy, holy, holy Lord.

The chords lift him higher, raising his spirit above the brass spires of the organ pipes, beyond the arches of St. Kolumban into the peace of a still blue Heaven. The Earth, with its man-made sorrows, seems to dwindle below.

Spare the people, Lord, we pray,
By a thousand snares surrounded:
Keep us without sin today,
Never let us be confounded.
Lo, I put my trust in Thee;
Never, Lord, abandon me.

He doesn't realize he has sung aloud until he reaches the end. As the last chord echoes in the nave, he hears the song's final words coming from his throat, thin below the confident harmonies of the organ. He falls silent and takes his hands reluctantly from the keys. He waits on the bench, humble and still, but filled with a satisfying ecstasy, an unexpected nearness to God.

When silence fills the church again, Emil says, "You sing beautifully."

"Thank you." Anton's face is hot; he has seldom sung in front of anyone, except to guide his students to the correct notes on their horns, and that hardly counts as singing.

"And you play as if you were born to it."

He laughs, self-deprecating. "I was not born to it, I can tell you that. But the priest of my church—I mean, the one my family attended when I was a child—he let me experiment until I learned how it was done, more or less."

"More or less?" Emil says wryly. Then, "I'll pay you ten reichsmarks a week, if you'll play at service. It's not much, I know—and on weeks when the collection is small, I'll be forced to pay you even less. It's the best I can offer for now. But if you will do it, Herr Starzmann, I know the whole village will be grateful. We need to hear the sound of our own music again."

"I'll be glad to," he says. "And please, call me Anton."

Emil brushes his hands together, a businesslike gesture. "As for your music lessons—there are two families in Unterboihingen who own pianos."

"So many? Here?" Who would think to find such luxuries as pianos in this quaint old village?

"It seems unlikely, I know, but the Schneider and Abt families are well off. They always have been. They're blessed with—what is the phrase?—*Altgelt*." Old money. "It seems the war has hardly touched them, lucky souls. I must say, they have been unfailingly generous to everyone around them, and have shared their good fortune with those in need. I can't fault them one inch. A priest can ask nothing more of his parish than kindness and generosity."

"And you think they'll pay for music lessons?"

"It's worth asking. Both families do seem to place a certain emphasis on culturing their little ones. To tell you the truth, I wonder that they never moved to Munich or Berlin, generations ago. But perhaps they simply feel Unterboihingen is too pretty to leave."

It is a lovely place. With his newfound prospect of a little pay, Anton likes the village even better. "I'll speak to them," he says eagerly. "I'll pay a visit to both families today, unless you think I had better wait."

Father Emil squeezes Anton's shoulder. "Let me find a pencil and some scrap of paper. I'll give you their addresses. But if you'll come and play at tomorrow's service, you can impress them with a display of your skills firsthand."

Anton spends the remainder of his Saturday inside the body of the organ, among old shadows that smell of ancient wood and dark grease. He tunes, adjusts, tests the notes until the sound is perfect and clear, until it slips down the length of St. Kolumban smooth as a silk ribbon pulled through your fingers.

The next day, when he enters the church beside his family, he pats Elisabeth on the hand—she glances at him, surprised by his affection—and says, "Excuse me, please."

"You aren't going to sit in the back again," she says, "now that we're married."

"No." He winks at the children. Then, because he is brimming with confidence, he winks at his wife, too. "I'm going to sit all the way in front."

"Anton? What do you mean?"

But he makes off without answering, straight up the aisle to the heart of the church. He has worked out the details with Father Emil already—when he should begin, which songs he will play—and when the moment comes, when the nave is half full, he touches the keys and raises from his instrument a cascade and a rumble, a chorus of bright, fulsome praise. He cannot hear the parishioners exclaim, but he can feel it—their wonder unfolding, their shudder of awe, shared in his own warming heart.

When the morning's music has concluded and Father Emil takes his lectern, he tells the congregation, "We are blessed to have a musician among us again—our new neighbor, Anton Starzmann, husband of our beloved sister Elisabeth." And at the end of the service, when the last hymn is finished, Anton rises from the organ bench to find Elisabeth standing at the foot of the chancel steps. She's holding their children's hands. She smiles up at him with appreciation, with unrestrained pride, and the light of her happiness is the most beautiful sight he has seen since he turned his back on Riga and marched the other way.

He thinks, *I might, after all, avoid making a mess of this new life. I might even excel at this husband business—who can say?*

Two other women join Elisabeth below the chancel. They are dressed as humbly as anyone else in the church—no bright colors, no diamonds or furs—but there is a newness to their dresses, a freshness of style, an unfaded quality that sets them apart. These, then, can only be Fraus Abt and Schneider, the *Altgelt* mothers of Unterboihingen.

"Vater Emil told me you are available to teach the children music," one says. She is the taller of the two, dark-haired and dark-eyed. Her face seems to hold an expression of natural gladness, for the corners of her mouth turn up on their own, even when she isn't smiling. She must be of an age with Elisabeth, but there are no weary lines around her eyes or her mouth, no trace of a permanent frown crossing her forehead. She is unmistakably pretty; yet somehow, Anton can't help feeling his wife is more beautiful still.

The woman clasps her hands, eager and hopeful. "I am Frau Abt. I regret we haven't had occasion to meet until now, *mein Herr*. But I have a piano, and I would be grateful if you would come and teach my children how to play. Once or twice a week would be ideal—or whenever you are available."

"And I," Frau Schneider adds. "I've a piano, too. Will Wednesdays do for you?"

12

The new wool cost Anton dearly—eight hundred reichsmarks, well more than a good pair of shoes might cost in a black-market Berlin alleyway. But for that extravagant price, he secured an entire bolt of plain brown tweed—enough to last the family through two winters, he prays.

Elisabeth is thrilled with the acquisition. She sends Albert to his room to try on his new trousers, and when he reemerges, she kneels beside her son to fuss with the cuffs, smiling in satisfaction. "They look splendid on you, Albert. Hold still, now, while I pin everything in place. With a little luck, you won't outgrow these quite so fast."

"I'll try not to," Al says.

"Off you go, then, and bring these back to me. Be careful not to prick yourself on the pins when you take them off."

When Albert returns the trousers, Elisabeth moves two candles close to her sewing chair and begins fixing the carefully rolled cuffs in place.

"You make the finest stitches I've ever seen," Anton says, watching over her shoulder.

"Flatterer."

"It's not flattery if it's true."

"I never had to work while my first husband was still living, of course. But after he died, I had some hope that I might support the children by sewing alone."

She might have succeeded, had the war not dragged on so long. "I am sure, if people had any money to spend, you would be the most popular seamstress in all of Württemberg."

"Now that is flattery." Her smile fades as she works a few more stitches. "If *we* had more money to spend . . ." She trails off, her cheeks coloring.

"Don't be afraid to speak," Anton says, not without a twinge of wariness.

"We could do with a few more things. But when not? I don't want to seem ungrateful, Anton. I know this cloth was expensive."

It was. The Abts and Schneiders paid generously, but even so, Anton was obliged to dip into his meager supply of money to afford the wool. Precious little remains. The cloth is not a miracle he can repeat. But what has he come here for, if not to provide? "Tell me, Elisabeth."

"Paul needs shoes. His old pair are pinching his feet something terrible. He tries to hide it from me—he's such a dear little heart—but I can tell, all the same."

"Every child receives shoes from the rations."

"But only once a year, and Paul is growing almost as fast as Albert."

"I see. And you've already asked around town, I suppose—"

"Of course." She doesn't look up from her needle and thread, not wishing to be confrontational. But Anton can sense the impatience in her words. It was a ridiculous question to ask. Who doesn't seek a trade before spending precious money?

"I could find larger shoes for Paul," Elisabeth says. "Something man-size, or close to it. But then I would have to stuff the toes with rags, and he wouldn't be able to run and play. It would be as good as hobbling him. I'm sorry, Anton—I know it's a burden to you. But what else are we to do?"

"Don't apologize. The boy needs what he needs." And what is a father for, if not to give his children whatever they need? Heaviness settles in his chest. Lessons from the two families won't be enough. He will need train fare to Stuttgart and enough reichsmarks to convince the back-alley traders to part with a good pair of shoes—just big enough for a boy to grow into, but not large enough to keep him from running. Anton must find more work, and soon.

He goes to the hook beside the door and fishes for his pipe in the pocket of his jacket. It's only now he sees how thin and patched his coat has become. He won't bring it to Elisabeth's attention; let her keep the precious wool for the children's clothes.

"Where are you going?" Elisabeth asks.

Anton holds up his pipe. "The tobacco rations are still useful, at least."

"You aren't angry?"

"No, Elisabeth—no." Only worried. What else should he be? "A man merely needs some time alone with his pipe and his thoughts, now and then." Time to plan. Time to fret where no one can see the despair hardening his face. He steps outside and descends to the dusky yard.

Strange, how quickly warmth vacates the world, how ready the season is to sink into darkness. Every year it takes him by surprise— the shortening of daylight hours until it seems the natural state of the world, since the day of first creation, is twilight or the time just before it, the soft gray dullness of a sunset lost behind a wall of cloud, and a smell of promised rain.

He has been working for two weeks now, but what has he to show for it, really? For a fortnight, he has been able to call himself a teacher— something he'd thought he never could be again. The work lifts his spirits, when spirits can be lifted, but darkness still catches him now and then. That's the nature of darkness. It comes at the end of every day, predictable as the striking of a clock's chime, even in the heart of summer, when the light is full and lingering. You can never quite escape the night. Perhaps that's as God wills; this must be His design. How are we to know when our lives are good and when we are blessed, if we have no sorrow, no deprivation for comparison's sake? There is, he believes, a purpose to all the Creator's ways. But the mind and heart of God are beyond the understanding of Man. You can know your suffering serves a purpose—that the suffering of others plays some inscrutable part in the grand drama of Creation. But knowing brings you little comfort. When night drops its heavy curtain across the world, darkness is cruel and unforgiving. The way all your happiness can snuff itself in an instant, like the flame of a candle pinched between a licked finger and thumb—it can shake your faith, or strip faith away entirely, if you let it.

On the long march to Riga, the men had often sung. Whenever that straight, unvaried road passed by empty fields or forests instead of homesteads—whenever they could feel sure no one was listening—they would take up the thread of some old-fashioned tune. They held to the music, clinging to it with chapped and trembling hands—and like a guideline, it pulled them through the cold and the dark. The songs were simple. Folk music, reminders of times long ago when the country was something different from what it is now. When we could find real pride in the mere fact that we were German. And sometimes they sang hymns, Catholic and Protestant, with every man joining in. They sang songs written by that Lutheran hymnodist, and "Warum sollt'ich mich denn grämen." They sang "In Christ There Is No East or West." The Lutherans have such lovely music, Anton can forgive them for their heresy.

But singing while you tread the endless road, just to keep warm—your wool uniform soaked with dew and your teeth chattering in the Prussian night—isn't the same as playing. He hasn't played, not like this—the organ at St. Kolumban and even the piano beside his young students—since well before the order was disbanded. There was no time for playing in the Wehrmacht, though, Lord knows, he spent as little time in service to the Party as he could contrive. When you play music, when you put an instrument to your lips or merge your hands with ivory, the act transforms. It makes of you a conduit between Heaven and Earth.

There are some feelings, some states of mind, that cannot be expressed in words. The transcendent beauty of moonrise over a quiet field, when your soul stills itself for a time, just long enough to remind you that you are still alive, still human, in a world that seems ravaged by inhuman beasts. And the deep, haunting song of loss, with its crossed harmonies and poignant discords, the way it reaches to the inside of you and turns your spirit out, everts the essence of your being through your heart or through your mouth and leaves it to hang there, vulnerable and exposed. There are some refrains that have taken up residence in his heart and mind and become a permanent part of him—and sometimes he likes to imagine that the men and women who composed those works felt exactly what he feels when he listens or plays. His very thoughts are theirs, and through the spell of rhythm he can sense, across the improbability of time and space, every throb and ache of the composer's heart. Music is a way of transporting emotion from one breast to another. It is a way of knowing the unknowable, of feeling what we can never allow ourselves to confront in any other way. These agonies and ecstasies—they can break us, use us up, burn us away unless we shield our hearts with music.

Even if we speak uncommon tongues, sound grants us the mercy of understanding. That sympathetic quiver of the heart, when a harmony rolls in thirds or a seventh resolves into the octave—it's the greatest miracle God ever wrought, for it shows us that we are one. There isn't a person among us, German or Tommy, Aryan or Jew, whole of mind or simple, who doesn't feel what you feel, what we all feel. In his most naïve moments, he thinks, *If I could only play for the Führer, I might make him see it, the unity of God's creation. And once he sees, how could he continue in this course of evil?*

He shivers. The evening is cold; winter is already here, though no snow has fallen yet. In the bare branches of the apple trees, he can hear some animal moving, the hop and rough slide of a bird's feet against bark. But he can't see the bird, and it has no song to sing now. He pulls at his pipe, blowing the smoke in the bird's direction. Smoke fades itself to nothing between dark branches.

In the deepest part of night, or even in the paleness of twilight, the fact that he goes on living often takes Anton by dull surprise. His life is undeserved, he knows, and any happiness this new arrangement brings is wholly unmerited. But that's the way of life, isn't it? You go on. You live. Even when grief turns your insides to lead and a featureless black sea rises. Men aren't supposed to cry, not even friars, but who in this time and place doesn't weep when he thinks no one else can see? Along the side of your nose, a track of red, the permanent chap of salt burn. And in your eyes a ready well, deep as the center of the Earth. Regret will do it, raise a flood of tears—regret for the words you might have said but didn't, and the things you might have done, the touch of kindness on the back of a shoulder or on the top of a small, sun-warmed head. And regret for the gestures you might have made—tied a loose shoestring or buttoned a winter coat up closer to the chin. Everything you might have done but didn't. Everything that might have been but never can be now. So many bodies lie in their graves, but not yours— not yours. Even when you think yourself motionless, when you try to strike the bargain: *Lord, if I trade places with them, the ones You allowed to die—if I stay here, just as unmoving as they—will it be enough to appease You? Will You raise them back to life?* But no matter how you concentrate on nothingness, on the great and hungry void, you are never as still as the dead. Your pulse trembles your limbs. It whispers in your ears, taunting and relentless. It nods your head—the slightest movement, a forced confession: *Yes, I am still here. Yes, I go on living. My God, why have You forsaken me?*

He tips the pipe out, taps it hard against his heel. Red sparks die against bare earth. The sudden movement startles him, though it's his own body that moves. Still, he didn't expect it. The bird in the orchard takes flight; he can hear its abrupt leap into darkness, the faint whistle of its wings through stiff night air. He thinks, *I should go back inside, talk to Elisabeth, tell her what I'll do. How I'll earn more money, whatever we need.* But he has no idea how he'll do it, and he can't face Elisabeth's careful silence now, her way of not looking at him and the resolute movement of her needle. Instead, he goes to the old shed and eases open the damp-swollen door.

Inside, his breath is a cold mist, and the mist is all he can see as he waits for his eyes to adjust to the darkness. He finds one of his trunks by feel and lifts the lid. A cornet is the first object that comes to hand—*his* instrument, after the piano and organ. The metal is cold; early winter and early night have intruded here. He rests the cup of the mouthpiece against his lips and breathes into it, livening the instrument with the heat of his body. You can't tune cold brass. It resists you, until you have given enough of yourself to let it know you are committed, that you will not leave it cold. His breath rushes through the cornet's compact, elegant curves. The metal warms in his hands, and the three pearlescent keys spring eagerly beneath his fingers.

A footstep at the open door. Anton turns, guilty, lowering the cornet, holding it stiffly like a child caught in some mischief. He had expected to see one of the children standing in the doorway, but it's Elisabeth, a dark silhouette backlit faintly by the gray remainder of sunset.

Blinking in the dim twilight, she comes farther inside. "Is that . . . a trumpet?" Surprised—wary, as she often is.

"Yes." *More or less.* Caught in the sudden grip of possessiveness, he resists the urge to step between his wife and the open trunk. These are instruments of his heart, his memory. They are relics, imbued with a fragile and sacred past. Why should he let her see, when Elisabeth has shown so little of her own heart? He reaches out to close the lid of the open chest, but Elisabeth crosses the space between them, too quick for Anton to stop her, and holds the lid open. She stares in astonishment at what the trunk contains. Another cornet, a French horn, a baritone horn, disassembled. There is a clarinet, carefully wrapped in thick felt and tied with twine to protect its delicate pads and springs. She can't see the clarinet through its wrappings, but what she can see is enough.

"Anton! I remember the boys chattering about musical instruments the day you mended Maria's dress, but I thought that was something from your past. What's in the other trunks?"

He doesn't want to admit it, protective of the places where his pain resides. But she is his wife now. He knows he must deal with Elisabeth honestly. "More of the same."

She looks up at him, astonished and pleased. "I've heard the Party are paying good money for brass. The Schutzstaffel want it for casings—ammunition."

The mere suggestion is a blow, a stab deep and vicious enough to bleed him dry. He struggles to keep the hurt and anger from showing on his face. He is failing in that—he knows he is. He flexes his fingers on the cornet's keys, depressing them one by one, fighting to control his temper. "I can't sell my instruments to the Nazis, Elisabeth."

"Why can't you? We need the money, Anton. Yes, I know Father Emil has been paying you to play at Sunday service, and you play beautifully—but you know we need more."

"I . . ." He falters, heart constricting. This is what he came to do, isn't it? Provider for those in need, protector of the helpless. But he could never have imagined God would be so cruel as to demand this sacrifice. "I can't, Elisabeth. I can't sell these things."

"Why not?"

Because they are memory. And miracle. They're the last proof I have that God exists, that He ever existed in this cold, bleak world. He says, "It's the wrong type of brass. It's thin and adulterated with other metals. It would be useless to the SS. They wouldn't pay."

The hard press of her mouth, the narrowing of her eyes—she is desperate, worried. And most of all, she is disappointed in Anton. She gambled on him—committed to him. She took a holy vow that can never be rescinded. And yet this man persists in a stubborn failure to provide. "Scrap metal is always useful," she says. "The SS will pay something for it. Something is better than nothing."

"Damn it, Elisabeth, this is not scrap metal!" He lurches away from the trunk, his fist tightening protectively on the horn he's still holding. The sudden movement frightens her—and why not? He is still largely a stranger; she doesn't know him, doesn't know what he is capable of. He isn't capable of *that*—violence. Never; not he. But his anger has boiled over, and he can't control it now. Unknowing, she has ventured too close to the source of his pain, and any animal in pain will react when provoked—will lash out or gnash its teeth or howl in agony. A small part of him is aware of the look on Elisabeth's face—the fear, the way she shrinks with hands up, clasped in front of her throat. He regrets his haste in the instant. He hates himself for frightening her. But he is more frightened than she. He forces himself to stand still, giving her room to flee if that's what she chooses to do. With an effort, his voice strangled by distress, he speaks to her more calmly. "This is not scrap, Elisabeth, and it's not for sale. It never will be. You'll have to make peace with that fact, because I will not sell these instruments."

Seeing now that he intends her no harm—other than the damage already done to her pride and her feelings—Elisabeth gathers herself, icy and calm. "Very well. If you will not do right by your family, let it rest on your conscience, not mine. It is for you to take up with God, Josef Anton Starzmann, not me."

She turns and strides out into the dusky yard past Albert's hens, small round shadows scratching in the mud. Anton takes a few useless steps after her, but he knows she wants no comfort—and what comfort can he give? He is as unused to making up with a woman as he is to quarreling. He watches her march stiffly through the orchard, through trees stripped bare of their leaves, standing gray and skeletal against a darkening sky. She knocks on Frau Hertz's door. In a moment, the door opens, and Elisabeth is admitted to the bosom of sympathy. Only the angels can say when she might emerge again.

Anton turns his back on the farmhouse. He walks out past the hen yard, past the stone wall that sometimes contains the goats, when they agree to be contained. He walks without seeing, moving beyond this present place, this point in time; he feels himself pulled back, or picked up and dropped suddenly into an unwelcome past.

He is standing in the courtyard outside St. Josefsheim. Memories wash in, a flood tide that threatens to rise above his head—drown him. Yet he is reluctant to banish that memory, despite its danger. It's as if he hopes that by reliving his pain, he can make some sense of it. As if by sinking willingly into black water, allowing the current to take him, he might come to understand his past. It's the instruments that have done this to him. He has touched them, and remembered. He has absorbed what they contain, like poison through his skin. If he were to do as Elisabeth wants and rid himself of the things, perhaps the memories could never haunt him again. But forgetting—that would be another pain altogether, and a far greater shame than the one he already bears.

Here, in a wide field stripped of its harvest and far from the farmhouse, he is as alone as one can ever be in a small town. And alone, there is ample space for pain to crowd in. He lifts the cornet again. He plays a long, low, melancholy tune and prays the sound will drive away remembrance. But remembrance takes him in its knife-sharp talons, more forcefully than ever before.

The bus. The children, queuing up, smiling and laughing—most of them—certain they were about to go on a grand adventure. A few—a few were bright enough to realize something was amiss. They looked about with lost expressions, wringing their hands or flapping their wrists to calm their fears. That was the way, for some of them; nothing else could ease their anxiety but to flail their soft little limbs in a soothing rhythm and cry out wordlessly—fragile birds. One of the SS, in his precise black uniform, watched a girl for a moment as she waved her hands in the air—it was Rillie Enns, one of her braided pigtails untied and unraveling. She called out, a high-pitched whine eloquent with fear. She had few words; that cry was the best she could do. But who has words at a time like this?

The man's face darkened with disgust. He muttered, "'Life unworthy of life' is correct."

We should have seen this coming. We have known; we have heard. Since 1939, Hitler has scoured what parts of the world he holds, searching for the deficient, the unwhole, the meek and innocent. It began by scrapping adult institutions, where nurses administered to those who could not care for themselves—those who remained like children all their lives. In those days, there were forced sterilizations, so those deemed unfit couldn't breed and contaminate the pool of perfection, the Germany Hitler would shape from our imperfect union if we allowed him to do it. And we have allowed it. We have sat by, complacent or disbelieving or relieved that it was happening to someone else, not to us—not to the people we love.

It began with sterilizations, but it followed a terrible black crescendo, a rising scream. It became something worse. We have read the stories in the papers and in the pamphlets passed hand to hand by the White Rose. Caretakers answered the knocks at their doors and found men in SS uniforms, come to take their helpless charges away. Redistribution. *We're going to place them in a facility better able to care;* that's what the SS say. *We will lift the burden from you; there is no need to trouble yourself any longer.* But everyone knows, everyone sees (even in our blindness) that those called "life unworthy of life" are only redistributed to their graves.

We have known, and we have heard—but somehow, we thought it could never happen to us. Or perhaps we willfully blinded ourselves, preferring ignorance and fantasy to the terror of reality. And one day, you look out the window of the classroom to see the gray bus arriving, with the handprints of ghosts clouding its windows, and the trucks emblazoned with the swastika, and men with guns and deadened eyes.

Rillie Enns looked up at Bruder Nazarius. She had few words, but she was not so simple that she couldn't see, couldn't understand. Her cheeks were red with fear. Her expressive mouth opened and she wailed, again and again.

Anton, in his gray friar's guise, moved past the muttering SS man to another, one whose face betrayed, just for a moment, a terrible anguish of despair.

"Please," he said to that man, the one who had allowed himself to feel. "Please don't do this."

From the steps of the school, someone barked, "Get them onto the bus. All the children, every last one. Check inside, somebody. Search the grounds. Be sure none are hiding. Be sure none of these gray Catholic rats have hidden them away."

The anguished man held a Karabiner across his chest. But he couldn't meet Anton's eye—Anton, a man of the cloth, armed only with his rosary. "It's not my choice," he said quietly, hoarse with shame. "It's not my doing."

"But you know it's wrong. These are innocent children. Their parents have entrusted them to our care. Who will take care of these unfortunates, if not we?"

"They're only being sent off to another facility," the man said, and it was all he could do to speak now. He was trembling.

"You know that's not true. We all know it."

"Step aside, Brother. We all must do what we're told."

Anton shook his head. Light, drifting, scarcely believing what he was doing, he placed himself between the SS and the children. "I can't. I can't just . . . *let* you. You know this is wrong. You know it's a sin. You know you'll answer to God for it, someday."

His fury rising, sudden and swift, the man thrust the muzzle of his rifle against Anton's chest. Somebody cried out in a panic—one of his fellow friars—"Brother Nazarius!"

"Stand in my way again, and I'll run out the bayonet." But the man choked on his words. Tears lined his eyes.

"What have they done to you?" Anton whispered. "How have they made you consent to this?"

The man shook his head, too pained to speak, but his rifle still bit into Anton's chest. He breathed raggedly, half sobbing, but quietly, so only Anton can hear. "I have a wife. I have two daughters, nine and twelve. They told me . . . they said . . ."

The man could say no more, but anyone with a heart could infer. They had told him what they would do if he refused. This man's wife, tortured. His little girls, raped by dozens of men. This is the knife they hold to your throat. This is the precipice to which they drive you. In the name of making Germany great, we have forced our men to choose between the lives of innocents and their own wives and children. We have cut the flesh of our women while their husbands look on. We have branded them with irons, disfigured them with beatings until they beg for a bullet to end the pain. We have thrown little girls to the rapists' queue. *Deutschland über Alles.*

Because the man's pain was too much for him to bear, Brother Nazarius stepped aside. No—that was not why he did it, but it was what he tells himself later. Every night when regret wracks him and keeps him from sleep, he tells himself, *I let those men take my children because the act was no easier for them than it was for me. Because the men in black uniforms also suffer, and are haunted by what they are made to do.*

But the Karabiner lowered in the man's shaking hands, and the moment it fell away from Anton's chest, relief overwhelmed him. That was why he let them take his children away: to save his own life. What redemption can he ever hope to find for such a sin?

"I am sorry," Anton said to the man in black. "I'm sorry. For what they've done to you. May God have mercy on you, my brother."

And on all of us. On us as well, merciful Christ.

13

When the music is gone, when he has played out the last wringing ache of memory, Anton walks back to the house. The cornet hangs from his hand; it drags through the tall grasses that grow along the irrigation ditch. He has no strength left to raise the instrument. In the distance, small and pale against the night, he can see Paul and Al herding the milk cow into the pen beneath the old cottage. Locking the animals up for the night—life on the old farm goes on, whether Anton is there with his family or no. Life everywhere continues. It is inexorable, and in its persistence, mysterious and infuriating. Life proceeds stubbornly, heedless of one's wishes, as long as you avoid the men in black uniforms and keep your curtains closed by night.

Their evening chores finished, the boys scramble up the steps and disappear into the house. No doubt Elisabeth has supper waiting for them, a tough old laying hen stewed over the woodstove or rabbit roasted with potatoes. Has she set out a plate for Anton, or is she still too angry to feed him? As he comes closer, he can smell onions and the faint, warm comfort of freshly baked bread. He's hungry. It seems absurd, to be hungry, for one's body to want nourishment. How can we insist on living when so many are dead, when we did nothing to save them?

Twilight has yielded to darkness. A few determined crickets still sing in the winter weeds. As he rounds the corner of the house and makes for the staircase, he finds Elisabeth sitting on the lowest step, waiting for him. She is wrapped in a winter coat with a brown rabbit-fur collar. It's the kind of coat a woman in Berlin would wear, or in Munich, and it's the first time he has seen it—but then, it hasn't been cold enough for winter coats until now. Elisabeth rises when she sees him. In the dimness, Anton can make out another garment folded over her arm—a man's coat. It must have belonged to her first husband, for it isn't Anton's.

She holds the coat out to him. "Put this on. It's cold, and that old thing you're wearing looks like it wants to fall apart."

Anton does as Elisabeth bids. "We had such a long summer, but it's over now." The coat is warm and heavy, perfumed with cedar to keep the moths away. "Thank you."

"I heard you playing, out there in the field."

He laughs, quiet and rueful. You're never alone in a small town.

"You play that trumpet as nicely as you play the organ."

"God has given me a few gifts, I suppose."

"I think God has given you a great many gifts, Anton." She hugs her body tightly and turns away to gaze out into the black orchard. Beyond the trees, a faint suggestion of Frau Hertz's house barely stands out against the night sky. "I'm sorry we quarreled."

"I am, too." Is it this easy, making up with a woman?

"I can see, Anton, how important music is to you. But we do have needs as a family. There must be a compromise somewhere."

"I know. You're right; there must."

She looks at the cornet for a long time. Then she bites her lip, a gesture that seems entirely too girlish for her. He thinks for a moment that she'll ask him to play again, and he wonders, in his dark mood, whether he can conjure up any song that isn't melancholy. But then she glances up the stairs to the cottage above. Maria's squeals come down; her brothers are tickling her at the supper table. The children are rowdy enough tonight; there is no reason for music. It would only distract them from their meal or drive them further from sleep.

She says, "Paul—I mean, my husband, not Little Paul—" Then she hesitates, offering a shy, apologetic smile. He is her husband now. She has forgotten it, momentarily. "My *first* husband, Paul . . . We often enjoyed music together."

"Did you?" Gently. In the five weeks of their acquaintance—and three weeks of marriage—he had never learned Herr Herter's Christian name. He is glad to know that his charming, lively little stepson was named for his father. It keeps the man's memory alive, now that he is gone.

"We listened to the radio shows every Tuesday night. When we first left Stuttgart, I mean." She laughs, uncomfortable with the memory, disbelieving that she's sharing it with him now. In a heartbeat of stunned silence, he can all but hear her thoughts: *What has possessed me to speak of something so private, and why now?*

"When you left the city? You make it sound like you ran away."

"We did. My parents didn't approve, because there were rumors, you see—my reputation was in danger." She narrows her eyes. "But I never would have done anything sinful. They were only stories."

"You are the last woman I would suspect of sin."

"We came here, to Unterboihingen, but the radios were so bad back then. They aren't much better now, to tell the truth. We could hardly tune anything in, but for some reason, on Tuesday nights only, one particular station would come in, clear as a bell." She smiles, remembering, softening completely for the first time since Anton has known her. He is gripped by the sudden urge to touch her—not in any carnal way, only to lay a hand on her arm or her shoulder or on the fur collar of her coat, so that he might experience a part of her joy. As if he might capture in his hand the rarity of her happiness. "We would dance, then, just the two of us. The music was like something from another world, from dreams. It always seemed to me as if that music could pick us up and move us anywhere we wanted to go." She stops and shuts her eyes tightly. "I sound foolish."

"No—I understand. I know just what you mean."

"After we were married, Paul bought a phonograph. I sold it years ago, after he died. I don't know now why I sold it. I suppose I assumed the war would be over soon, and the money from its sale would be enough to keep us going until then. Until better times came. I wish I still had that phonograph now."

Silence. They are both caught in the past, snared by their private recollections of the time when we all thought this war would end.

"Did you have a favorite song?" He doesn't know why he asks it. Perhaps he only wants to see her more clearly—Elisabeth as a glad young bride, in a time before the world beat her and burned her with its irons. "One you liked to dance to?"

She shakes her head, refusing to answer. The memory is too dear. But after a moment, after a pensive silence, she says quickly, "Marlene Dietrich. 'Ich bin von Kopf bis Fuß auf Liebe eingestellt.'"

Then she turns and climbs the stairs, climbs back up to her children. She goes with steady, marching steps, arms wrapped tight around her body. She moves like a woman who never expects war to end.

14

Three days before Christmas Eve, the moon is shining clear and bright on blankets of snow, knee-deep across sleeping fields. There is light enough to see for miles, so the family walks to the church. They're carrying gifts for Father Emil, who has been so kind to them all. This night is peaceful, and though it's cold, it's as beautiful as the world must have been on the night of the Nativity, when the Christ child first came down to grace us.

The children skid their feet along the road's packed snow, while Elisabeth and Anton walk more sedately behind. Tucked beneath her arm is a loaf of cinnamon bread, wrapped in waxed paper; Elisabeth has saved the paper carefully through countless prior uses, and now it's soft and creased like parchment, like the pages of an old book. The scent of warm spice asserts itself against the flat gray smell of winter. Anton is carrying a small box. Inside, the little figures he has carved for Father Emil rattle with every step—a camel and a donkey for the church's crèche.

When they arrive at St. Kolumban, stamping their feet in the cold yard, the children sing a rough chorus, a Christmas tune. Anton and Elisabeth join in. They laugh more than they sing, all of them, and when Anton lays his hand on his wife's arm to stop her slipping in the snow, she doesn't pull away.

Emil opens the door. The church inside is dark, of course, for the sun has set. Stuttgart suffered a major bombardment only a few weeks ago, one of the worst it has faced thus far. With the bombing so recent, one would expect no planes tonight, but one can never be sure. We must always be cautious in times like these. But even without a golden glow spilling from the open door, a fulsome warmth still emanates from the nave. It's the spirit of the place, love and hope gathered over centuries, graven in the very stones.

"Come in, come in," Emil says. "I'm having a humble little celebration inside, only reading my scriptures by candlelight—but you are always welcome to join me."

The priest takes Elisabeth's arm and guides her through the dark. The children hold to the hem of her city-fine coat, and Anton stumbles along behind. Emil leaves them at the front pew, then rustles down the length of the nave; there is a rattle of drapes being pulled across windows, their metal hoops sliding over curtain rods. The children whisper and kick their feet—excited by the novelty of being here, in the dark and without the congregation, but conscious of parental expectation: we must be reverent at church, even when it's not Sunday, even when it's dark as the inside of a shoe.

Father Emil makes his way back to the front of the nave, feeling his way along the pews. A moment later, he strikes a match, and a great white candle blossoms on the altar. Its singular light seems to draw in all the appointments of holiness, pulling them into a close and intimate proximity. The humble gilded crucifix, the brass candlesticks without ornamentation, the censer hanging from its tripod, close at hand. The church has never looked more beautiful than it does now, in this quiet amber glow. Its divinity tonight seems private, singular, a gift softly bestowed on this small, new-made family. Their offerings of cinnamon bread and carved animals are embarrassingly small by comparison to friendship and candlelight, but Father Emil exclaims over his gifts with unrestrained gratitude.

He holds up the carved camel, admiring the workmanship. "I didn't know you were a carver, Anton."

"I'm not much of one."

"There, I must disagree." He turns the camel in his hands; the newly exposed wood is pale in the candlelight, so the little figure stands out against the shadowy nave. "He has so much expression. I could almost believe this is the very camel who witnessed the Savior's birth."

Maria reaches for the figure. "Let me play with it. I want to see!"

"Now, now," Elisabeth scolds. "You had your chance to see it while your stepfather was carving it. I won't have you breaking it."

"I don't mind," Emil says to Elisabeth. "She can't do these little beasties any harm." He gives Maria the camel and its donkey companion. "Do you know where the crèche is? Up there, at the front of the sanctuary."

Maria holds the carved animals to her chest. She blinks past the pool of candlelight, peering anxiously into darkness beyond. "I can't see it."

Emil rises, laying his hand on the girl's head. "Don't be afraid, little one. I'll go with you and show you where it is. You can set the camel and donkey up wherever you please."

A few moments later, Anton can make out Maria and the priest seated beside the dim crèche, playing with the wooden figures. Father Emil gives the Wise Men funny voices; he makes the angel sing until Maria giggles herself into breathlessness. The boys soon join in, pausing first to break off pieces of cinnamon bread. Father Emil has said they might eat as much as they like.

"The *Vater* has always had a special bond with Maria," Elisabeth says, watching them all at play. "I can't understand it; she's such a naughty girl. One would think a priest would prefer a good, obedient child, like Albert."

"Maybe he sees something in her—" Anton is about to say, *Something that reminds him of the boy he was, long ago.* But Elisabeth says, "No doubt, he sees a little sinner in need of salvation. I don't know what I'm to do with her, Anton."

With the children well into their game, Emil returns, a trace of reluctance in his sigh, in the slow way he sits on the pew. "It's good to forget, for a few minutes," he says quietly. "It's a great blessing, to laugh and play. Children are so resilient, in times like these. Would that we could all bear up as well." He tastes the bread and nods in appreciation. "It has been too long since I've had something so sweet. Where did you get so much cinnamon, Elisabeth?"

"I've been saving it for someone special."

"I have done something right in this life, if God has deemed me worthy of such an honor." He turns to Anton. "How are you faring with your music lessons, my friend?"

Just before he answers, the air chills around Anton and Elisabeth. He hopes Emil can't feel that moment of tension. The matter of the scrap metal—the brass relics of memory—still lies unresolved between husband and wife. The family does need more money; Elisabeth was right about that. Unless he finds some way to provide it, Anton must be counted derelict in his duty to family and to God. But where is the sense in spoiling this night with such unpleasant talk? Let us not dredge up the old quarrel—not here and now.

"Lessons are going well," he says. "The Beckers have hired me, too, once a week."

"That's three families," Emil says. "Six children in all, unless I'm mistaken."

Elisabeth says, "It's a good start."

"I never would have thought," Anton begins. He's about to say, *I never would have thought Unterboihingen was hiding so many well-off families in its hills and dells.* But before he can finish, a low moan interrupts the conversation. It's coming from somewhere high above the nave's arches, above the roof of St. Kolumban. It's coming from the sky.

The children drop the wooden figures. They look up from their play with wide eyes and open mouths. The moan intensifies; it rises, deepens. It becomes a hoarse, angry roar, fast approaching. There isn't a soul in Germany but knows what that sound means. Even the smallest children understand it.

"Quick," Emil says, standing, spreading his arms wide as if to shepherd them all. "Into the shelter."

"Where is it?" Al cries. They know where to shelter at home—in the space below the house, alongside the animals. And at school there is a cellar; every week they practice going down into the darkness. They practice staying calm. When we are out there in the countryside, walking along the roads and fields, any ditch will do. But where can we go now?

Something snaps, whatever force of terror tethers the boys to immobility. They bolt in the same instant, darting off in opposite directions. Elisabeth is quick; she catches Paul by the hand as he runs past in blind terror. The boy flies to the end of her reach, and his feet go out from beneath him. He screams in surprise and pain as he collides with a wooden pew, but at least he is safe with his mother. When Paul is on his feet again, Elisabeth spins him about and points him toward the priest. She says, loud and stern enough to cut through his fear, "Follow Vater Emil, Paul. Don't leave his side."

Al has already sprinted down the center aisle, quick as a deer; he is lost somewhere in the darkness near the church's entry doors. He'll run out into the night next, out into the snow—his dark coat visible from above, vulnerable against the pale ground. Anton shouts, raising his voice in a hard, commanding tone for the first time since becoming a father. "Albert!" A moment later, Albert returns, and Anton's heart lurches with relief. The boy's eyes are huge, strained; his face, as he reappears in candlelight, seems all eyes. Anton shoves him toward his brother.

Gathering the boys close, Emil calls over the increasing roar, "Where has Maria gone?"

Anton glances at the crèche; the figures lie where they have fallen, but Maria has vanished.

"Mother above!" Elisabeth cries. She goes to her boys and takes the youngest again; Paul squeals as her grip tightens on his arm, but she holds him closer. The airplanes scream closer, too, rattling the windowpanes. One of the drapes, Anton can see, is not quite closed. How much light have they revealed? He imagines the plane, the pilot; the view from above. A streak of gold reflected on the snow, betraying the life cringing below.

Emil sees the curtain, too. "The candle, Anton!"

"But Maria—"

"Be quick!"

He runs up to the altar, no time to pay proper respects. He crosses himself as he goes, a terse bid for the Lord's forgiveness—for mercy, if any is to be had. He blows out the candle, and the sanctuary plunges into darkness. Anton calls over the roaring engines, "Where are the children?"

From somewhere close by, Emil answers. "The boys are with Elisabeth; I told her where to go."

"Maria! We must find her!"

Just then, Anton hears the girl crying. She is somewhere below his feet, but he can't see her, can't feel her when he drops to the ground, pawing through darkness. Father Emil is beside him in a flash, falling to his knees, pulling the cloth from the altar. The blackness is so dense, Anton pushes his hands through it as if he might part shadows by force and reveal his small daughter, cowering and afraid, in a shaft of protective light. But there is no light here. The dark is everywhere, stifling and thick.

Maria screams, *"Machen Sie die schlechten Bomben weg!"* Make the bad bombs go away! Beneath the altar table, her voice is everywhere, splitting Anton's head, strident with fear. But still he can't find her. His hands grasp only emptiness. *Where is she? Merciful Lord, give me back my child!*

"I have her," Emil says. "Come!"

One hand on the priest's shoulder, Anton follows him, stumbling through the darkness. Emil knows where to go. There is a dry rasp of old door hinges, barely audible over the sound of the planes. Emil murmurs soothing words to Maria, who wails wordlessly, her cries muffled, face pressed hard against the priest's shoulder or chest.

"Reach down, Anton," Emil says. "Directly down from where you stand. The door to the shelter is just below."

"I can't see."

"You'll find an iron ring near your feet. Pull it straight up."

The planes roar closer, closer. This is the night when Unterboihingen will be seen, when our perfect village, our sanctuary of brotherhood, will be struck, destroyed, undone. In the morning, we will find it broken, shattered houses bleeding children's cries into icy streets. Someone has left a candle burning. Someone has left a curtain open. It's all over now.

He finds the ring; he strains upward. A creak of wood and age, almost as loud as the planes, and something opens below. A gust of cold, damp air pummels him in the face, a smell of decades and mildew.

"Careful, now," Emil says. One hand steadies Anton, strong on his upper arm. "Take Maria from me. I'll go down first and get a light burning. I know where the candles and matches are kept."

The girl is stiff with terror when Anton scoops her against his chest. He rocks her, singing a lullaby close to her ear, but she doesn't hear him. She hears nothing but the thunder of death, feels only the rattling of the church's fragile old bones. A moment later, a spot of light appears, down in a pit beneath the floor. The light is dim, but it's enough to illuminate the tiny room in which they're all standing. Elisabeth is cowering by a wall; the boys have buried their faces against her body. At Anton's feet, a ladder descends into the darkness, six, seven, rungs down.

"Boys, quickly," he says. They don't move, too frightened to obey. He speaks low and calm, firm and commanding. "Boys. Do as I say. Now."

They tear themselves from their mother and scramble down the ladder into the cellar. Anton nods to Elisabeth; she follows, and as soon as her feet are on solid ground, she reaches up for Maria. He passes the girl down to her mother. Only when his family is tucked away does Anton crouch and find the rungs with his groping feet. He descends into the shelter as quickly as he can and then slams the trap door overhead.

Even here, buried beneath the floor of St. Kolumban, in a passage hidden by some ancient closet, the engines with their hellish screams overwhelm every sense and all rational thought. Still clinging to the ladder, Anton fights against his fear, forcing himself to observe, to know. Emil's small candle lights the whole room. The room is close, lined with shelves. There are four sturdy benches, one along each wall, and on the shelves, a supply of food and water in jars and tins. The family huddle with their priest on a single bench, pressed close together. Maria is curled in a ball on Father Emil's lap, still screaming with a fear that can be expressed no other way. Anton staggers to his family. He stretches his arms wide, sheltering his wife and sons—as if he can protect them, as if he can do anything to stop the bombs from falling. And after the bombs, the bricks and masonry and timbers of the church. He can feel the weight of the building overhead. Through the engines' roar, he can almost hear St. Kolumban grinding, sighing, ready to fall.

No one speaks. They wait; they shiver. They count their heartbeats, listening for the blasts, wondering whose houses and lives will be gone, wiped out, when they emerge from the cellar, if they emerge at all.

The roar thins and dwindles. The planes are still out there, but they have passed over Unterboihingen, passed the village by. Did they never see us huddled here, or are we merely unimportant? Anton fills his lungs with cold, wet air. He releases his family slowly, his hand sliding over the fur of Elisabeth's collar. We will not be bombed—not tonight. He thinks with great effort; he orients himself by force of will, dragging his mind out of terror, sequestering what remains of his fear in an unused corner. He mentally retraces their steps as best he can, the route they took as they fled the nave. He believes they are on the south side of the church. That means the planes are headed west.

The fist of this family unclenches. They sit up and move apart, just enough so that each can breathe, and Maria's sobs taper off to whimpers.

And then the bombs fall. The impacts come first as vibrations through the earth, low, dull thuds like the distant tread of giants. They are followed moments later by the sound waves, a tin-can crash of far-away explosions.

"Stuttgart," Anton says, both saddened and relieved.

Elisabeth murmurs, "Again," and crosses herself.

Father Emil pats Maria's back until she sits up, sucking her thumb. "One would think poor Stuttgart has had enough by now." Then he prays for the souls who will lose everything tonight. "Lord, extend your mercy. Let no one suffer; take those who must die quickly, and comfort those who must go on alone." The family murmur as one, "Amen."

After a silence, a pause to honor the newly made dead, Anton says to the priest, "Back there in the nave, I thought you were going to take us outside."

"Outside?"

"To the door set in that wall, all covered with ivy. When I first saw the door, I thought it was a bomb shelter."

"No." Father Emil's face darkens, and he turns his eyes down to the hard earth. "It's not a shelter."

Al says, "What is it, then?"

"An old, old tunnel, dating back to the age of kings."

The boys rustle on the bench, intrigued, already forgetting the bombs—the resilience of youth.

Emil brightens, settling into the story. "The tunnel was used by messengers. There are other tunnels, too, running from one town to the next. The messengers could go from one village to another without being seen, and warn their friends if danger was approaching."

Paul says, "But it's dark in a tunnel. How could they see?"

"The same way we see now." He indicates the candle, burning with a light that seems too cheery, forced and false.

Watching the candle's flame, Anton sees suddenly beyond it, past the jars that line the shelves. There are deep, square shadows back there, set behind Father Emil's prudent supplies. The walls of this pit are lined with recesses, all of a size, reaching back into the stone foundation of St. Kolumban. The candle's flame jumps for a moment, stirred by a child's breath, and in that brighter flash, light just illuminates the gray curve of a skull, the black of an eye socket peering out from behind a tin of potted meat. St. Kolumban has an ossuary—the final resting place for generations of priests who have served here, long before Father Emil's time. And someday, Emil's bones will lie here, too, sleeping among his predecessors.

Unsettled, prickling with chill, Anton looks away from the skull. He doesn't want to bring the thing to the children's attention. Let them be comforted, distracted by Emil's stories of times long past, the age of kings. But he can feel the relentless gaze of that dark socket. He can feel its set gray grin. Death has one eye on him.

Maria has recovered herself enough to talk. "Can't we go up now?"

"Not just yet," Emil says. "We should make certain there are no more planes coming."

"Then you must tell us everything about the old kings!"

The boys agree; they pepper Father Emil with questions, and the priest has an inexhaustible supply of answers. Elisabeth sighs to see Maria restored to her old ways, as if she can finally release a mother's fear—as if she believes that one day, the planes will steal away her children's spirits, leaving them as dry husks, empty shells. Today is not that day, thank God. Anton has seen children like that, their souls ripped away by horrors even a grown man can't contemplate. He would rather see these children—his children—dead than broken. He wonders how many empty husks will be made tonight, and how many orphans. How many children of Stuttgart will go dull-eyed and quiet, with all the anticipation of Christmas forgotten, and tainted forever?

"Tell us about the knights," Paul says, "in the time of kings."

"Yes," says Al. "Let's have a story about knights with swords!"

"It's Christmas," Elisabeth says suddenly.

"Not yet," Maria says, sulking. "I want a story about knights!"

"Let's hear about the Nativity instead."

"That's a fit tale for Christmastime," Emil agrees. "Long, long ago, in a land far away, the Lord chose Mary to be the Holy Mother, for she was better than all other women—the kindest and most caring, the most faithful and good."

The children resign themselves to the familiar story. They settle back against the shelves, and Maria snuggles against Emil's shoulder, listening as he tells of the Annunciation, the Mother's long journey on the back of a donkey, her travail in Bethlehem. Emil makes the great star shine brightly in their imaginations; he decks the roof of the humble stable with a choir of angels.

"And do you know what song the angels sang when the Christ Child was born?"

The children shake their heads. The night is still and quiet, Stuttgart settling into dust.

Father Emil sings:

> *Break forth, O beauteous heavenly light,*
> *And usher in the morning:*
> *Ye shepherds shrink not with affright*
> *But hear the angels' warning;*
> *The child now born in infancy,*
> *Our confidence and joy shall be . . .*

Anton can't resist the music. He joins the hymn, lending his voice in harmony with the priest. Elisabeth sings, too, entering on the same word, the same note. Husband and wife glance at one another, shy and surprised by this unexpected unity, but they do not cease to sing.

The power of Satan breaking,
Our peace eternal making.

PART 3

The Ways a Man Might Earn His Pay

February–May 1943

15

The earth lies hard and dead under layers of compacted ice. Along the road, up the slope of its verge, across the flat breast of distant fields, whatever is blanketed by snow is grayed by clinging dust, the thick, colorless residue of coal smoke and woodsmoke, of bombings and fires carried in from the cities by the steady seasonal winds. And everything is covered with snow. February is the coldest part of the year. Why should it be so? It's the winter solstice, days before Christmas, that marks the darkest hour—that fearful time when night seems to swallow all the world, when even at its best the sun is weak and low, riding through a sky burdened by cloud. Why now, when the days have lengthened enough that you can notice the change, when there is just enough light to see by—why should the cold be so bitter, so persistent? St. Kolumban is flattened against the landscape, and the gentle yellow of its aged stucco walls is paled and whitened by winter. The bell tower is laced in frost.

A footpath, trampled through the snow, crosses the churchyard, a slash of white through the dull, gray stillness of the cemetery. Anton takes the path and knocks on the little side door, the one Father Emil uses to come and go.

"My friend." That's how the priest greets him when he opens the door. "Come in, my friend."

It is Tuesday; the church is empty. Father Emil leads Anton past the small chamber that serves as the priest's living quarters to the stone stoop, where they cross themselves with wet fingers, and into the grand, sweeping arches of the sanctuary and nave. No matter how many times Anton sees the interior of St. Kolumban, it never fails to impress him. The wooden pews, gleaming from eight hundred years' worth of polish, bisected by the perfect aisle, roofed over by a dark brick web of sexpartite vaulting. The altar, framed and glittering with what little gold Unterboihingen possesses. To gospel side and epistle side, arching above the chancel, Mother Mary and her saints process toward Heaven. They are painted in flowing robes with halos of brilliant color.

Together, the two men bow to the altar and make their reverent approach. The organ waits in peaceful stillness, tucked behind its rood screen in the shadows of Mary's statue and Father Emil's pulpit. That quiet corner, hidden from the congregation, is as familiar now to Anton as the palms of his own hands. He takes his accustomed seat on the bench and plays a few experimental chords. The church swells and echoes with the sound.

"What is the problem, exactly?" He tries another chord, and another. He can detect no sour note, no wavering vibration.

"I don't know, precisely," Emil says. He leans against the rood screen's dark upright beam. Casual, yet without the least air of disrespect—how does he manage to do it? "I was only amusing myself yesterday, plinking about on the keys—I'm not an accomplished musician like you, Anton—and something sounded off."

He runs up a scale, then down. His fingers know the way, unthinking, like scratching an itch or tying the laces of your shoe. "Which note sounded off? Which key?"

"I, er . . ." Emil shuffles his feet, clasps his hands behind his back. "I'm afraid I don't know."

Patient as always, Anton smiles. "White or black? Or was it one of the pedals?" He tests those, too, depressing each long plank of wood in turn with the toe of his wet boot. The bass notes rattle St. Kolumban's bones, but the sound is true.

He plays a verse, then another: "Mary Walked Through a Wood of Thorn." What did Mary wear beneath her heart? *Kyrie eleison!* A little child, free from pain. That's what the Mother carried in her heart. *Jesus und Maria.*

"Everything sounds fine and well to me," Anton says. Hands and feet go still, and the chords' echoes murmur up there in the arches, among the high ceiling like birds in a sleepy roost.

"My mistake, then," Emil says. *"Entschuldigen Sie."*

"Think nothing of it." He is reluctant to rise from the bench. He never likes to leave his music.

"It was good of you, to come tramping all this way in that bitter cold, to humor me with my complaint about a broken organ."

"We should only be glad it's not damaged. Who knows where we might have found the parts to repair it?"

"Some other church, in some other town, might have had a part to spare. But I never would have known what to ask for. I'd have been obliged to send you off to another village, carrying the message on my behalf." Emil turns away, heading back for the pews, but the movement is too abrupt. It catches Anton's attention, holds him in a tense grip. He sits, fingers of one hand spread across the ivory keys from the low G to the octave above. The silence Emil leaves behind is lively, crackling with unspoken meaning.

When he does rise from the bench, Anton finds the priest sitting in the front pew, as is his habit, gazing up at the procession of painted saints. He's staring at Mary in particular, standing below the rest with her benevolent hands upraised, pointed up a ladder of clouds.

"You don't need to head back yet, I assume," Emil says.

"Not just yet, no. I told Elisabeth I'd be gone for an hour at least."

"Then sit with me a while, my friend."

He does, though not without some trepidation. Father Emil is not his usual self today. There is something chary about the old priest; his jovial light is smothered under a clandestine bushel.

"How are you and Elisabeth faring?"

"Well enough." It's not a lie; since their argument over the hidden brass, there have been no further quarrels. Yet he can't help feeling he has deceived Father Emil. In all things, Anton and Elisabeth have been cordial, cooperative, respectful. Anyone would call their relationship admirable—if they were neighbors instead of husband and wife. She hasn't mentioned the instruments again, but her knowledge and her need have hung over Anton all those weeks since the end of October. At night, he hears unspoken accusations whispered in her sleeping breath.

"I wish I could pay you more for your services on Sundays," Emil says. "You play so beautifully, and I can see how much the congregation enjoys your music. You have brought considerable light to us in a time of grave darkness."

"It's my pleasure. I know a parish can't afford much in the way of pay. Not in times like these, when all of us struggle for our daily bread."

A pause. "Just how much are you struggling, Anton? The children—do they have enough to eat?"

"We get by." Now, in the deadest and coldest part of winter, there are times when Maria and Paul cry because their bellies ache with hunger. But although sometimes the food is less than filling, Elisabeth sees to it that her family eats three meals a day. It seems disloyal, ungrateful, to mention any small lack when so many in the country—indeed, in the world—suffer far worse. "We're luckier here in Unterboihingen than we deserve to be. Even in the winter, the hens still lay a few eggs, and our shed is full of roots. We're blessed, aren't we, to be able to trade with one another. It makes our ration stamps stretch a little further."

"The trading is good," Emil agrees. "But for you, a man on your own, to take on the support of four other souls—and three of them helpless children. Well, I imagine you find yourself in a difficult place. That's why I say, 'If only I could pay Anton more.'"

He lays a hand on Emil's shoulder. "Really, there's no need to worry. I'm still teaching Frau Becker's daughters the piano."

"Only the Becker girls? What happened to the Abts and the Schneiders?"

He withdraws his hand, sighing. "They've had to delay lessons until the spring, I'm afraid."

"Ah. Even those families feel the pinch, I see."

"Don't we all?"

Those words open a door. Emil turns to him, wordless, but his stare is forceful and direct, laden with meaning. For a long moment, they merely look at one another, the priest pressing his lips as if fighting the urge to speak again, Anton prickling under a wave of caution.

At length, Emil says, "Spring is a long way off."

"Not so long. Six weeks, perhaps."

"I think about how much can happen to a man—and to the world—in six weeks. The thought makes me shiver."

Anton shivers now. Is it only this strange turn in Emil's mood that has set him on edge, or is some other force at work? There is a tremor in his soul, a quaking fire as before the presence of the Holy Spirit. This hour, this moment, is important. He waits for the priest to speak. In the silence, in the dense winter stillness of the air, he feels two unseen hands upon his head, and a wash of holy fire.

Woe to them that devise iniquity, and work evil upon their beds. When the morning is light, they practice it, because it is in the power of their hand.

Emil says, "There are other ways a man might earn a little pay. Something to stretch the rations."

And they covet fields, and take them by violence; and houses, and take them away: so they oppress a man and his house, even a man and his heritage.

Anton nods. Go on; speak.

"I tell you this only because I consider you a friend. I am right in that consideration, I hope."

"You are."

"These ways to earn a bit of money . . . they amount to no more work than walking from one town to the next." Emil turns back to Mother Mary. Casually, he says, "Or if it's too far to walk, you might take the train, or a bus. Sometimes business may take you farther afield."

"Business?"

"Walking. Just walking. And carrying something for me."

A pause, long and cautious. "Carrying what, Father?"

"Only words."

"Messages." He is robbed suddenly of breath. Anton's voice, a whisper, barely fills his own mouth. But the fire that fills his soul, the ice that floods his heart and makes his body quake . . . He says, stronger now, "Whose messages? Which side do you serve?"

Emil smiles. "Anton, my dear friend. The question does you credit, but how can you doubt that I serve God? I always serve the Lord."

That can only mean—aided by the Spirit, illuminated, Anton sees with the bright-white clarity of a bolt from Heaven—Father Emil does not serve the National Socialists. He is no gauleiter, no fat Franke in his furniture shop—no lapdog of Hitler. "You resist?" The words tumble out of him, half laughter, and his eyes burn with tears. "There is a resistance?"

And now it's Emil who takes Anton by the shoulder and bolsters his spirit with a firm grip. "Of course there is, my friend. You *are* my friend, in truth. Of course we resist. Christ's love can't be blotted from the world so easily, not by the hand of any man. It will take a power far greater than the NSDAP to put out our light."

"It seems there is no greater power. I've almost come to believe that." The tears are falling freely now, but he is not ashamed. The Spirit doesn't allow for shame, in His healing and holy presence.

"You have *almost* come to believe, but not entirely."

Anton shakes his head, slowly. For the moment, he is bereft of words, hollowed by awe and relief.

"There is a greater force, Anton—I promise you. There is a power in this world that no evil can overcome."

Day after day, it rises. Like a tide, it swells. Every outrage, every death, each new act of inhumanity wrings from us another drop of resolve, even when we think our spirits dust dry and deadened. We flow together; we merge; the burning-salt wash of our tears and the breath of our sobbing voices, the tension of our tightened jaws, our current of despair. We are a river eroding its banks. We will no longer be contained. There is a greater force. Its name is *Widerstand*, resist. We call it White Rose, and Grauer Orden; we call it Non-Compliance. In the streets of Munich and Berlin, the boys, unbroken, take fists to the faces of the Hitler Youth, and we call them Edelweiss Pirates. We call the force Unbowed, Unbent, and Father Emil, and Anton.

"Will you do it? Will you carry my words? The pay is very good, I can tell you."

He nods. What else can he do but accept? "I won't do it for the pay, though—not only for that."

Again, Emil smiles. "No, of course you won't. You of all people— you listen to the voice of the Lord."

Truly we are full of power by the spirit of the Lord, and of judgment, and of might. Hear this, we pray you, ye heads of the house of Power, and princes of the house of Oppression, that abhor judgment and pervert all equality. You build up our nation with blood, and stain the world with iniquity.

Certainty, a conflagration in his spirit—his ears ring with the sound of God's call. He says, "When do I start?"

16

His first assignment takes him to Wernau several weeks later. The town lies only a few kilometers away—near enough to walk—but it feels like another country, another world. The town is much like Unterboihingen, with its old stucco buildings and medieval air—though even at first glance, Anton can tell the population of Wernau is at least twice that of his home village. It's not the buildings or the people that leave Anton feeling like a foreigner but rather the eerie sense of being watched. On the long walk from Unterboihingen, he never imagined he would feel the prickle of eyes upon his back. And now, with that sinister itch burning between his shoulders, he can't decide whether the danger is real or conjured up by his own feverish thoughts.

Father Emil coached him on the work, made Anton rehearse the casual stroll, the friendly nod and smile that would allow him to pass unnoticed in Wernau. They practiced, too, a smooth handshake, the passing of a small slip of folded paper from one palm to another. Emil had pronounced Anton ready, but now that he has arrived in Wernau, uncertainty wracks him, makes him twitch at every sound—the blow of a hammer from a carpenter's shop, the barking of a terrier from an upstairs window.

Easy, he reminds himself. *You're natural as can be. There's nothing unusual about paying a visit to Wernau.* He has only come to pick up a copy of sheet music from Wernau's priest—they, too, have an organ.

That's the excuse Father Emil has arranged for this foray. Sheet music, and one other small, insignificant mission . . .

The bell tower of Wernau's Catholic church rises above the town's dark rooftops. Anton makes his way steadily toward it, weaving through a group of schoolchildren who are enjoying an outdoor lesson. He dodges a flock of geese being driven from the front of an old *Oma*'s cottage to her vegetable patch out back; he nods in greeting to the midwife on her bicycle, though she pedals with obvious haste, eyes squinting toward her urgent destination, and takes no notice of Anton at all. No one in Wernau, in fact, looks twice at Herr Starzmann. But still, he can't rid himself of the queasy sensation that everyone is watching, everyone knows.

He passes a fruit seller with a few apples and pears on his cart, a woman unraveling an old sweater on a stool beside her front door, an old, stooped man carrying a string of dead pigeons over his shoulder. There are two fellows near his own age, talking earnestly over a single-page newspaper as they walk—and right behind them, a boy no older than fifteen in the brown uniform of Hitler Youth, the red blaze of a loyalist's armband drawing Anton's eye like a stain of blood. Three little girls in an alley, stringing wet stockings on a line. They are old enough to be in school; it's a shame duties keep them at home. Has the war made them orphans, he wonders, or has it merely widowed their poor mother?

He looks at every person he passes, but never for long. He must locate his contact, but he mustn't draw attention to his presence. There is no sign of the man Father Emil described, and he has almost reached the church, almost passed through the whole of Wernau itself. He has just begun to ask himself what excuse he'll find to remain in the town for another hour when he sees his goal: a man of middling height but broad build, ambling from the nearest corner toward a small public garden. He's wearing a bowler hat of the same iron-gray as his suit—just as Emil had said. With a tingle of dismay, Anton realizes his contact had been walking the long street nearly its whole length, some dozen paces ahead of Anton himself. He must develop a sharper eye and quicker wit if he's to have any hope of succeeding in this new role.

Anton continues to the church—not as lovely on the inside as St. Kolumban, for all its ornate exterior—and retrieves the sheet music from its priest. "Father Emil sends his warmest greetings," he tells the black-robed old *Opa*, "and his thanks." The music goes into his knapsack the moment he's in the churchyard again. He has no need of music, anyway; he memorized all the best hymns when he was still a child. He straightens, tossing the sack on his shoulder, and looks around anxiously. The contact remains in the garden, slouched on a wooden bench, arms folded tightly over his chest.

Anton must restrain himself from running to the garden. Even a brisk walk would be unseemly; he meanders from the church to the garden's little arched gate and pauses to read the new bronze plaque set into its post.

THIS PUBLIC GARDEN HAS BEEN CREATED AND MAINTAINED FOR THE
ENJOYMENT OF OUR CITY.
THE LEAGUE OF GERMAN GIRLS, WERNAU CHAPTER

He suppresses a shudder. The garden isn't large, but it is tidily kept, and planted with ornamental foliage, the only color allowed by early spring. Anton sees nothing but a blur of coppery reds and smoke green as he wanders among the beds. His thoughts are all for the girls who built this place.

In the days of his youth, there were myriad clubs for children—camping clubs and music groups, scouting societies and improvement associations, every sort of service organization one could imagine. All of them dedicated to a single goal: the wholesome occupation and education of children. Now, the Party has disbanded the old clubs and replaced them with only two: the League of German Girls, for the indoctrination of young women, and Hitler Youth, whose primary function seems to be the manufacture of cannon fodder for the front lines. Every boy between the ages of fourteen and eighteen is required to join.

His leisurely circuit of the garden finally brings him to the bench where the man in the gray suit is waiting. Now Anton can see that the fellow has pulled the edge of his bowler hat down across his eyes. His breaths are deep and slow; he gives every impression of having fallen asleep, though how anyone could sleep in this damp, chilly air is a mystery to Anton. He sits on the far side of the bench, rummages in his knapsack, and pulls out his modest lunch, packed for him by Elisabeth. He unwraps the paper to reveal a few slices of hard sausage, boiled eggs, and a small round of soda bread.

"One would think we'd have snow again, with this cold," Anton says quietly, peeling an egg, "but it smells more like rain to me."

There is no response from the man in gray. Anton drops the eggshell on the ground and crushes it beneath his foot. He waits, but still no reply is made.

Should he speak again? Should he get up and leave? Perhaps he is mistaken; he has found the wrong man in the wrong gray suit. He taps the second egg on the bench and is about to peel it, too, when the man tilts his head, just far enough to peer at Anton from beneath his hat.

"I do feel rain in the air," he mutters.

Anton is so relieved, he nearly laughs. But that would make him entirely too conspicuous. He takes a bite of egg instead and, with his other hand, slides the folded paper from his coat pocket. He lets the scrap fall on the bench between them. The man in gray makes no move to retrieve it.

"You're new," he says, still slouched in feigned slumber.

"Yes."

"You've done well so far. Didn't stick out too badly, here in Wernau, though you are so damnably tall and thin."

Anton finds it disconcerting to carry on a conversation while eating—and a conversation with a stranger, at that. Moreover, this man insists on huddling beneath his hat—not a posture conducive to friendly terms. He turns to face the man as he speaks. "Thank you. If it was meant for a compliment."

The man in gray tuts. "Don't turn toward me. You'll draw eyes."

Anton straightens on the bench, working away at the dry sausage.

"That's better. This is dangerous work, New Fellow. There's no room for error."

"Error?"

The contact's shoulders shake, a silent laugh. "Plenty in our line of work have slipped up, believe me. You've heard of von Gersdorff, I assume."

"I can't say I have."

"No fault to you; it happened only a few days ago. He decided he was willing to die, himself, if he could end the ultimate evil in the bargain."

The sausage is too dry to swallow; it sits like a rock halfway down Anton's throat. "What do you mean?"

"It was at the old armory museum in Unter den Linden," the gray man says. "Our dear leader and a few of his closest friends were to tour the place, take in the glory of military might, all that sort of thing. This Gersdorff fellow loaded his pockets with explosives and set a timed fuse, and then he followed *that one*, whose name we all know, around like a puppy." Better not to say *Hitler* where any passing person may hear. One never knows who is keeping a sharp ear out for betrayal. "But wouldn't you know it? The man has no patience for glory or military might. He was in and out of the exhibit before Gersdorff's pocket bombs could detonate. Imagine the poor fellow's agony, standing there with his coat pockets ticking away while *that one* strolled off unharmed!"

"Lord have mercy," Anton mutters. "Was Herr Gersdorff killed?"

"Not this time. He ran to the bathroom, where no one could see, and managed to defuse the devices with mere seconds to spare. It would be enough to make a man roar with laughter, if it weren't so deadly serious. So you see, *mein Herr*—no room for error. In this business, our business, it comes down to seconds. Heartbeats."

Anton whispers, "I understand. I'll be more careful next time."

The gray man shifts on the bench and stretches his arms. When Anton glances down, the folded message has disappeared. He never saw the man take it.

"I've a lot to learn," Anton tells him.

"But you will learn. Everything depends on it—everything depends on all of us being as clever and as careful as we can. Only with great caution will we carry out our mission. We all wish for a speedier conclusion to this mess, but haste makes waste, as the Americans say."

"What is the mission, exactly? That's one thing I don't quite understand."

This time, the man's laugh is not so silent. "*Mein Herr*, don't force me to remove my hat and give you a scornful stare. I find this hat to be a brilliant disguise."

Anton amends his question. "Obviously, the ultimate goal is—well, what Herr Gersdorff attempted. But we—you and I, and the man I work with back in my village—what part do we play? That scrap of paper I dropped from my pocket . . ." His voice sinks even lower, barely audible now even to his own ears. "Do we send information to the Tommies?"

"Some of us are spies, yes. Some of us transmit whatever intelligence we can glean to the Tommies and Americans—anyone at all, provided they might help us undo what has been done to Germany. Others pass around leaflets, when it's safe to do so. Literature might inspire our friends and neighbors to stand up and fight alongside us. There are those who move people in secrecy—Jews and Romany, homosexuals, nuns, journalists—anyone the Party has fixed in their sights.

We have networks, you see—chains of cellars and attics and spaces between walls. By night, we guide the refugees from one hiding place to the next until they are over the border and can finally seek real aid from friendlier nations."

"And you?" Anton says. "What do you do? What do we do?" Something in the man's speech has told him that this work—Anton's work—has little to do with these efforts. They are driving at a different goal entirely.

"We, my friend, are hard at work on the most dangerous and most important task of all. Without telling you too much, you understand."

"Of course." It's unsafe to know too much.

"Thanks to us, there will be no wolf left to terrify us. I would say 'Soon there will be no wolf,' but it would be a lie. We might not act soon—or we might, if the right opportunity arises. But we will act, and when we do, the leader of the wolves' pack will howl no longer."

Assassination. That is their goal.

"You've stopped eating, *mein Herr*," the gray man says, though he hasn't lifted his hat to see.

God has said, *Thou shall not kill*. But God never stopped the gray bus from coming. Perhaps there are times, Anton thinks, when the Lord makes exceptions. He won't allow it to trouble him for more than a moment. As the gray man has said, it comes down to seconds in this business—heartbeats. Anton's heart goes on beating, and the warmth of righteousness settles over him like a cloak. He picks up the soda bread and takes half the round in a single bite. He doesn't look at his contact, but he grins at the man all the same.

17

Late April. When the sun finds a hole in its clouded shroud, the light glares off what remains of the snow, off the surfaces of puddles in the ruts of the road. It's enough to make you squint, looking out the window at a world wet and striving, struggling to renew. The green and growing things are winning that fight. Everywhere, they push up through crusts of old ice, the shoots of sapling trees and spikes of crocus flowers yet to unfold. Winter can't keep its hold forever. As he stands beside the sitting-room window, watching the lane beyond the Hertz farmhouse, Anton can hear the running and dripping of meltwater from the eaves. This weather, cold and wet, with a forbidding, iron-gray sky, keeps the roads almost as empty as they have been all winter long. Who will venture out or roam between villages unless urgent business compels him?

The strong odor of cooked cabbage fills the small house. The children are gathered around the table, dunking eggs into bowls of boiled red cabbage or onion skins. Later, they will tie the eggs with ribbons and hang them from the willow branches Elisabeth has brought inside.

"Look, *Vati*." Maria holds an egg above her head for Anton to see. The blue-green dye runs down her arm into her sleeve.

"Your eggs are very pretty." He kisses Maria on the cheek and gives each boy's hair a tousle. To Elisabeth, stirring more cabbage dye on the stove, he says, "I'm off now. I'll try to be home by suppertime, but with the roads so muddy, you know—"

Without looking up, she says, "Who looks for piano lessons the Friday before Easter?"

"It may be unusual, but we need the money." He kisses her cheek, too, but she doesn't turn toward him, and never stops her stirring. He can feel her tense waiting, the stiff, upright posture of her irritation. Piano lessons don't bring in enough money to bother with. He knows it, and Elisabeth does, too. How, then, will he explain the money he'll bring home tonight? The bounty that will spill from his pocket.

"I think I may have found a buyer."

She stops stirring the cabbage. Her brow pinches as she looks up at him. "A buyer? What do you mean?"

"The brass. You remember."

The frown lifts from her face, and a radiance of relief alights in its place. "Anton! Are you sure?"

"Nothing is certain yet. I'll need to discuss it . . . negotiate. After I give my piano lesson."

She sighs happily. "That's a weight off my back. Have you sold all the instruments?"

"I've sold nothing yet. Remember that; it won't do for you to expect more than I can deliver. But I think one or two might sell."

"It's a start." She smiles at him, briefly, almost shy. Then she returns to the cabbage. Anton tries to ignore the pressure of guilt swelling in his stomach.

"Which town are you visiting today?" Albert asks, rolling his red-orange egg in a towel.

"Kirchheim." He tells the truth—in this, if nothing else—before he realizes he ought to lie. The secret work is still too new; he hasn't learned the nuances of being a message carrier, a resister. He must be more careful—discreet. Surely the gauleiter sees every coming and going. No one tramps through a puddle in Unterboihingen without Möbelbauer noticing.

Paul says, "Is there any chocolate in Kirchheim?"

What is Easter without chocolate? Outside, near the foot of the staircase, the children have built their *Hasengärtle*, the rabbit garden, a round plot of grass fenced by broken twigs and bedded with soft green moss. Overnight, the visiting rabbit will whisk the dyed eggs from the willow branches and lay them out in the children's garden, making a pretty picture to welcome the spring. If the rabbit is fortunate enough to find the traditional sweets—scarce, bedeviled as we are by war—then he'll leave treats in the *Hasengärtle*, too, hidden among the eggs and flowers. What a thrilling thing to discover in the morning light. Anton has not yet asked Elisabeth how she managed Easters past, especially since the war began. He has a feeling the Easter rabbit hasn't brought these children a bite of chocolate in years.

He tells them, "I don't know whether there's any chocolate in Kirchheim. I suppose only the Easter rabbit can say."

Al tilts his head, too old now for such fantasies. "We don't need chocolate. There are heaps of other things we should spend our money on." But Anton can hear the longing in his voice.

"Your mother raised you well. You're a good, sensible boy." He makes a private note: *Find chocolate in Kirchheim, at all costs—the biggest, sweetest bar in all of Germany. Give it to Al and tell the boy he must eat the whole thing himself.*

"You don't buy Easter chocolate, Albert," Maria says. She is condescending, with all the lofty wisdom of a girl on the verge of seven. "The rabbit brings it if you're good."

Albert rolls his eyes and sinks back in his chair. "Then I won't waste my time wondering why the rabbit never brings you any."

"I had better be quick," Anton says, "if I hope to make Kirchheim in time to speak with the rabbit."

Paul's eyes widen. "Do you know him?"

"I've met him a time or two."

He doesn't attempt to kiss Elisabeth again. She is always stiff when he tries it; he suspects a brick wall would show more appreciation for affection.

Settling his old-fashioned hat in place, wrapping his coat tightly around this body, Anton descends the stairs and faces the bite of spring-time wind. The breeze stirs the scraps of dirty ribbon the children have tied to their *Hasengärtle* fence. In minutes, he is strolling down the main road, Unterboihingen at his back and his duty lying somewhere ahead.

He hasn't yet carried a dozen messages for the *Widerstand*, the resistance. Father Emil has assured him that with time and experience, the awkward sensation will dissipate—the feeling that a hundred pairs of eyes are fastened to his back, that they chase him through the streets, they scrutinize his every movement and expression. Anton prays the priest is right. *Lord, give me confidence, for my stomach is always knotted and sour by the time I reach my destination.*

At least Anton has had one cause to thank God. He has never been required to take the tunnel—that musty old passage from the age of kings. Since the night just before Christmas, when he huddled with his family in the moldering ossuary below the church, the steel door has given him a shiver every time he has passed it. Dreams have often haunted his sleep—of groping through a blackness deeper than night with a folded piece of paper gripped in his teeth, while above, countless tons of earth sag, ready to fall, saturated and stinking with the coldness of death.

One would think such nightmare visions—he has them both sleeping and waking—would leave him all but crippled by anxiety, hour after hour. They did, at first. But day by day, he has come to accept this new reality. Now the fears only plague him when he works—when he boards the buses that take him to Kirchheim or the train to Aichelberg. The fear of being followed pursues him down the tracks. On the bus, he sits in the back row so he can't feel a stranger's eyes on the back of his neck or imagine he senses a knowing stare. But other times, going about the minutiae of a father's life, he has never felt freer or livelier, not since 1933. He has taken action; he has made his stand. With a hidden fist, he has struck back at the Party. And though he is only one man, and can strike no blow that will devastate like a British bomb, in his heart he believes the Reich will feel his wrath.

He knows little about the messages he carries. They are, of course, encoded. Emil, too, remains comfortably in the dark. It's better this way; they are links in a chain. If one link is apprehended and the connection is snapped, another can easily be forged—the mission will continue. Success is more important than knowledge. As for trusting the sources of their information and the safety of their orders, both Anton and Father Emil have already placed the fullness of their faith in God. It's the best they can do, given their circumstances.

As winter gave way to spring and the earth burgeoned again with new life, Father Emil found, among his various friends and confidantes, yet another source of work for Anton, beyond carrying the messages. Along the banks of the Neckar and in Wernau and Unterensingen—yes, even in Kirchheim—more families have hired Anton to teach their children music. Whether the parents are sympathetic to the resistance and offer up their homes as a convenient cover for the message carrier, or whether they truly wish their children to acquire a little culture, Anton hasn't the least idea. Perhaps both motives are at play. Each family pays him a pittance apiece—no one can really afford music lessons now, not here in the country—but it's not their pay he needs. It's the excuse to visit their towns, to stand at the ordained street corner at the appointed time, and to say to the man in the gray felt hat, "A fine day, but do you smell rain coming?" just as the church bells ring. A friendly chuckle, as one would give to any talkative stranger on the street, and a polite handshake—no more than that—but it's enough for a scrap of paper to pass from one palm to another.

In Kirchheim today, the message changes hands more rapidly than usual, and his contact saunters casually away. His piano students are not in—they and their parents have gone to the church, making some preparation for Easter service—so he is free to hunt for his chocolate. He finds it at the bakery, though he must convince the proprietor to part with it. She is reluctant even to admit it exists. He pays dearly for the stuff, but the compensation from the *Widerstand* has been ample thus far. His family can afford this one small extravagance. Easter only comes once a year.

The bus ride back from Kirchheim is always long, and it stinks of exhaust. He is glad to find himself at the crossroads where Austraße meets Ulmer Street. The walk home is more than an hour from here, but the day has turned fine, with a brisk spring wind sweeping the clouds off to the west and puddles shining silver in the ruts of the road. He whistles as he walks, hands in his trouser pockets, the chocolate tucked away safely in an inner pocket of his coat. His top hat is smart, if it is old-fashioned. How long has it been since he's whistled?

The day has gone so perfectly that he might feel tempted to apprehension, if he were a superstitious man. The chocolate seems a blessing from on high; he can already see the children's faces when they find it in the rabbit garden—this miracle enough to make even Albert believe. The morning's ice has melted; the banks of ditches are lush with new spring growth. This is the season of renewal, of hope unfolding, and optimism blooms for him now. Vaguely, with a kind of sheepish inner grin, he thinks he ought to disguise that outrageous upwelling of hope if he cannot stem it. It's unseemly, in this time and place, when so many people despair.

But those who are heavy of heart don't know what he knows—that there is a resistance, that Germany has retained, in the smallest, thinnest capillaries buried deep inside its flesh, a lifeblood of essential goodness. Righteousness still flows, and ever will, Amen.

Whistling, humming, he takes the track that runs toward the heart of the town, along a field newly plowed and carpeted by the first flush of early weeds. The field belongs to the Kopps, the three brothers

Kartoffelbauer. They made thorough work of their spring plowing, and the earth is richly black where they have turned it over. The air smells of clean soil, mineral and damp. The brothers will have a fine crop of potatoes come the early summer. Food for all their neighbors' tables.

Across the field, he sees two small figures near the dark line of a hedge. They are young and slight and some distance off, but near enough that Anton recognizes the habits and movements of his two young sons. He stops on the road, content to stand and watch them at their play. He is—all the world is—suffused with a rosy gladness. What a miracle it is, that he has come to know the children so well already. And what a pleasure to see them making up stories and games as all children do, in better places than this war-ravaged nation. The boys face one another. They each step back. What are they doing? Tossing something between them, back and forth, at every throw taking another step backward. What is it they're throwing—a rock? No, it's too light for its size. The object flies too easily, hanging at the apex of its arc before falling back into their hands. It must be a ball, then. Seized suddenly by an appetite for play, as if he is a boy himself, Anton thinks to call out to them, to run through the field and join in their game. He sets off, taking long, reaching steps across the furrows.

But as he draws closer, Anton can see that it's no ball the boys are tossing. Gray-green and oblong, as it hangs in the air he can see, as if it's frozen in ice and magnified before his eyes, the score marks running down its sides like the scales of some deadly viper. His body goes cold. Where did the boys find a grenade? He staggers to a halt, staring, helpless with shock. Ought he to shout? If he does, will one of the boys miss his catch, and will the damned thing strike the ground with enough force to explode?

Just in that moment, as Anton hesitates halfway across the potato field, Albert catches sight of his stepfather. Thank God, he catches the grenade, too, and says something to Paul, quick and urgent. They drop the thing on the ground—as it falls, all the world seems to constrict around Anton, crushing him with a weight of fear and helplessness—but it rolls harmlessly into a furrow. The boys turn their backs and run. They know they've done wrong.

"Damn it!" It's the closest he ever comes to cursing, but he bellows it now, roars those two hard words across the field. The sound only spurs the boys on; they fly over the field like a pair of hunted hares. Anton leaps into pursuit, does his best to catch them—to keep them in sight—but even the rawness of his fear and anger can't make his aging body move any faster. If ever he needed a reminder that he is a man on the brink of middle age, he has it now.

Nevertheless, he chases the boys through the potato field, his sluggish legs burning with the effort. Al and Paul dodge through a scratching gap in the hedge into forestland beyond. Anton follows, though the hedge tears at his coat and the backs of his hands. Too breathless to beg them to slow down, to stop and talk it out, he can only run, striving desperately to keep the frightened boys in view.

The forest closes overhead, a deep-green canopy rustling with sound. Anton can no longer see the boys, nor can he hear them running. The trees are too dense; they offer too much cover for small, slender bodies and youthful feet. He halts in a small clearing, heaving for his breath, and stares around the wood. The boys must have gone to ground somewhere; otherwise, he would hear them running still, crashing through the underbrush. He may be aging, but he hasn't yet gone deaf. Then he sees the little trail off to the right, new buds of a hazel broken off, the shoots of some small woodland flower crushed under hasty feet. He takes the trail.

The forest path leads from one clearing to another—and in this one, he finds the boys' lair, a childhood kingdom so fascinating it forces a reluctant grin of admiration. The forest floor has been swept clean of detritus, and a fire ring made of charred stones stands at the center of the clearing—Al's doing, that meticulous preparation, the attention to safety. A great stump of some long-fallen tree has been hacked and hollowed and roofed by evergreen boughs, and its splintered gap of a doorway hung with a scrap of fabric, the same heavy dark-green wool Elisabeth uses for her curtains. Torn pieces of colored cloth and cutout magazine ads, faded by the elements and spotted with mildew, swing on lengths of twine that have been strung like a cobweb, this way and that, across the clearing. Anton wonders rather mischievously whether Elisabeth has noticed the disappearance of so many clothespins from her wash line.

"I know you're in there—in your fortress," he calls. "Come on out, boys. I'm not angry. Not anymore."

There is a furtive shuffling inside the stump. He waits, patient but firm. After a moment, they appear, eyes on the ground as they scramble from the stump. They stand with heads bowed and kick their feet in the dirt, unwilling to meet his eye.

Still breathing heavily, Anton sits on one of the logs near the fire pit. His knees crack as he does. Inside the fire ring, the earth is carpeted with dry ash and bits of charcoal. "Come here; sit with me. We need to have a talk."

"Are you angry?" Paul says, hanging back. The cautious note in his voice says he might take off running again if Anton answers, *Yes*.

But Al scolds his brother: "He said he's not. Don't you ever listen?" Even so, shame and wariness narrow Albert's eyes.

"Sit down, boys. I won't bite, I promise."

They sit, leaning elbows on their scraped knees, still turning their faces away.

"Do you know what that thing was—that you were tossing back and forth?"

"A grenade," Al says at once.

He stares at the boy, taken aback. If he hadn't known, then perhaps Anton could have understood such foolishness and forgiven him. How did this boy—his thoughtful, cautious one—think it wise to play with a grenade? "Don't you understand how dangerous it is? I expect better sense from you, Albert. Where on earth did you get that thing?"

"One of the boys from our class found it in his grandfather's fields, out near Stuttgart. He brought it back, and he told us where he hid it."

"We only wanted to see it up close," Paul says.

"Your friend brought it back from Stuttgart? It's a wonder he didn't get himself killed—his whole family, too."

"He showed it to his father, and his father said it's dead. Disarmed."

Anton isn't likely to trust the opinion of any old Unterboihingen man. These farmers and simple laborers—what do they know about weaponry? As for Anton, he has seen enough grenades in his lifetime, and more guns and bombs than he can bear to recall.

"I'll have to learn the best way to dispose of it safely."

"You can't get rid of it," Albert says, fists clenching at the injustice. "We were only playing. It couldn't have hurt us."

"We never have any fun!" Paul wails on the verge of tears.

"Do you call that fun, playing with a dangerous weapon? Would you think it fun to blow off a hand or a foot?"

"No." A sulky chorus.

Al adds, "But it's exciting, to play soldiers. We didn't mean any harm. We only wanted some excitement."

There is nothing exciting about a soldier's life. He wants to tell them the worst parts, the grueling, dull hours, numberless and blank—the way the nothingness grinds away your spirit and erodes your judgment, your humanity. Worse than the dullness are the times when you must see suffering close at hand—when you must cause it yourself, if you are unlucky. But Anton is wiser than to speak of it. His sons won't listen; boys never listen to the grim lectures of older men, men who know better than they. If he wants to prove to his boys that there is a better way to be, something to aspire to beyond soldiering, he must take a different tack.

"I admit," he says, "life can get rather dull out here in the country."

They turn to look at him now, wary but willing to listen.

"What do you suppose is the best part of being a soldier? What do you imagine they do, in the Wehrmacht?"

"Running!" Paul says. "And climbing in and out of trenches."

Al adds, "And being brave, and doing things no one else can do."

He says thoughtfully, "I suppose that does often come into it. I would know, having jumped from an airplane."

The boys are with him now, attuned to his words.

"But you know, there are ways for boys like you to have a good time without bringing grenades into it. And there are ways for a fellow to find more fun than he can ever get from the Wehrmacht."

"How?" Paul squints at him, skeptical.

"You might go fishing, now that the streams and ponds have thawed."

"We haven't any fishing rods."

"I'll show you how to make them. It's simple, and you can dig up worms for bait around the *Misthaufen*. Muck heaps always make fat, juicy worms, the kind fish can't resist. Or, if fishing isn't to your liking, you might hunt."

"But we don't have a rifle," Al says. "Nobody can own one, unless you're a soldier or a loyalist. You know that."

The boy speaks the truth. Anton well remembers the Weimar Republic with their registry of firearm owners. They started the registry when he was a young man, freshly ensconced in the Franciscan Order. It had seemed like a wise idea at the time; Anton, committed to the order's peace, had even praised the registry. But it had run quickly out of hand, as do all things touched by the NSDAP. If all citizens had abided by the law—or if every citizen had broken it—we might not find ourselves here now, a people quivering in the sights of the Party's confiscated arms. But in '31, they used the registry to target and disarm the Jews, and in '33 the constitution was suspended while the NSDAP scoured every home and business, cracking safes and slicing open mattresses, breaking down pantry doors. They took every firearm they found and revoked the legal license of every man and woman deemed *not politically reliable.* And by that time, what could a few rebels do—that ragged handful who refused to comply with the Weimar registries? Nothing but stand by and watch while their defenses were seized, their right to resist burned to the ground. What can one man do against an army bristling with guns? What can half a dozen do, or a hundred? Now, since 1938, it's only avowed members of the National Socialists who may own private firearms. What might a thousand men do, or ten thousand, if they had the strength to match their adversaries?

To the boys, he says, "You don't need a rifle to hunt. What do you suppose people did in the days before guns were invented? You can make slings easily; I've a book somewhere that shows how to do it. We'll need to find some leather soft enough to work with, but Möbelbauer might have a few scraps he's willing to part with, left over from covering chairs."

"We can't kill a deer with a sling," Paul says. "And even if we could, a deer is too heavy for us to move."

"Deer! Who likes deer meat, anyway? No, boys—I'm talking about rabbit."

They glance at one another, considering.

"It might be fun to hunt," Al admits. "But it's far more manly to be a soldier."

Anton covers his mouth with his hand, trying to hide his frown. How to tell them—how to make them see, in a world that praises the unfeeling killer as the height of masculinity? We celebrate the man who bristles with arms, who paves for himself a path of violence. But there are other men, other lives, other ways for a man to be. What of the teachers and the priests? What of doctors and artists, who heal and create where other men destroy? What of our fathers? *And how do I tell them,* he wonders, *that the soldiers they revere sweat beneath their helmets and wake screaming in the night? How do I tell them that the Party leaves their soldiers little choice, or none at all?* By force, the Wehrmacht commit such acts that destroy their souls, as surely as a bullet destroys flesh. By force, the Führer manufactures ghosts that will haunt forever those who serve him.

He cannot say these things, not to boys so young and innocent. Let them stay this way for as long as fate permits, gamboling and unconcerned, with their heads full of dreams, not nightmares. He says, "It's most manly of all to do kindness to one another. You remember, Al— you don't want to hurt anyone, or see harm done to your fellow men. You told me so on the first day we met."

Al nods. He remembers.

"I must take you both hunting," he says with finality, though he has seldom hunted in his life, and not since he was a boy himself. When can he do it, busy as he is with the *Widerstand* network? He must simply find the time—find it, or make it. He must show these boys, entrusted to his care, that there are more rewards to be found in mercy and love than in mindless fighting and killing. We gain more by emulating Christ than his persecutors.

"I would like to go hunting," Al says.

Paul jumps to his feet. "So would I! Let's do it tonight."

"Not tonight." Anton climbs to his feet, stifling a groan. His legs and hips ache from the run, and there is still a rough, burning sensation deep in his lungs. "We must make our slings first. You boys must promise me with all sincerity that you will never play with any sort of weapon again. And if you see anything of the sort, you are never to touch it, but tell me at once."

"All right," Al says, still a little sulky. "We promise." A darker thought occurs to him, and he grabs Anton's sleeve in alarm. "You won't tell Mother, will you?"

"Seeing as how you've given me your solemn vow never to do it again, I think this time we can leave her in blessed ignorance." It's a mercy to poor Elisabeth; she would take sick with fright at the mere thought of her boys meddling with a grenade. "But if it happens again, you won't be so lucky."

As he turns to go, he says, "I like your fortress. You've done well with it. Don't stay out too long; it will be cold this evening, and your mother will be worried."

The sun has nearly set by the time he finds his way out of the woods. He eases through the gap in the hedge, and there is the grenade, lying mute and small in its furrow. He stands frozen, half crouched, his blood humming with a tight, uncomfortable energy, half expecting the damnable thing to explode unprovoked, like a curse. When he can relax by inches, he steps around it, cautiously, slowly, circling and staring like a skittish dog. He can see now that the boys were right: it's only an empty shell. Someone has disarmed it; the steel plug is gone from one end, the pin from the other. There is nothing inside but a void.

He lets his breath out slowly. He picks it up, feeling the cold of its metal skin in his colder hand. This grenade will harm no one, but it's still a hateful thing, a tool of destruction. He turns it over in his hands, rolls it between his palms. Its size baffles him. How can something so small contain such deadly force? How can so simple an object unmake a body, a life, the world? He looks down the hole in the grenade's tapered end into its hollow heart. Light shines through the other side. Then he whips back his arm and throws the thing hard, as hard and far as he can. It lands with a small, insignificant splash in the irrigation canal that runs along the edge of the Kopp field. The water, flowing high and fast with spring's thaw, takes the grenade and pulls it under. In moments it is buried, vanished into soft and fertile silt.

18

Spring slips rapidly away into summer. Anton would be glad of the change of seasons, the lengthening light and the growing warmth, if not for this persistent feeling—a kind of whispering dread, always murmuring behind his thoughts—that he has accomplished nothing since taking up with the resistance. Father Emil has told him, "Be patient. We can't change the world overnight." But still, he expected by now to hear some news from Berlin or from the Prussian outpost where the Führer often goes to ground. Our cities, our citizens, face bombardment nearly every day. But when the assaults prove too much for our great leader to bear, he tucks himself away in his Wolf's Lair and shelters from the storm.

On a blue day in May, when the air is sweet with the perfume of flowers, he meets his contact in Wernau. Anton sees the man reading an NSDAP paper on a bench near the bus stop—gray suit, blue tie, spats covering his shoes. This is the very man he was told to find.

He passes the bench, muttering the key phrase as he goes. "Do you smell rain coming?" Without looking up from his paper, the man in the gray suit gives the expected response. "No one can keep the rain away forever." Anton circles the block, taking his time, lingering at shop windows and lifting his hat to the women he meets. He flashes his charming grin. He makes as if he has nothing but time, as if his only concern is whether the sun will pink the tops of his ears.

When he returns to the bus stop bench, the man in the gray suit is still there. He has finished his paper—it's only one long sheet, printed front and back, as are all papers now—and he sits gazing down the street, as if searching for his bus. He has folded the paper into a perfect square. It lies on the bench, forgotten.

Anton looks the contact over more carefully. Of course, the man declines to meet Anton's eye; that much he expects. But the fellow waits patiently, allowing Anton to study his face while he scans the long street. Anton has seen him before. This is not the first time he has exchanged messages with this man. He is, in fact, the first man Anton ever met in the secret work, the one who told him the story of Rudolf von Gersdorff frantically defusing his bomb in the museum bathroom. He is glad to see Herr Pohl again. It's always a pleasure, to know someone you admire has survived.

As he sits, Anton lets the folded message drop from his hand onto the bench. A moment later, Pohl uncrosses his legs, recrosses them. He shifts, he sighs; distracted, he picks up his folded newspaper and the message with it. Anton's note tucks into the paper square and slides between its overlapping leaves. The message has vanished.

"A beautiful day," Anton says. "Any news from Berlin?"

Pohl gives the briefest of smiles. "Not the kind of news you and I are looking for."

"Soon, though. I can feel it in my bones."

"You are a tireless one. And optimistic."

"My faith in God compels me. I believe in the work God has given me, and I believe in His power to right all wrongs."

"A Christian," says Herr Pohl. He sounds amused.

"You're not?"

"If I say I'm not, will you stop coming to speak with me?"

Anton searches the street, too, gazing in the opposite direction, never meeting Herr Pohl's eye. "Not in a thousand years. I believe too strongly in my mission."

"More strongly than you believe in God?" There is no sting in the man's voice. In fact, there is something of a chuckle. It's a boyish game, this teasing, but Anton feels compelled to answer forthrightly.

"I will admit, there are times when I have my doubts about the Lord."

"How not, with so much evil in the world?"

"Once, on a train, I heard a man say he didn't believe in God because he had never seen Him."

Herr Pohl laughs, dry and quiet. "A clever man, that."

"But just because we can't see the Lord—that doesn't mean He isn't there."

"Can't see Him, can't feel His touch. He has no influence in this world, or you and I wouldn't be here, now, doing what we do. If God ever existed, He is dead, my friend. Hitler himself killed Him."

What can Anton say to that? He has scarcely felt the Lord's presence since this war began. He believes because he wants belief—because without it, he will crumble in despair. God is not dead, only absent. Whenever He deigns to return, Anton will be waiting to embrace Him. He will take God in his arms and say, *Look what I have done while You were gone. Look how I have tried to uphold Your glory. I am only one man, but my God, I tried.*

After a pause, Pohl says, "My name is Detlef. My Christian name, I mean."

Anton turns to him, grinning. "Your Christian name—then are you a Christian, despite yourself?"

Pohl only shrugs and refuses to look at him. Anton understands his uneasiness. They aren't supposed to know one another's names, the men and women who carry out this great and deadly work—except when two resisters work closely together, and on a regular basis, as in the case of Anton and Father Emil.

"I know," Pohl says, apologetic. He looks up and down the street, casually but with a keen eye. "We aren't supposed to tell. It's safer that way—of course it is. But sometimes I find my job rather lonely, don't you? Sometimes I think, 'If we don't remember each other's humanity, and recognize individual worth, then we aren't much better than . . .'" He leaves the rest unspoken, but his meaning is clear.

Anton has felt the same way, now and then. He has shared Detlef Pohl's dark thoughts. He sees, too, that this is Pohl's apology, an earnest attempt to mend what this talk of God has broken. "I'm Anton Starzmann. Pleased to meet you—properly, I mean, since we have crossed paths before."

"Don't tell me if you have a family," Pohl says quickly. He toys with the folded newspaper. He spreads it open again, glances over its lines. The scrap of paper with Anton's message is gone. If Pohl concealed it in his hand or in his pocket, Anton never noticed the subtle motion. Pohl is a man of long experience. "If you have a family, I don't want to know. In case they ever catch me, you see. I don't want to tell them how they can get to you, if they force me to reveal whatever I know."

"I understand," Anton says. "They can't force you to say what you don't know." He leans back on the bench and turns away again, searching now in earnest for his own bus. Outwardly, he is unconcerned. Inside, his throat has gone tight with fear. *Don't ever tell how they can hurt me. How they can force me to their will.*

Pohl says, quite suddenly and with the hint of a laugh, "They call us the Red Orchestra, those of us they know about, those they keep their eyes on. Did you know?"

"I didn't."

"It's their secret code. Or they think it a secret, but we know—we know nearly everything." Pohl's voice falls even lower than the cautious murmur he'd been using before. In that sinking pitch, Anton hears the unspoken words: *Knowing as much as we do, one would think we could have acted by now. One would think we could have cinched this business up last spring. Von Gersdorff and his damnable bomb.*

Anton says, "Why an orchestra?"

"They give us each a special name, those they know about. We are all musical instruments to them. Herr Violin, Herr Clarinet, Fräulein Oboe—that sort of thing. Do you know why? Because they think if they ever capture us, they can make us all sing."

"They don't know us half as well as they fancy." It's a brave thing to say, but Anton has seen firsthand what the SS can do, how they can break a man and force him to their will. He says, "How will this all end, do you think?" He dares not ask when.

"The kingdom can't be overthrown until the king is dead. What he has built is too deeply rooted in Germany now." The Party is too thoroughly entrenched, and the people are too cowed, too frightened to resist. They are all too willing to shut their eyes, to pretend nothing evil has happened. They are even willing to accept that these things Hitler does, these things he says, are normal—that the Party has the right of it, and has been right all along. They are ready to believe, now, that mankind was always meant to hate his neighbor, to kill the weak and the outcast, since God first dreamed us into being.

But those of us who resist—we remember what the world was like. There were times before—all the long history of our nation, before Hitler's rise—when we behaved less like wolves and more like men. We remember; we know. The purging of the press, the suspension of our constitution, the rallies and marches and the Reichstag fire—this is not who we are. Anton sits in silence, listening to the slow rustle of Herr Pohl's paper. He stares down the road for the bus, but in his mind, he walks backward through time, searching as he did before for the place where Germany went wrong, where we turned aside from our humanity. It was when hunger came in 1918. It was when our jobs vanished, when a man could no longer expect to feed his family, when any crust of bread was a miracle. His efforts are misplaced, in searching for the origin of evil. He knows it's so, yet he can't stop asking: When? And why? But when and why don't matter. If not now, then some other date. If not for Hitler's reasons, then by the will of some other man. Satan is alive and well; he lives in the hearts of all people. He waits, his sharp ear cocked, for the whisper from a sly politician, or a general's shouted order. He is always ready to reach out his sulfur-stinking hand and beckon us toward the unforgivable.

Walking home from his bus stop outside Unterboihingen, Anton considers what Detlef Pohl said. The Red Orchestra, and all the secrets the Nazis think they can keep. *Do they know about me yet, or am I still invisible? What name have they given me; what will my voice sound like when they take me, and make me sing?*

The bells of St. Kolumban ring out the hour, and the sound carries across the distance, familiar and soothing, a beacon to guide him home. Despite his worries, Anton smiles to hear it. For a moment, that gentle tolling overwhelms the dread that murmurs ceaselessly in his mind. The bells drown out the frantic chorus of his imagination, the blood-red orchestra playing.

He reaches into the pocket of his unbuttoned jacket. The Easter chocolate went over well; he has found more candy to give the children—peppermints, this time—and he feels compelled to check on his small treasure, to be sure it's still there. Tucked beside the peppermints, he finds the folded letter from his sister, Anita. He received the note two weeks ago, a welcome surprise, but he'd forgotten slipping it into his coat pocket. He pulls it out and unfolds it to reread Anita's words as he walks.

He'd written to her belatedly, months after the wedding. *You will never believe it,* he told her. *I am a husband and father now. I am sorry it has taken me so long to tell you. I'm kept busier than I'd imagined I could be, caring for the little ones.*

Anita's response is amusing—she was always a funny girl—but between her humorous lines, he can read the sobriety of her thoughts.

My dear little brother,

It is I who must apologize to you. You may have taken three months to tell me you ran off and got married (I would have expected something like this when you were a boy of seventeen, but now that you are practically old . . . !) but it has taken me three more months to write a reply. That's six months of shame on us both. It's a good thing neither of us is in our orders any longer; otherwise, we would have to assign penance to one another, and I hear nuns are terribly cruel to their little brothers. I would be obliged to uphold that tradition.

Since we saw each other last, I have found work as a secretary here in Stuttgart. Can you imagine, a nun taking dictation and typing off memos! It's too ridiculous to think about. I can hardly believe it myself, and yet I get up every morning and put on my city-girl clothes and go off to do my work. But it's work or starve, for me. I won't take a husband (not that many men chase after me; I am forty-two now!) for I am still faithful to Christ.

Yes, you read it correctly. We are still estranged, but I am willing to take Him back once He's ready to reconcile. I am faithful to Him forever.

You mustn't think I judge you for your decision to marry, Anton. I am sure your wife and children are delightful. I trust your heart to lead you in the right direction. I hope you trust your own heart, too—and God. Someday, when this boring war is over and we can re-form the orders, you will not go back, now that you are a Vati. *But I believe you have ended up exactly where the Lord means you to be.*

I wonder, is Christ truly divorced from me now, or has some worse fate befallen Him? Am I a woman cast off, or am I a widow, like your Elisabeth?
    Your loving sister,
    Anita

Anton smiles down at the note, as he did the first time he read it, and a dozen times after. But Anita's pain strikes him afresh, so evident in the letter's final lines. Even the most devout have begun to believe that God is dead. He can hardly blame them. What kind of Lord allows this iniquity to taint what He has made? Only a weak God or a nonexistent one—perhaps Herr Pohl is right. Perhaps it's Anton who is strange, he who is unusual, buoyed by his relentless, unforgiving optimism, pressed ever onward by his conviction that this regime can be overthrown. Even when logic and common sense tell him, *Give up, Anton, it's impossible. Shut your eyes and accept*—still he presses on.

He tucks Anita's letter back in his pocket. He has written her since receiving this note—in fact, they have exchanged several more letters each. But for some reason, it's this letter in particular that moves him time and again, this one he keeps as a reminder never to accept that God is dead.

He passes the lane to a small cabin, tucked several yards back from the road behind a paling fence with a thick backdrop of tall cottage flowers. The flowers are woefully overgrown, an untended jungle of color and sweet perfume. The little house hasn't been used for some time—it is, or was, the country home of some wealthy city dweller. Who can say whether the owner is still living? But he hears a voice coming from the cabin, high and thin and small. He pauses, straining to listen, caught by some instinct he can't yet identify. Then he realizes it's Maria's voice. Maria is singing—to herself, as far as he can tell—inside the little house.

Anton checks his pocket watch. It's barely past the lunch hour; the girl should be in school. A vague yet pressing fear needles him. This is not routine, not right; wary of some half-formed danger and with a sudden, protective energy, Anton hurries through the gate and up the lane, brushing the overgrown flowers from his path. Petals scatter in the uncut grass.

The cabin's door swings on its hinges, left carelessly ajar. He calls out, "Hello? Who's there?"

Maria stops singing.

"Maria? Is it you?" No adult answers his call, so he opens the door wider and steps inside.

"I'm here." Maria sounds annoyed, and disappointed at being found.

He turns in place, searching the sitting room, but the house appears empty. Dust lies thick and pale on the furniture.

"Where are you, girl?"

"I'm here, *Vati*."

He finds her sitting cross-legged behind the sofa, a great pair of black scissors in one hand and a magazine in the other. The floor is covered in a snowfall of paper scraps.

"For goodness' sake, what are you doing?"

"Cutting," she says. As if to prove her point, she snips at a page of the magazine, clumsily cutting around the outline of a woman's body. The woman, fresh-faced and smiling, leaves the artificial realm of her soap ad and trembles in Maria's hand.

"You naughty child!" Anton whisks magazine and scissors out of her hands; she looks up at him, her hard, affronted eyes filling with tears.

"I'm only making paper dolls!"

It's then that Anton sees all the girl has done. More magazines poke out from beneath the sofa—a few books, too. Some lie open, their

169

illustrated pages mangled with ragged cuts. Anton shifts his glasses and rubs his eyes. He can only hope the books weren't valuable.

"Maria! Don't you know it's wrong to enter a house that isn't your own?"

She climbs to her feet and braces belligerent little fists on her hips. "That's not in the Bible! God never said so."

"That doesn't mean you aren't doing wrong." She is only seven. How has a girl so young developed such contrary habits? Elisabeth spoke the truth when she said Maria was as mischievous as the Lord ever made a girl to be. "Why aren't you at school?"

"I don't like school. I haven't gone in ever so long."

His hand falls from his face; the glasses drop too low on his nose. He stares down at the girl, astonished. "How long, exactly?"

Maria shrugs. "Since it got sunny and warm. I decided it was funner to be out playing, so I go out and play."

"But your brothers walk you to the schoolhouse." He'll have to speak to them, and sternly, too. The boys must drift off, playing soldiers along the road, failing to keep their eyes on Maria. Such neglect of duty is dangerous at the best of times, but now, when any moment a plane might appear over the crest of a hill, laden with bombs—

"They do walk me, and Al holds my hand the whole way."

A sigh of relief. "Then why are you here?"

She beams at him, pleased with herself. "I tell the teacher I must go to the bathroom. She lets me go, because if she doesn't, I'll pee myself."

"And then you never return?" He fights to hold back a laugh. She may be a bad little girl, but at least she is clever.

Coolly, with a decidedly grown-up air, Maria nods.

It's a wonder the girl's teacher hasn't yet spoken to Anton and Elisabeth. The poor woman must be run ragged, keeping up with all her students—and Maria can easily make as much trouble as five ordinary children.

"A few times," Maria says proudly, "my teacher said, 'I'll go with you, to see that you find your way back from the bathroom.' But I just stayed inside and said, 'I'm not done yet!' until she went back to the classroom."

"Merciful Mother. That poor woman."

"She's not a poor woman! She's dreadful and I don't like her one bit."

Anton suspects the feeling may be mutual. "Your teacher must be onto your tricks by now."

"She is harder to fool now. Last time, she told me she would make me sit in my chair and she didn't care if I wet myself in front of the whole classroom; I would have to sit in my own mess until school was out."

"What did you do, then, to escape?" Anton isn't certain he wants to know.

"Once I faked a sick stomach and ran outside to throw up in the bushes. But I didn't throw up. I kept on running, and she couldn't catch me."

He resists the urge to cross himself, to plead with the Lord for mercy.

"And this morning," Maria goes on, "I told her as soon as class started that my *Mutti* is sick and I must go home to help her with the chores. She said, 'Then go, you bad little girl! It will be a mercy to me, to be free of you for the day.' I don't think she likes me, but I don't care. She's the worst teacher you can imagine, *Vati*."

"It's very wrong for you to deceive your teacher. And you've been deceiving your mother and me, too—and your brothers." A thought occurs to him. He sinks down to her level, eye to eye. "But you always come home with your brothers, at just the right time. How do you manage it?"

"I listen for the church bells. I go meet the boys in front of the schoolhouse when the bells ring the right hour."

The girl is too intelligent for her own good. Perhaps he ought to take her along on his errands; keep her under his thumb, and well supervised.

But of course, that would be far too dangerous. If Unterboihingen has a gauleiter, why not Kirchheim or Wernau? If he were to be seen with his daughter, spotted by a man possessed of more ambition than mercy, the Party would know at once how to trap Anton Starzmann. They would have no trouble making that instrument sing a pretty tune of betrayal.

"You're coming home with me now."

"I'm not done cutting!"

"Oh yes, you are. And once we reach home, you'll write a note to whomever owns this house, apologizing for ruining their books and magazines, and you will leave it where they can find it." Assuming the cabin's owner ever returns to Unterboihingen, Anton will owe him money to replace what Maria has damaged. *Angels, defend me—let her not have cut up some priceless antique book or a family album.*

"Can I take my paper dolls?" She pulls from beneath the couch an astonishing stack of colorful figures, two inches high—men and women snipped from countless pages. The girl must have been at this particular mischief every day for weeks on end.

"Absolutely not! Put them in the stove."

Tears spring to her eyes again. "They'll be burned up!"

"That's the consequence of deceit. Just be glad I don't turn you over my knee and give you a worse punishment."

Anton carries Maria home. She has gone limp in his arms, in protest of his cruelty—though she stopped crying at once, as soon as she realized tears could not move him. Thinking of the money he may owe the cabin's owner, his stomach curdles with frustration—but despite lingering sourness, he can't help feeling a melting glow of love as he holds the girl, as she tucks herself trustingly into his arms.

That evening, when the supper dishes are washed and the children are readying themselves for bed, Anton takes Elisabeth outside, into the warm summer night, to discuss Maria.

"I found her hiding behind the sofa, shearing a stack of magazines as if they were sheep. I almost swallowed my tongue when she showed me her handiwork—weeks' worth of cutting. You should have seen it." He bites back the smile he can't quite conceal.

Elisabeth is not amused. "Frau Hertz always says, 'Maria is a handful.' But I can't keep hold of her with both hands, let alone one. She'll get herself into real trouble someday, and then what will I do?"

Elisabeth's look of pale distress moves Anton. He pats her shoulder, awkward as always, and wonders if he ought to risk embracing her. "The girl will learn. We must be firmer with her, that's all—and show her that virtues have their own rewards."

"No virtue has enough natural reward to tempt Maria into proper behavior." Elisabeth sighs and presses the fingers of one pale hand to her forehead. The ceaseless pain of motherhood. "I'm only grateful, to you and to God, that I have you to help me through this, Anton."

He blinks in surprise. It's as close as Elisabeth has ever come to a tender word.

She says, "Maria alone was more than I could handle, when I was by myself. And now the boys are getting bigger; they'll soon be teenagers, and boys of that age are never easy. Even Albert and Paul, sweet as they are, will soon be more than I can manage alone. Without you, this family would fall apart."

"Well, I . . ." Lost for words, embarrassed by the swell of warmth in his chest, he pulls at his tie, loosens it, leaves it hanging askew. He takes his pipe from his pocket, lights it, and puffs once. He lets the ember die out, and the pipe parts with a final trace of smoke. "I'm only doing what I promised to do," he says at last.

"And now that we have the money from your music lessons—it's such a blessing. The extra income has relieved so much of my burden. I admit, when you first said, 'I'm going to teach children how to play the piano,' I had my doubts. I thought, 'He'll never find enough work to keep a steady income, not with the war on.' But I was wrong, Anton. I don't mind admitting I was wrong."

He swallows hard. He has only just delivered a lecture to Maria about the sins of deceit. Some of his money does come from the lessons, of course, but most is paid by whoever keeps the Red Orchestra together—whatever shadowy figure pays Father Emil, who passes Anton's cut along to him.

I should tell her, he thinks. *I should let her in on the secret. We're a family now; we must rely on each other, trust one another. How can I expect my wife to ever trust me, or love me, when I hide this from her?*

The next moment, he dismisses that idea. Elisabeth would prefer not to know the truth—he's sure of that. She wants nothing more than to keep her head down and muddle through the war. Keep her family safe and whole until, God willing, this madness finally ends.

And Elisabeth and the children are safer in ignorance.

"I've had a harrowing enough day," Elisabeth says, "even without Maria's naughtiness. Möbelbauer has been at it again."

"At it? What do you mean?"

She sighs heavily and turns her face away. "That man is a pig. He shits on all the women of the town." She blushes at her own coarse language. "I'm sorry, Anton. I know you don't like those kinds of words. I don't, either—but Möbelbauer has put me so much on edge, I can't help myself."

"Has he done something to you? Said something?" He will go and see Franke, if that's the case. Man to man, they will thrash it out. No one may speak a harsh word to Anton's family and get away with it. Strange, the instincts God puts in a man, once he's a husband and a father. It's no wonder all the world fights wars. Look how many men are married, and the guardians of children.

Elisabeth stares down at her feet, then out at the orchard, its late blossoms still visible in the twilight. She glances up at the cottage roof, then out across the field. She looks everywhere, anywhere but at her husband. "You know, Möbelbauer has never been faithful to his wife. Never. I wouldn't be surprised to hear that he spent his wedding night with some other woman—he's that fond of straying. He has gone through every woman in the village, nearly—everyone who's still young enough to catch his eye."

"You can't be serious." He wants to say, *Why do the women permit it?* Franke is not so handsome or charming that he would catch most ladies' attention and tempt them to infidelity. But as soon as the thought enters his head, he understands. He says, "It's because he's the . . ." He almost can't make himself say the word. "Gauleiter." The eyes that watch for disloyalty, the ears that strain to hear the smallest whisper of resistance.

"Yes," Elisabeth says. "That. The women all go along with him, and give in to his advances, because they're afraid. What might Bruno Franke say about them, or about their husbands, if they don't? Unless they comply, he will write one of his letters to his contacts in Berlin. He's a disgusting man—*disgusting*."

Anton has seen village women with haunted looks and distant eyes. He had assumed it was only the war that affected them—*only* the war, as if it is a small thing. But now he understands there is something else at work here, a greater darkness moving. The sharp ear of the Devil has turned toward their safe little town. In the cities, they force men to run out their bayonets, and herd children off to their deaths. The women, they force to break their marriage vows and dirty themselves with shame. There is no remorse, no care for the consequences. And no thought for what it says about us, as a nation and a people, that we turn our eyes away from our neighbors' suffering. But of course, the pride and reputation of Germany mean nothing to the Party, or the dogs who lick their boots. They care only for what they may gain. The powerful take ever more power. They will remake the world as they see fit.

"If Franke ever comes after you," Anton says, "tell me."

Elisabeth flares up suddenly. For the first time that night, she looks directly at him. Her eyes are two points of anger, glowing in the dusk.

"I'll never break my vow. I said holy words before God; that means something to me."

It means something to all the women Herr Franke approaches, Anton is sure—but these matters are never as simple as one thinks when one is on the outside, looking in. It's only when they come to your door—when the gray bus arrives—that you know for certain what you will do. When they present you with the choice that is no choice at all—in the moment of truth, when the lives of the people you love hang in the balance, will it be easier to break a vow made before God, or condemn your children to the gas chambers?

"Tell me if he tries anything. I'll sort it out with him, so you won't have to." And God help me if he has already noticed my comings and goings.

Troubled, sleepless through the night, Anton goes to Father Emil the next day. Did he already know about the town's gauleiter—what Möbelbauer does with the women, married women, mothers of the village?

Yes. Emil knows. "Ambition makes the best of men dangerous," the priest says, "but I'm afraid Herr Franke was never the best of men."

"Elisabeth seemed quite upset by him, when I spoke to her last night."

"That's no wonder to me. You know this is a small town, Anton." He says it apologetically. "We know everything about each other."

Anton takes his meaning, but he has to hear the words before he will believe. "Tell me."

Emil pauses and sighs. He doesn't like to say it. "Herr Franke has already approached Elisabeth with the same foul proposal he has made to most of the other women in Unterboihingen."

Anton's mind is a flash of whiteness, blankness. He freezes on the church pew, motionless, stunned.

Emil says, "I am not breaking the sanctity of confessional by telling you this. I never would do such a thing. Elisabeth hasn't brought me this news herself, but a few of her friends have told me. They were troubled by it and sought my advice—wondering what they ought to do, how they could help her. I'm glad you came to see me about this matter, my friend. I have considered going to you and Elisabeth and offering my counsel. I know your marriage is unusual, and not especially warm. But for the sake of the children you both love, it must hold together."

"Poor Elisabeth. To face such a thing . . ."

Emil chuckles. "Poor Elisabeth? She sent Franke packing! Her friends all agreed on that point. They were proud of her, awed by her—doing what few other women have had the fortitude to do."

She would send Möbelbauer packing, and with a kick to his stout behind. Elisabeth's faith is a tower, a monolith. Woe betide the man who expects her to violate vows made at the altar.

"But now Franke will be angry with her," Anton says.

"Yes." It's clear from Emil's sober expression that he understands what Anton has left unspoken. How much does Herr Franke know? Is he even now scratching out a letter to whichever Nazi dog he reports to, implicating Anton as an instrument of the Red Orchestra—purely for vengeance against the only woman who has dared to spurn him?

He says quietly, "Father Emil, what do we do about this?"

Emil lifts his hands in a gesture of surrender. "We keep on, my friend. Is there anything else you would do?"

No. There is nothing else.

PART 4

Death Has One Eye

October 1943–April 1944

19

Fall crisps the air again, leading in the winter. How has a year passed so swiftly? Woodsmoke hangs in the orchard, a blue haze caught among the dry, rattling leaves that still cling to the branches. It's almost too cool now to dry the washing outdoors, but Elisabeth persists. She likes it when the scent of autumn smoke works itself into her dresses and old, threadbare jumpers. She has told Anton so, and now he has come to associate the smell of the season with his wife. The autumn is like Elisabeth—solemn, austere, a touch chilly, but not without its flashes of brilliant color.

Anton rests on the cottage's lowermost step, transferring his pipe from one hand to the other, watching Elisabeth hang up her clothes. Every article is spaced along the drying line at precisely the right distance. Nothing is crowded, and not a hand's width of line goes unused. She bends to her laundry basket, lifts a damp dress, and pins it to the line with a casual grace she doesn't even know she possesses.

When she pauses in her work—every time she rests—Elisabeth's eyes wander up to the peak of the cottage roof. Still, she is thinking of the tiny attic space, the unused void above her family's heads. Still, she wonders. There are those in Unterboihingen who would call Elisabeth cold, but Anton knows she is not—not where it matters most, in the center of her soul.

When she has hung the last garment on the line, Elisabeth wanders to the stairs with her laundry basket balanced on her hip. She lets the basket fall to the dry golden grass and then lowers herself to the step beside Anton, sighing.

"You know I don't like it when you smoke that thing."

"I know." He puffs and grins at her, teasing.

"I suppose I can't complain, though, after the wonders you've worked with Maria."

Anton has convinced the girl not only to attend school daily but to maintain her best behavior, too. He still can't credit his own achievement. When he looks back on the complex web of scolding, religious lectures, and bribery—largely involving old magazines, which Maria may use for her paper dolls—the route to his daughter's reform makes him quite dizzy.

"I don't suppose Maria's teacher has had any cause to complain recently," Anton says, cautious.

"Not a bit. She seems quite satisfied with Maria's behavior. So you may smoke away, as far as I'm concerned."

The boys' shouts carry, thin and distant, across the pasture. Anton and Elisabeth turn to watch as Paul and Albert scramble through knee-high dull-yellow grass. The two white goats leap away from the boys and run to the farthest corner of the field. The sun will set soon; the goats must be penned in before dark, bedded down with the milk cow in the stone foundation of the cottage.

"One would think those boys would have learned how to manage goats by now," Elisabeth says. "They'll never catch them by chasing."

"They're only playing. The good Lord knows, it's no easy feat to find some fun nowadays."

Elisabeth watches the boys in silence for a moment. Albert gestures, and Paul runs in a wide arc across the pasture, trying to outflank the goats as they mill and dart. Al waves his arms; the goats break toward

Paul, then dodge in another direction when Paul springs at them like a tiger from the tall grass.

"I'm glad they have one another," Elisabeth says. "I'm glad they're close."

"As close as brothers ought to be. Imagine what an Eden our world might be if we were all as close as brothers."

"I've seldom seen brothers as tightly knit as Paul and Albert. The Kopps, maybe—but few others."

Perhaps it's the war that has tied Paul and Albert so closely together. In a world that might upend itself at any moment, blow itself inside out in a ball of fire and noise, maybe brotherhood seems all the more precious.

"I'm worried about them," Elisabeth says suddenly.

Startled, Anton takes the pipe from his mouth. "What—worried about Al and Paul?"

"Yes. They haven't been eating as much as they used to. Haven't you noticed? At suppertime, they don't take as much food. Could they be ill?"

"We'd know for a certainty if they were ill." Anton frowns across the pasture. Al and Paul have captured the white goats at last. They lead the animals by their collars, moving quickly through the tall grass. The boys seem as energetic as ever. "I can't find a thing wrong with them—except now it's Al who's struggling with his shoes, not Paul. Look; can you see him limping?"

"Yes." Elisabeth rests her chin in her palm and props her elbow on her knee, the very picture of dejection. "It never ends, does it? I should be grateful to God that He has allowed my children to thrive on little more than rations. Instead, all I can think is, 'They grow like weeds, and how will we ever keep up?'"

Anton reaches into his pocket and counts out a few reichsmarks, which he hands to Elisabeth. "We'll manage. Don't worry, my dear."

She tries to refuse the money. "There will always be more things we need, more we must spend."

"If Albert needs shoes, there's nothing to be done but see that he gets new shoes."

Elisabeth takes the bills and crumples them in her hand. "You're right, of course." Then she brightens. "What would we have done if you hadn't sold those instruments? The extra money has been such a blessing to us, Anton. I almost feel rich."

He smiles, but he can't quite meet Elisabeth's eye. He should tell her—confess everything—but the thought of it makes him blanch. He hasn't sold a single horn—not one. He never even considered it. The instruments are too dear to him, the memories they hold too intimate and raw. Silence stretches at the tail of Elisabeth's remark. In another moment, Anton's stillness will come to feel like secrecy, and then she will question him, then she will pry—

In the heart of the village, the bells of St. Kolumban ring the hour. Anton and Elisabeth turn as one, savoring the sound. The low, rich music spreads itself across the land. It drowns out the memory of airplanes' engines, of the dry, rattling blasts from Stuttgart. It even silences, for a short time, haunting cries of vanished children and the sound of a gray bus idling outside St. Josefsheim. In the field, the boys stop to listen. Even the goats prick their ears.

When the last peal rolls past the cottage and out to the distant hills, Elisabeth wraps her arms around her knees and speaks. "I love the sound of those bells. I sometimes think I'd go mad without them. They make this place feel like a home, don't they?"

Anton nods. He chews the stem of his pipe.

"It's funny—these bells don't sound quite like any others. Have you noticed?"

"Every bell has a different voice, I suppose. It must depend on how it was made."

"Or perhaps," Elisabeth says, "it has more to do with our surroundings. The countryside—perhaps the wide-open space allows them to sing more beautifully. There were church bells in the city, of course, but I never truly loved the sound of bells ringing until we came to Unterboihingen. In the city, they always sounded harsh to me—clanging like some terrible alarm. But here, they truly sing. Here they sound like home." Wistfully, she smiles. "I remember those bells ringing at Maria's christening. I remember everything about that day—how glad we all were, how full of hope. The world seemed new, and . . . not so dark as it seems now. The bells seemed to say, 'Goodness will come again—goodness like this new baby girl. The darkness can't last forever.'

"And I remember how the bells rang at my husband's funeral, too." She hangs her head. "I shouldn't talk of it, I suppose—"

"Go on," Anton says. "I don't mind."

For a moment, she sits in pensive silence, her face turned away. But then she rounds on Anton with sudden, despairing passion. "I'm glad he didn't live, Anton—and I know it's terrible to say it, terrible to think it, but I can't help it, all the same. I'm glad. He was such a kind man, so good, so sweet. I'm glad he never lived to see what the world has become." She sniffs and wipes her eyes with the heel of her hand. "But I don't know how to explain it to his children. How do I tell them what the world was like before, and why it has changed?"

His children—my children, Anton thinks sadly. How do we tell anyone?

Elisabeth shakes her head, laughing without humor at her own reaction. "I'm a fool. There's no point carrying on so."

"It's understandable."

"But it does no one any good." She straightens, and seems to lift her own spirits by force of will. More brightly, she says, "Every hour, I feel I can't go on any longer. I feel the world is too wicked to bear, and too broken to be made whole. And then—every hour—I hear the bells of St. Kolumban ring, and I know I can go on. Sometimes I even think that God will manage to patch up this wreck of a world, after all—somehow. Do you know what I think it is about those bells that makes me love them so much? It's because the whole village hears them, too. It's something we all share, isn't it?"

Not a soul alive doesn't love to hear those bells ringing. And not a soul alive doesn't feel, between one peal and the next, hope and peace return to the world, if only at the close of the hour.

20

Anton has delivered, by now, more messages than he can count. To Herr Pohl; to a handful of other barely familiar men and women in the towns scattered around Unterboihingen. The woman of fifty or so, with the bent spine and spectacles that are always spotted with dust. The man with the red hair, who appears in Kirchheim whenever Pohl does not. The youth who can't be older than eighteen—he looks so much like Anton did when he joined the Franciscans, fresh and eager, confident that he could change the world. Countless messages, innumerable handshakes, more folded scraps of paper falling from Anton's hand to the sidewalk than there are stars in the sky. And still no word from Berlin or Prussia. Still, the Führer goes on.

Returning from his latest assignment, Anton passes the Kopp field on the edge of town. The brothers brought their harvest in early last week; now the spent vines lie flat and brown, wilting down the length of the field. Far across the sleeping ground, Anton can see Paul and Albert loitering near the hedge, just as they'd done that day last summer when he caught them with the dead grenade. As before, he stops to watch. The boys aren't playing now. They are squatting at the field's edge, shifting aside dry potato vines. They reach into the soft earth and paw through it. Puffs of dust rise on still air.

What on earth are they doing? Anton squints across the distance, as if that will help him make sense of the strange activity. Then he understands: they are pulling up potatoes, digging them out, turning the tubers over in their hands. He watches as the boys brush soil from yellow-brown skins.

A weight of sorrow drags at Anton's heart. This is theft; his sons are stealing. Even if the harvest is over, and these potatoes were overlooked, it's still theft. Without permission from the Kopp brothers, what his boys are doing now is a sin.

He waits in the shade of a roadside oak, careful not to move. He doesn't want to draw the boys' attention. He remains there until Paul and Albert rise, brushing the dirt from their knees as they did from the potatoes. They disappear through the leafless hedge—heading toward their forest stronghold, as Anton suspected they would. This time, when he follows the boys, he does it with more dignity than he managed at Easter. The October wood is warm, spiced with the smell of fallen leaves. Its fragile, fleeting beauty wracks him with pangs of melancholy. Death is the very heart of this season—the passing of summer warmth, the fading of all that is young and green. A long, cold spate of colorless dark stretches before him.

When Anton enters the hidden clearing, the boys look up from their fire. There is a moment of dry, quiet tension as they sit, hunched upon a damp log, waiting for him to speak. Their eyes are bright and round in their solemn faces. The fire snaps, releasing a drift of sparks, but no one jumps at the sound, no one moves. Then, as if coming to an unpleasant decision, Al rises slowly. How tall the boy has grown; he will be a man soon. Anton can see very little of Elisabeth in his face, though Al has inherited his mother's meticulous nature and her habit of quiet observation. But it's the boy's biological father Anton sees now. Albert, watching Anton with a man's sternness and knowing. There is no mistaking the determination in his eyes, the somber paleness around his freckles. His height, his posture—he is strong, growing stronger and more his own man every day.

Anton thinks, *Herr Herter, you and I could have been friends, in another life. Your children are good people—even little Maria—and through them, I have been gifted with fatherhood, a blessing I never thought to receive.*

He doesn't wish to anger Herr Herter's shade, nor insult him. But it has fallen to him, Anton, to teach these children whatever the war has not taught already.

"I saw you take the potatoes," he says. He can feel Paul Herter's spirit there beside him, likewise mournful.

The boys hang their heads—even Al, tough Al's eyes flash up, briefly and only once, to gauge or challenge Anton's severity. In that moment, for the first time, Anton feels as if all the work he has done—the trips to other towns, carrying the coded words—everything he has wrought and risked to bring down this damnable regime—all is for naught. What is resistance for, if we fall back into evil?

Paul says, "They were left after the harvest."

"But they weren't yours to take."

"We know," Al says. "We talked it over. Didn't we, Paul? We never felt good about it—we knew it was wrong—but we thought, in the end, it was more loving and kind to do it. Even though it's wrong to steal. And we thought, if we only took the potatoes left at the end of the harvest, it wouldn't be so bad. Then we wouldn't be hurting the Kopp brothers. It's wrong to steal, but if we're not hurting anyone . . . and if it's more loving to do it . . ." Al trails off, biting a dirty nail. His gaze shifts to Anton's feet and stays there.

"More loving? What do you mean?" Then Anton notices the small white bones strewn around the clearing, kicked to the edges where carrion birds can pick them clean. Rabbit bones. As Al shifts restlessly on his feet, Anton sees the sling trailing from his trouser pocket. It's a homemade affair, fashioned from scraps of soft leather. He thinks, *I never went to Möbelbauer for the leather. They must have done it themselves.*

I never helped them make the slings. I never taught my sons how to hunt. What kind of a father am I?

"We remembered what you said, that day—you know, with the grenade—about hunting and fishing." Al swallows hard, but now he meets Anton's eye directly. "We would have liked for you to teach us, but you haven't had the time."

"That's true," Anton says hoarsely. "I haven't found the time."

"We thought, if we could hunt up our own food, and take the potatoes no one wanted anyhow, we could leave more on the table for Maria and Mother."

So his boys are no soldiers, after all. This is the act of a teacher, a father. Their generosity—and his soaring relief—move him almost to tears. "I only regret that it wasn't I who taught you how to hunt. But in truth, it has been so long . . . I would have been a poor instructor. I'm afraid you wouldn't have liked learning from me. Who taught you?"

"No one," Paul says. "We figured it out on our own. Well—there was a magazine we found at school, a boys' magazine. We read how it's done, and tried it."

"We worked at it for weeks," Al says. "We made little houses out of sticks and practiced knocking them down."

Paul pulls his sling from his pocket and holds it up for Anton to see. He has warmed to the story, swept up in the excitement of the telling. "Every time we hit a stick house, we had to take a step back. That was the rule. Soon we could hit them all from fifty paces away!"

"That is impressive," Anton admits. "But rabbits run; they don't stand still and wait for the hunter to come."

"That was the hardest part," says Al. "We had to learn how to aim all over again. But we've done it; either of us can bring down any rabbit in the forest."

Paul whirls his empty sling, a demonstration. "I'm going to hunt partridges this winter."

"Look," Al says, suddenly stubborn, as if he expects Anton doesn't believe his boast. As if Anton can't see the bones among the tree roots. The boys shift aside, revealing their fire. A rabbit, pink-brown and spitted on a long, charred stick, sizzles over the flame.

Softening, Al says, "Do you want some meat? The potatoes won't be done for a while yet—we've buried them in the coals—but the rabbit is good."

"Thank you; I'd be glad for a bite."

Anton joins them on the log beside the fire. The spit is wedged between two large rocks; Paul works it free and rolls it in his hands, twirling the roasted rabbit in the air to cool the thing down. When the fat no longer hisses and snaps, Al tears off a shoulder, carefully, then holds the spit so Paul may do the same. Then it is Anton's turn; he takes a haunch, still hot enough to burn his fingers, but smelling like the first meal out of Eden. The meat is delicious, even unspiced, flavored only by forest and field. When they have picked the rabbit clean and licked grease from their fingers, the boys poke at the embers with broken branches; they roll the potatoes roasting in the ashes. Anton finds a branch of his own. He stirs the ashes alongside his sons and helps them fish out the stolen potatoes, leaving them to cool on a bare stone. He cuts the potatoes open with his pocketknife. When they're no longer steaming, Anton eats alongside his boys, all sins forgiven and forgotten. After, they snap their branches into pieces and toss them on the smoldering fire. They talk of slings and hunting, of fishing in the river. They talk of trucks and mountain paths and love and generosity—things boys like, things men like—until the sun has almost set.

When night's chill has settled over the wood, Anton rises reluctantly. He stretches his stiff back. How he feels the cold, these days. It's getting late; Elisabeth will be wondering what has kept him so long.

He says, "You must teach me how to hunt. Refresh me. You know more about it now than I do."

"So we're forgiven for the potatoes?"

"You should probably confess the theft to Father Emil and do your Hail Marys, just to be on the safe side. But I think God will look the other way. You had good intentions, after all, and you are helping your mother and sister."

Paul says insistently, "But will you forgive us?"

A bright pang of adoration stalls him for a moment, cripples his heart. It's his pardon the boys want, not God's. A father's acceptance means more to them now than any religious absolution. Anton lays a hand on each boy's head. The unexpected flash of warmth has stolen his speech away, but a touch says what his voice cannot.

21

Twilight is fast approaching. Hurrying through town, Anton passes the bakery. It's closed for the night, black shutters drawn over its windows and the shade pulled down to hide the front door's glass. But the wrought-iron table is still sitting outside with its two simple chairs. He remembers the first time he saw Elisabeth there. He remembers the way she held her teacup and watched him without drinking, wary and speculative. He sees again the way her forehead furrowed as she picked up the newspaper and read her own advertisement. Who would have thought, on that day, that he would fall in love with the woman in the blue dress, the woman who never sipped her tea until it had gone cold?

He stops beside the iron table and drops his hand on its rusted surface, as if he might find in the spaces between the iron some remedy to his confusion. His own thoughts are puzzling him. What is this sudden lump in his throat, the pounding in his chest? Does he love Elisabeth, after all? And how strange, that any husband must ask himself whether he loves his wife! If he were less patient and less committed to God, he might shake his fist at Heaven for leading him here, to this strange place. But he is determined to forebear, to persist, even though there is an ache below his heart, a sweetly hollow pain, this realization that he loves her—or thinks he does—while she feels no affection for him. They have never exchanged more than the most cursory of kisses, the briefest touch. Why should it pain him? All is in accordance with their agreement, the bargain he foolishly offered more than a year ago, here at this cold table. He had still been a friar, then—in his heart if not in practice—and had wanted no more of her than she'd been willing to give. But now he is something more. Elisabeth's husband.

"Herr Starzmann." A thick voice, calling from across the street, pulls Anton from his thoughts. He turns away from the bakery table, quickly, swallowing hard, as if he has some reason to feel guilty.

It's Bruno Franke—Möbelbauer. The man lifts an imperious hand—in greeting, or as an order? *Stay where you are.*

Möbelbauer comes toward him, scuttling across the empty road. Anton grips the lapels of his jacket, resisting the urge to hunker down in his coat, to hide from this man. It's a ridiculous thought: tall, lanky Anton Starzmann can't hide from anyone. Instead, he makes himself release his grip. He waves to Franke, giving the man his most disarming smile. And all the while, as Franke lumbers toward him, Anton thinks, *You swine of a man. You're lucky I'm an instrument in the Red Orchestra, lucky I can't risk smashing in your smug face for what you've put Elisabeth through—and all the other women of our town.*

When Möbelbauer reaches Anton, he folds his arms across his chest and smiles in a satisfied manner, a cat with a mouse pinned beneath its paw. "I've been meaning to speak to you," he says.

Anton slides his hand into his pocket. He has already delivered the day's message, over in Kirchheim. If Möbelbauer jumps him, manages to overpower him, he will find nothing on Anton but Anita's letter, a pocketknife, and a pipe. And his rosary, of course. His fingers tangle in the beads for a moment, but he soon abandons them and takes the knife instead. The tortoiseshell handle is cool and smooth, reassuring even if it is small. Should he pull his only small weapon now, or keep it snug in his palm? No, there's no reason for that—not yet. Anton draws his pipe from his pocket instead. He upends its bowl and taps it, though it is clean, nothing inside to fall out. He smiles at Möbelbauer again, patient, disarming, waiting for his doom to come.

"A fine evening," Anton says, as if nothing in the world is wrong. He puts the pipe in his teeth, just for something to do. He doesn't pack it or light it—somehow, it seems unwise to occupy both his hands, to let down his guard in this man's presence. But at least he has something to bite down on, something other than Möbelbauer's face.

Möbelbauer does not return the greeting. He says brusquely, as if presenting a delinquent customer with an unpaid bill, "You've got two boys, now that you've married the widow."

"Albert and Paul. Yes." The heat of fear suffuses Anton's spine. He feels first weak, weak enough to collapse—and then, with a mad rush, he is a tower of anger, a bulwark of rage. He bites down harder on the stem of his pipe. The smile fades; in another moment, Möbelbauer will see the resistance in Anton's eyes. Does the gauleiter plan to use the boys against him? Is this the start of it, the first whispered threat? He should have kept the knife in his hand. *You won't take them. You won't harm a hair on my children's heads. I'll kill you first, I swear it.* Anton doesn't bother to repent of the terrible thought. God will understand; and if He doesn't, then Anton has no use for Him.

But if Möbelbauer notes a change in Anton's demeanor, he doesn't show it. He says, "It's long past time we brought some youth programs into our town, don't you think? As the stepfather of two growing boys— boys who came to me to get leather for their slings—surely you agree."

Marginally, Anton relaxes. Not enough to trust Möbelbauer—never that—but enough to unclench his jaw before he chews the stem of his pipe in two. "What sort of programs do you mean?"

It's the wrong question to ask. Möbelbauer narrows his eyes. "Hitler Youth, of course. And the League of German Girls; I suppose we ought to start that group, too, if we hope to guide our girls along the proper path. What other programs are there?"

Casually, Anton laughs. "Ah, of course! I only thought—well, in my day, you see, growing up in Stuttgart, we had a few other clubs. But there are far better programs now, more streamlined, more organized."

"Organized, yes. That's what I mean, exactly."

It's only by the grace of God that Anton calls the smile back to his face. He resists the urge to snarl, to crack his knuckles under Möbelbauer's nose. He says, "Do you think Hitler Youth will really catch on, though? Here, in this sleepy little village? It seems the sort of club city boys might enjoy, but—"

"I don't see why not. Wernau has had its Hitler Youth program in place for years now—and the League of German Girls, too. The clubs had better catch on here. The children of Unterboihingen need a dose of morals every bit as much as city youth. I've seen your stepsons grubbing in other people's fields. They need direction and guidance." He says it in a manner that implies, *If you and your wife won't provide that guidance, we've no choice but to call on Adolf Hitler to raise your children properly.*

"My work, you know." Anton amazes himself with his perfect imitation of an apology. "It takes me out of town so frequently; I'm not with the boys as often as I'd like. And Elisabeth has both her hands full, with Maria and the sewing." Why does he do this, explain himself, excuse himself to this man?

"Yes, your work. About that." Möbelbauer pauses, considering his next words. In the brief silence, the fear and fighting anger return to Anton's body. He trembles with the need to lash out at the detestable beast before him, but he shifts his pipe instead, from one corner of his mouth to the other. "Since you're only teaching music, and not building anything or contributing to a healthy economy like the rest of us, I thought you would be the right fellow to lead our youth programs— the boys' program, at least. We must find a woman for our League of German Girls, but that can be arranged." Möbelbauer adds belatedly, "And because you were a schoolteacher, once. I suppose that also qualifies you for the role."

By God, it's the last thing Anton will ever do. What the youth of this town need is an example of Christian charity, of gentle love. And don't we all need it, everyone across this nation? If we learned that lesson in the proper time, years ago—generations ago—where would we be now? His sons have learned charity and love—they have dug up goodness and generosity along with their stolen potatoes. Grubbing in other people's fields, they have uncovered better ways to be better men. What a miracle, that Paul and Albert have found morality, surrounded as they are by hatred, by violence and war.

But Anton can't refuse Möbelbauer—not if he wants to keep his family safe. He can't even voice his loathing for Hitler Youth, for the crime of indoctrination. That detestable club amounts to the murder of fine young minds, and Anton will never support it.

He responds the only way he can, given how Möbelbauer has trapped him. "It sounds very promising." He must forestall this dizzy twist of fate—give himself a chance to dodge Möbelbauer's bullet. "I will need time, of course, to arrange all my affairs. I must be sure my schedule will coordinate; all those lessons I teach in other towns—"

"This is important, Starzmann." Möbelbauer jabs a finger into Anton's chest—he dares to touch him, this man who has propositioned his wife. "We need to show our allegiance. Even here in the small towns, we are still German."

"We are still German. How right you are."

"I can't let this slide any longer—we can't. Let us not put it off past Christmas. You'll be ready by then, won't you?"

"Certainly." He adds, smiling, "Thank you for thinking of me. It's such an important role, shaping the minds and hearts of our youth."

Möbelbauer extends his hand, and they shake. Inwardly, Anton recoils from the touch, and more so when he considers what he has agreed to do. But how could he refuse this man's request—his order? Even if Möbelbauer hasn't yet discerned the reason for Anton's comings and goings, the gauleiter's eye has already narrowed its focus on Anton's family. Elisabeth's refusal will not sit well with a man of Möbelbauer's sort. They walk the razor's edge, now—Anton, his wife, and their inno-cent, unknowing children.

As he makes his way home through the dusk, Anton scrubs his palm against his trousers again and again, trying to erase the lingering feel of Möbelbauer's grip. He must find a way to stop the gauleiter's plan. He will not see his sons, nor any other children of Unterboihingen, indoctrinated into hate. They will not become a part of the evil that spurs on our government to ever worse and ever more horrific deeds. Anton can't save all of Germany—he is only one man. But he can, he must, save this one small town.

He only needs to find some way to do it—some way that won't end with Elisabeth and the children loaded onto a gray bus, with Anton choking on the smoke left behind.

22

Anton rises early the next morning, long before the sun is strong enough to seep around the edges of the wool curtains. His family is sleeping. In the un-light, quiet as a shadow, he dresses and takes his jacket from a hook beside the bedroom door. Across the small room, Elisabeth moves in her sleep: a rustle of bedding, a brief, baffled sigh. He sees her through the gray dawn gloom. Her hair is in disarray; she has thrown one hand up on the pillow, as if defending herself from her dreams. But her face is peaceful in sleep, as always. When she's sleeping, it's the only time she looks entirely fearless. She has grown used to sharing a bed with Anton. She no longer goes rigid when he lies beside her, and there are times when he would like to hold her, comfort her if he can. But he knows she will never accept comfort—not from him. Each night, as they lie side by side, as he edges into the blurred world of sleep, his arms seem to hold the ghost of his wife, a small, warm body grateful for protection. He can feel her, pulled close to his chest, and yet she is never there.

Anton slept very little last night, and when he did drift off, his fragmented dreams were all of the children he had already failed—those at St. Josefsheim. The calls of night birds, distant over the forest, echoed the wails of little ones torn from the friars who had sworn to protect them. They are lost souls now, frightened and unsheltered, vulnerable and small. By night, they weep across the dark and endless fields.

Anton leaves his cold bedroom behind and slips from the cottage, down the stairs into the damp chill of dawn. Sluggish with despair, he pushes the old shed door open and moves through the space inside, dragging dark and heavy thoughts.

It has been many months since Anton brought his clothing into the house—his other small possessions, too. His humble belongings now share the dresser and closet with Elisabeth's things, though everything he owns, what he has brought to this marriage, seems to crouch in the presence of her life, frozen and panicked, like a rabbit that has forgotten to run from the hunter. Between what is hers and what is his, there is always a margin of emptiness—a gap between their hangers in the closet, a gulf between their folded sweaters and matched stockings, as if she can't bear even for her possessions to touch his. But Anton has left the instruments in the old chests, locked up now so no one can find them. Cobwebs shroud the old trunks, clinging between wooden ribs. No one has touched the trunks for months, but they are not empty, despite what the spiders would have you believe.

He finds his key ring in his pocket and unlocks the nearest chest. There they all lie, cold, dull, and silent. They are creatures from a fairy tale, cast into endless sleep by a witch's sorcery. He touches one, the cornet, and runs a finger along the rolled edge of its bell. *Do they call me Herr Cornet, they who wait for the Red Orchestra to play?*

I can't do this, he tells himself. *I can't lead children into sin. I can't teach them to do evil, to worship anyone other than God—especially not the beast who calls himself the Führer. I swore in Riga I would never again work for Hitler's good. I can't do this. I cannot, my God.*

But what choice does he have? The gauleiter, with his notes and letters, with his contacts in Berlin . . . if Anton doesn't obey, Möbelbauer will surely bring him to heel.

And that will be the end of Anton's family.

Something is stuck between the cornet and a French horn below. Small, gray, papery, its dry leaves are bent and soft around the edges. He pulls it free of the horns and turns it over in his hands. It's his workbook from his Wehrmacht days. In this small book, in a neat teacher's hand, Anton recorded all his doings, the everyday drudgeries of military life. Struck by a sudden urge to see what kind of man he was then—longing to find some difference in his spirit, some proof that he is someone better now—he goes to the doorway, where pink morning light spills in. He opens the workbook, but the lines of his writing bleed together into black and formless shapes, and he can't make out the words.

His service in the Wehrmacht was not long—one ill-fated march and then his escape, with his injured back for an excuse. Nevertheless, his leap from the plane and the march on Riga come back with vivid clarity. Against the dawn sky, he can see a tower of flames, a church spire wreathed in fire—and to either side, darkness rolling out toward a faraway horizon. He is trapped now in that same snare, forced to do the Reich's bidding. No matter which way we turn, no matter how we resist, there is a fist of power ready to close around us. The road is straight and unvaried. It leads us on, merciless, toward ash and fire.

Since he took Father Emil's offer and joined the resistance, there have been times when Anton has felt himself beyond his depth. When he was new and inexperienced, he couldn't deny that he had flung himself into treacherous water, and it was far above his head. But he never doubted his ability to swim. No matter how deep the mire, no matter how swift the current, he could fight his way up to the surface—he knew it; his faith was unshaken. But this—the gauleiter assigning him a repellent task, and no safe way to refuse . . . For the first time since taking up the secret cause—indeed, for the first time since coming to Unterboihingen—he feels he can do nothing but fail. It leaves him stunned and absent, with a taste like copper on his tongue. He is weak, powerless, as all men are against the forces that assault our humanity.

Leaning against the doorframe, he breathes in the scent of morning. Dew hangs heavy in the air, and the irrigation ditches are thick and fragrant with water. The earth is wet and weeping. The ground exhales the moisture of sleeping children's breath; memory of the ones he lost hangs between Heaven and Earth, an unseen mist he can feel brushing his cheek, as he once felt their small hands, patting, holding to his habit, slipping into his own large, protective grasp. He is too tired to cry, too far surrendered to his grief.

He turns a page in the workbook; the lines unblur. The words assert themselves with brutal clarity. In his own handwriting, he reads: *Church burned at Riga.* And the vision is still there, beyond the page—flames leaping up the side of the spire, black smoke billowing, the road straight as truth, never bending, never changing.

Anton's hand trembles as he turns another page. This one is blank. The pages after are blank, too, all the way to the end of the book. They had intended him to fill this book with accounts of his doings, his brave service to the Party. But he never set his pen to the workbook again.

We are troubled on every side yet not distressed. We are perplexed but not in despair. Persecuted but not forsaken; cast down but not destroyed. Not yet. And until they do destroy me, I can fight on. I can always fight, even knowing it is futile. Always bearing in my body the dying of Lord Jesus, that the life, also, of Jesus might be made manifest.

Anton cannot win, but they haven't destroyed him yet. What is he now, if not a resister? If not a father and a husband, protector of widows and children? God's command is the only one he will obey, the only voice he will hear, until they take him, too, and redistribute him to his grave.

He closes the workbook. There is a coin in his pocket, a five-reichs-mark piece, with the worn-down face of von Hindenburg, all disappointment and jowls. Coin in one hand, he stares for a moment at the book's cover, chestnut brown against military gray. The eagle, hard-eyed and angular, spreads its wings below the words "Deutsches Reich." In its talons, it holds the oak wreath and the swastika, symbol of Hitler's ascendancy.

Anton touches the swastika, traces its clawed, broken arms with the tip of a finger. The paper is dry and ordinary. It whispers beneath his touch. This book is a small and simple thing. Why should it hold power over him or his family? He presses the edge of the coin against the cover. The fibers yield. A hiss of paper, a rasp of metal, and the swastika is gone, scratched away as if it had never existed.

A high, thin scream erupts from the house, from somewhere just outside it. For a moment, he believes he has been found out already, that some demon from Hell has come to seize him in this moment of rebellion, to drag him off to Dachau. But then he knows it's Maria crying. He drops book and coin on a dusty shelf beside the door and runs. The girl has tumbled down the stairs; her nose is bleeding, and her face is red from her screams. He scoops her up in his arms, kissing her, talking close to her ear so she can hear him over the sound of her own cries. "What's wrong, Maria? Where are you hurt?"

Elisabeth comes running down the stairs, her mouth round with panic. Her nightdress billows behind her legs. The boys are just behind, still in their pajamas; they hug themselves against the chill.

"For goodness' sake, Anton, what has happened?" Elisabeth cries. She dabs at Maria's bloody nose with the sleeve of her nightdress.

Maria chokes on her sobs. "I thought *Vati* went out to get the eggs, and I came to help. I fell down the stairs."

"How far did she fall? How many stairs? Is she badly hurt?" Elisabeth pats her small daughter, prodding her little bones, but Maria's tears are already dissipating. She wipes her face against Anton's shoulder, leaving a smear of blood.

"She's more frightened than hurt, I think." He kisses her cheek again. "There, you see? Her nose has already stopped bleeding. You're all right, aren't you?"

Maria nods, sniffling.

Elisabeth heaves a deep sigh, a mother's shuddering relief. Then she begins to scold. "You are the most careless girl I've ever seen! And naughty, to go running outside before you've had breakfast. Before you're properly dressed!"

Maria whimpers, "You aren't properly dressed, either."

"No back talk. I won't put up with it, not today. Not from you."

Albert and Paul, assured that their sister will survive, scuttle down to the old shed, drawn by its open door. Boys are always ready for adventure, even first thing in the morning. Since they are already up, they may as well have some fun before school begins.

"Put her down, Anton. If she's not hurt, then she doesn't need any coddling. She needs a good swat on her backside, that's what."

Maria, on her own two feet now, hides her face against Anton's leg. She mutters, "I don't need a swat. It's bad enough, falling down the stairs."

"Then go up to your room and get dressed."

Maria goes, climbing the stairs with assiduous care, both hands clinging to the rail. Elisabeth watches her for a moment, tense, like a horse ready to shy at any rustle in the grass. When Maria is safely inside, she turns to Anton with a frown. "What were you doing up so early?"

"I couldn't sleep."

The nature of her frown changes, from annoyance to concern. She tilts her head one way, then the other, examining his complexion, eyeing his brow for beads of sweat.

"I'm not ill," he says. "I'm perfectly well." He almost says, *Möbelbauer expects me to tell our children—and all the children in this town—how to be good National Socialists. How to worship Adolf Hitler above even God and Jesus. It's enough to rob any man of his sleep.* But he stops himself. He remembers his dignified, very proper wife saying, *He shits on the women of this town.* The last thing she needs now is a reminder of Herr Möbelbauer.

"Well," Elisabeth says at length, "even if you aren't ill, you should try for another hour or two of sleep. You look pale and tired."

He tries to smile. "I feel pale and tired."

"Boys," Elisabeth calls, "come out of that shed. Go get ready for breakfast. It will be time soon for—"

"Look, Mother!" Paul emerges from the shed, running, holding something up above his head as if in victory. "Look what we found! What is it?"

It is small, papery. Newly scraped clean.

Anton pulls the workbook from Paul's hand as the boy passes him. He presses it against his chest, cover side in, as Paul gives a wordless whine of disappointment.

"What is that thing, Anton?" Elisabeth fixes him with her eyes. The air has gone still around her.

"It's nothing important." To the boys, he says, "Do as your mother tells you."

They grumble, but they run upstairs. Elisabeth is in no mood to deal with recalcitrance; the boys can sense it, and they are wise enough not to take the chance.

Alone now at the foot of the stairs, Elisabeth and Anton watch one another in silence, she wary, he anxious. He slides the workbook down toward his pocket, but the motion only makes her press her lips together, and her face reddens.

"What is it?" she says quietly.

"Only my workbook, from my Wehrmacht days."

"Why are you so quick to hide it?"

"I'm not hiding it," he says, edging the thing farther from her sight.

She holds out her hand. "If you're not trying to hide it, then let me see."

What can he do? He passes the book to Elisabeth. She turns it over, cover side up, and for a moment she sees nothing unusual. A look of mild confusion crosses her face, a pinch of her brow. Then she sees—she understands. She stares in horror at the place where the swastika should be. Slowly, she lifts her face to meet Anton's eye, mute and afraid.

She returns the book to his hand. Anton prays this will be the end of it, nothing more will come. But then she brushes past him, moving stiffly, and enters the shed.

"Elisabeth, wait . . ." He hurries after her, too late to alter fate's course. He has left the trunk open; its lock lies undone upon the shelf. Elisabeth approaches the open chest as if it might contain a nest of vipers. When she looks inside, Anton thinks she might have preferred to find a writhing knot of snakes than the musical instruments.

She whirls, stares at him, her mouth hanging open. "You never sold them. I thought—"

He shakes his head.

"My God, Anton—where has the money come from, then?" She glances at the defaced workbook in his hand. He can see the moment when realization dawns, the moment when she fits every piece of his puzzle together. Her face flushes red with her rapid pulse. It glows like a fire in the darkness.

Elisabeth all but runs from the shed. The nightdress flutters in her wake, a bird's startled wings. She bends as she passes Anton, fitting herself against the doorframe so she will not touch any part of him. She takes the stairs two at a time, as if the Devil is after her—as if the Devil stands there in the yard, helpless and bewildered, curling the workbook in his clenched fist.

"Wait," Anton calls up to her. He runs up the stairs, but he can't catch her. "Listen to what I have to say. Please, Elisabeth—only listen!"

Inside the house, the children are dressed, though their hair is still uncombed. They look up from the table, where they are helping to make breakfast, spreading butter on slices of bread.

"You aren't going to school today." Elisabeth speaks shortly, words clipped and angry. Paul and Maria cheer, but Al looks pale; he glances from Anton to Elisabeth. "Pack up your clothes in your knapsacks. We are going away."

Al says at once, "Is Anton coming with us?"

Elisabeth doesn't answer him, only goes to her room and shuts the door. He can hear her opening and closing drawers, the rattle of closet hangers as she pulls her dresses down.

Anton taps on the door. "Elisabeth, please. May I come in?"

She doesn't answer. He decides to take her silence for acceptance, and he lets himself in.

"Don't do this," he says quietly when the door is shut behind him. "My heart will break. I should have told you all about this; I'm sorry I kept it from you."

She wheels from the closet, crumpling a dress in her distressed hands, crushing it against her chest. "And what do you imagine I would have said, if you had told me?" Her eyes are burning with outraged disbelief. "How could you think it was safe, Anton? How could you think it was wise?"

The door creaks open; the children are clustered there, Paul and Maria staring at them both with wide, teary eyes. Albert tugs at their hands, but the younger children will not look away.

"I didn't think it was safe."

Elisabeth cuts off his next words, whatever he'd thought to say. "Don't talk about this in front of the children." She turns to them, hard-faced and determined. "Go and pack. Be quick."

The children weep as they go off to their rooms. Al says to Maria, "I'll pack your knapsack for you."

"Where on earth do you think to take them?" Anton says quietly.

"Anywhere that's far away from you and this . . . this thing you do."

"There is no place safer than Unterboihingen. You know that, Elisabeth!"

"Even this town isn't safe as long as you're doing . . . *this*! You could get us all killed!" She blanches as a terrible thought overtakes her. She wavers where she stands, and for a moment, he thinks she might faint. But Elisabeth is not the fainting type. She rights herself before Anton can reach for her. "Oh, merciful Mother—what about Möbelbauer? Herr Franke . . . he knows. He *has* to know."

"I'll leave," Anton says. "It's better for the children to stay here." He would rather risk himself in the cities, with the bombs falling, than Elisabeth or the little ones. "You aren't thinking clearly, Elisabeth. You stay in Unterboihingen; I'll go away."

She pauses in the act of stuffing her bag. She turns slowly and gazes at him, fighting to swallow her tears. For a moment, he believes they will reconcile now—easily, just as easily as they did the first time. For a moment, he thinks she'll say, *I don't want you to leave, either.* But what choice do they have now? His dangerous secret is exposed. He has made trouble for them all.

"I only wanted to help you and protect you," he says. The words sound weak, ineffective, even to him.

"You've done a remarkable job of it." She throws the last of her things into her bag and storms out to the sitting room. The children are there, weeping and clutching their knapsacks. "Come, now," she says, dry-eyed, and leads them down the stairs.

Anton follows them. The stairs rattle beneath his feet, hollow as loss. He knows it's useless to plead with her, but he can't simply stand and watch his family go. Elisabeth makes for the lane, and the main road beyond, the one that leads to the train station.

He dodges into the shed and pulls his cornet from the trunk. There are things a man can't say with his voice, wounds only music can heal. The instrument is cold, and there is no time to warm it; the sound will be sour. But as Elisabeth marches the children toward town, he follows her out into the lane. He stands there while she walks away, while she leads the little ones farther and farther from his side.

Anton lifts the cornet to his lips. As the music follows her retreating back, he hears the lyrics in his head. He feels them in his heart.

Falling in love again, never wanted to. What am I to do? I can't help it.

It's the song Elisabeth danced to with her first husband. Marlene Dietrich, "Ich bin von Kopf bis Fuß auf Liebe eingestellt." I can't help falling in love. The music speaks in his place. It finds the words that evade him; it reaches across the gulf that separates these two wounded hearts and takes hold.

Elisabeth stops in her tracks. She stands for a long time with her back turned to Anton. The children mill and shuffle about her, looking back at their stepfather with pleading eyes while he plays and plays but doesn't speak. There is a stone-hard resolution in the set of Elisabeth's shoulders, the straightness of her back. She yields nothing to the music, nothing to memory.

But then, with a shudder so small Anton isn't certain he has seen it, she turns. She faces him, eyes cast down to the dirt road. One step, then another, slow and deliberate, she walks back to Anton, chin quivering. By the time he plays the final chorus, Elisabeth is standing close enough to touch him, but she will not lift her eyes. He can see her jaw clenching, the muscles behind that round, pretty face hard and resisting.

When the song is done, Anton lowers the horn and Elisabeth lifts her eyes to his. They are so blue, bluer than summer. He has never noticed their depth before, their purity of color. But they have seldom looked at one another this way, lingering and close. In the softening of her look, he can tell Elisabeth sees his remorse, and reads his apology in his own eyes.

Anton waits. He tells himself that whatever she does next, whatever she chooses, he will accept with no further complaint, and no attempt to stop her.

Elisabeth leans forward, so subtly he isn't quite sure she has moved. But then she creeps closer. She rests her head against his chest, just as Maria does when she is hurt or sad.

Thank you, God. Thank you. Anton wraps his arms around her, his wife.

"This is dangerous." Her tears soak hot through his shirt.

"I know."

"But you are my husband. I took a vow. God protect us, you are my husband."

His heart expands, a sudden, forceful, grateful pressure. What has he done—what has he ever done, in this shameful life, to deserve such a good woman, a wife so brave and strong? She knows in her heart that resistance is right, even if it is dangerous. She is steadfast in her faith, as ever—and he loves her for it.

"I am your husband," Anton says quietly. He presses his lips to her bowed head. "You are my wife. And I know God will protect us, Elisabeth."

So I pray.

23

He prays, and the answer comes to him.

Tuesday is Hitler Youth day. Across the nation, our young people meet on the same day of the week, at the same time of the evening. Order, lockstep, we do as we are told. Compliance and uniformity make us great—that's what they would have us believe.

Monday: Anton is in Kirchheim, a village not exactly near Unterboihingen, teaching the children of that parish to play the organ. No one in Kirchheim wanted organ lessons, but Father Emil has made the arrangements. Emil has insisted, has worked his influence among the Kirchheim priests—and so every last child in the parish will learn to play. It keeps Anton well clear of Unterboihingen until late into the night, every Monday night.

Wednesday: The buses are always slow, so he tells Frau Müller in Wernau that he must shift the time of her daughter's piano lessons back to five p.m. He can just catch the last bus back to Unterboihingen; he won't be home until half past seven.

On Thursday, he volunteers at the bakery, lifting pans for Frau Bösch, whom the children have nicknamed Frau Brotmacher—"bread maker." The Frau has recently hurt her back, wrestling with an ill-tempered milk cow. If she can't bake, then our town will have little bread, and we will all be the worse for hunger. Who can do this work, if not Anton? Every other man is busy on Thursdays, by Father Emil's suggestion. If anyone remembers that Anton injured his own back in the Wehrmacht, no one mentions it now. He is careful to walk straight and unbent, to move without the least impediment, lest anyone recall his aching back and comment on the strange arrangement. He fetches and carries for Frau Brotmacher in the heat of her bakery, sweating through his shirt to his vest, almost until midnight. And so Thursday nights are out of the question.

Friday: He adds three lessons to his roster, with Father Emil beating the hedges and alleys of the parish to scare up more students. The families are among the poorest in Unterboihingen; Anton suspects Father Emil is paying their fees himself, but he won't shame the parents by asking, nor will he expose Emil to scandal. He accepts the situation for what it is, what he needs it to be: tight commitments that can't be broken, every Friday until late in the evening.

Every Saturday, he minds the children of the Forst family—eight dirty, ill-behaved brawlers. Both Herr and Frau Forst must work now: he at the train yard, she at the distribution center, sorting our weekly rations. No one is left to care for their brood. Who can do this task, save Anton? No one; there is no one else who can spare the time. That's what he tells the village, and the village comes to believe it. A dozen different people might have taken to minding the Forst children on Saturdays. Frau Hertz, or Frau Bösch, even with her bad back—Elisabeth herself might have done it, and her stern discipline would have done the Forsts a world of good. But that is not the point. That is not a part of this quiet, careful design.

When his schedule is impossibly full, Anton goes to Möbelbauer, hat in hand.

"It has been such a busy winter for us all," he says to Franke, smiling his pleasant smile, the one that can put anyone at ease, can convince anyone that Anton Starzmann is trustworthy, your dearest friend. "I'm so disappointed, because I've been looking forward to leading the Hitler Youth program since you first told me about it. But, well . . . as you can see . . ." He passes a paper to Möbelbauer: his impossibly tight schedule, scrawled and annotated, marked up, crossed out and rewritten, as if he has made an honest attempt to rearrange his life. As if he tried every conceivable way to accommodate the Führer's plans.

"I don't see the problem," Möbelbauer says. "Your Tuesday evenings are free. It's perfect; Tuesday is Hitler Youth night."

"It would be youth night, if you only want Unterboihingen to participate in the usual program. If you don't aspire to anything greater."

Möbelbauer squints up at him. What is the ex-friar talking about?

"I thought, friend—wouldn't it be something truly special if we were to give a real gift to the Führer?"

Möbelbauer waits, pursing his lips below his truncated mustache. Confused and wary, his eyes shift from Anton's smile to the schedule in his hand.

"We don't exactly stand out here in Unterboihingen," Anton says. "Who ever gives us a second thought? Who minds any of us—you included, although you're a genius furniture maker? Consider for a moment all the talent we have here, concentrated in this town. All the great things we can do—we alone can do. All the ways we can honor the Führer with our gifts."

"I don't know what you're getting at," Möbelbauer says shortly.

"Herr Franke, what would you do—who would you be, *how high could you rise*—if a man of your quality, with your talents and ambitions, were actually recognized by those who matter? Those with power. Where do you see yourself? There is no limit, as far as I can tell. A good, clear-headed, loyal Party man like yourself . . . You're everything the NSDAP wants, everything they look for in an officer or a politician. All you lack is visibility. And who can expect visibility in Unterboihingen?"

Möbelbauer stares at Anton openly now, his hunger conspicuous. The force of the man's craving, the power it has over him, nearly makes Anton step back and throw up his hands in defense. As Father Emil has said, a man ruled by ambition is dangerous. All Möbelbauer wants in this world is power—to be recognized, to be feared. Why else has he set himself up as gauleiter, if not to work his way ever closer to the source of power? He says, "Go on."

"Here is what I propose. Here is how you stand above the crowd. The Führer loves music; we all know that. And I am a music teacher. What's more, I have instruments—I saved them from my old school in Munich. Wouldn't it be a shame to throw away such an opportunity, such a resource? How many other towns have marching bands dedicated to the glory of our Führer? Forget the little villages—how many *cities* have bands to play for our leader? None—that's how many. We could have Hitler Youth meetings, like all the other towns and cities, like everyone across the nation. Or we could create something new. Something no one has done before."

Möbelbauer's eyes widen. Now, at last, he sees the great vision.

Anton presses his advantage. "Think of it: good, strong, German songs, celebrating the old culture, the old ways. Through music, we can teach our youth what it means to be real Germans. What better tool of culture? What better way to honor the Führer and celebrate everything he has done to elevate us? Music is his greatest love. With a youth band, Unterboihingen would certainly stand out. And any fellow who can say, 'This band, this special salute to the Führer—*I* made it happen,' well, the Party would notice a man like that. You can be certain."

Slowly, thoughtfully, Möbelbauer nods. Anton can see it: the gauleiter is ravenous for recognition.

"But," Anton says, weighting his voice with regret, "as you can see, the only time I can manage to lead a band is Tuesday evenings. Hitler Youth night. You could find someone else to lead the club, I suppose . . ."

"But then none of the boys could join your band."

"That's so. What a quandary; what a difficulty. I suppose we'll have to decide whether it's better for us to make ourselves known to the Führer, or stick with the tried and true."

Möbelbauer passes the schedule back to Anton. "You say you have the instruments already?"

"I have everything I need."

"Why don't we give it a try, Herr Starzmann, and see where it gets us?"

Anton smiles easily. Herr Starzmann is every man's friend. He reaches out to shake Möbelbauer's hand, and it's all he can do not to tighten his fist and crush those greedy bones. "I'm glad you're agreed."

24

When Anton left the cottage for this first afternoon with the band, Elisabeth pressed a lunch into his hands, wrapped in one of her coveted pieces of waxed paper. She said almost nothing to him in words. Only, "When shall I expect you home?" and, *"Viel Glück,"* but the lunch spoke on her behalf, a volume of gratitude and worry she couldn't bring herself to express. The packet is heavy in his hands, so heavy he wonders how he can ever hope to eat it all before reaching the *Gymnasium,* the secondary school. When he unwraps the paper, he finds a thick slab of liver, seasoned with pickled onions and yellow mustard, between two skimpy slices of bread. Stacked neatly atop the sandwich, there lies an orderly arrangement of dried apples, still laced on their oven-black string.

He examines the apples as he walks toward the school, purely for a distraction from his rioting nerves. The apples are soft and going softer by the moment; they have absorbed some of the sandwich's moisture. When he bites into one, he can taste the tang of onions alongside the bitterness of curing smoke, the fumes from the sulfur candle with which Elisabeth has preserved the fruit. But after he chews a few times, the apple's natural sweetness comes through. The overall effect is not unpleasant. He prefers the apples to the sandwich; he has never shared Elisabeth's fondness for liver and onions.

His stomach is so tight with anxiety that he considers tossing the sandwich into some ditch or hedge, leaving it for the birds to peck. But he discards the thought almost as soon as it occurs. With such deprivation as we now face, it would be an unthinkable waste, almost a sin. Besides, he has no desire to throw away his wife's gesture of affection. When he'd told Elisabeth about the band and his newly hectic schedule, she had understood at once. She said little then, as this afternoon—but for days after, she carried herself with a kind of grim confidence, a straightness and coolness that said she approved, that she, too, resisted. There were times when she smiled at Anton or touched his arm with a gentle warmth that surprised him. He can feel her touch now, an unseen hand on his shoulder, guiding him. He has no great love for liver and onions, but Elisabeth is another matter. He eats his lunch with all the steadiness he can summon.

He is licking mustard from his fingers when he reaches the school. Like nearly everything in Unterboihingen, the building seems plucked from another era. Its high-peaked roof is outlined in dark timbers. Ivy has climbed the white walls and been pulled away, leaving brown scars crisscrossing the stucco. And more vines have grown up again; one corner of the school is curtained in green, a spot of cheerful color in the January gray. Lessons have ended for the day; he had expected to find the schoolyard teeming with children, but it is empty, save for one slender figure in a high-necked charcoal dress.

When the teacher catches sight of Anton, she hurries down the path to the road. He removes his top hat before taking her chilly hand. She is young—early twenties, no older than Anton was when he first went to St. Josefsheim.

"Herr Starzmann," she says, "I can't tell you how glad I am to see you. I'm Fräulein Weber—Christine." She's a pretty woman, tall and blue-eyed, with glossy chestnut hair and painted lips. Her pale cheeks are flushed from the winter's cold.

"I'm glad to be here," Anton says, not at all sure he is. His stomach is churning on the liver. It has been three years since he has entered a classroom, since he has stood in front of so many children as their teacher. Does he still remember how to do it?

Christine leads him toward the school. She keeps her eyes on the path as they walk and keeps her voice low, but she doesn't hesitate to speak. "I have prayed, night after night, that our town—our children—would be spared." No need to specify. From lessons this earnest young teacher would rather her pupils never learn. From doctrines of purity and perfection. From the pledges of fealty to Our Leader, repeated week after week, every Tuesday night, with an arm flung out in salute. If you force a man—or a boy—to recite words often enough, sooner or later he will come to believe what he says. "When I learned what Bruno Franke intended, I was outraged." The way she says the name, with a growl of disgust, makes Anton believe that she, too, has been the recipient of Möbelbauer's lust, his foul propositions. Of course she has; look at her. Lovely, young, and single, this teacher is an apple too tempting for Möbelbauer to leave on the bough. Anton can only hope she hasn't suffered overmuch.

"I was furious with Herr Franke, too," Anton says. *I am furious still.*

She stops outside the door, beside the spray of ivy. The green leaves set off her red hair with luminous intensity; for a moment, Christine shines at him, a youthful beacon of hope. "But there's no need for either of us to be angry now. You've come to save our children from that fate."

He holds the hat against his chest, pressing it to his fluttering heart. "If I manage to save anyone, Fräulein, it will be by God's grace."

From the moment she opens the school's front door, Anton can tell where the children have gone. Conversation bubbles out into the foyer from a classroom; laughter hangs in the air, the music of children forgetting to be afraid. They have lingered inside the schoolhouse rather than running home. They have waited there for Anton.

"That room, there," Christine says, gesturing to the open door, "will be yours entirely, this time every Tuesday, for as long as you need it."

"It's very generous. I'm humbled."

"Think nothing of it, *mein Herr*. We are all too happy to oblige."

"The instruments . . . ?"

"The Kopp brothers brought them over on the back of their truck, just at the start of the lunch hour. You'll find them all inside the classroom."

She grins at him suddenly, buoyant with an expectation that is almost childish. He thinks, *Where did this teacher grow up? Munich, Stuttgart?* Christine is young enough that she couldn't have escaped mandatory participation in the youth programs when she was a schoolgirl. It makes his jaw clench, to think of this bright, hopeful young woman—any young woman—pressed into the Bund Deutsche Mädel, the League of German Girls. In the BDM, they teach our girls to sing "The Flag on High." They teach our girls to work the farms—*Blut und Boden*, soil and blood. They teach our girls, above all else, to guard against racial shame. To love a man insufficiently German, to bring forth a child with tainted blood, is a crime worse than murder. He can only thank God such teachings didn't stick in the heart of this brave young woman.

"Thank you, Christine," Anton says.

"Call if you need me. I'll be out here in the foyer; I intend to listen to the music."

"Don't expect too much, this first day."

Laughter and horseplay end abruptly when Anton enters the room. There is a hasty rustle, a scrambling for seats—the children have pushed their wooden double desks into a half circle. Two dozen eager faces turn toward him; some of the younger ones have come, he sees, from the other schoolhouse down the road, the one Maria used to escape in favor of butchering magazines. The Kopp brothers have deposited the trunks at the head of the classroom, just below the blackboard. A remnant of the day's lesson still shows on the board, a sentence partially erased. The smell of the place leaps to the forefront of Anton's awareness. Ink, the old wood of well-used desks, chalk dust, and a faint trace of mildew from the pages of aging books. The scents are familiar to him, all of them, as natural as if he'd never left his first classroom behind.

Al and Paul are there among the other children, elbowing each other, glowing with pride, for it is their stepfather who has caused so much excitement. This is almost as good as his story about jumping from the airplane.

Albert—twelve years old. In a few short years, he'll be as old as the biggest boys in the classroom, and they are old enough to be conscripted, sent away to fight and die, fodder for the Führer's machine. Most of the older boys would have been sent already, if they'd been made to join Hitler Youth. That program has degenerated into a convenient Wehrmacht reserve, nothing more.

Well, that's why I'm here, isn't it? Even with my band, I can't prevent these boys from being taken off to war if their names are drawn. I can't stop their being forced to fight and kill. Nor can I stop them from dying. But I can stop their hearts from turning. I can keep them anchored to love and righteousness. That much I can do.

Anton turns the top hat over in his hands. He sets it on the teacher's desk—or tries to. He has misjudged the distance, and it falls to the ground. Amid a ripple of nervous, testing laughter, he retrieves it, sets it firmly in place, and then rocks on his heels, looking out at his pupils. Uncertain what to say.

One of the boys calls out eagerly, "*Mein Herr*, are you going to teach us how to play?"

Anton chuckles. "God willing." The boys and girls shuffle their feet; they murmur with excitement.

Where best to begin? He opens the nearest trunk and picks up the first instrument to hand. He holds it up so all the children may see. "This is a cornet. Pretty, isn't it? It can play the highest notes of all the

brass—that is, the kind of instruments you must buzz your lips to play."
He demonstrates, pressing his lips together and letting out a rasping
vibration. The children laugh. "I'll pass it around, so you all may get a
feel for it. No one try to play it—not yet. None of us wants to go home
with a headache." More laughter.

The cornet begins to make its rounds. The children test its weight
in their hands, imagine what they must look like holding it, capable
and proud. Anton retrieves the next instrument from his trunk. "French
horn. Look at the curves, and see how the keys are different from the
keys on top of the cornet. This one sounds mellow and sweet."

He names each instrument and explains its role, what purpose it
will serve in their band. The baritone horn, the trombone with its long
slide—he must assemble that one while the children watch. Clarinet
and piccolo, oboe and flute, the bright cymbals that flash when he
raises them. The children cringe with hands over ears, expecting him to
crash them together, but Anton only laughs and passes a single cymbal
around the room.

When he has shown them every instrument, he says, "Now you
each may try the ones you like best, so we can learn what suits you. I
don't have enough instruments for everyone, so even when you've made
your choice, most of you must share. I'll have your teacher, Fräulein
Weber, help me make a schedule. How does that sound? Stand up
now, and arrange yourselves in order of height." The children of St.
Josefsheim used to like that method of sorting. Brother Nazarius seldom
picked them in order, from tallest to shortest. Sometimes he would go
the other way, and sometimes he would work from the middle out, so
everyone had a chance to be first.

They begin only with mouthpieces. Anton pulls the metal cups
from each brass instrument; the children take turns buzzing, and the
room fills with a chorus of duck quacks. The students are nearly beside
themselves with laughter, the sound is so ridiculous—but Anton notes
how quickly they are learning. Soon enough, he fixes the mouthpieces

back onto brass bodies. The children play—or try to play; the discordant honks and feeble squeals would be enough to make them laugh all over again, but a serious air has fallen over the classroom. They are doing their earnest best to learn, every one of them. And this is like nothing they've ever done before. Rapt in the development of this new skill—what will be a new skill, with practice—they are committed, serious, as children seldom are. Those who are not playing encourage the others. They applaud each other's first attempts at C and A and G. A sense of cooperation forms, trust and camaraderie forming fresh new buds. Someday, those buds will open, flowering into reliance and unity, the magical forces that bind a music group together.

Two hours of lessons fly by. While Christine Weber checks off names on her list, Anton sends half the children home with an instrument—all except those who will be his drummers. They must obtain their parents' permission to learn percussion. Anton won't surprise the parents of Unterboihingen with cymbals or his little snare drum. He would never be so cruel; the trumpets and piccolos will be torment enough.

"Next week," he tells them, "each of you must be able to play all the notes I've shown you, so practice well, and be sure you meet up with your partners midweek to trade the instruments. Those of you who have the instruments first: it will be your responsibility to remind your friends how to play the correct notes. Drummers, you will practice on your knees until your parents agree to let you keep the drums." He shows them how, tapping out a paradiddle until the whole classroom takes it up, even those who haven't been assigned to percussion.

Anton strolls home in the blue twilight with Al and Paul at his side. Paul carries the cornet, which the boys will share; he can't resist squawking out a few notes now and again, and every time he does it, a rabbit bolts from the road's verge or a flock of partridges clatters into the air. Anton can scarcely recall feeling so satisfied. His heart brims over with a rich, warm sense of accomplishment—and the certainty that he has laid the foundation for something miraculous, something he will build.

He had expected it would only bring him pain, to stand at the head of a classroom again. But he needn't have feared. In a world steeped in sorrow, he has found a small portion of joy. It's worth more than gold, in times like these.

When they reach their home, Elisabeth comes down the stairs to meet them. Anton pauses in the yard while the boys run ahead, clamoring to show their mother the cornet. She has seen it before, but never in their hands. Anton watches her descend from the cottage in a wash of pale moonlight. At first, he thinks, *How lovely she looks, with that silver glow along her crown, sparkling in her dark hair. She is even prettier than Christine Weber.* But as Elisabeth draws closer, he sees that her eyes are tight, her mouth thin and troubled. She barely pauses to admire the cornet. Then she lays a hand on Paul's head, halting his chatter. "Go inside, boys. Supper is waiting."

The boys clatter and bump up the stairs, jostling and laughing. Paul plays a final squeal on the instrument before he disappears inside.

In the silence that remains, Elisabeth looks soberly at Anton. Something is terribly wrong.

"What is it? Has something happened to Maria? Is she sick?"

"No, Maria is perfectly well. It's nothing like that, nothing of that sort." She glances up the stairs, to be sure the door to their home is well shut and little ears can't hear. "I've heard the news this evening, while you were at the school. Frau Hertz came over and told me." For one wild moment, still riding on his wave of hope, he thinks the Red Orchestra has finally played its deadly chord, and someone, the chosen assassin, has made his move against Hitler. But if that were so—if they were liberated, as suddenly as that, Elisabeth would never look so grim.

"What is it?" he whispers. "Tell me."

"It's about those students from Munich—that group that called itself the White Rose."

"Yes?"

223

"The SS arrested two more students today, Anton. They aren't even proven to be White Rose members; they're only suspected of having some connection to the resistance." She pauses, fixes him with an unblinking, significant stare. "You know they'll be executed."

"I know."

He can sense the fretful storm inside her, the need to say more. Still, she hesitates, drawing a deep breath. She presses her fingertips between her eyes, as if fighting back a headache or her own dark thoughts. The words claw their way out at last, though she won't give them more than a whisper. "It's too dangerous to fight back. We can't stand up to the Party."

"It is too dangerous; you're right about that. But we must fight, all the same. You know in your heart it's right. I haven't forgotten the ham—do you remember? You were beside yourself, fearing you'd insulted that poor, hidden family with your gift. I've seen the way you look at our house sometimes—the way you eye the attic. I know you've wondered whether we could hide any innocents there."

"But I would never go that far. I have my own children to think of—our children, Anton. I can't risk their safety. Neither should you."

Anton knows Elisabeth is right. But neither is he wrong.

Once, in Munich, he found a pamphlet published by the White Rose. It was a small thing, a leaflet, and what's more, it was half burned and discarded behind a wall when Anton came across it, as if whoever dropped it there had been ashamed of having read it and had tried to destroy the evidence. But what shame could those words have roused in any honest soul? What he read on that charred scrap of paper still blazes in his heart. He has never forgotten those words—not a one. Like scripture, they rise whole to the surface of his thoughts. Like his wedding vow.

Nothing is so unworthy of a civilized nation as allowing itself to be governed, without opposition, by an irresponsible clique that has yielded to base instinct. It is certain that today, every honest German is ashamed of his government. Who among us has any conception of the dimensions of shame that will befall us and our children when one day the veil has fallen from our eyes and the most horrible crimes—crimes that infinitely outdistance every human measure—reach the light of day?

Those students were children when they started the White Rose and laid the foundation of resistance. Only children, hardly older than Albert and his friends. He remembers a building in Munich, the great green letters painted on its flat, windowless wall, the words of the White Rose: *"We will not be silent. We are your guilty conscience. The White Rose will never leave you in peace."* When he came across the graffiti, the paint was still wet and dripping. He pressed his fingers against the words to feel the life in them. Threads of vibrant green remained embedded in his fingerprints for days.

The Schutzstaffel, with their hard eyes, their guns, their black boots marching in lockstep—they may put us all on trial. They may try to break the spirits of our youth, but the young people are Germany's guilty conscience, the teeth gnawing on the bone. And we are Germany's conscience. The words of the White Rose are truer now than when they were written. The longer this party remains in power, the harder we must work to tear away the veil of our shame.

"You can't keep doing this," Elisabeth says, "whatever it is you do for . . . them."

He hasn't told her, *I am only a messenger, and surely messengers are in the least danger. We only carry words.* He hasn't told her; it's better if she knows nothing. One day her ignorance may preserve her, if God is merciful. He has only reassured her that his involvement is periph-eral, incidental, and that much is true. But these days, mere association with suspected White Rose members is enough to get you arrested. In Munich, they will kill you for who you know. There is no point trying to reassure her, no point in telling her, *I am safe.* It would be a lie, at any rate—and Anton has promised himself he will never lie to his wife again.

She says, "I can't lose you, Anton. I need you. I need you in my life."

He takes her hand. He risks a careful touch, running his thumb along her knuckle. Her hands are roughened by endless work. "I will stay safe. I promise you that."

But he will not give up this work. *Wir schweigen nicht, wir sind euer böses Gewissen.*

25

It is a bright Sunday morning. The birds of early spring are singing as beautifully as they ever did in the days before there was war. Maria, dressed in her white finery, a little bride-like figure ready for her First Communion, can't leave the breakfast table alone. Elisabeth tries in vain to keep Maria distracted from the porridge and apples to which her brothers attend with their typical appetites.

"You can have your breakfast after church," Elisabeth reminds her. "You mustn't have anything to eat before your First Communion. That's the way it's always done."

Maria sags against the back of Albert's chair, wilting for sympathy. "But I'm so hungry!"

"Think of how proud Vater Emil will be," Anton says, "if you can be brave and strong, and take your Communion on an empty stomach."

That does the trick. Maria dances away from the table, twirling so her white skirt lifts and floats around her quick little legs. "I'm glad I'll take my First Communion from Vater Emil."

"Who else would you take it from?" Paul says. "He's the only priest we have."

"But I'm glad, anyway. I like him best out of all the grown-ups I know . . . except for Mama and *Vati*."

Anton suspects she has only added that last as a sop to his and Elisabeth's feelings.

"I'll go outside and play," Maria announces, "so I won't have to see the rest of you eating."

"You'd better not," Anton says. "You might stain that pretty white dress, and then what would Father Emil think?"

She throws herself down on the faded sofa, arching her back and rolling her eyes in a display of intolerable suffering.

Al edges close to Anton's chair. "When you're through eating, will you show me how to clean the cornet?"

"Of course. It's fairly simple."

"I've been practicing," Al says eagerly. "I can play a whole octave now without having to stop and think about it."

Paul adds, "I've practiced, too!"

"I've heard you both, out there in the orchard."

From the bathroom, Elisabeth calls, "It's a wonder Frau Hertz hasn't evicted us. You boys shouldn't subject her to all that ungracious honking."

"But we'll never learn if we don't practice," says Paul. "I want to play as well as Vati Anton someday."

"You will," Anton says. "I have no doubt. When I was your age, I—"

Elisabeth emerges from the bathroom, fastening her pearls around her neck. "Where has Maria gone?"

Anton and the boys turn to look at the sofa—empty. The cottage door is hanging open, morning light spilling inside.

"No," Al groans.

Elisabeth clicks her tongue. "Go out and catch her, boys, before she can get into trouble."

"I'll go," Anton says. "The boys are already dressed for church." And he's wearing only his workaday trousers—simple, faded blue, with his mauve shirt half tucked in.

He steps outside and peers down from the staircase. He can see the edge of Maria's veil below as it disappears beneath the house. Anton would allow her to play, if he could—let her frolic in the springtime warmth.

Let him witness this joy, at least, for he will miss the rest of it—his little girl's First Communion. He hasn't yet told Elisabeth that he won't be at the church to see it. Last night, as he made his way home from the Forst place, Father Emil met him along the road and passed an urgent message with his handshake. He has never been required to carry a message on a Sunday before. That, he assumes, is one of the perquisites of working with a priest. But today's duty can't wait until after the Sabbath. It must be today. Elisabeth will be angry and hurt when he breaks the news, but there is nothing to be done. The fire of resistance burns hotter by the day; the secret networks are boiling with sudden activity, with an intensity that heightens his hope and his fear in equal measure. Something is going to happen, and soon. We are on the verge of a great change. We can only pray we will come through this trial alive and unbroken.

If only he could linger, enjoying Maria's happiness for a few moments longer, before he must admit it all to Elisabeth and ruin the day—but if Maria stains her dress, the day will be ruined anyhow.

He hurries down the staircase, circles the cottage, and steps across the ditch that drains the muck out into the *Misthaufen*. He searches across the grazing yard, but the only whiteness is the goats' hides; there is no sign of Maria in her Communion dress. Then, as he faces the house again, he spots the girl. She is walking along the stone wall, the one that forms the downstairs pen where the animals sleep. Maria puts one foot in front of the other, arms flung wide for balance. She hums as she walks. Stunned, Anton stares; Maria teeters, and her little arms spin like the blades of a windmill. That spurs him into action; he dodges around the corner of the foundation to where he might be able to reach her. Should he call out to her? Should he shout and scold? The last thing he wants is to surprise the girl into falling.

Maria turns her head, golden curls bobbing. She sees him now—squints at him, and quickens her pace.

"Get down from there," Anton says. "Your mother will be angry. Running around in your Communion dress—what are you thinking?"

"I won't fall!"

"I've seen you nearly fall half a dozen times already." He edges closer and reaches up to grab her around the waist, but she darts from his hands, bright shoes tapping gaily along the stones.

"You must get down at once! Go back inside, and wait for the rest of the family to finish dressing. It will soon be time to walk to the church."

"It's boring inside! I don't want to be there."

With an effort, Anton smooths the anger from his voice. All sugar, he says, "I know it's boring, but you won't be there for long. Then you'll get to see Father Emil and stand up in front of everyone in your fine white dress. Isn't that something to look forward to? Come along, now, *mein Schatz*. Let me help you down."

But at that moment, the door bangs open and the boys run downstairs, shouting Maria's name. There is an urgency in their voices; Elisabeth has sent them off to catch their little sister and bring her to heel. Distracted, Maria turns toward her brothers—and misses her step. In an instant, she dips to the side; her arms flap helplessly in the air. Her little face is all round eyes and round, open mouth as she topples from the wall, falling on the inside—where the animals sleep. A tremendous crash follows the little white figure's disappearance. And then, a moment later, a cloud of stench rises from the *Misthaufen* trench.

Anton sprints to the back of the house and throws open the gate of the pen. He hurries through the straw bedding, kicking it this way and that. The dairy cow, dozing in her bed, lumbers to her feet with a frightened bellow. He finds Maria at the bottom of the muck trench, lying flat out in the urine and dung. The poor thing has smashed right through the light wooden planks, a perfunctory screen that, until now, has hidden the trench and its unappealing contents. For a moment, Anton fears she is seriously injured, perhaps fatally—she lies so very still. But then Maria sits up slowly. She looks down at herself—at the Communion dress, so lovingly made by Elisabeth, brown and reeking now, ruined with filth. She sucks in a tremendous breath, throws back her head, and lets out a long, piercing scream.

The boys join Anton below the house just as the cow trots away, driven off by Maria's earsplitting cry.

"What have you done?" Albert cries, while Paul shouts with entirely too much glee, "Mother's going to burn your backside!"

Anton reaches for the girl. The boys move as if to help him, but he waves them back. "Don't you get filthy, too. Your poor mother has enough to worry about." He lifts Maria in his arms, though the smell nearly chokes him. "Are you hurt?"

"No," she wails, "but now I'm all dirty!"

"Didn't I tell you this would happen?"

"Yes, but I didn't believe you! I didn't think God would be so mean to me on my First Communion day!"

"It wasn't God who did this, you silly girl. You've no one to blame but yourself. This is what disobedience gets you!" Still cradling Maria, he carries her out from under the house. His own shirt is smeared with the same foulness, but there's nothing to be done about it now. He stands Maria upright in the grass, surveying the damage. The filth is everywhere—soaking the front of her smocked dress from bodice to hem, splattered on her red face, matted in her hair.

Elisabeth has come to the sound of her daughter's cries. Maria's distress has summoned Frau Hertz, too; she runs from the farmhouse, already talking to no one in particular and wringing her hands. Out of breath, Frau Hertz can only cluck with worry, but Elisabeth is mute from shock.

After a few moments of useless gasping, Elisabeth musters her words. "We have only half an hour before we must leave for the church! Maria, you will be the death of me!" Tears spring to Elisabeth's eyes. Anton is surprised—he hasn't seen her weep since that day in the lane, when he played his cornet. "Whatever can we do?"

Frau Hertz takes Elisabeth under her comforting arm. "Be calm, my dear. It's not as bad as you think. I still have my old Communion dress; I know just where I've stored it. It should fit Maria. It's old-fashioned, of course, but it will serve."

"I want to wear this dress," Maria cries. "It's so pretty!"

Paul says, "It's not pretty anymore," which only makes Maria cry all the harder. Elisabeth clouts Paul on the back of his head, sending his blond hair ruffling. The boys bite their lips to stifle their laughter.

"Come along." Frau Hertz guides Elisabeth toward the big farmhouse. "We'll get her cleaned up and dressed. There will be enough time, Elisabeth; don't you fret. Albert, run ahead and fill up that big copper tub, the one I keep in my kitchen. The water will be cold; there's no time to heat it. But we must wash her hair. There's muck all through it. Anton, you carry Maria."

As Frau Hertz marches her away, Elisabeth glances back at Anton. "You must change your clothes as soon as we've got Maria into the tub, Anton. She's smeared dung all over your shirt; you can't go to church in such a state."

Anton does change, when he is free to do so. But when he enters the Hertz home several minutes later, freshly dressed, he is still not wearing his Sunday best.

Wrapped in a large towel and shivering, Maria is bent over an ironing board with her hair spread flat along its length. Already she has been thoroughly scrubbed; Frau Hertz can work wonders when wonders are called for. Elisabeth has clamped both arms around Maria's middle, trying to keep the girl from wiggling. Frau Hertz applies a hot iron to Maria's hair. The iron hisses like a serpent, and a cloud of steam rises, beading moisture on the windowpane.

"I was about to start my ironing when I heard Maria scream," Frau Hertz says. "The iron was already hot. That was good luck; otherwise, we couldn't hope to dry her hair in time. I'm afraid you won't have curls today, Maria, but straight hair is better than muck-covered hair."

Albert and Paul sit at the ends of Frau Hertz's velvet-covered sofa. Between them lies a painfully old-fashioned Communion dress, spread out to air. Time has yellowed the fabric, and even at a distance, Anton can smell the residue of mothballs.

"Hold still," Elisabeth says to Maria. "If you don't, you'll only burn yourself on the iron. Wouldn't that be a fine addition to the day?" She glances at Anton—then looks again, dismayed. "You aren't going to church in that outfit, are you?"

He feels like a dog who has made a mess of the rug. "I'm . . . not going to church today, Elisabeth. I must work—in Wernau."

Her mouth falls open. "Not going? Anton! It's bad enough, working on the Sabbath, but missing your daughter's First Holy Communion?"

"I'm sorry. If there were any way . . ."

"There is a way. Go to church. Don't abandon your family for mere work."

They can't discuss the matter in front of Frau Hertz and the children. "You know I can't do that. This work is too important." What must the Frau think? She has no reason to believe Anton is anything other than a music teacher. But she minds her own business, goes on pressing the damp out of Maria's hair while the girl struggles and complains.

"I'm sorry," Anton says again. "I'll find some way to make it up to you. To all of you."

Elisabeth will no longer look at him. The lines of her face—what little he can see of it, turned away—are hard and forbidding. "It's Maria you owe an apology to, not me."

Maria seems untroubled by the news. "Why can't I wear my hair in curls?" Then, as Frau Hertz pushes her head down again, she shouts to Anton, "If you're going to Wernau, I want paper dolls!"

"I'll bring you some paper dolls to celebrate your Communion. Boys, help your mother mind Maria. Don't let her get into any more trouble."

He edges close to Elisabeth, meaning to kiss her cheek, but she pulls back. "You had better go." She flicks one cold look at him, then her eyes dart away again. But he can see more than anger in her eyes. There is fear, too.

26

In Wernau, the shops are all closed. In a secluded alley, Anton manages to find a few discarded sewing catalogs stacked beside a garbage bin. The covers have faded, but the pictures inside—of ladies in smart dresses and men in tailored suits—are bright and cheerful enough to please any little girl. He tucks the catalogs under his arm and makes his way toward the bus stop, eyes open for his contact.

He sees Detlef Pohl before the man sees him. Pohl is carrying a cane this time—he is fond of adding elements to his various disguises, not that any message carriers rely much on disguise. Pohl walks with the dignity of a king in a procession. He pauses now and then to gaze in the windows of shops; he checks his pocket watch with an unhurried air, then tucks it away again. When they pass on the sidewalk, Anton and Pohl tip their hats, as polite strangers do. The folded paper falls from Anton's other hand; the tip of Pohl's cane comes down, pinning the message to the pavement.

"A lovely Sunday," Pohl says.

"It would be lovelier if my wife didn't want to skin me alive."

Pohl's mouth tightens. Too late, Anton remembers what the man said once, back in Kirchheim: *Don't tell me if you have a family.*

His cheeks burn. It was a careless mistake. "I should be on my way."

But as he turns to go, Herr Pohl says quietly, as if he can't help it—as if it burdens his spirit, "A shame about Egerland."

Anton glances back. "What has happened? I haven't heard the news. Our town is so small, you know—we don't always hear what happens in the world beyond." But we heard about the students, arrested for contact with the founders of the White Rose. That fear still hangs over Anton, and over Elisabeth, too.

"The Czechs have pushed back," Pohl says. "A rebel faction. They won't last long; the Reich will lay into them soon enough. But for now, they've expelled at least a hundred German families—maybe more."

"That is a shame," Anton says.

Pohl lifts a single brow. "All those people, cast out of their homes. Women and children, wandering the countryside, homeless, hungry. I hear they've taken to sleeping in barns—when they can find them—and eating weeds. Like cattle."

The picture of tragedy resolves before Anton's mind, grim and clear. Now he says with real feeling, "How terrible. Can anything be done to help them?"

"They need homes, the poor souls—at least until their land is reclaimed and they can return to Egerland. Assuming the Czechs leave something for the exiles to return to, that is . . . something worth calling home. I have heard there is some relief effort planned, but it amounts to transporting the homeless here, to the Württemberg countryside, and turning them loose again."

"Not much of a plan."

"No, not much. But we don't expect better from those at the helm, do we?" Pohl shifts his cane, pulling the message closer. When Anton has gone, he will bend and pick it up. He will make his way to the next contact; the words will flow, a trickle, a quiet stream. Pohl lifts his hat again. "I had best be going."

"And I."

"Be safe, *mein Herr*."

235

By the time Anton finally reaches home, long after sunset, a spring drizzle has set in, soaking his coat and chilling him to the core. But rain and hours have cooled Elisabeth's anger. She looks up from the stove as he enters, and when he bends to kiss her cheek, she doesn't pull away. Whatever she is cooking smells delicious: savory, yet lightened with a pinch of the cinnamon she guards with such jealous attention. The children have gone to bed.

Anton takes the sewing catalogs from inside his coat. He stacks them on the table, neatly, the way Elisabeth likes.

"How did Communion go?"

Faintly, Elisabeth smiles. "Maria did well. She took the matter seriously, thank the Lord. She treated the ceremony with reverence. You would have been proud of her, if you'd seen it."

"I am always proud of my Maria." He hangs his wet coat on a hook beside the door, then pages through one of the catalogs. "She can cut these up to her heart's content."

"She'll like that. Sit down; I've reheated the stew. When I noticed the rain, I thought you'd be terribly cold by the time you came home."

The stew is delicious, and the cinnamon has been added just for him—Anton feels certain of that. Between bites, he says, "I regret missing Maria's big day. If it had been any other work, you know I would have let it rest until Monday."

"I know." She sighs, ever weary, and sinks onto the chair closest to Anton. "I'm glad Maria wasn't hurt by your not being there."

"I'm sorry you were hurt, though. It wasn't an easy decision to make."

For a moment, she blinks down at the table in silence. "I worry, Anton—how often will you choose this work over your family? Where will you draw the line? When will we be more important than this?"

How can he make her understand? He can't disentangle his commitment to the resistance from his commitment to the family. They are two edifices in his heart, each built from the same stone. He fights because he loves his family, because he needs to believe that they will see better days. There is nothing he can say, where the children might hear. He can only hold her hand, briefly—all she will permit—and pat her shoulder, a silent promise of unity.

"I heard news from Egerland while I was away. The Czechs have retaken the place. They've turned all the Germans they could find out of their homes. So many have been displaced—women, children—it turns my stomach to think of it."

Elisabeth's face lengthens with pity. "Those poor people. We have so little here, in the country, but imagine being cast out from your home—imagine having nothing."

"The NSDAP plans to bring the refugees here, you know."

"What, to Unterboihingen?"

"Not precisely. They're being carried by train to Württemberg."

"And then?"

Anton shrugs. "Then left to fend for themselves again, I suppose—left to scratch out some bare existence in the fields and forests."

"How can the Party do such a thing? It isn't as if these refugees are *impure*." She weights that word with all the scorn it deserves. Only Party wolves could think any person impure—and those like Bruno Franke, who quiver with a base eagerness to lick Hitler's jowls. "They are Germans, full citizens, with every right to the Reich's protection, according to the Reich's own decrees. It disgusts me, how anyone can support these devils—even now, when they plan to drop German mothers and children like trash on a refuse heap. I feel ill."

"I suppose they justify it—the Party and their supporters—by saying, 'We're at war now. Where will we find the money to care for refugees?'"

"Money shouldn't matter. It's the right thing to do, to care for them. And so it should be done, no matter the cost, no matter who must make the sacrifice."

He takes her hand again. "When, *mein Schatz*, has this regime done what is right?"

"Never." Tears spring to her eyes. She turns her face, ashamed, and tugs her hand free from Anton's grip. She wipes her eyes before the tears may fall. "Never, Anton; from the start, they have done only evil. And we have gone along with it—all of us, the whole country. We could have stopped them long ago, but we didn't. We hid our faces behind our hands. We told ourselves, 'This won't continue. It won't be allowed. Someone will stop them; someone must. The Reichstag, or an assassin, or the Tommies. Or God Himself. It won't be allowed to continue.' But it *has* continued, and now it seems there is no end in sight. We can't go back to the time when we might have stopped this all; we let that chance pass us by. What does that make us? What will God think, when we stand before His judgment?"

There is nothing Anton can say, no comfort he can offer. The chance has passed; a hundred chances more lie in the dust behind us. The miles we might have marched in protest, the votes we might have cast. The mercy we might have shown but withheld, fearful of what our neighbors would think. There is nothing left for any of us but to stand firm on what little ground remains. To say to the Party, *You have gone far enough already. Now you will go no further.* We will stand, and we will know that we'll be ground beneath their heels. We'll be like grains to a millstone. But until the moment when we fall, we will stand.

Elisabeth looks up to the cracked plaster ceiling. Her eyes are drawn, as if by instinct—as if by hope—to the tiny space above, the empty attic she cannot see. But she knows it's there.

"Surely our attic is far too small," Anton says quietly. "This house is hardly bigger than a tinderbox. There can't be enough space above our heads for a man to stand upright. What kind of life would it be, crawling about on all fours?"

"It would be life." He can hear his wife's unshed tears wavering in her voice.

"And Elisabeth . . . if we were found out, the Schutzstaffel would take our children. You know they would." *They would make us watch while they shot our sons, our brave little daughter. They would put your hand on the rifle and force you to pull the trigger.*

"I know," Elisabeth says. "I won't do it, Anton—I won't hide anyone from the Party. I would never risk the children. But it will haunt me for the rest of my life, the fact that I didn't do it. I never tried." A new thought occurs to her. She sits up straight in her chair, and now all traces of tears have gone. "But the Egerlanders. The refugees. You've said they'll be left here in Württemberg. We must take *them* in, if we can't take Jews or Gypsies or Poles."

He considers. Slowly, he mulls it over. "Can it displease the Party at all? I want to believe they would permit it, but what if they feel we've crossed them somehow—gone against their designs?"

"You cross them every day, as far as I can tell."

"But I do this in secret. We could never hide it, Elisabeth, if we brought refugees into our home."

"What can anyone say about it? What protest can they possibly raise? Those Egerlanders are our fellow Germans; we wouldn't be aiding any of the *impure*."

"If we take in the Egerlanders, we'll draw attention to Unterboihingen." No longer invisible. We will shine like a torch from the night sky.

Elisabeth considers for a long moment, brushing her lips with her fingertips, gazing up past the ceiling, to the space she cannot see. "You're right; it will draw every eye in Germany to Unterboihingen. And that's why we must gain the whole town's approval. Everyone must agree, or none of us can do it at all."

"I meant to pay a visit to Father Emil, first thing in the morning. I want to apologize for missing Maria's Communion. Perhaps I'll take the matter to him."

"I wish you would. If anyone can convince our town to help those refugees, it's Father Emil."

This time, when Anton takes her hand, she allows him to hold it a little longer.

"You deserve a better husband," he says, "one who is on hand whenever you need him. Whenever you want him near."

Elisabeth makes no reply, except to squeeze his fingers. But in her touch, he feels a marginal warming, a thaw in her habitual chill.

27

Father Emil has called a meeting, and St. Kolumban is full to groaning. Every man and woman who is well enough to leave home has come to the church. The nave is loud with restless chatter, and although the arches of the ceiling soar high above their heads, the air is close with the breath and heat of so many people.

Holding to Anton's arm, Elisabeth tightens her grip in surprise as they enter. "I never expected so many people would come to this meeting."

"You said yourself," Anton replies, "Father Emil can move hearts."

She glances around uneasily. Anton can see it, too—the agitation in men's gestures, the loudness of their voices, the emphatic shaking of women's heads. Father Emil's work is cut out for him.

"They seem reluctant," Elisabeth says quietly as Anton leads her to a front pew.

"Some undoubtedly are. But keep faith, my darling. Let's give the father a chance to work his miracles before we despair."

They settle beside Frau Hertz just as Emil emerges from behind the rood screen. He steps to his lectern, and a hush falls across the nave. Villagers find their seats; there is a murmur and rustle like wind through a forest.

"My friends and neighbors, my brothers and sisters," Emil begins, smiling, "I am so gratified to see all of you here this evening. I know it's unusual, to assemble this way, but we find ourselves in unusual circumstances—or about to be touched by unusual circumstances, I should say."

A mutter rises again from the nave, with a distinct note of protest. But it dies back just as quickly. Someone among the pews hisses, "Let the father speak before you judge!"

"Many of you have already heard the dreadful news from Egerland," Emil resumes. "It's true, I'm sorry to say: the Czechs have taken over there, and pushed German families from their homes. We've good reason to believe that the refugees will be redistributed to Württemberg.

"A member of our flock"—Father Emil does not look at Anton or Elisabeth—"suggested that we might open our homes to those in need, and welcome the Egerlanders among us. I've brought you here tonight with the hope that we might seek consensus, and act as one body in this matter."

Across the aisle, Bruno Franke rises to his feet. It's all Anton can do to keep a scowl from his face as he listens to the man speak—listens to him bellow.

"It's a terrible idea. We oughtn't even to think of it."

Cowering beside her husband, Frau Franke keeps her eyes fixed to the floor. She is a small woman, wrapped in a dark woolen shawl, sober-faced and pale. When a woman to her left murmurs something close to her ear, Frau Franke quivers as if the very proximity of another woman burns her.

The poor thing, Anton thinks. *What must her life be like, shackled to the town gauleiter? Does she know how her husband carries on with the wives and unmarried girls of the village?*

One of the Kopp brothers stands, too. "Come, now, Herr Franke. You aren't suggesting we turn away women and children in need?"

Anton recognizes many of the voices raised in support—the Abts and Schneiders, the baker and her two red-cheeked daughters.

But someone else shouts, "Bruno is right. It's a bad idea—dangerous!"

Anton burns to crane his neck, to find out who called out such folly. But he can't draw attention to himself with the gauleiter so near. He forces himself to remain casually in his place, eyes on the priest at his lectern.

Emil raises his hands until silence has been restored. But Bruno Franke remains standing.

"Herr Franke," the priest says, "please tell us more. If we know why, exactly, you are concerned, then perhaps—"

Möbelbauer cuts Emil off with an impatient jerk of his head. "We don't need more mouths to feed here in Unterboihingen. If we let in a great herd of strays, they'll eat us out of our homes."

"Strays?" Frau Abt cries. "For Heaven's sake, those are little children you speak of, not dogs!"

The woman seated near the Frankes adds, "Show some humanity, Bruno." When she elbows Frau Franke, the Frau only huddles deeper into her shawl.

Janz Essert lifts his hand. "Franke has the right of it. We've kept ourselves out of trouble here in this town. Refugees will only complicate our lives. Who needs the bother?"

A murmur of disapproval rises like a flood. Someone shouts over the noise, "We can't turn away people in need!"

Now more are on their feet, voicing their support of Möbelbauer— men and women alike, six, seven. Then ten, then a dozen. Anton never dreamed the gauleiter had so many admirers. Frantically, he takes stock, trying to impress their faces and names upon his memory. His life might depend, one day, on staying on the right side of Bruno Franke's friends.

Franke says, "Listen, listen, all of you. Let us talk sense. I'm not a heartless fiend"—Elisabeth's legs twitch, and Anton fears she may leap up to confront the man—"but consider our situation. We've just enough, among all our little farms and shops, to keep ourselves in good health and good cheer. If we open our homes to these Egerlanders, every one of us will be stretched too thin. There will no longer be enough surplus for trading. We'll all be back to living on ration stamps and nothing else. Is that really the life you want to lead?"

Elisabeth springs up before Anton can restrain her. She faces Franke across the aisle, shivering with anger and disgust. "All of Germany has tightened its belt," she says. "We can do the same. We've had an easy go of the war, here in Unterboihingen. Now it's time we share our good luck with those less fortunate than we."

The roar of assent is gratifying; it raises a prickle of triumph along Anton's spine.

Franke has nothing for Elisabeth but a twisted sneer. "You would take food from your own children's mouths to feed strangers?"

There is no hesitation in her reply. "I would rather send my children to bed hungry than teach them to harden their hearts. What good is a comfortable life if we don't know the meaning of love or mercy?"

"Hear!" someone shouts in admiration. Applause ripples around the nave.

But those who have stood in support of Bruno Franke haven't backed down yet.

"We don't even know what kind of people these Egerlanders are," Janz says.

The man standing beside him—Hofer Voigt—nods eagerly. "That's right. They're strangers to us; who can say what they intend?"

"What they intend?" Elisabeth cries. "Herr Voigt, how can you say such things? They are homeless! You make it sound as if they've had any choice in this matter—as if they were planning an invasion!"

"And as for what kind of people they are," says another Kopp, "they're Germans. What more do you need to know?"

"Plenty of unsavory types have called themselves German." Franke casts a sly look around the church, the muttering crowd. "Plenty of impure types. Just because they claim to be German, that doesn't make it so."

"That's the truth," Hofer says. "Listen well, all of you. How can we be sure these Egerlanders wouldn't bring Jews or Gypsy rats among us?"

Anton seizes Elisabeth's hand to silence her. He can all but feel his wife's hotheaded reply, for it's burning on his own tongue: *I'd take in a Jewish family, too, if I could—and call myself blessed for the chance.* But it would never do to admit such a thing here and now. Not with Franke's eyes narrowed and darting around the room, searching for sympathizers and traitors.

"Peace," Emil says from his lectern. "Peace, my friends, peace. It's plain to see that we all feel strongly about the Egerlanders. Yet we must decide what's best to be done. For the refugees are coming to Württemberg, whether we like it or not. Do we offer them shelter, or do we leave them to roam the countryside, fending for themselves?"

Carefully, Anton rises to stand beside his wife. "There is one consideration no one has yet raised. We've gone largely unnoticed, here in Unterboihingen—but if we take these families into our homes, word will get out. In the cities, they will learn the name of our quiet little village. Newspapers will run the story; they'll talk about us on the radio. We will no longer be invisible, as we once were. Do we accept that risk?"

"No!" Franke shouts, and his supporters join him, shaking their fists above their heads.

But when a semblance of quiet has returned, Elisabeth speaks again. "It's true what Anton says. We must be prepared to lose some of our safety. But ask yourselves this: If you leave the homeless to wander without shelter, will you be able to meet your own eyes in the mirror without shame? If you do what's easy, instead of what's right, will you ever hold your head up again when your spouse speaks your name? If you turn your backs while children starve in your fields, can you ever again touch your own child's face without agony?

"Ask yourselves this: Are we good people, here in Unterboihingen? Do we heed the words of Christ, and care for our brothers—even for strangers among us? Or are we selfish as Judas, selling what is holy and good for a few pieces of silver?"

The remainder of the village rises now, shouting support for Elisabeth, for the Egerlanders.

Heart welling with pride, Anton tightens his grip on her hand. He can feel Bruno Franke's stare on his face—on Elisabeth, too, darkly assessing. Anton will not look at the gauleiter—let him flounder in his defeat. But he takes note of the men and women who storm from the church on Möbelbauer's heels. Never would he have suspected this serene little village harbored so much hate. And never will he know what's to be done about it.

The rest of town agrees; only Franke and his handful of supporters are openly against it. Even Bruno Franke's wife—harried and sad, refusing to meet the eyes of other women—remains in the church. She, too, is in favor of helping the refugees.

From the lectern, Father Emil catches Anton's eye and smiles. The matter is settled. Let Unterboihingen open its doors and welcome the refugees in.

28

Shoulder to shoulder, Anton and Emil relax in the orchard, their backs against the trunk of the largest tree. Smoke from Emil's pipe rises and hangs among the new leaves. Dapples of light chase themselves, back and forth, across pools of violet shadow. The grass in the orchard is green and sweet, dotted where Anton sits with curls of soft, pale wood. The chunk of pine in Anton's hand has become a prancing horse, a gift for the Egerlander girls to share.

"You're a genius with a carving knife," Emil says. He exhales a slow stream of smoke.

"This?" Anton stands the horse in the grass. It tips over. "I think I must disagree. This is hardly proper carving. Better call it whittling, and nothing more."

"Have you always been a whittler?"

"My father taught me when I was a boy." He shaves a sliver from one hoof. This time, the horse remains on its feet.

"You should teach your boys how it's done."

Anton laughs. "I've more to learn from Al and Paul than they'll ever learn from me. And they're natural teachers. Look at them."

Across the orchard, in an opposite swath of shade, the boys sit on an old, thin blanket with the two refugee children, Millie and Elsie, who have come to live on the farm along with their mother, Frau Hornik. Albert is showing them how to play the cornet. He demonstrates, playing a high, clear note. He depresses one of the keys, and the note changes. Millie and Elsie look at one another, giggling, and when one takes the cornet from Al's hands, the boy flinches back as if burned. The girls are twins, so much alike Anton can never tell them apart. They are of an age with Albert, and if the way Al blushes and fidgets in their presence is any indication, they have each given him a kiss or two when no one is looking. One of the girls tries to play. The cornet emits a weak, breathy honk, and all the children collapse into laughter.

Emil sighs. "What a blessing, to see young people so full of happiness. With everything these girls have been through—losing their home, the ravages of war—it's a wonder they aren't damaged in some way."

"I'm constantly amazed by the resilience of children."

"I suppose you saw that resilience often enough, teaching with the order."

Anton nods. He plucks up the curls of pine and sorts them into a tidy pile. He still doesn't like to speak of his days at St. Josefsheim—how they came to an end.

"This work, opening up her home to others—it suits Elisabeth well."

Anton follows Emil's gaze to the flat yard outside their old cottage. Elisabeth and Frau Hornik are busy with the washing; they have rolled their sleeves up past their elbows and covered their dresses with thick linen aprons; they splash in the tub and wrestle with the washboard, giggling like a pair of twelve-year-old girls. Maria is making mud pies beside the women's feet.

"I haven't seen Elisabeth so happy in all the time I've known her," Anton says. "She likes Frau Hornik tremendously, as you can see. They've hit it off like sisters. Frau Hornik's husband died several years ago, before the war got so bad—just like Elisabeth's first husband, so they've got something in common. But there's more to it than simply liking our guest."

"Yes," Emil says. "I've always known her to be warmhearted, but I never knew what great love was in Elisabeth, until now—until she could be of some real service to those in need. She finds her strength in love."

Again, Anton nods but says nothing. Elisabeth is prepared to love everyone, it seems, wholly and without reservation—everyone except him. If he knew the way to win her heart, he would have done it by now.

Emil says, "Elisabeth would be one of the brave ones—the ones who hide Jews in their own homes—if she hadn't any children to think of. It's only the little ones who have prevented her from opening her heart so wide. But what a big heart she has, all the same. The children must take priority, of course—that's the way God made mothers. I suppose He knows best about such things."

"She is brave, nonetheless—even without any Jews sequestered in the attic. But I know she would do more, save more people, if she could. It eats away at her soul, knowing she must choose between her children and someone else's." *As it eats at my own soul.*

"I admire her very much. She has lived a hard life—losing her first husband, facing poverty with three children to care for. Yet she never fell into despair. And the way she spoke for the Egerlanders—the way she stood up to Bruno Franke . . ."

"I fear that man," Anton says. "I don't mind admitting it to you."

Emil draws on his pipe. He nods, exhaling.

"I fear him, and I hate him."

"Anton, we mustn't hate."

"I know." Hate is a foul and useless thing. It taints too much of this world. "You can give me my penance when next I come to confess."

Emil smiles. He blows a smoke ring. "What do you know? I've always wanted to make a smoke ring—tried for years, and never could get it right. Now I do it without even thinking about it."

The children come running through the orchard. "Ah," Anton says, "the very girls I wanted to see." He holds up the carved horse; Millie or

Elsie takes it, and both girls admire it in silence. They bite their lower lips in exactly the same way when they smile.

"Vati Anton," Paul says, "on market day, may we bring Millie and Elsie with us?"

"They want to see how we do the trades," Al says.

"I think that's a fine idea. Albert, you'll be just the fellow to show them how to drive a bargain."

Al's freckles disappear as his face heats red. He won't look at the twins, but he nods and says, "I'll show them."

"I might join you, if you'll have me," says Father Emil. "I need to pick up a few necessities—I've six single men from Egerland staying at the church, sleeping on bedrolls in the nave. They do go through candles and bread rather quickly. Would it suit you boys—and you girls, too—if I came along?"

"You are always welcome in our family," Anton says. "There is no need to ask, my friend."

◆　◆　◆

When they reach the market square, Al hands his basket of eggs to one of the Hornik girls. He leads Paul and the twins into the crowd, explaining as he goes: "My eggs are the best in town, because my hens are the best, so my eggs are worth more, you see. We must be careful to get only the best things in trade."

The boy and his voice disappear in the noise of the market square. Anton remains with Father Emil; Elisabeth and Frau Hornik have already sought out a gathering of women. They will put out word that Maria needs bigger shoes. Who has a child's shoes to trade, and who needs a small pair, worn but still useful?

"It has been weeks since I came to market last," Emil says. "Does Herr Derichs still have candles?"

"The best in Unterboihingen. He has been sick lately, but even so—"

Abruptly, Anton falls quiet. Over the bustle and noise of the crowd, a jolly sound rises. A skip and bounce of rhythm, the bright, smiling notes of brass. He and Emil thread across the square—and there, at the edge of the crowd, in the mouth of a narrow alley, he finds a handful of his music students playing a march. Their eyes light up when they see their teacher. Some of them blush. But they don't stop playing, even when the notes fall sour. More people gather beside Anton and the priest, watching, listening, pausing to set down their cares for a moment of guiltless joy. When the march has finished, the crowd applauds. The boys bow to their admirers and then scatter into the alley, thrilled and embarrassed, laughing.

"I can scarcely believe how far they've come," Anton says. He calls, "Well done, boys!"

Emil says, "You work even more wonders with your band than you do with your carving knife."

"The children deserve your praise, not I. They've done the difficult work."

"Don't be so humble. It's unbecoming."

"Unbecoming?" Anton grins. "Doesn't the Bible tell us we should be humble?"

Emil delivers a friendly blow to Anton's shoulder. "I forget you were a friar. There's no sneaking any point of doctrine past you. But accept a little praise, my friend; you deserve it. Your band has brought us all considerable happiness, when we have little other cause for feeling glad."

Anton lowers his voice. Even in Unterboihingen, one never knows who might be listening. "My band has achieved exactly what I set out to do. Those boys in the alley—they won't be pinning swastikas to their sleeves anytime soon."

"Let's pray they will not." Smoothly, Emil changes the subject. "I was just thinking, 'There never was a crowd so big at the Saturday market. When did our town grow?' But it's the Egerlanders, of course."

"Thirty-six families in all," Anton says. "And how many single men, like the fellows who sleep on your pews? Frau Hertz has taken in four young men; they're a great help around the farm."

"There are twenty young fellows, at least, and five old gentlemen that I know of. These Egerland folk fit right in. One would never know they haven't been in Unterboihingen all along."

As much a part of the landscape as the ancient houses and blue hills beyond.

Once more, a sharp sound rises above the din of the crowd, but this time, there is no glad music. It's a coarse shout like the bark of a dog, hard-edged with anger. Anton and Emil glance at one another, and there is a sudden tightness in the eyes of the priest. Caution has eclipsed his happy mood. They jostle through the crowd toward the market's eastern edge. There stands Bruno Franke—Möbelbauer—confronting two of the newcomers, refugee men. A handful of Unterboihingen fellows stand behind Franke, lending their support. They watch the Egerlander men with narrowed eyes. Anton makes note of their hard, hateful faces. They are the same men who rose in opposition at Father Emil's meeting, the day Unterboihingen voted to take in the refugees.

"Those are two of mine," Emil says quietly. "They're brothers—Geißler is their family name. They were the first to take shelter at the church."

The Geißler brothers are no older than twenty-five. They're standing side by side, arms folded over their chests, holding their ground against Franke and his friends. Brave, for men so young. But then, if they knew they confronted the town's gauleiter, would they be so bold?

"These two wretches took too much flour," Möbelbauer shouts. He intends the whole town to hear, an impromptu tribunal. "I said two measures; they took three."

The elder brother says, "You told me to take three." The younger adds, "At least speak honestly, now that you've got the attention of the whole village."

"Do they know?" Anton murmurs to Emil. Do they know they're speaking to a gauleiter?

Emil shakes his head. "I don't think so. I haven't told them. I should have thought to tell all the men at the church—warn them to be careful. The blame lies with me."

Anton lays a hand on his chest. "No time now for regret. We need to help those boys. If they fall too far on Franke's bad side—"

Möbelbauer has puffed himself up at the younger brother's cheek. Like a toad roused from its burrow and jabbed with a stick, he has inflated himself. He takes a menacing step toward the Geißlers. "Look at you, the both of you—young and hale, but here you are, hiding from your duty with the women and children. You should be fighting for our country, defending the German way. You should be on the *Ostfront*—better men than you have died there already, for the sake of our land."

In the next moment, Möbelbauer will accuse the brothers of disloyalty. It's a short drop from there to the gauleiter's letter desk, a message winging off to the NSDAP.

"All right," Anton murmurs, stepping forward. "I'm going to speak to Herr Franke."

Emil catches his arm. "Don't. You know it's too risky for either of us to draw Franke's eye."

"If we don't intervene, those young men will—"

Before Anton can finish speaking, another figure has pushed her way out of the crowd. He recognizes the dark-blue dress, the stoic marching step of her walk, before the danger registers—before fear strikes him.

Elisabeth.

She stands beside the brothers. "Leave off, Bruno. It's only a misunderstanding."

"A misunderstanding?" The gauleiter's voice slinks low, low as a snake on its belly. "These disloyal dogs have invaded our land—"

"They are Germans!"

"—and you have let them in. Don't think I've forgotten it was you, Frau Starzmann, who convinced the rest to open their homes and their larders to this trash. You're the one to blame. Indiscriminate—that's what you are. If these useless mouths to feed had left me with a single reichspfennig in my pocket, I'd wager my last coin that you would take in any foul creature, any impure thing that came your way."

This talk is too dangerous. Anton can't allow it to stand. He breaks away from Emil, shaking off the priest's restraining grip. He strides across the cobblestones and steps between Elisabeth and the gauleiter. Then, heart pounding, he moves closer still, until Möbelbauer is forced to look up at him. The man seems quite small now, shrinking in the shadow of Anton's superior height.

"Say one more word to my wife, Franke," Anton mutters. "Just one."

Möbelbauer squints at Anton. His gaze slides to the crowd—the tense, silent watchers. He doesn't dare accuse Anton now. No one will believe that the man who brought us music, the man who gave us joy, is any sort of villain. Here before the eyes of the whole town, Franke can do nothing but back down.

He does, throwing up his hands and turning away. "Let the lot of you starve, then," Möbelbauer says as his friends fall in line behind him. "It won't be on my head."

Möbelbauer vanishes behind his shop door, taking his fellows with him. The moment the gauleiter has disappeared, the crowd relaxes, sighs, buzzes with conversation. Shielded by the sound, Anton rounds on Elisabeth.

"What were you thinking, confronting Möbelbauer that way? You know he's dangerous."

Elisabeth has gone pale. He can see the faint trembling of her shoulders. He takes them in his hands and presses, trying to hold her together.

"I know he's dangerous," she says. "But someone had to stop him."

"Leave it to someone else, then—anyone else. Not you."

"Why not me?"

"Because I love you." The words are out of his mouth before he can think better.

Elisabeth turns away at once. She will not meet his eye, nor speak to him, as she calls for Frau Hornik. She counts the children as they assemble around her. Then she points them all in the direction of home.

But late that night, after Elisabeth has seen to supper and tucked the children into bed, she finds her words. The house is quiet, soft with shadow. She carries a candle to Frau Hornik. Anton and Elisabeth have given their bed to the widow; the twins take turns, sharing the bed with their mother and sleeping on a straw-stuffed mat beside the dresser. Elisabeth steps from the bedroom, only one candle in her hand now. By its simple light, she glows in her humble white nightdress. Candlelight surrounds her with gold; it gleams in her hair, it makes fine shadows of the lines at the corners of her eyes. Once Anton had thought those lines were carved by weariness. Now he knows they are traces of her rare but luminous smile. She checks the curtains, pulls them more tightly closed. Then she sets the candle on the floor beside the pallet near the stove—their bed, since the Egerlanders came—and slides beneath the blankets. Cool air comes with her; it raises the hairs on Anton's arms and on the back of his neck. Elisabeth blows out the light, but she doesn't settle at the edge of the pallet, far from his touch. Instead, she presses herself against his shoulder.

"I also love you," she whispers.

He finds her mouth in the darkness. His kiss is long; she allows it to linger.

PART 5

Bell Song

July 1944–May 1945

29

Summer has unleashed a punishing heat on Germany. It is only the twenty-first of July, yet already the fields are wilting, going brown around the edges, and the scent of hay hangs over dusty roads and irrigation ditches run dry. The barley has begun to lean, weeks too soon. The first harvest will be poor, and with this heat, there is little hope for a second reaping.

Anton and the boys labor in the shade beneath the cottage, mucking out the pen where the animals sleep. A pile of new straw is waiting nearby, sweet and deep, ready to be spread across the floor. Stink rises from the *Misthaufen*, clinging to the workers' damp shirts. The shade is a mercy, but even so, the day is hot. Anton has rolled his sleeves as high as he can manage; the boys have stripped off their shirts entirely. Sweat trickles down their backs as they wrestle with pitchforks and reeking loads of soiled straw.

"Can't we have sheep?" Paul asks, not for the first time.

"Where would we get sheep?" Al rejoins. "What would we trade for them?"

"I don't know, and I don't care. But their dung isn't as hard to clean up as cow's dung."

Anton says, "Sheep don't give as much milk as a cow."

"I don't like milk, anyway," Paul says sulkily.

"Of course you do. You drink more than anyone else in this family."

"Well, I'd give it all up if it meant I never had to shovel cow's shit again."

"Language," Anton says, with a warning tone.

Paul is too hot and irritable to apologize. He stabs the tines of his pitchfork into a newly uncovered cow patty. Flies buzz around him.

"Herr Starzmann!"

The boys throw down their pitchforks and run to see who has called from the lane—any excuse to shirk this unpleasant task. Anton straightens, peering over the stone wall, and finds one of the Geißler brothers shouting and waving as he hurries through the orchard.

"It's an Egerlander," Al says. "One of the fellows who lives at the church. What do you suppose he wants?"

Anton goes out to meet him. The young man is panting, his shirt every bit as soaked as Anton's.

"Father Emil has sent me," he says, "to fetch you. It's urgent; you must come at once."

"Is the father well?"

Geißler nods, blotting sweat from his brow with a kerchief. "He said you must come quickly."

Anton glances at his sons, wary now. "Has . . . anyone come for Father Emil?" If the SS had arrested the priest, they wouldn't have permitted Emil to send for Anton. But might they have forced a confession? Have the SS set a snare for Anton?

Geißler shakes his head. "No one. He only told me to fetch you, as quickly as I could."

Anton can read no fear in the man's face. No slyness, either. He must take him at his word.

"Al, Paul—you'll have to finish the work without me."

Paul groans.

"Come, now; it's nearly done. And when you've finished, you can go swimming in the river."

"You aren't going to see Father Emil like that, are you?" Al says.

Anton takes stock of himself—saturated shirt, carelessly rolled sleeves, face and trousers streaked with grime.

"No time to change," Geißler says. "The father wants you straight-away, *mein Herr*."

"Then I must go to him straightaway. I hope he'll forgive my bad manners."

Anton sets off down the lane with the Geißler boy. The young man leads him at a rapid pace, almost a jog. The afternoon's work has worn Anton thin; he would beg Geißler to slow down, but quiet dread makes him push on, despite the trembling of his limbs.

"Have you any idea what this is about?"

"None," Geißler says. "The father said nothing to me."

"But you're certain no one *unusual* had come to the church?"

"No one whatsoever. I'm afraid I can't tell you more than that, *mein Herr*."

A host of possibilities tumbles through Anton's head, each grimmer than the last. Something has gone wrong within the ranks of the Red Orchestra. One of the other messengers has been taken. Someone has proven a traitor to the cause. Or the National Socialist rats have sniffed out Anton and Emil, and the gray bus is coming for them, headed this very moment toward Unterboihingen. By the time he reaches the church, Anton is sick with anxiety, and he has begun to sweat all over again.

Young Geißler leads him to Emil's side door. "I'll leave you here. The father is expecting you; he told me to send you straight in as soon as we arrived."

Anton shakes his hand and prays Geißler can't feel his shivering, the weakness of his bones. Then he lets himself into Father Emil's small private sanctuary.

The room is simple and spare, as one would expect of a priest's quarters. Emil is waiting for Anton, seated on the edge of a narrow bed. The only other furnishings are a small writing desk and an iron woodstove. Emil's hands are folded in his lap, his back straight and resolute. He looks at Anton, graying brows raised, but Anton can't read the priest's expression.

"What is it, Emil? What has gone wrong?"

"Close the door," Emil says softly. "These young fellows from Egerland—one would expect refugees to harbor no great love for the Party, but one can never be too careful. I've been shocked and dismayed more times than I can count, when someone I'd previously thought fine and sensible professed admiration for the Führer."

That's true enough. Anton hasn't forgotten how many people rose in opposition when he and Emil proposed sheltering the refugees. Even in Unterboihingen, there are loyalists. Sympathizers. Why not among the Egerlanders?

When the door is shut, Emil whispers, "What has gone wrong, Anton, is nothing you could have imagined. And yet, it's no cause for us to fear."

"I don't understand."

"I'll tell you. You know we work in a chain of sorts, we who do . . . this work. The man I report to—the one from whom I receive my orders, and your orders—he received a telegram this morning. Yesterday there was an *attempt*."

The wet shirt turns to ice against his skin. He takes Father Emil's meaning at once. No need to clarify; there is only one end we are working toward, we who resist.

"Only an attempt? It wasn't successful, then."

"No. Not this time."

Not this time, or any time before. They have tried it in beer halls and museums, on parade routes and in the air while the Führer flew back from Smolensk. Tried and failed, again and again. The beast will not lie down and die.

"What happened?" Anton says.

"It was at his stronghold in Prussia—the one he calls the Wolf's Lair. A briefcase, stuffed with explosives—carried in, would you believe it, by one of his own colonels."

"Did the colonel know what he was carrying?"

"Oh yes. He was quite complicit. No one is certain, yet, just what went wrong. The bomb exploded. Four men died, but not the fellow we want dead—not the one who counts. Though I dare say he was somewhat surprised. His trousers were ripped to shreds, I hear—he can't have escaped without injury. But he is as stubbornly alive as ever. Showing off his torn-up trousers, by my friend's account, and bragging that he is invincible."

Anton sighs. He can see what will unfold next. The SS won't hesitate to track down those directly responsible—surely they have names already. Soon enough, they will sing. And everything Anton and Emil have worked for—all they've built, one scrap of paper at a time—will crumble.

"It's over, then," Anton says. "We've failed. If it hadn't happened in the Wolf's Lair—if it had been a crowd on some city street, there might be some question of who was responsible. But now—"

"We?" Emil says. "No, not we. This was not our resistance, but another—one I didn't even know existed until I read the telegram. And, Anton, this resistance came from inside the Wehrmacht. It's no mistake, and no coincidence, that a colonel was involved."

Slowly, Anton sinks onto the stool at the writing desk. He'd had no idea there was resistance among the military. Nothing in his experience, his short but memorable service with the Wehrmacht, has led him to expect resistance. And to hear that senior officers are involved . . . The news robs him of sense for a long moment. He paws at his trouser pocket, searching for his pipe, before he recalls that he is in his shirt-sleeves, drenched in sweat and stained with grime—and at any rate, he is in Father Emil's private residence. He can't smoke here.

"The Wehrmacht?" Anton finally stammers. "How can this be? It's the last place I'd look for opposition."

Emil says, "The resistance is everywhere. Didn't I tell you once that love couldn't be erased from the world so easily?"

"Those brave, determined men—"

"Those poor men. The perpetrator must have been arrested already. How not? If the plan had come off, he'd be lauded as a hero. Now I'm afraid he'll meet a swift and unjust end."

While the Führer goes on crowing about his immortality.

Anton and Emil lapse into silence, a moment of reflective appreciation for the courageous soul who almost managed to rid the world of Adolf Hitler. May God grant him peace in eternity.

At length, Anton says, "What does this mean for us? How many times, now, have would-be assassins attempted to kill that creature with explosives? And if your telegram is accurate, this plan nearly succeeded. No one can hope to try again. He is already guarded day and night, I hear; no one will ever be allowed in his presence with any sort of package in his hands."

"You're right about that." Emil's smile comes very close to smugness.

"Even if one of our company wasn't responsible, it seems we still must give up all hope. His guards will be warier than ever before."

"We will succeed where the others failed."

"God help me, but I can't imagine how."

Emil leans toward him, across the narrow space of that small, humble room. He whispers what he knows. "We don't intend to use explosives, Anton. We'll rely on something far more subtle, when the time is right. Poison—slow-acting enough that it will never be detected by his food tasters, until it's too late to save him."

"Poison."

"I know very little, of course, for safety's sake. But I do know this: we've a man positioned already, capable of delivering our blow. It hardly seems right to call it a 'blow' at all. Only a small drop—perhaps two or three—and we'll claim our victory at last. Slow and steady—slow and unstoppable. That's how we'll win, my friend."

30

By the time the full heat of summer has descended, most of the Egerlanders have moved away. They have found jobs and homes in the cities, in Hamburg and Cologne, in Frankfurt and Düsseldorf. The Hornik family is no exception; Frau Hornik has found a steady job in a munitions factory in Cologne.

"I'll earn enough to keep the three of us alive," she says.

"That is something," Elisabeth answers, twisting her kerchief in anxious fingers. Beyond the railway platform, the train's whistle cries. The whole family has gathered to bid the Horniks farewell. The sun makes them all squint, but only Elisabeth blinks and dabs at her eyes when she thinks no one can see. "But are you sure you don't want to stay with us? City life can be so dangerous."

Frau Hornik takes her hands. "You've been so kind, Elisabeth—all of you have. You must know we aren't ungrateful. But it's time we made our own lives again. It's time we got on with it. Besides, you can't go on sleeping on the floor forever." She lays a hand on each daughter's head. "Millie, Elsie, say goodbye to your friends. The train will be here soon."

The girls begin to weep as they embrace Albert. Each gives him a kiss on the cheek—one the right, the other the left. Al can't bring himself to look at his brother or at Anton; his face is redder than a ripe apple.

"We'll write to you," says one of the twins. Anton thinks it might be Elsie. The other says, "Will you write back?"

"Yes, of course," Al replies, though he keeps his eyes on the ground and shuffles his feet. "I will, if you like."

The girls ruffle Paul's blond hair. They kiss little Maria on her forehead. Frau Hornik kisses the girl twice, and says rather sternly, "Be a little angel for your mother. Don't drive her to distraction. If you do, she'll write and tell me, and then I won't be able to send you any paper dolls from Cologne."

Frau Hornik takes Anton's hand. "I can't thank you enough for all the kindness you've given—you dear, good man."

"It's no more than anyone would do."

"It's a good deal more than most people would do. You saved us, you and Elisabeth—it's simple as that."

When it's time to say farewell to Elisabeth, Frau Hornik folds her in sisterly arms. Elisabeth presses herself against her friend's shoulder, trying to hide her tears. She remains in the woman's embrace for a long time, until the train pulls alongside the platform and hisses to a stop. Only then does Elisabeth lift her face and let Frau Hornik go.

The engineer calls the departure. The Horniks hurry onto the train before they can change their minds. The girls call out the window—*"Auf Wiedersehen, auf Wiedersehen"* and *"ahoj."* Anton stands in the hot sun with his wife and children, waving as the train pulls away, coughing in its smoke. The shriek of its whistle, the rumble of its wheels, cover the sounds of weeping, but nothing can hide the quick, darting motion as Elisabeth dashes tears from her eyes.

As they walk slowly home, Elisabeth waits until the children have run ahead before she speaks. There is no sense upsetting the children, causing them to worry over playmates. "I hate to think what may happen to them in a big city."

It has been several months since Stuttgart was last bombed, but no one who is wise ever feels complacent. And only the good Lord can say how Cologne fares, or what might be in store for that place.

Anton takes her hand. She doesn't pull away anymore, not since the Egerlanders came. Sometimes—rarely, when the children are not there to see—they even kiss. The briefest touch of their lips can set Anton's heart pounding. It still amazes his old self, the friar self, when he pauses to think of it. In the order, he was perfectly content with a chaste life. But now he knows it was only because he never knew what was missing.

That night, the bed is theirs again, and the house is quieter than it has been for months. It feels empty of everything, hollow and brittle as an abandoned snail shell. In their nightclothes, they slip beneath the warm covers, and, in unison, they sigh.

Elisabeth laughs—such a happy sound, a strange contrast to the air of melancholy. "You're thinking the same thing I am."

"We slept on the floor for—how long? Two months? Three?"

"Near enough."

"I always thought this bed was ordinary. Perfectly serviceable, but ordinary. Now I see it's soft as a cloud."

She rolls over and cuddles up against his arm. Anton's breath seizes in his chest; she has done this only once before, drawing so close of her own accord.

She murmurs, "It is a good bed, after all."

Slowly, fearful she will pull away or take flight like a frightened bird, he reaches across his body and lays his hand on Elisabeth's shoulder. She is warm through the cotton of her nightgown, and she smells like Frau Hornik's rose-petal soap. Elisabeth raises no protest. He slides his hand a little lower, tracing the graceful curve of her rib cage. He enjoys the feeling of a woman in his arms—and never thought to enjoy it until now. Oh, you friars and monks, you dedicated priests. If you only knew!

He asks her, "Will you be all right, now that the Horniks have gone? I know how much you loved caring for a family in need."

"I only hope I gave the Horniks more happiness than I got from them. God willing."

"You did, my darling—I'm sure of it."

"Then I will be well." She pauses. Crickets sing in the silence; from the sleepy orchard, a night bird calls. She says with a small, rueful laugh, "I'll be well once I stop worrying about them. Frau Hornik and I have promised to write at least once a week. I need only wait until she's settled in and sends me her address."

"I heard," he says with a chuckle. "Such oaths you made to one another, I have no doubt the mail carriers between here and Cologne will soon be staggering under the weight of all your letters."

The thought makes her giggle. It's such a girlish sound that it startles him. He has never thought to hear the like from his sober, quiet wife. It brings a smile to his face; soon Anton is laughing, too.

This is a small happiness, in a mad and dangerous world. But it's better than gold, better than music, to know you made another person happy. To know you've kept them safe.

31

No duty calls him out the following day—no message to carry, no organ lesson in a foreign parish. He walks to town alone, determined to spend a little of his money at the bakery—something sweet for Elisabeth, to conjure up one of her elusive smiles.

But just as he reaches the main street and turns past Möbelbauer's furniture shop, a familiar figure catches his eye, tall and blocky and gray. The man is walking on the other side of the street. There is no cane this time, no spats on his shoes—but still Anton recognizes Detlef Pohl in the space of one startled heartbeat. He blinks and darts his head to look again. Surely he is mistaken. But he can't deny what he sees: Herr Pohl has come to Unterboihingen.

This isn't supposed to happen. There is a fixed order to their dealings, a way things are done—a way things are not done. Anton goes to Pohl's towns, wherever the man is scheduled to turn up. His contact doesn't come to him. No one, so far as Anton knows, was ever intended to come to Unterboihingen. His pulse pounds in his ears, and his stomach swells with sudden sickness. Something has gone wrong. Or worse, something is about to go wrong, here and now, where any of his neighbors—or his children—might see.

Anton sees at once that he must speak to the man, find out what he is up to. But they can't speak where anyone may see. You're never alone in a town so small. He is uncomfortably aware of Franke's shop, just behind his shoulder. He can all but feel the gauleiter's eyes watching him, prying into his back, into his soul. He ignores the feeling and walks on without any show of fear or hurry until he has drawn abreast of gray Herr Pohl. By chance, each man looks up at the same moment. Their eyes meet across the street, briefly and blandly. Anton turns and goes casually toward the church. But before he reaches St. Kolumban, on an empty stretch of road, he steps across a drainage ditch—dry, in the late-summer heat—and hides behind the crackling hedge that conceals the oldest corner of the graveyard.

He counts seconds. Then minutes. He peers through tiny spaces between yellow brambles and twigs shedding their first leaves—autumn is already eager to begin. There is Pohl, turning down this very road, strolling unconcerned in the direction of St. Kolumban.

Anton waits. He saves his breath until the man is close enough to hear. Then he whispers, "Pohl. I'm here."

The man gives no obvious sign of having heard, but he alters course and slows. He bends near the drainage ditch, as if he has found something of interest in the dust—a dropped coin, some other artifact intriguing enough to catch a fellow's eye on a lazy day. He straightens and looks up at the sky, as if wondering whether rain might come. Anton could roar with the torment of waiting. Pohl takes his pipe from his pocket, fiddles with a box of matches, and strikes a single, pale flame alight and dips it into the bowl of the pipe, as if time is his for the spending. Anton can only tremble and pray. He has thought Detlef Pohl a friend—or if not a friend, then at least a reliable colleague. Has he misjudged the man? Have they shared too much information; does Pohl know too much? Perhaps the man has been on the wrong side all along—a sour note planted deliberately among the players in the Red Orchestra. Now he has come to seek Anton out, to exact the vengeance of the National Socialists. This is the way it all falls apart.

Pohl draws on his pipe. A tail of smoke drifts into the hedge and hangs here, overwhelming Anton's senses with its rich odor. He can just see the man's back—blocky shoulders, the gray wool of his tailored jacket—through the tightly knit branches.

Anton whispers, "Are we alone?"

"Yes."

"What are you doing here, man? I thought you weren't to—"

"Listen carefully, Herr Starzmann." Pohl pauses to enjoy his pipe again, but despite his casual air, there is no mistaking the urgency in his voice. "I haven't much time, and neither have you. I've taken a risk, coming to you—but I had to take it. I had to warn you."

Anton goes cold, down to the rapidly numbing soles of his feet. "Warn me?"

"There's a man in your town—a gauleiter."

Anton waits. He says nothing. The quiver of Möbelbauer's reddening face replays in his mind. That day in the market square, when Anton stepped between Elisabeth and that despicable man. When he said to Bruno Franke, *Say one more word to my wife.*

"He suspects you are up to treason."

"Of course he suspects. He's the gauleiter."

"Listen, my friend," Pohl says. "He *truly* suspects you now. This goes beyond a gauleiter's natural peevishness."

"All right," Anton says. "I'm listening."

"You convinced this fellow, this gauleiter, to give up his Hitler Youth program in favor of some musical group."

Anton tries to speak, but his throat has closed tight. Distantly, beyond the welling blackness of his panic, he feels a certain awe, amazement at what a network of eyes and ears can uncover.

"Your gauleiter has figured you out. He has realized you never intended this music program to honor the Führer, as you'd originally told him. He knows now that you only meant to keep the children of this town from participating in Hitler Youth and the League of German Girls."

"How?" His tongue, dry and thick, can barely form the words. "How do you know all this?"

"I only know what I'm told."

"Then how do *they* know—the ones who told you?"

The only plausible scenario plays itself out in Anton's mind, rapidly, dizzying him with the plain, clear sense of it. Möbelbauer himself told all of this to someone—spilled out his suspicions into some convenient ear or scrawled his foul report on a scrap of paper. It was only by chance that the ear Möbelbauer chose feels friendlier toward Anton than toward the NSDAP.

Another chilling possibility occurs. Has Franke already sent his letters? Has he notified his contacts in the Party, convinced them that the sleepy village of Unterboihingen harbors an enemy? The Red Orchestra knows Anton has been compromised—so, then, they must have intercepted one of Möbelbauer's letters. But how many did the gauleiter send? Was there only one, or are there a multitude of messages working their way across Germany, riding along the black tracks of the railway? How many have reached their destinations already?

"I have a family," Anton blurts.

"I know. You told me as much, once—poor fool. Your family is why I've come." He puffs on his pipe again, an act so leisurely it makes Anton want to scream with rage, with blind despair. "I've come to tell you that you should stop the work immediately. No more carrying messages. Stay here and lie low. Most of all, do not cross the gauleiter. We will find someone else to carry on the work."

"No." He says it quickly, but with utter conviction. He doesn't want to stop. He wants to be a part of this; he needs to be a part of it. The resistance is his calling, as surely as he was called to be a husband and father.

"Listen to me, Anton. The only thing that's saving you now is the fact that this town is an utter backwater. Who in the Schutzstaffel can afford to pay attention to what goes on in Unterboihingen? This place means nothing, not when there are students in Munich painting *"Widerstand"* all over the buildings, and feral boys roaming the streets, hunting down the leaders of the Hitler Youth. There was a resistance march in Frankfurt—did you know? It didn't last long, to be sure; I heard bullets were fired on the crowd, though I don't know if anyone was killed. As long as these disturbances occur in the big cities, where a greater number of people may heed the message of resistance, the SS won't trouble themselves with you. But make no mistake: as soon as our friends in black have cleared up their schedules, they will descend on this town and take you. They will execute you and your priest, both."

"Father Emil? They know about him, too?" It's an absurd question. Of course they do. They must, if they know so much already.

"Lie low," Pohl says again. "For the sake of your family, take no more risks. Now I must be gone; I've stopped here long enough already. May your God keep you safe, Herr Starzmann."

Pohl vanishes swiftly from the roadside, but Anton remains hidden. He can still smell the pipe smoke, trapped among the leaves of the hedge, but he is utterly alone. He crouches on his heels behind the hedge and prays, though his thoughts are a useless jumble. In all this time, through his months of buoyant hope, he never really understood that this was what he risked, that this might be his consequence.

Yet now the hour has come. Now he must decide what he will do. *God give me strength. God give me some clear direction. Do I fight on, or do I yield to the enemy? Have the forces of evil silenced me at last?*

When he has mustered strength enough to stand, he rises on trembling legs and takes to the road again. God has provided no answer to his frantic prayer, but there is no question in his mind what he must do next. He goes straight home and climbs the cottage's staircase in a daze. He finds Elisabeth sewing in her chair.

She looks up, smiling. There is a sheen to her dark hair, a bloom of health and happiness. "Back so soon?" But when she sees the desolation on his face, she drops her sewing in the basket and hurries to his side.

"What's the matter, Anton? What has happened?"

He won't keep the truth from her; he can't any longer. No matter what it costs him, he must come clean.

"Are the children in?"

"They're outside, playing."

"Good. I must speak to you alone."

They sit close together on the sofa, and, holding her hand—her hand which grows colder by the moment—Anton tells Elisabeth everything. Somehow, his voice remains steady. He speaks low and level, with a grim sort of calm, while Elisabeth stares into his eyes, pale-faced and frightened. When he has finished—when he falls silent, waiting for her judgment—she breathes deeply, struggling to summon her voice. She shakes her head slowly, as if trying to clear the fog of terror from her mind.

"You must stop," she says at last. "You can't go on defying the Party."

"Do you mean . . . stop the band?"

"Of course."

He had been prepared for her to say, *You must stop carrying messages*, as Pohl had done. He had even been prepared for her to leap up in fright, to try to flee with the children once more. But he'd never thought she would say this.

"I can't, Elisabeth. I can't do that." Take away the children's music— take away their joy. Take this town's voice, when we have only just learned how to sing.

"*Why* can't you?" she demands. "Why is it so important that you go on risking your life—your family's lives, Anton!—for some silly marching band?"

He opens his mouth to speak, but he can find no words—no explanation she will accept. He wrings his fists, a useless expression of despair. He must make her see what it means to teach again, to lead children away from the dark into the pure, sweet light of happiness.

But he can't make her understand unless he tells her the rest—why he is a friar no longer.

Anton has never confessed to anyone what happened at St. Josefsheim—what happened to him, and the children he lost. He never even told his sister. But Elisabeth's fear is there before him, written on her face. In the trembling of her lips, in the coldness of her hands, he can see that she has reached the end of her courage. She is ready to break from him and run to safety—or to the illusion of safety, a cruel mirage in a world distorted by war. That morning long ago, when she took the children—their little knapsacks stuffed hastily with their belongings— Anton had thought his heart would shatter as he watched his family walking away. Now it would only be worse if she were to leave. The love he bears for his family is greater now, greater than he can comprehend. It has grown until it has consumed him. It is all of him, the full weight and substance of his soul.

He must keep Elisabeth's trust at all costs. And so he must find the words, despite his fear. He holds nothing back.

This is why I am no longer a friar. This is why I can never be redeemed.

"I was eighteen when I joined the order. I felt so grown-up then, but I look at Albert now, and it shocks me. I was a boy—just a boy, Elisabeth, barely older than Al. But young as I was, I knew I'd heard the call of God. I went where He directed.

"Early on, when I was scarcely out of my novitiate, the leaders of my brotherhood noted my skill with music. I was entirely self-taught"— he smiles feebly—"as I still am. But they were taken with my humble talents. They asked me to devise a program for children, which I gladly agreed to do. But the father took me aside and said, 'These are not just any children, Bruder Nazarius. They are the most unfortunate innocents God ever made. They are not whole, not capable like so many other little ones. And worse, they have been abandoned—surrendered to our order for care. Some cannot speak. Some have twisted limbs, or little control over their bodies. They suffer from seizures, or blindness and deafness. Most will remain like children forever, no matter how long they live. They are not ordinary children, but I promise you, Brother, once you come to know them, they are extraordinary. And it is our calling to give these little ones everything their own families never could: a sound education, opportunities for happiness . . . and love.'

"When I first began my work, there were few people, even in my order, who thought those children were capable of learning. But music is a kind of magic, a miracle. It can reach into a person's mind, even into his soul, and touch the places words never can. Music is the great key; it can open any lock. My students took to their lessons readily. They embraced learning as wholly as any other children would. And the music—my teaching—gave voice to the voiceless."

Mute with sympathy, Elisabeth takes his hand. Anton draws an unsteady breath, reluctant to continue. But the story must be told. He presses on, no matter how it pains him.

"As the war came on and Hitler's actions grew more despicable, many in the order told themselves it couldn't really happen. Not to us."

"What couldn't happen?" Elisabeth's voice is dull, low. She knows how he will answer, but she must hear it for herself, to be sure.

"The T4 Program."

She covers her face with her hands. "Dear God."

Who can choose the worst of our government's crimes? If you point to any execution, any plan of extermination, and you say, *This is the worst, the vilest thing we have ever done*, then you excuse, in part, all the rest. There is no darkest deed for Adolf Hitler and the wolves who follow him. He is one deep pit of foul black evil, and day by day, we sink farther below the surface. There is no act more terrible than the rest.

In the T4 Program, they called the broken ones, the imperfect, *life unworthy of life*. Little children, even infants, were torn from their mothers. When families protested, they took the rest of their children, too, even the healthy and whole. Or they sent the fathers off to war, to the front lines in the east, to be ripped apart by machine-gun fire.

Bishop von Galen, in Münster, called the program plain murder. And when his loyal priests distributed his sermon, the SS took three of those good men into the public square and cut off their heads, like rabbits ready for the spit. The summer of '41 was dark. The sky reeked of oily smoke, black with the stench of burning bodies.

"I knew . . ." Anton goes on; God alone can say where he finds the strength to continue. "I knew they would come for our children some-day. Some of my brothers denied it could really happen, but somewhere in my soul, I knew. I also knew there was nothing I could do to stop the SS when they came. So I went on with my life, teaching my little ones as best I could, giving them all the love the world could not. And I prayed; I begged God, night and day, to spare my students—and me."

He falls silent. After a long, trembling pause, Elisabeth says, "Did you oppose them? When they finally did come?"

"We did, every way we could think to do it. We pleaded, we threat-ened, we made barriers with our own bodies, even knowing what they would do to men of the cloth who crossed the Führer. But they were armed, when they came . . . and the brothers, of course, were not." He shuts his eyes, grappling with the pain, the terrible, sharp rebuke of memory. "But what haunts me, Elisabeth—what I can never forgive—is this: I did not fight as hard as I might have. When my time came to face judgment—when the gun was pointed at my chest—I chose my own life over theirs. I saved myself, instead of the innocent."

She says nothing. Her hand twitches in his grip.

"But I knew, Elisabeth—I *know* what they did, what they still do to the men who wear the uniforms. Those men are victims, too—some of them, anyway. Not all are consumed by evil. Some do only what they must, to spare their own children from death. Knowing that, I stepped aside. I didn't resist as forcefully as I could have done, because in that moment, I couldn't choose between the soldier's pain and my own. But I made the wrong decision. I know that now; I have known it every moment I've lived since then. I should have forced that man to kill me.

I should have made his every move an agony; I should have plagued him with guilt. It wasn't his choice, to take the children, and he took no pleasure in his work. But who suffered? Who died that day? The little ones. The ones I was meant to protect. God may forgive me someday, but I will never forgive myself."

Elisabeth seems to know there is more to his story. She squeezes his hand gently, a gesture that says, *Go on.*

"After they took the children, my order was disbanded, of course. I went back home to Stuttgart and lived with my sister for a time. She had been a nun, and her order, too, was dissolved. We were a comfort to each other, but we were both grieving for what we had lost.

"Then I was drafted into the Wehrmacht. You know about that, I suppose; you've heard me tell the boys. There isn't much to report, beyond that one jump over Riga. My injured back got me out of the service, and once I was free, I swore I'd never go back."

"Your back isn't injured. You're fit as can be."

Despite his sadness, Anton smiles. "I suppose that was my first act of resistance. I felt a coward, leaving the Wehrmacht when so many other good men, conscripted like me, remained. But my entire soul, my whole being, revolted at the thought of aiding the Party in any way. They had taken everything I'd loved. I would never serve them again. They could kill me for it, but I wouldn't serve."

He has talked this well of memory dry. He sags back against the sofa, his chin falling toward his chest, crumpling in despair. Elisabeth takes his arm; she braces him. "Let's go out for a walk. It's a lovely day."

It's the last thing Anton wants, to be among sunshine and blooming flowers when he knows he has failed. He has drawn the eye of the enemy to his sanctuary, and now it all must end. He thinks, *If I hear the laughter of my children now, my heart will break; my mind will turn itself inside out; I will become a ghost where I stand.* But Elisabeth pulls him to his feet and leads him toward the door. He can't let go of her hand, and so Anton follows.

They walk in silence down the lane, past the orchard full of breezes and whispers. There is a fresh smell in the sky, a crisp blue scent of rain to come. From the pasture behind the cottage, he can hear the milk cow lowing. In the distance, as if in lazy reply, the bells of St. Kolumban ring the hour.

Elisabeth stops. She turns toward the sound, listening to the bells chime with her face to the easy wind. The notes roll fat across the land, golden and round. Anton watches her, that resolute face softening with pleasure, softening so fractionally he could miss the change if he weren't her husband, if he didn't love her beyond reason or life. As the bells die away, leaving only their echo behind, Anton thinks he should speak— apologize, perhaps, or make some excuse as to why he can't stop, why he must fight on. But Elisabeth speaks before he can.

"I met Paul when I was very young. I had just moved out of my parents' home; I was only seventeen. I took a job as a maid, at one of those grand old castles—Lichtenstein." She smiles and lowers her face for a moment, sheepish at the memory. "I thought it would be romantic to work in a castle, silly girl that I was. But the work was very hard; I cleaned day and night for the owners, forever on my feet, and all of us—the maids, I mean—were expected to be on our best behavior. Even when we weren't at the castle, when we came and went on the trains, we were required to look flawless and modest, and behave with perfect obedience and charm. The strain was enough to drive a girl mad.

"Paul was a botanist, fresh out of university. He'd been hired that summer to tend the gardens at Lichtenstein. It was his first job, too. He had seen me across the grounds and—" She laughs, suddenly shy, and tucks a stray curl behind her ear. "I suppose he liked me when he first saw me, though I still can't think why. There were prettier girls on the payroll. I knew I was nothing special.

"One day, I went into a servants' passage to clean it—you know, one of those dark, narrow ways between the walls. They always made me think of a mouse's burrow; I shivered every time I had to enter one.

But there was Paul when I opened the door. He'd been coming from the other direction, with his gardening tools in a bucket and dirt all over the knees of his trousers. He dropped his bucket when he saw me standing there in my prim little uniform, with my dusting rag in my hand." She laughs softly. "I'll never forget the sound his bucket made. I thought we would both be in trouble for it. But no one came to see about the noise. We were entirely alone.

"Paul said some sweet words to me—I can't remember now just what he said—and my heart was captured. I was sure I'd never seen a man so fine in all my life. From that moment on, I did everything in my power just to catch a glimpse of him. I must have washed every window in that castle ten times a day, merely for the excuse to look down and find him in the garden below, digging in the soil.

"It didn't take us long to realize we could meet in the servants' passage. We had absolute privacy there, as long as we were careful to whisper. And we did meet there, almost as often as we liked. But we never did anything sinful. It was all holding hands and gazing into one another's eyes—just the sort of things a foolish girl of seventeen dreams of doing in a romantic old castle.

"It looked terrible, of course, to meet in secrecy. I can see that now, as a grown woman—but neither Paul nor I understood it then. We were in love; that was the only thing that concerned us. But when our employer realized what we were doing, he sent me back to my parents with a scorching letter in my pocket. I was meant to give the letter to my father, so he could read all about my low morals and punish me for it. I didn't know what to do. Of course, I planned to burn that letter before my parents could see it, but even without the note, I would be obliged to explain why I'd been sent away from my work, and I didn't know whether my parents would really believe I'd done nothing wrong.

"I was on the train, heading home with tears in my eyes—absolutely certain I would never see Paul again—when I realized he had boarded the very same train. He came down the aisle of my car, looking for me, calling my name. I remember he even lifted one man's hat, as if he thought I might have hidden beneath it. I jumped to my feet; I'm afraid I jostled everyone around me terribly, but I didn't notice at the time. When Paul saw me, he said nothing more, but he pushed his way to my side, and I kissed him, right there in front of everyone. I didn't care one bit who saw or what they thought of us. I was done caring what other people thought. All that mattered was that Paul and I were together.

"Paul took the letter and tore it up, right there in the aisle of the train car. He threw it out the window. I'll never forget the sight of those bits of paper fluttering away in the wind as the train left the station. He said, 'There's no shame in anything we've done. We can't let that sour old Herr push us around.'

"I told him, 'I can't go back to my parents. Even without the letter, they'll know I was dismissed, and they'll soon guess why. My reputation is ruined.' And Paul said, 'Then don't go home. Marry me instead.'"

She pauses. Still holding Anton's arm, she stoops toward the tall grasses and picks a simple blue flower. She twirls the stem in her fingers; the flower spins.

"We did marry. That same evening, in fact, as soon as the train stopped at Stuttgart. We scarcely had two coins to rub together, but with each other, we felt we were more than blessed. Those were some of the happiest times in my life, though we were so very poor. We made do with what we had and never felt we lacked the finer things in life. What does one need, beyond love?

"Soon enough, Albert came along, and little Paul not long after. We moved here to Unterboihingen when Paul was a baby, just before Maria was born, because of his allergies. He couldn't take the city air, the poor little mite—he used to cough all night until he was too weak to cry. I feared if we didn't get him out of the city, he would die—and once we arrived in Unterboihingen, he began sleeping through the night again. He thrived. We all thrived here, in fact, though I'd been sure I could never come to love country life—not truly. In a farming community, there was always plenty of work for Paul; he improved many of the farmers' holdings, with his knowledge of plants and the earth.

"But then, shortly after Maria was born, it all fell apart. Paul cut himself—such a simple thing. The cut wasn't deep, but the wound festered. And then . . . he was gone, almost before I could realize that his death was a possibility.

"I look back on the time I spent with him, and it seems a miracle. I knew things weren't right with the nation—beyond the boundaries of our private happiness, I was aware the world was falling under some dark shadow. But I still felt safe, secure, for I had my husband, and I thought, 'God will soon set everything right. He won't allow evil to go unpunished.' I had my little family—what could truly go wrong? I would give anything to go back to those times."

She turns to him, eyes brimming with a sudden, forceful passion. "Do you think me terrible? Because I—"

"Because you still love Paul? No." Anton brushes her cheek, tucks the stray curl behind her ear before she can reach for it. "He sounds like a wonderful man. If I'd known him, I think I would have loved him, too. Your devotion does you credit."

"I wonder, when I get to Heaven someday, will I be his wife, or yours?"

Anton doesn't ask which she would prefer.

"I understand," Elisabeth says. She bends the stem of her flower, crushing it in her fingers, and the scent of green sap rises between them. "I understand why you're doing it. What you said about the children you taught—I understand why you can't leave the Party alone. God knows, none of us should leave them in peace. None of us should allow them to work this evil without any resistance. But it's all I can manage, to care for my children. To see that my children survive." She pauses and closes her eyes. In the silence, a dove calls from the trees overhead, nasal and lazy in the August heat. "I think, sometimes—sometimes, I am sure—that God will punish me. For not doing more. We are meant to care for our neighbors as if they're our brothers and sisters, aren't we? What kind of a Christian am I, if I turn my back on the persecuted? But unless I turn my back and look to my own home, my babies will suffer. I can't, Anton—I can't do better than I'm doing now. God will damn me for it, but at least my children will survive."

There is only so much one person may give before it exhausts your shallow well of courage and leaves you damned and dry. Before outrage becomes commonplace, and you grow used to the horrors of this life. They count on it, the Nazis—and other villains, too. Mussolini in Italy and Baky in Hungary, Ion Antonescu, purging the streets of Old Romania—and those who, in some future time when civilized people think themselves beyond the reach of moral failings, may rise to stand on foreign soil. They want you tired and distracted. They plan to burn this world down—our old ways of being. From the ashes they will build the world anew, after a fearful pattern, after their own bleak design. But the flames can only devour what we leave unguarded. So they will force you inward, if they can, to huddle over whatever small treasures the Lord has given you. When your back is turned, that's when they'll strike the match.

"God will not damn you," Anton says. "You gave up your bed to refugees. You taught your children right from wrong. You stood by your husband, when you knew the extent of it—what I've tangled myself in, the dangers I've exposed us all to."

"About that." Elisabeth opens her eyes. Unclouded now by fear or regret, they skewer him in his place. "I don't know how much longer I can take it."

"Let me do the work you can't do. Let me fight, let me resist, when you cannot."

"You endanger my children by doing it—our children, Anton."

"The last thing I want is to harm our children."

"Then you must stop. You must. No more carrying messages, or whatever it is you do. No more visits to other towns. Möbelbauer isn't stupid. He sees the way you come and go; he must see it. How long until he realizes—?" A thought comes to her, too terrible to speak aloud, though this can't be the first time it has haunted her. She presses the tips of her fingers against her mouth. What if Möbelbauer has already realized?

"I can't stop now. We're so close, Elisabeth—so close! Everything is in place now. We're positioned to act."

"Act?" The word rises on a panicked note.

He is quick to reassure her. "Not me personally. I've done my part already. But he'll be gone soon. Dead." The Führer.

Elisabeth flinches away, recoiling from his touch, as if the suggestion is one only a madman could have made. They have ground her down so thoroughly that she can't imagine Germany without Hitler; she no longer remembers this world without war. This is how they succeed, one person at a time: one frightened mother beaten down, too exhausted to resist. And then another, and another.

"It's true," Anton says. Now, at last, he knows his wife well enough to trust her. He tells her the secret, quietly, standing so close his voice never carries beyond the rustle of the oak leaves. "We've finally got a man on the inside. Not one of the kitchen workers but someone with reliable access. It will be poison. On his food, or in his tea." You can't do it any other way. No one owns a pistol anymore—the NSDAP were quick to excise that right back in 1938. A bomb would better express the rage, the pent-up fury that pounds in our heads day after day. A length of black pipe, not much longer than a human heart, filled with jagged things like fear and nails, shards of glass and desperation, capped on either end by the hopelessness of forced silence. But there is the problem of access, now that the July attempt has failed. The Führer surrounds himself with loyalists. Like drones around a queen bee, they circle him in a tight orbit, each one ready with his sting. Anything to shield the pulsing, breeding thing at the heart of the hive. We will only have one chance to strike, so we must not miss our target. "It's a slow-acting poison, so the ones who taste his food won't know until it's too late."

"Are you sure? Is this real?"

"I'm as sure as I can be."

"When?"

"I don't know the date; I wasn't told. But now that we are poised—"

"Because I don't know how much longer I can stay, Anton. It's too much for me to bear, knowing the risks you run, and what they'll do to you if you're found out."

It's the first suggestion, the first faint intimation Elisabeth has ever made, that he matters so much—that she can't picture life now without him. She hides her eyes behind her hand and turns away.

To spare her the embarrassment—a raw emotion, suddenly exposed—Anton says, "And the danger to you and the children, of course. If I were caught, they would try to apprehend you, too." They would try. They would succeed.

"Yes," she says, briskly, glad for the rescue. "That's my point exactly. We can't risk the children any longer."

"Well, it won't be much longer now. My part is done, and the plan is in motion. Any day now, we'll read it in the newspapers: *The Führer choked to death on his turnip stew.*" With the fist of Anton Starzmann locked around his straining, crushable throat.

"Promise me," Elisabeth says, "promise me you won't do any more. Nothing else to raise suspicion, or give them any cause to . . ."

"I won't."

"Swear it, Anton. Make me believe it's really over, and I can feel some hope for peace."

"I promise you, I won't cross the Party again. We'll lie low, all of us, until we hear the news." He takes the broken flower from her hand and tucks it in her hair, just above her ear. "It's nearly over now, Elisabeth. We've almost won."

32

Practice day. The children are lined up in smart rows on the street outside St. Kolumban. They're holding their instruments before them; they're standing at eager attention. Anton promised his band that if they rehearsed their parts well, they could play at the equinox, parading down Unterboihingen's main street in their first public display. Now they await their conductor's cue with military poise. It's remarkable how still and attentive children can be when they have good enough reason for it.

He raises his baton. The horns snap up, ready. He counts them down, and in perfect unison, they begin to play.

The piece is "Schön ist die Nacht," a popular and rather sentimental tune. He allowed the children to choose their song; he suspects it must be a favorite of one of the village girls, the sweetheart of some teenage musician—Denis, perhaps, who is big and broad enough to carry the baritone without fatigue, or Erik, trombone, with his roving eye and mischievous smile.

A few students approached him rather tentatively, suggesting something from Duke Ellington or Cab Calloway. Anton had been quick to stamp out the idea. Jazz has been strictly outlawed since 1938. It is *fremdländisch*—foreigners' music, reeking of American filth and British impurity. We must give every appearance of being good and loyal Germans—outwardly, at least.

"Where have you heard Ellington and Calloway?" he asked his students, then quickly cut them off with a shake of his head. "Never mind; I don't want to know if you've gone and joined the Swing Youth. No, the band must play something solidly German, from a German composer. Nothing else will do."

"Schön ist die Nacht" has a simple, square, four-four time. It's slow enough that beginners can march to the tune, so once his students showed some enthusiasm for the safely German piece, Anton agreed they could play it.

"And now to march," Anton calls, keeping time in the air with his white baton. "Left, and left, and left—"

The band shuffles forward, their first fledgling attempt at marching. This is not a skill that comes to anyone overnight. It's far harder than it looks, to step in time while you play, and more difficult still to coordinate your movements with the fellow beside you. Anton leads the band from the church toward the town square. He can hear the occasional clash of one horn colliding with another, and now and then, a sour note as the children lose their place in the music. But they are trying; practice brings perfection.

"Schön ist die Nacht" finishes just as the band arrives at the square. A few villagers have stepped from their shops and houses to applaud the effort, to cheer the band on. Someone shouts from a balcony, "Bravo!" and one of the Kopp brothers hoots wordless approval from his truck, idling in a narrow lane.

The children shift on their feet and mutter to one another, both embarrassed and thrilled by their grand foray into the public sphere. "Well done," Anton tells them, but even as he says it, he can feel a sly prickle between his shoulders.

He turns. There is Möbelbauer, lounging against the door of his shop. Two men linger beside him: Hofer and Janz. They'd been among Möbelbauer's supporters months ago when the gauleiter shouted down the Egerlander boys.

Anton makes a note of their presence now—the loyalists creep from the woodpile day by day, emerging from beneath their hidden stones, emboldened to wear their hate proudly and openly, even here in Unterboihingen. But he only nods at them, a pleasant greeting.

Möbelbauer grunts in reply.

"What do you think?" Anton says.

Möbelbauer stands up straight. He tugs at his lapels, certain of his own importance, and swaggers out into the square. "You want to know what I think? I'll tell you. I was just standing there, wondering when you plan on teaching these youngsters some real German music."

"'Schön is die Nacht' is German."

Möbelbauer spits into the dust. "It's modern trash—practically jazz. You should be ashamed of infecting our youth with such filth, Herr Starzmann."

Hofer and Janz mutter their agreement from the sidewalk.

"This is a simple piece," Anton says. "We're working up to more complex music. Besides, one can't march to Wagner. It's not the right kind of music."

"I thought this band of yours was going to provide a way for Unterboihingen to honor our dear leader, the great values of the Party," Möbelbauer says. "That's what we agreed to. But you seem more interested in playing your Catholic tunes and this American-tainted filth. What am I to think of that? Eh? Answer me that, Anton: What am I to think?"

Even the children in the band have begun to shift uncomfortably. Anton raises a hand to settle his students, to calm their fears.

He longs to say to Möbelbauer, *You thought this band would raise you up, so Hitler could see you and honor you. Or if not the Führer, then some other man of great power. And why not? I told you to expect as much. But I've played you, better than I play the church organ. This is my band now, my group. And I will keep these children safe.*

But then he remembers Elisabeth, her desperate plea never to cross the Party again. He's already walking a thin line, where his wife is concerned. If she decides the band is too dangerous, she'll convince Anton to stop, one way or another. He knows when Elisabeth delivers her final ultimatum, begs him earnestly to give it all up, he won't find it in his heart to deny her again.

"What about 'Horst-Wessel-Lied'?" Möbelbauer demands. "'The Flag on High,' our Party's anthem? Surely that song is not too complicated for loyal German children to play."

"If you want to hear us play good German music, approved by the Party—by the Reichsmusikkammer itself—we will be happy to oblige." Anton lifts his baton; the instruments snap to position. "'Emperor Waltz,'" he calls to the children, and before they can collect their wits, he counts them into the piece.

The arrangement of the Strauss piece is far more complex than the tune they have just played, yet not nearly as difficult as the children make it seem. They understand the importance of playing poorly now—such is the connection between a leader and his band. We anticipate one another; we carry our friends. With one mind, one body, we move. The children honk and chirp through the waltz, each losing time and picking it up again, careless and unconcerned. The display of ineptitude draws a satisfying cringe from Möbelbauer.

When the band has struggled through a few more terrible bars, Anton cuts them off. His back is turned to the gauleiter; he winks at the children, and slyly, his band smiles behind the bells of their horns.

"As you can hear for yourself," Anton says, "we need more practice before we'll be ready to do justice to real German music—the great old classics in particular."

Again Möbelbauer spits. He slinks back to his friends, back to the lair of his shop. "I hope to see some improvement soon, Herr Starzmann. Otherwise, I'll be forced to believe you never had any intent of making music to honor the Führer. You should know by now, I don't consider liars to be my friends."

33

A week later, the band assembles again outside St. Kolumban.

Father Emil, leaning against the graveyard fence, calls out to Anton. "Your musicians have come far, my friend. The whole village is impressed."

"Not quite the whole village, I'm afraid."

Emil chuckles. No need to specify who is dissatisfied. "But will they be ready for the parade?"

Young Erik answers in Anton's place. "We'll be ready, *Vater*—just wait and see!"

"I have every faith in this group," Anton says. "They'll do Unterboihingen proud."

The band's marching skills have certainly improved. They can step along to the music with a respectable degree of coordination. At least they no longer run into each other; he'd begun to fear for the safety of his brass. Too many dents, and the sound will be affected forever.

Facing the band, walking backward, he counts the children into their song, and they begin in near-perfect unison.

"And here we go," he chants, in time to their music, "and left, and left, and—"

The band hasn't progressed more than a few yards when the horns stutter to a stop. One awkward crash of the cymbals rings out and is hastily silenced. Anton spins on his heel to learn what has distracted his students—and freezes, disbelieving what he sees. Beside the old church, the ivy curtain on the hillside wall shivers and stirs. The steel door creaks, groans, and then screams on its hinges as it opens. Emil staggers back from the fence into the middle of the street.

"Lord preserve us," Anton mutters.

The priest makes a hasty cross over his chest.

In the sunstruck metal doorway, a man appears. He staggers into the churchyard on legs as weak as a newborn colt's, one arm thrown up to shield his eyes from the pain of sudden light. The man breathes hoarsely; Anton can hear the rasp of his lungs from where he stands. The newcomer is wearing a brimmed helmet and the unmistakable green-gray uniform of the Wehrmacht. A soldier.

A soldier, come up like a demon from the depths of the earth.

As the man stands panting in the graveyard, wiping sweat from his brow, another appears in the doorway. Then another. The hill disgorges them more rapidly by the moment, two by two and three at a time; they scramble to get through the door, clawing at its steel jamb, tearing at one another like rats. They fight their way out of the tombal earth into fresh, clean air.

God have mercy, what are they doing here? Will Unterboihingen soon be overrun with soldiers? The Wehrmacht has resurrected the warren of tunnels, the passages that have laced the unseen depths of Germany since the time of kings. If this village becomes a regular hub for the transport of soldiers, the town will lose its precious invisibility. The bombs will find us, without fail.

Anton can't allow himself to fret about it now. There is no time for fear, no time to stand and wonder. His mind leaps into action, seizing the strange opportunity God has presented. In the unexpected appearance of the soldiers, Anton finds his chance to put Möbelbauer in his place—to disorient the gauleiter and prove to the man that his band must play on. As the soldiers assemble in the churchyard, awaiting the emergence of their commander, Anton lifts his baton again. His students, well trained, raise their horns in response, though they can't take their eyes from the spectacle unfolding outside St. Kolumban.

"'The Flag on High,'" Anton calls.

"But we stink with that piece," Denis protests. The other children mutter agreement.

"Time to stop stinking. Come on, now—" He flicks the baton, setting the rhythm, and the band begins to play.

And they play well—as well as one can hope for, considering Anton has allowed only the most cursory rehearsal of the nation's new anthem. The soldiers mass together in the shade of an oak, milling between the gravestones. They stare at the band, transfixed, as more of their number struggle up from the tunnel. Tentative smiles appear on a few soldiers' faces. The music is already making them forget the horror of the tunnels, the groping through cold and damp, the weight of the unseen earth bearing down from the blackness overhead.

But the soldiers aren't the only ones drawn to the band. A handful of spectators arrives from the center of town. They had thought to cheer the children on as they marched—but when the villagers see the Wehrmacht soldiers pulling themselves up from the earth, they stop and stare, disbelieving. They whisper behind their hands. What does this mean?

"Keep playing," Anton calls. The children's eyes dart about, and a few notes land false, sharp from tension. But they trust their conductor. They keep the rhythm. They do as their leader tells them and play on.

When the children arrive at the anthem's bridge, Anton hears a rumble on the road, feels it pulsing against the beat of the song. He knows the sound of that truck's engine. He heard it on the first day he came to Unterboihingen.

Anton glances over his shoulder. Möbelbauer, the only man in town who could possibly have known the soldiers were coming, scowls at Anton as he cuts the engine, gets out, and slams the door of his truck. Anton pins the gauleiter in place with a challenging stare. *You thought you had me, Herr Franke, but here's the proof you wanted. Here: my band playing the National Socialist anthem, even though it kills me to glorify those devils. But better this than Hitler Youth. Better this than all these boys' minds and hearts rotted by your poison. You thought you could put me out of the way—and punish Elisabeth for rebuffing you—but I've outwitted you. Now, even Wehrmacht soldiers believe I'm loyal to the cause. You can't touch me. The Red Orchestra will play the final chord. We'll outwit the whole damned lot of you.*

Möbelbauer's face darkens; it's as if he can hear Anton's thoughts, as if Anton has shouted the words for the whole village to hear. Then, with a toss of his head, Möbelbauer breaks Anton's stare and reaches into the bed of his truck. He lifts something long and black; it cleaves the air in a terrible, slow-motion arc, and comes to rest on Möbelbauer's shoulder. A rifle.

A woman in the crowd screams. Father Emil crosses himself again. The soldiers shout, rip pistols from their holsters; the music clatters to a graceless end. With dull curiosity, caught in sluggish time, Anton watches Möbelbauer point the rifle in his direction. Of course the gauleiter is armed. He is loyal to the Party, and all those loyal to the bleak cause may take lives at will. This is their privilege, power over life and death; this is the banner of terror under which the Reich marches on. Neighbor turning on neighbor, brother oppressing brother. For this power, men like Möbelbauer have blackened their souls. Their hearts are bitter with the stink of burning powder. Anton wonders, *Should I duck?* Then, with a stab of helpless agony, he thinks of his son Albert, too far back in the ranks of the marching band for Anton to reach him. He can't protect Al, but he can save whichever child is closest to hand. He moves without looking, quick as a bullet despite the shattered blankness of his mind. He grabs the nearest child by her shoulder and pushes her to the ground—and in that moment, Möbelbauer takes aim and fires.

The shot cracks the air high above Anton's head; it splits sound, muffles his ears, and an instant later leaves a high, stinging vibration wailing inside his head. But he is unharmed; his chest flushes hot, as if to prove to him that every drop of blood remains inside. He looks up, over the heads of his scattering band, following the trajectory of the shot. When his neighbors gasp, Anton breathes with them, a long, indrawn sigh of sorrow and shock.

The stork on the bell tower has burst. A cloud of feathers curls on the wind. The bird's body hits the roof tiles and rolls down the slope; where its heart should be, there is a slash of red, dark against white feathers. Its wings spread like the rays of a broken fan. The stork's body falls into the graveyard below.

The watchers, even the soldiers, give one collective groan of pity. Father Emil presses a fist to his mouth in horror. Children sob; the people of Unterboihingen shout Möbelbauer's name, clutching their chests in disbelief. The soldiers stare at the gauleiter, wide-eyed.

A few feathers drift down to the earth. They land near the lifeless bird and tumble in the breeze. Cold, robbed of his breath, Anton watches the feathers in the grass. Nothing else moves. The world has gone still.

He finds Father Emil beside him. "Our luck has fallen," the priest says quietly. "Dear Lord, what will become of us now?"

34

There are no messages to carry. Even if there were, Anton would not take them; he promised Elisabeth that much. If he broke his word and forged on with this doomed resistance, Herr Pohl would refuse to meet him, Anton has no doubt. God has left him to hang at a loose end, restless and irritable, consumed by his own dark thoughts. There must be some reason, some pattern to discern in the Lord's grand design. But if there is a lesson he is meant to learn, it's beyond Anton's means to puzzle it out.

Nothing feels more futile than hope. Armed only with that weak weapon, he marches through his days. He hopes, and he tunes in the radio, searching through the hiss of static for words he is desperate to hear. He hopes, and he scours the newspapers every day. Papers and radio alike are in the hands of the NSDAP, but surely, when our deliverance comes, even the Party will admit defeat. They will recognize their downfall. They will concede. He hopes, and he imagines the headline: *Our dear leader has choked to death on his turnip stew*; *The fury of the Reich has succumbed to his morning tea.* Hope is all that remains to Anton, so he plies it with ever greater force. He wields it even as it wanes, as it crumbles in his hand. September passes, then October. News fails to come. Hitler and his men go on, as untouched and untouchable as before. After the briefcase bomb in the Wolf's Lair, the July attempt that left him scarred but still ruthlessly alive, the Führer has taken to bragging that he is unstoppable. No hand can touch him, not even God's; no man can take his life. Even as he clings to his fraying hope, Anton has begun to believe the Führer's tale of immortality must be true.

What, then, became of the Red Orchestra's plot? Did his contacts mislead him? Were they misled by some other party, a person unknown who has played them all for fools? Little by little, the dregs of Anton's confidence drain. What's left to him is a shallow, stagnant pool. It's an insufficient supply for resistance; soon his spirit will thirst, and he will find nothing there to sustain him. How long now, until the SS remembers Unterboihingen and the two frail rebels the village contains? How much life is left to him?

As autumn gives way to the dark of winter, he turns his full attention to the children. To them, he gives the time he never gave before, the care they should have had from their father. If he had known all hope would shatter, he would have spent more time in their company. He would have built for them a world of warmth, memories to shelter them when harsher winds of war rise. He would have prayed that they might survive this endless winter and know peace someday.

They say almost five hundred thousand have died in the cities, and even in the countryside. Five hundred thousand. He must devise some way to move Elisabeth and the children to safety—to a greater illusion of safety. He must do it before the walls come down; that hope of safety will be the last and most important thing he gives his family. He will place it, tattered, in their hands, transfer hope to their keeping, and beg God that it will be enough to sustain them. Can he wait until after Christmas to send them away? Will God and the Party grant them one last Christmas together before he must tear this family apart?

But Anton hardly dares to wait so long. There is no telling when the SS will come for him. Elisabeth and the children must be gone before the SS arrive; they must be well beyond his enemies' reach. If any place in this world is beyond the reach of evil.

As the snow falls, muting the earth, he still delays what must come. *Grant me one more day of love, God, and one more, and another. One more blue afternoon with my children's voices filling the sky—this, my only music. One more sight of their breath rising in plumes against the cold, so I may know they're still breathing. Give me time enough to fix these memories in my heart. Let me write this love upon my soul. These memories will be my only comfort. This is all I may bring with me into the gray camp, and later, the chamber. This love will keep me warm inside my grave.*

Now—now that he has made time for them at last—the boys have taught Anton how to use a sling. He has learned the rhythm of the spin and the feel of the stone's weight departing. He can knock over a little house of twigs from twenty paces, fifty. There is something comforting about the action, something soothing in the way the sling and the stone and the target steal all your thoughts away. The escape is all too brief, but it is an escape. A relief, while the leather whirls in your hand.

On a bright Saturday, when the sun is glaring white on snow, Albert and Paul take him hunting. In perfect silence, except for the slow crunch of their feet on the icy crust, they follow a rabbit's tracks from the heart of the wood out into the Kopp brothers' field.

"There he is," Al whispers, pointing.

The rabbit is small, a dark spot in a sea of brightness, moving slowly along the line of the hedge, searching for any green thing in this colorless, barren season.

Al nudges his father. "You take the shot."

Anton loads his sling with a stone from his pocket. He spins it until it hums, but when the time comes to release the stone, he finds he can't do it. He can't take the rabbit's life. He looses his shot, but it lands wide, and the rabbit springs into flight. It bounds over the field, swift and afraid but with its life intact. Anton watches it go with a painful sort of satisfaction.

One morning, when the light is gray and low, he walks with the children past the home of the town eccentric, a wild-eyed old man called Eugin. Eugin is seldom seen outside his home, but today he is perched on a tiny stool just this side of his door. Each spring, the swallows nest in Eugin's eaves—they have done so for generations—and layers of old droppings have coated the ground around the house's foundation whiter than the snow. The old man's breath makes beads of ice in his heavy mustache. He is shaving pieces from a chunk of lard, clutched in his greasy hand. As Anton and the children glance his way, Eugin takes the lard delicately from the blade with his teeth. He chews with gusto, smacking his lips in that tangle of beard.

He proffers the lard in his fist. "Want some?"

"No, thank you, *mein Herr*," Maria says politely. "I've already had my breakfast."

Anton would laugh at her remark. But now, all he can manage is a faint, disbelieving gratitude that the girl has learned some manners. *I have left her something, taught her one good lesson at least. Thanks be to God for that.*

The old man's rasping laughter fades as they hurry past his house. St. Kolumban rears before them, a white edifice in a silent white world. They can see the stork's nest, a damp, black tangle of sticks piled high with snow. Untouched, unoccupied since the bird fell.

Albert says, "I don't like to see the nest like that, all covered in snow." The poor boy has been unable to forget the stork since the day the steel door opened. Anton can only imagine what violence fills his son's dreams—visions of red ripped through white.

"What do you suppose it means for us now," Al says, "since the stork is gone?"

Paul sighs heavily, kicking his feet in the snow. He doesn't like to talk about it, but Al persists: "Father Emil said it was the luck of our town."

"There is another stork," Anton reminds them. "The other one still lives."

Paul blurts out an answer suddenly, as if, all at once, something has loosed his reservations and freed his little spirit to confront that senseless death. "But the other stork will never come back. Father Emil says they mate for life. It will never come back because the nest reminds it of its dead mate, and it will never take another mate, either, because it's too heartbroken now."

Maria stares at her brother for a long moment. The vapor of her short, rapid breaths rises ever faster as she struggles not to cry. She gives up the fight and covers her face with her hands, keening. Paul blinks and shuffles his feet again. He wipes away his own tear.

"Is it true?" Maria clings to Anton's hand. "*Vati*, is it true?"

"No, darling. It isn't true." He bends to stroke her hair, to kiss her hot forehead. "Storks do find love again. In time, when it's not so sad, ours will take another mate. Perhaps they will even come back here, to our town. They might take up in the same old nest on our bell tower."

"I don't want them to come back to St. Kolumban," Paul says. "It won't be the same! It won't be *our* stork, the one we lost."

"There, there." He gathers them all in his arms, these three precious children, gifted to him by God and fate. "After a time, you won't cry over it anymore. The pain won't hurt so badly."

And spring will come, you'll see. The snow will melt away. Winter's dark can't last forever.

35

That night, Anton is sitting alone on the last stair outside the cottage. The dampness of the step has soaked through his trousers, and he is chilled, but the cold seems too insignificant to notice. He tries to blow a ring, as Father Emil did that summer when the Egerlander girls laughed in the orchard, but he can never manage it. He sends up one trail of pipe smoke after another to vanish among the stars. The red ember of his pipe is too small, surely, to be seen from above.

How has Anton been allowed to linger into winter? He knows well enough. The Americans have kept Herr Hitler distracted in France, in the Ardennes. Now Bastogne is surrounded, and Germany's recapture of Antwerp is no longer the easy maneuver it once seemed. But it's like Pohl said: as soon as their schedules have cleared up, the SS will turn their attention to Anton. There are more pressing matters now, but even in this endless war, matters will not press forever.

He thinks, *I must tell Elisabeth: Once I am gone, she should look for another man. Find a third husband who can pick up where Paul Herter and I left off.*

He must make her understand. Once they part ways, it will be forever. There can be no hope that Anton will return.

When finally the night is cold enough to make him shiver, Anton goes back inside. Elisabeth has gone to bed, but she has left a candle burning on the old kitchen cupboard. He checks the curtains to be sure they are tightly drawn. Then he sorts through the wood beside the stove until he finds just the right piece, long and heavy with a dense, fine grain.

By candlelight, in the old chair with his wife's sewing basket near his feet, Anton begins to carve. Christmas is almost here, but he has yet to make a gift for Elisabeth. He will work all night, paring away one resinous sliver at a time, until exhaustion drives the thoughts from his mind and lures him to his bed. And each night thereafter, while his family sleeps, Anton will do the same. In amber light, with one small flame, he will sit with the ghosts of memory. On the fifth night, the gift has taken recognizable shape: a figure of Saint Elisabeth, praying with her neat hands folded. On the sixth, he gives the figure Elisabeth's own face—his Elisabeth, his good wife, his brave and loyal love.

He speaks to the saint as he carves her. He whispers everything he regrets and everything he does not. In the curls of her hair, in the pleats of her gown, in the traces of a smile around her eyes, he scribes his inmost thoughts, committing them to the small, freshly made body. As if someday, in the act of running her hands over smooth, polished wood, Elisabeth will find the secrets Anton has embedded there and will finally understand.

He tells the saint, *I loved you. Never forget that. Whatever you felt for me, I loved you, every bit as much as I loved the children. Our children who live, and the children I lost—and all the people who command my love, though they are strangers. The ones who cry from their graves for justice and those whom we may yet save, if we can stop what we started long ago. Everything I have done—for you, Elisabeth, and for God—I have done out of love.*

Christmas, when it comes, is quiet. No bombs fall on Stuttgart, and, thank God, no bombs fall on our village. The children are happy with their nuts and oranges, the simple wartime toys for Paul and Maria. Albert is too grown up now for toys, so Anton gives him books instead. He has saved another gift for his eldest son, his quiet, thought-ful boy—but he must wait to present it until the time is right.

Anton has decorated Elisabeth's box with the blue silk ribbon, the one his sister gave him long ago. Elisabeth unties it; she looks inside. Her eyes shine with tears as she takes Saint Elisabeth in her hands. She already seems to read with her fingertips the words Anton prayed into the fragrant wood, and when she lifts her eyes to thank him, she is smiling.

36

The new year is cold and hard, bitter with frost. Elisabeth has been tense and irritable since just after Christmas, as if she can sense all the things that must change, if life is to go on: the loss of Anton, the dissolution of her family. Soldiers have been through the tunnel again, breaking free of the frozen earth on New Year's Day. Little by little, the world is stripping away our shelter, tiny Unterboihingen. The world is tearing back the curtains. Elisabeth's eyes turn to the sky at the slightest sound, the booming of grouse in the fields or the rumble of a truck's engine down Austraße Road. No place in all the world is safe, if Unterboihingen is not.

In her vigilance, her wariness, it's Elisabeth who hears the news first. She went to town with chicken soup and fresh-baked bread, a relief for Frau Sommer, the mother of a sick child. But she hurries home with the news on her tongue, and finds Anton cleaning his old pocket watch beside the fire. Her cheeks are still chapped from the cold.

She says, "Do you remember when I told you to sell the instruments—when the SS was paying for brass?"

"Yes." How could he forget?

"They aren't paying anymore, Anton." Her brow furrows. "They're *taking* brass now. Confiscating it."

He shakes his head. A small worry, now—and a wonder, that he'd ever been troubled by something so insignificant. "They won't take the band instruments. It really is the wrong type of brass; I told you the truth when I said as much."

"No." She drops to her knees beside him, clutching his sleeve. "Anton, they're taking church bells. They've already taken the bells from Wernau and Kirchheim. Frau Sommer's family lives in Wernau. They've written her and told her all about it. She showed me the letter."

The watch falls from his hands and thumps the wood floor. Elisabeth retrieves it, but Anton hardly knows what to do with the thing. He winds its chain around his hand, tighter and tighter still.

He will not let Hitler take St. Kolumban's bells. But how he is to stop it from happening, Anton hasn't the slightest idea.

Elisabeth can see his resolve building, breaking through weeks' worth of surrender, and it frightens her. "Anton, you mustn't—"

But he must. They are coming for him, anyway. It's only a matter of time, a matter of freed schedules. His destruction is assured, his death written in stone. What can it matter now, if he rattles Hitler's cage?

I may as well make myself a thorn in the wolf's paw. One last time. God willing, he will succeed in this, if in nothing else.

"Anton, your hand!"

The watch chain has bitten deeply into Anton's flesh, and his fingers are turning purple. Trembling, he unwinds the chain. Elisabeth takes his one hand between the both of hers and rubs it until feeling returns.

"Listen, Elisabeth. This is what we must do."

"No, Anton." She can sense what's coming. She shakes her head, but the protest is weak. She knows already what must be done.

"Yes, my darling. Listen to me. You and the children will go to Stuttgart. You'll live with my sister." He hasn't asked Anita to take them in—this desperate plan has only just occurred to him—but he knows his sister will agree. Anita would never turn away Anton's family.

"Why?"

"It may be safer for you there."

"Safer in Stuttgart? Anton—"

"Now that soldiers are coming and going through that damned tunnel, Unterboihingen isn't the haven it was."

Elisabeth shakes her head again, more adamantly now. "No place is as safe as Unterboihingen."

"Then no place is safe at all. Elisabeth, you know it's true." He pauses, gathering his thoughts and his quailing heart. He says carefully, "You can't be here when—"

"Don't say it. Don't think it. If we go anywhere, you'll come with us."

"They'll find me." The SS. The rifle against his chest. "They already know my name. What was that business with the stork if not some kind of threat? An attempt to silence the band, to warn me . . ." He sighs and works his fingers up under his lenses to press hard against his eyes. His thoughts are tumbling, impossible to sort. "Möbelbauer must have told them about me—*them*, whomever he speaks with, his friends in the Party. He hates me—"

"If he hates you," Elisabeth says, resolute, "it's only because of me. I told him I would never betray our marriage. That's why he's bent on destroying us both. So you see, it's my fault. If you stay here, then I will stay, too."

He takes her hands, muted for a moment by his admiration for her. What strength, what bravery! If only he were half as courageous. He kisses her palms. "It's not your fault—never blame yourself. But think of the children, Elisabeth. We have a duty to keep them safe."

She doesn't try to argue; she knows he is right. "How much longer do we have? Together?"

"I don't know. But the sooner you leave, the better. We've waited too long already, and the waiting is dangerous."

She looks away, refusing to see the sense in his words. Tears have burned her cheeks. But still, she doesn't argue.

"Can you have the children ready to travel by tomorrow morning?"

"I suppose, if I must."

"Good. I'll write a letter for my sister. You must give it to her when you meet."

Elisabeth's eyes flash. "She doesn't even know we're coming? Anton—"

"Anita will take you in, and gladly . . . but she'll want word from me, too. And I want to say my farewells to her, before I'm taken. She was always good to me."

◆ ◆ ◆

At the train station, he tells the children brightly that they are going to visit their aunt Anita—though they have never seen her before. They do not know her.

"We'll all be back together soon," he says. But he can feel Al's hard stare as he says those words. The boy can tell when he is being deceived.

Anton takes Albert's hand, as you would do with a grown man. "I'm proud of you, son. Proud of the man you're becoming, the man you'll be someday."

He removes the watch from his pocket. Albert takes it, startled, and turns it over and over, tilting it so the polished casing gleams.

"My father gave this to me," Anton says. "I want you to have it now."

Al nods. He closes his fist around the watch. "I'll try. I'll try to make you proud." The boy is struggling not to cry, fighting with all his strength to hold back his weeping.

Anton takes him by the shoulder and leans close, so only Al can hear. "Men cry, son. All the time. Never be ashamed of your feelings. Your feelings are your compass. They guide you to what's right."

The tears break at last, spilling down the boy's freckled cheeks. "I won't tell them what's really happening," he says. "Paul and Maria."

"Not until they're old enough to understand."

He holds Paul for a long time—he is crying, too, but a boy of his age hasn't yet learned to feel shame over sorrow. Maria he scoops into his arms and covers with kisses. She is sad to part with him—she tells him so—but her eyes are dry. She pats his cheek. "You'll come be with us at our aunt's house, won't you, *Vati*?"

"Of course," he says, heart breaking. "Just as soon as I can."

Elisabeth clings to Anton. Her mouth is sweet and trembling, but her kiss tastes of bitterness and salt. There is no more time to hold her. The whistle blows; it's time for them to part.

He thought no pain could surpass that of his first great loss—the children of St. Josefsheim, boarded onto the gray bus and torn from his life forever. But as the train pulls away, rolling toward Stuttgart, a terrible emptiness settles in Anton's heart in the place where his family should be. The vastness of that void, yawning, opening wider by the moment, frightens Anton far more than any SS man with his bayonet, any tumble from a roaring plane in the sky above Riga. He stands, small and alone, waving uselessly after the train until it has shrunk to a speck in the distance.

Long after the train has disappeared below the horizon, Anton remains on the platform. He stands, hands in his pockets, rosary tangled around his fingers, watching the place where his heart vanished as the evening grows late and cold around him. He can't bear to think that one of his children might look back now and find him gone.

37

When he locates Father Emil later that night, the priest is half hidden among the ivy, with his back turned to the churchyard. He is busy with some task Anton can't see—busy at the steel door set into the ancient wall, the tunnel that runs from one village to the next, the damp hollow artery hidden under Germany's skin.

"Father?"

Emil turns. His face—Anton has never seen the priest look this way, hard and tight-jawed, fixed with a determination he seems to know is as dangerous as it is futile. His lower lip, tense, pulls open to reveal a set of bulldog teeth, small and crooked with shadows in between, avid to bite.

A second before he sees the trowel in Emil's hand, Anton smells the cement—wet and cool, with a grainy note of mineral dust.

"In mercy's name, Father—"

"There's nothing to say, Anton. I've had enough." He turns back to his work. Lifts another thick pat of cement from the bucket at his feet and slides the trowel down the line of the door, pushing the stuff deep into the crack. He smooths it with care, and with a graceful, competent motion of arm and shoulder, as if he'd been made to set bricks in mortar rather than men on the path to righteousness.

"Is anyone in there—in the tunnel?" Anton's detachment does him no credit. If soldiers are within, creeping blindly through the earth or huddled in a small white kerosene sphere of lamplight, they are still men. Men who will reach their destination after hours of terror, only to find a door that refuses to open. Men—unless they're loyal to the NSDAP. What do you call a person, a creature, who loves our dear leader more than he loves what is good?

Emil says, "If so, they'll turn around and walk back to wherever they came from."

And if someone has sealed the door on the other side? Anton can't bring himself to think of it.

"This is dangerous," Anton says, but not scolding, not warning. Merely a statement of fact. Everything is dangerous—the music; the messages; the scrape of a coin over dry paper, the black arms of Hitler's sigil erased as if they'd never been.

The trowel lowers slowly and drops into the bucket. Emil stares at his handiwork for a long time. He takes something small and white from behind his wide sash—a stork's feather. He presses the feather into wet cement and says, "They're coming for us, you know, Anton. For us—you and me."

"I know, Father."

Emil straightens his back, stretching it slowly. His gray head tips up to look at the stars, turning in their courses over black silhouettes of trees. He sighs. Then he says, slow and tired, "I'll have one last stab at the bastards before they take me down."

Anton knows he ought to clean off that trowel and use it to scrape away the cement before it sets. He ought to pull the steel door open, break the still-wet seal. Those are men down there in the tunnels, and Anton knows all too well that not all of them serve by choice. But if he opens the door, the Nazis will come pouring through. Long has he pitied men who were forced to choose between their own children's lives and another's; now he finds himself facing the same decision. And so he leaves the trowel where it lies. His loyalty is here, in Unterboihingen: with the children in the marching band; their mothers, with hollow cheeks and eyes; Frau Bread Maker, and Möbelbauer's quiet, pinch-faced wife; Christine Weber, who learned a dearer truth than "Blood and soil." Eugin, with his breakfast of leaf lard and his garden white with bird shit, and the Kopp brothers bowing, as if they are one, over a homemade wedding cake. Anger the SS enough, and they will come for us all. They will take us away to the places where we can be broken and safely contained.

"Thank God Elisabeth and your children are out of it," Emil says. "Thank God they won't be here to see." He picks up the bucket. It's heavy; it drags at him, tilting his shoulders and unbalancing his stride. He sets off through the dark yard toward his church.

Anton hurries after him. "They're coming to take the bells. Before they take us, I mean—or maybe after; I don't know."

Emil sets the bucket beside his door, the little side entrance only the priest ever bothers to use. "I'm sorry to hear it," he says, flat and defeated.

"But I won't let them do it, Father. They can't." Through the darkness, Emil watches Anton. The priest's eyes pinch at the edges with sympathy, but not enough, not enough understanding. He doesn't understand.

They already took the children. They can't have music, too. They can't have the full bronze throat of joy and sorrow. They can't take the light from the world. He remembers the parachute opening above him, the calm of his fall toward Riga.

"Those bells have rung since before the Reich existed," Anton says, his voice cracking with the strain. "And by God, I will see to it that they will ring long after Hitler falls."

Emil pauses, one hand on the doorknob, and the hard lines of his face soften. His silence says, *You really believe he will fall?*

Anton takes him by the shoulder. The rules that govern men don't permit him to do more, but Emil seems to understand. The priest nods, heartened—as much as one may be uplifted, knowing the gray buses are coming.

"You should plan how to do it," he tells Anton. "We should both plan. Tomorrow. Can you find your way back home in this darkness?"

"I can. But there's nothing for me to go home to."

"Then stay here." Emil opens the door. "I've got candles enough to work by."

38

It takes six nights for Anton and Emil to dig their pit in the unused field behind the church. They do it under cover of darkness, or by moonlight and starlight when the clouds part, for no one must know, no one must see, even those whom they call friends. They take it in turns, one swinging an old pickax into hard, frozen earth, the other working with a spade, clearing away the loosened soil. When they strike layers of stubborn, ice-hard frost, they boil kettles of snow over Emil's tiny stove. They carry the water out into darkness and pour it on the steaming ground, and in this way the earth is made to yield.

Six nights of work; they sleep by day, so weary from the digging that they dream no dreams. And then, when the pit is as deep as Anton is tall, and wide enough that a farm wagon could fit inside, they know their plan is ripe.

On the seventh night—the night of their final act of resistance—Anton and Emil ascend the bell tower together. They have draped their shoulders with lengths of heavy felt, which trails behind them as they climb. Up there, by the light of one tiny candle in a pierced brass shutter, they examine the bells. Even in virtual darkness, the ancient bells are beautiful, gleaming wherever a speck of light slides along their metal. A holy air hangs about them, captivating, sublime. Anton runs his hand over the nearest, tracing its graceful curve, and the bronze trembles beneath his palm. He can feel, in that caress, the echo of a thousand peals. The memory of these bells reaches back hundreds of years and more to a different world, when we were a different people. In the curve of their deep-bronze flanks, you can sense all the lives, long gone, that have listened to their tolling. He could never count the people who have heard the song. But he feels their presence, more numerous than stars, shuddering faintly under his touch.

He thinks, *I will take this with me, too, into the gray that waits. I will feel memory and music alive in my hand.*

Carefully, working on their knees, Anton and Emil wrap the heavy clappers in felt to silence St. Kolumban's bells. When they have finished, Anton rests his hand on one of the old bronze singers again. This time, his touch is an unspoken apology. *We must silence you for a time, my friend, though not forever. One day, when we know we are free, we will hear your voice again.*

It seems impossible, that two men should be able to move the four massive bells—especially Anton and Emil, who are no longer young. But by the grace of God, the strength comes. They free the knots in the ropes and lower each bell carefully, laying hard against the great, rough lines, struggling and panting as they ease each sacred relic to the ground. It takes half the night to coax the bells out of the tower and the other half to roll them over the ground to the dark, frozen pit. With their ropes, they lower each bell again, until it stands upright at the bottom of the grave. Down there, not even moonlight can reach them. They are invisible, swallowed up by the earth.

The first light of dawn pinks the sky; time is running out. Exhausted, aching, trembling with weakness, they shovel soil over the bells, flatten all evidence of their work, and push snow atop the disturbance. Then, wracked with weariness, they kneel on the spot and pray. They ask that God might divert their enemies' eyes from this place—make Unterboihingen invisible once again.

Neither man presumes to ask the same mercy for himself. It's too late now to evade their fate. They can only beg the Lord to send them swift and easy deaths, and to shelter those they love when they have left this world behind.

39

Anton drops into sleep on a small cot in the corner of Emil's room. When he wakes, groggy and disoriented, the low yellow light of a late-winter morning pools beside the window. The smell of old snow hangs heavy in the air—snow and fresh ink. He thinks, *I've had an hour or two of rest, at least—a small but notable blessing.*

Father Emil is across the room, sitting up in his own narrow bed, back propped against his pillow. He is writing a letter on a small wooden lap desk.

"Anton. You're awake."

Anton prods his own forehead, baffled by the thick fog that has swallowed his thoughts.

"How long did I sleep?"

"An entire day and half of another."

So long? Anton sits up quickly—too quickly. He groans at the pain in his body, stiff and aching from their week of work, their nights of mad rebellion.

"Easy," Emil says. "Move slowly. Trust me on this; I seem to have come through the worst of the pain."

"Elisabeth and the children—they should be with my sister by now." How will he know for certain? He must return to the cottage behind Frau Hertz's farmhouse—the only place the letter carrier will think to find him. But the thought of entering the cottage, emptied now of everything he loves, is far too painful to bear.

"I slept, too," Emil says, scarcely looking up from his letter. "Almost as long as you. The neighbors were concerned; they came knocking. I told them I'd caught a nasty cold and to keep their distance so it wouldn't spread. That ought to explain my stiffness and absence. It kept their eyes off you, too."

Emil finishes his letter, seals it in an envelope, and writes out the address in a slow, unhurried manner. Then he rises—slowly—and takes something from his desk.

"A letter for you. I sent a friend around to Frau Hertz's place. She kept this, in case you ever came back. I've put your glasses there, on the little stool beside your cot."

The letter is addressed in Anita's unmistakable hand. He opens it hastily, greedy for news, and lies back on the cot to read.

Dear little brother,

I was only too happy to meet your Elisabeth and the children when they came knocking on my door. She gave me your note. You mustn't apologize for surprising me this way, and you mustn't feel any guilt. Of course I will take your family in, Anton, and give them all the care and protection I am capable of giving.

We make a tight bundle here—Elisabeth shares my bed, Albert has the sofa, while Paul and Maria sleep on the floor at night. But we are cozy, and no one is ever lonely. I think we can count that a great blessing in times like these. Your children are dear to me already; I love them as much as if I'd known them all their lives. I never looked to be an auntie, but now that I am one, I'm glad to be.

Elisabeth means to write you, I know. But she has been so sad. She cries all the time—I don't tell you this to hurt you, only so you will know how much she loves you. I will see to it that she writes you soon, so you will have some word directly from your wife.

I know from your note, and from what little Elisabeth has told me, that there has been some fearful trouble. I don't like to think of my baby brother in that sort of trouble. But whatever has happened, whatever you have done, I know you have done it with your whole heart, and with righteousness your aim.

You mustn't worry about your family, Anton, whatever may come. I will care for them and love them, even if there comes a day when you cannot.

We will meet again, Brother, in this life or the next.

Love,

Anita

He lets the letter fall. Relief strikes him so hard and fast that he shakes as if in the grip of a fever. His glasses fog with the heat of his tears. They will be well. They will be safe—as safe as anyone can be.

Emil takes a long breath, on the verge of speaking, but he leaves his words unsaid. After a moment, Anton hears the priest's pen scratching again, beginning another letter, telling his story all over again to whomever must know. He is content to leave Anton be, with his grief and his joy. Men cry—all the time. Our tears are the glass of our compass case, and the needle that points our way.

40

When the day comes—when the SS finally arrive—it's the loud stir of the village that draws Anton and Father Emil out into the street. The sound pulls them from an afternoon prayer at the feet of Mary's statue—not a sound of shouting, exactly, but of loud disbelief, a surging instinct of denial. When he hears it, whispering outside the walls of St. Kolumban, Anton rises from the prayer bench. Father Emil crosses himself, and then he stands, too. They consider one another in silence. Neither man sees fear in the other—only readiness to face what has come.

"That sound," Emil says. "Someone has arrived in the village, someone who doesn't belong."

Anton nods. It can only be the SS. "Come for the traitors at last. Shall we go out and greet them?"

They need not go far. As soon as they step outside St. Kolumban, they can see the black truck approaching, dark canvas rolled down to cover its bed. The truck comes to a stop in the dirt road opposite the church door. A crowd of townsfolk follows on foot, shouting objections, raising their fists, though surely they must know it's dangerous to do so. Any show of resistance, no matter how small, is apt to be punished.

To Anton, Emil says, "God keep you, my friend." Then he strides forward, head up, to meet his fate. The black robe of his office flares at the hem, fanned like the stork's wings. Anton hurries after his priest.

How his throat tightens with despair and hate when the officer steps down from the truck. Black from head to foot, his long coat falling just above his polished crow-dark boots, the Schutzstaffel man seems some hellish twin to Father Emil, made in the image of mockery. He is every inch as tall as Anton, but the eyes that narrow in the shadow of his cap are harder than Anton's could ever be.

The officer nods a curt greeting to the priest. "You're here; excellent. I've come to claim your church bells."

Not come for them—Anton and Emil. Not yet.

Anton slides a wary look in the priest's direction. Their eyes do not quite meet, but Anton can feel a fresh current of hope running through his friend—running between them, shared.

Anton says to the officer, "But . . . *mein Herr*, you already took our bells."

"Nonsense. I haven't come through this town yet."

"Not you exactly, *mein Herr*." He gives the man a grin, wide and friendly. Anton Starzmann is every man's friend; his ready smile proves it. "It was another captain of the Schutzstaffel. When did it happen, Father—a week ago? Ten days?"

Emil taps his chin. "I believe it was—"

The officer silences Emil with a terse gesture. "No one came here. No other officer would intrude. This shit hole of a village is in my territory; it's my responsibility. No one would be foolish enough to canvass my towns without seeking my permission, and I do not shirk my duties."

Anton lifts his hands in a gesture of bafflement. "But it's true."

Father Emil nods. He points, indicating the bell tower—empty, a perfect square of blue sky showing at its peak. "You can see for yourself, *mein Herr*—our bells are already gone."

The crowd murmurs and shivers. The villagers break away in little groups, making for the heart of Unterboihingen as quickly as they dare to move. The arrival of an SS officer would not have gone unnoticed, seven days past or ten. The villagers know Anton has lied. They know their priest has lied. And none of them wish to be questioned.

The officer's voice rises an octave. "Do you think us fools? Do you think we can't keep our affairs in order?"

"Certainly not," says Emil calmly.

"Those bells were mine, meant for my quota. Why didn't you stop the man who took them?"

Emil shrugs. "We had no idea our town wasn't in that man's jurisdiction."

"And," Anton adds, smiling again, "you don't think we would say no to an officer of the SS, do you, *mein Herr*?"

The captain is rigid with anger, his jaw clenched so tightly Anton can count the striations in the muscle of his cheek. Then he leans close to Anton, so close he can smell the man's breath. "Wipe that grin off your face, you small-town scum. This isn't a laughing matter." He turns to the few people who still dare to linger near the churchyard. "Who among you can corroborate this man's story? Speak with care; I have ways of sniffing out lies."

No one speaks. No one dares to move. Anton breathes deeply. He thinks, *I gave it my best effort. From here, I'll go to the camps, like my students before me. But I can be proud of the work I've done. A thorn in the wolf's paw, however small that thorn may be.*

From among the small crowd, a familiar voice speaks. "I can vouch for their story, *mein Herr*. I was here when the officer came. I saw it all; it was nine days ago, not ten."

Elisabeth. She has come back. Anton can't take his eyes from her face as she walks toward the officer—that familiar way she has of moving, her back strong and unbent. He clenches his jaw to blank his face, so the captain won't see love in his eyes. He tightens his fists at his side to keep himself from moving, keep himself from standing between Elisabeth and danger.

"Who are you?" the captain barks.

"My name is Elisabeth Herter. I'm a widow; I've lived in this town eight years."

The last watchers finally scatter. They won't remain as witnesses while Anton and Elisabeth lie to this dangerous man—but neither are they willing to betray two members of their tightly knit community. And these two are better loved than most.

The captain stares at Elisabeth for a long time, searching her face for a flinch, a draining of color, any sign of weakness or fear. She stands her ground. She gazes back unfazed, the very picture of a good German woman, open and honest, loyal to her country, with nothing to hide.

Finally, the captain turns away. "If the bells aren't there, then they aren't there. But I will get to the bottom of this. I'll know the truth of what has happened here, and then we'll see who's to blame."

The truck's door slams, and the engine coughs to life. The next moment, the truck is rumbling away, its canvas cover flapping, back down the main street toward open fields, toward Stuttgart beyond.

Anton and Elisabeth hold themselves apart, though for him, the urge to run to her is crushing, overpowering. He watches as she closes her eyes, still and silent, composing herself, bracing for whatever will come next. As soon as Emil whispers, "The officer is gone; I can't see the truck any longer," she flings herself toward Anton and throws herself into his arms. She weeps with relief against his chest.

"Merciful Mother." Anton's voice trembles. "Why did you come back?"

"I couldn't leave you to face your fate alone."

"But the children—"

"Your sister has them in her care. She agreed, if anything should happen to you and me both, that she would look after them."

Gently he pushes her away, holding her by her shoulders. "You must go back, Elisabeth. You can't stay here with me. We had a close shave just now—but we won't escape a second time. Whether they learn the truth about the bells or not, they will be back, someday, for Father Emil. And for me."

She smiles at him through her tears. "God willing, we will escape."

"The children need their mother."

"God willing," she says again, stubborn as ever.

Anton wouldn't gamble on God's willingness. "When Möbelbauer hears what you said and did, he's sure to write to his contacts. He'll tell them you and I are married. They'll arrest you, too, for lying to an officer."

"I know they'll learn the truth," she says, "sooner or later. I know they'll be back. You don't think it was easy for me—do you?—to leave my children."

He is almost weeping now. "Then why did you do it? Why return?"

"You are my husband. We will stay together, no matter what happens."

He pulls her tightly to his chest and wraps his arms around her body. If only he could be her shield and spare her from what will come.

Emil places a hand on each of their heads, a silent blessing. "Go home," the priest says. "Go and be together, while there's still time."

Together, Anton and Elisabeth walk the dirt road. They turn down the lane that leads to the old farmhouse, the orchard, the raised cottage beyond—their home. The whole way, Elisabeth holds on to him. She doesn't release Anton's hand until they reach their bedroom door.

41

It is easier to hope with Elisabeth beside him, but still Anton wishes she were back in Stuttgart. Winter gives way slowly to a gray, wet spring. The crocuses bloom, painting the milk cow's pasture and the yard at the foot of the stair with strokes of purple and white. There is no one to build the rabbit garden this year, but with the few coins that remain to him, Anton buys a bar of chocolate from the bakery and sends it to the children in Stuttgart.

The crocuses fade, the season of resurrection passes, and still the papers bear witness only to the Führer's immortality. But where there is love, there is hope. In his moments of despair, Anton takes Elisabeth's hand. He tells himself, *Be patient. In hope, we are saved.* Hope that is seen is no hope at all; who asks for what he already has?

Anton and Elisabeth, husband and wife, fall into a quiet pattern of waiting. They rise in the morning, and they go about the business of life. Between the greetings they exchange with their neighbors, in the meaningful spaces between words, they search for the miracle they're still waiting for. The radio broadcasts and papers all proclaim that Germany is mighty, Germany is strong, our dear leader is indomitable. But whispers tell another tale. In January, the camp at Auschwitz was relinquished to the Soviets, and what prisoners had survived were freed. In March, the Americans took Cologne—there is no word yet from Frau Hornik. Himmler is gone now, replaced by General Heinrici; the stronghold in Copenhagen has been bombed and destroyed. On the last day of March, General Eisenhower demanded Germany's surrender. You won't hear it on the radio, but that's what rumor insists, and rumor has made its way even here, to our insignificant village.

The black tide is turning, but not swiftly enough. The NSDAP still holds Germany, but when a wolf is cornered, it's far more apt to bite. Anton and Elisabeth listen and wait, but they don't allow hope to bloom. In the evenings, they hold one another, surrendering for an hour or two to the fear that never abates. Sometimes she cries, already mourning what she has not yet lost—and sometimes it's Anton who weeps. When sleep comes, their dreams are black and gray, shot through here and there with spots of light, like a candle hidden in a pierced shutter. And in the morning, they rise again. They pull back the curtains; they read the news. But still, news of Hitler's fall refuses to come.

First the crocuses, then the daffodils. Then the tulips, blushing pink. Anton dreams at night of a place underground, deep in the earth, where only the roots of flowers may go. The dark ground shakes from a ghost's voice, a memory's voice. He wakes to the sound and feels its echo ringing in his palm.

He lies still, watching the sun's light move slowly around the edge of the curtain. It's late in the morning. He should wake Elisabeth, but she looks so peaceful in sleep. Let her have the mercy of dreams for a while longer.

He woke to a sound, and it comes again—so faint, so distant, that he mistakes it for a memory. He'd heard the toll of a bell, and it had sounded like a boy's voice calling.

"Father!" The voice is closer now. Louder. And there is no mistaking to whom it belongs. "Father! Vati Anton!"

Albert. Anton could swear he has actually heard the boy, out among the orchard or running down the lane. He sits up slowly, but the movement is enough to wake Elisabeth. She stirs, yawns, and rubs a knuckle in her eye.

"Anton? What is it?"

"I thought I heard—" He won't say, *I thought I heard our son.* They have lived without the children for months now—four cruel months, when it seemed winter would never end, a new spring would never come. Every day he has seen the pain in Elisabeth's eyes. Every day he has known what it costs her to be here with him. He won't raise hope without cause.

But she murmurs, "I had the strangest dream. I dreamed I heard Albert calling for me."

Then, waking fully, she hears the boy again. They both hear. "Father! Mother!"

Elisabeth stares at Anton for a moment, pale and frightened. He can read her thoughts, for they are his own. *Is this a trick of the Devil? Or has the boy died? Is our child's spirit trapped between Heaven and Earth?*

They leap from bed in the same instant and fly to the window. Elisabeth's teeth are chattering with shock and fear. The children cannot be here. It's too dangerous for them now. If they've truly come, Anton must send them away, and both their hearts must break all over again.

But when they look down to the lane, there is no mistaking Albert—taller than when Anton saw him last but just as pale, just as freckled. He is no ghost. The boy is running, his arms flung out like wings. Behind him, Paul comes skipping and singing, holding Maria's hand.

"Mother Mary!" It's all Elisabeth can say. She runs for the cottage door and the staircase before Anton can caution her. He can't catch her, either; he can only hurry along behind, reaching for her, trying to steady her as she bolts down into the yard. Barefoot, her hair a mess, clothed only in her nightdress, she sprints across the wet grass and catches her children in her arms.

Frau Hertz is running from the farmhouse, waving something above her head, something white and black and fluttering. A newspaper.

"Anton!" He looks up, and there is Anita, in her laywoman's dress, hustling down the lane, red-faced and puffing. There is an auto parked behind her, round-hooded, soft gray. She jingles a set of keys in her hands, as if to say, *Look what I've got; are you jealous?* Then she squeals with happiness like the girl she used to be, catching him in a tight embrace. She spins him around and around. "Look at you, in your nightshirt. You slept in too late, Little Brother. You missed the news!"

"What news? For goodness' sake, what has happened? Why are you here—and the children?"

The children squirm out of Elisabeth's arms, run to Anton, and throw their arms around his body. He is squeezed and patted to within an inch of his life, and he laughs—laughs with the gladness of it until he is wheezing and breathless.

"You haven't heard yet?" Albert cries, face alight. "It's done now. It's all over!"

"What? Speak sense!"

Frau Hertz arrives then. She thrusts the newspaper against Anton's chest. He takes it and holds it out—he hasn't put his glasses on, and he can barely read the neat headline. But through his blurred vision, the words seem to advance upon him, resolving with startling clarity.

FAREWELL TO HITLER

"He's dead," Anita says. She laughs wildly and thrusts a fist in the air. "We heard it quite late, yesterday evening. The Party tried to suppress the news, of course, but the streets of Stuttgart are flooded with talk. Our dear, brave leader took his own life, rather than face surrender. How do you like that?"

"Are you sure?" Anton clings to his children, gripping them so tightly Maria twists away and runs back to her mother.

"No one's sure of anything yet," Frau Hertz says. "But I suppose the paper wouldn't have printed this story unless they were certain at least that he's dead. Dead and off to Hell, where he belongs." She spits in the mud.

"You know the Party will deny he took his own life," Anita says, "until they can't hide the truth any longer. But it seems the sort of thing he would do, doesn't it? After all the misery he's spread, all the people he's made to suffer, he hadn't the courage to face the trials and a proper punishment."

Did he really take his own life, Anton wonders—*or did he choke on turnip stew?* It hardly matters now—now, in the morning light.

"I have to go see Father Emil," Anton says. "I must know if he's heard the news."

Elisabeth laughs. Tears of joy have thickened her lashes. "Not like that; look at yourself. You can't go to the priest in your nightshirt."

In their home—what a joy it is, to hear the old house ringing with the sound of the children's voices—Anton and Elisabeth dress as quickly as they can. Elisabeth makes a cursory attempt at tidying her hair, then finally smashes a hat atop her head. "Good enough," she says. "Let's go."

Anita drives them to the church while the children run along behind the car, hooting and dancing, turning cartwheels between puddles.

But when they arrive at St. Kolumban, Father Emil isn't there. The nave is empty. So is his little room in the back of the building.

Elisabeth's smile fades. "Has something happened to him? Oh, merciful Lord—they didn't come for him last night, Anton? Not now!"

"No, darling—no. Come; I know exactly where we'll find him."

He leads Elisabeth to the field behind the church. The earth is lush with new growth, the soil soft and yielding. A smell of dew fills the air—dew and unfurling blossoms. Emil, in his black robe, is on his knees, pawing through the soil with his bare hands. He looks up at Anton's shouted greeting. When he sees the family approaching, he jumps to his feet, spry as a boy of eighteen. "Anton! Have you heard the news?"

"I have!"

More people must hear; the whole world should know. Anton brings the shovel from the churchyard, and he and Emil dig into ripe, dark earth. Soon Elisabeth and the children join them, moving soil with their hands—Anita and Frau Hertz, too. More hands arrive, more help. Two and four, a dozen, twenty—the field fills with neighbors, all those who have come to the church to give thanks for this new morning.

"Dig!" Anton tells them. "Everyone, dig!"

The youngest Kopp brother asks why.

"You'll soon find out," Emil tells him. "Anton will show you where. Bring spades, if you have them. Pickaxes—anything!"

The field rings with laughter and the shouts of children. Anton straightens from his task, his hands caked with earth. Across the pit, he sees Frau Franke laughing as she tries and fails to brush the mud from her palms. He has never seen the woman smile before, but she is beaming now, though the hem of her dress is ruined with soil. Her husband is nowhere to be seen.

"Where's Möbelbauer?" he asks, of no one in particular.

One of the Kopp brothers throws his arms around Anton, crushing him in a hug so tight Anton loses his breath. "Möbelbauer's gone," the young man says. "He left last night, running like a dog—running to his SS masters, no doubt."

Another Kopp adds, "If he ever tries to come back here, he won't find a warm welcome."

Someone has brought more shovels, and the people of Unterboihingen dig deeper into the earth, and deeper still, though they can't know what Anton and Emil know—what they will soon uncover. The whole town is laughing, breathless with disbelief. Is it really over? Can it be?

When the first shovel strikes bronze, the crowd goes still. They back away; Anton jumps down into the pit and clears the last of the earth with his hands. The first bell shows itself through wet black soil, its proud height and strong curve, its domed crown gleaming. A great shout goes up from the townspeople. They cheer with one voice, and the echo of their gladness rebounds from the blue, blue hills.

"A parade," Emil shouts. "Let's have a parade!"

The villagers cheer again.

The Kopps bring their two great flatbed trucks out into the field. The people of Unterboihingen lift together; they raise the bells up. Children pick armfuls of flowers and greenery from hedges and ditches, and skipping and singing, they strew petals over the earth; they cover the bells and the beds of the trucks in sweet, bright swags of green.

"Albert," Anton says, "run to every house. Knock on every door. Bring all the children here with their instruments. You heard Father Emil; we must have a parade!"

When the bells are all but buried under wreaths of blossom, the band assembles. Anton heads toward his students, intending to lead the march—but Emil catches him by the arm. "Let them play without a conductor today. You've taught them well enough; they can manage." He gestures to the nearest truck bed. "You belong up there, my friend—up where the whole town can see you."

Grinning, accepting the praise, Anton climbs up beside his bells. Flowers and new leaves cling to his wet shoes and to the cuffs of his trousers. The air is rich with the scent of honey. He waves to the crowd; they lift their hands and cheer again, and fill the air with petals.

Anton reaches down for Elisabeth, intending to pull her up beside him. But she steps back with a shy smile.

"Come, now. You ought to be the queen of the parade."

"I can't. I'm afraid I'll fall."

"I'll make sure you won't. I'll keep my arm around you the whole time."

Elisabeth lowers her voice; he can barely make out her words over the cheering crowd. "No, we can't risk it, Anton." And she lays a hand low on her stomach.

The clamor of the music, the honking horns, the waving banners of color—all that glad madness dies away. Elisabeth is all Anton can see, all he can hear—her happy laughter and the tears shining bright in her eyes.

He leaps down from the truck bed and pulls her into his arms. She kisses him, unashamed and unreserved, there in front of everyone.

This is the world as it was before, the life we used to know. And this is the world we will make again, in love's lasting image.

HISTORICAL NOTE AND
AUTHOR'S REMARKS

It might surprise you to learn that this is a true story. What's more, this is a family story: Josef Anton Starzmann was my husband's maternal grandfather, and I could have written a novel about him twice the size of *The Ragged Edge of Night* without running low on material. Anton was a fascinating and inspiring man.

I first heard the story of "*Opa* and the bells," as my in-laws say, in 2010 over Thanksgiving dinner. I had only recently begun to date my husband-to-be, Paul, and he had just left on a nearly yearlong deployment to Kuwait. I had fallen in love with Paul far more quickly than was prudent, and even though our relationship was still quite new, I was heartbroken over his absence. When his family invited me to spend Thanksgiving in their company, I accepted, but not without some trepidation. I barely knew Paul at that point, even though I was in love with him; his family were total strangers to me. To make matters worse, Paul had told me of his thoroughly Catholic roots, so I was fairly sure his family wouldn't approve of the fact that I was still technically married to my first husband. We had been separated for some time, but I hadn't been able to secure a divorce yet. I knew if I hoped to gain acceptance from Paul's family, I would have to avoid too many personal questions and tread with care.

Fortunately, I've always had a convenient, conversation-diverting ace tucked up my sleeve. When I arrived at the home of Paul's eldest brother, I broke it out immediately.

"So, what do you do?" someone asked.

At the time, I was working at a bookstore, and told them so. "But," I added, "I'm also a writer. I'm trying to make a career out of it. My specialty is historical fiction."

Most people love books, and historical fiction has a broad audience. My ace worked its magic; soon I was bonding with Paul's family over a shared interest in history, and no one skirted too close to any potentially damning information.

Paul's eldest brother, Larry, said, "You should write about *Opa* and the bells. I think it counts as history, and it would make for really good fiction."

Over turkey and mashed potatoes—and with an ever-increasing sense of being thoroughly gobsmacked—I teased out this family's most incredible story, though it came to me piecemeal. The conversation went something like this:

"My dad hated Hitler," said Rita, Paul's German mother. "Absolutely *hated* him."

"Well, who doesn't?" I chuckled uncomfortably.

"Yes, but *Opa really* hated Hitler. I mean, he was willing to do whatever it took to get the guy's goat."

Getting Adolf Hitler's goat sounded like it had to be an understatement.

"What do you mean?" I asked.

"Well, the Nazis almost killed *Opa* because of what he did." I love my mother-in-law to death, but it has never been easy to extract a story from her.

"It wasn't the Nazis," Larry said. "It was that jerk in town. What was his name?"

"He was a Nazi," Rita insisted. "He might as well have been. It was the same thing as being a Nazi."

I cut in. "Wait . . . what did your dad do, exactly?"

"He hid the church bells. He buried them in a potato field so the Nazis couldn't take them. They were claiming all the church bells, so they could melt them down and turn them into ammunition. But he wouldn't let them have the bells, on top of everything else they'd done, so he hid them. And then, when some SS officer came to get them, he said, 'Look, the bells are already gone. Somebody else from the SS took them.' The guy was so mad, but Dad said, 'What, you didn't want me to say no to an SS officer, did you?'" Rita laughed heartily.

"They almost killed him for that?"

"Oh yeah. You didn't cross the Nazis. Trust me—you think you know about the Nazis, but you don't. They were truly evil, and *crazy*. They'd do anything, for any reason."

I wasn't about to argue. I believed her.

Larry's girlfriend, Julie—now his wife, and my sister-in-law—spoke up then. "I thought the Nazis tried to kill *Opa* because of his band."

"Yeah, that, too." Rita waved her hand, as if defying the Nazi Party not once but twice was nothing remarkable.

"His band?"

"He started a marching band to keep the town's boys out of Hitler Youth," Larry said. "That didn't make Hitler very happy."

"I imagine not."

"Anyway," Rita said, "they still remember my dad for what he did. He's the hero of Unterboihingen."

In fact, after the restoration of the bells to St. Kolumban's tower, Anton wrote a beautiful song celebrating their music and history, which is still performed annually by St. Kolumban's choir in remembrance of *Opa* and the bells he helped save. In early 2017, I had the privilege of translating his lyrics, titled "Bell Song," from German to English. As far as I know, it's the first English translation of the work.

After that Thanksgiving dinner, the years passed and I came to know Paul better—and his warm, wonderful family (all of whom are far more accepting and open-minded than I had originally assumed). As I learned more about Anton's life, I pieced together a clearer picture of *Opa* and the bells. And the more vivid *Opa's* story grew in my mind, the more certain I became that I would write it all out as a novel . . . someday.

Josef Anton Starzmann was born in 1904 in Stuttgart, Germany, to a devout Catholic family. His sister's real name was Korbel, which my editor and I decided to change to Anita, since she plays a minor role in this novel and Anita is an easier name for English-speaking readers to manage.

Anton joined the Franciscan Order as a very young man, and was happy in his work for many years, until Germany began to alter itself subtly—and then, in 1933, not so subtly. A lifelong and self-taught musician, he developed and implemented musical programs at St. Josefsheim, a residential, Franciscan-run school for developmentally delayed and disabled children.

Anton—who, in his Franciscan years, was known as Bruder Nazarius—took great joy in his work. The order was his whole identity. I have a striking photo of him, taken when he was twenty or so, dressed in his Franciscan garb, with his little round spectacles balanced on his long, thin nose. The photo is dear to me, for my husband, Paul, looks almost exactly like his *Opa*, a resemblance that's almost eerie in its perfection. Take a photo of Paul in 1940s clothing, pass it through a black-and-white filter, and even Rita would be hard-pressed to tell the difference between her son and her father.

In 1939, Hitler initiated the T4 Program, his campaign to rid the Fatherland of all people physically and intellectually disabled or delayed. The measure began with forced sterilization of adults, but soon progressed to "euthanasia," carried out in Germany's many death camps or in hospitals where Josef Mengele and his ilk performed their experiments. As the tide of war slowly began to turn against Hitler, he ramped up his extermination of the disabled and developmentally delayed. Sometime in 1940 or 1941, the children of St. Josefsheim were taken and "redistributed to other homes." Anton, of course, knew what that meant. I've been unable to learn whether his particular order was disbanded at that moment or whether he left of his own accord after the children were seized. Rita and her sister Angela, the only remaining members of Anton's family—and the only two biological children Anton and Elisabeth shared—don't know whether their father left on his own or was forced out of the friar's life by decree of the Nazis, as so many other friars, monks, and nuns were.

When his happy days as a friar ended, Anton found himself conscripted into military service, forced to fight for the government he hated, the people who had taken and destroyed everything he had loved. He did complete one paratrooper's jump and the march to Riga but left the Wehrmacht immediately after, with an injured back for an excuse. Both Rita and Angie maintain to this day that his back was fine; the lie was his first overt resistance against the Nazi Party (known in this book mostly as the NSDAP, short for the German name: Nationalsozialistische Deutsche Arbeiterpartei, or the National Socialist German Workers' Party.)

No one is entirely sure why he did it, but at some point after leaving the Franciscan Order, Anton answered a personal ad in one of the few remaining Catholic newspapers, exchanging letters with Elisabeth Hansjosten Herter, a widow struggling to care for her three children in the tiny village of Unterboihingen. Elisabeth's past—and the story of her first marriage—were exactly as I portrayed them in this novel. My only alteration to Elisabeth's past was to change the date of her marriage to Anton. They married in April instead of October, and in 1941. As far as I know, Anton never proposed a companionate marriage, nor faked any incapacity—that was a device I added at the recommendation of my editor, who felt truth was stranger than fiction, and their first meeting needed a little more tension.

That was all I knew of Anton's life for many years, and goodness knows, it's interesting enough on its own to carry a novel—the story of a slowly blossoming wartime romance between two unlikely partners, the widow and the ex-friar. But despite my publisher prodding me to dip my toe into World War II, I didn't feel the time was right to develop my notes about Anton and Elisabeth into a book. Most of my historical fiction has focused on figures whom history remembers as larger than life—powerful, important, far from ordinary. I didn't yet feel enough drive to tell *Opa*'s story—the story of an ordinary person who fought back against some of the worst impulses of the human heart.

It wasn't until the 2016 election that I knew the time had come.

As I watched the US I thought I knew devolve, seemingly overnight, into an unrecognizable landscape—a place where political pundits threw up Nazi salutes in front of news cameras, unafraid—a place where swastikas bloomed like fetid flowers on the walls of synagogues and mosques—I knew the time had come. I called Jodi Warshaw, my first editor at Lake Union Publishing, and told her I'd finally found a World War II subject I wanted to write . . . and I wanted to write it *now*. Jodi agreed that the time was right for a story of resistance—of an ordinary person taking a stand against hate. Within weeks, my proposal for *The Ragged Edge of Night* was approved, and I began to research and develop the book in earnest.

I have written many historical novels over the years, and have enjoyed researching them all, but never has the research process touched me so deeply. Rita and Angie were both excited that their family history would soon be a novel, and I was humbled that they trusted me to tell the story well. My mother-in-law and aunt were overwhelmingly generous with their knowledge, time, and irreplaceable family artifacts. Rita gave me a whole bag of Anton's personal items, and while I worked on *Ragged Edge*, I kept them spread out across the bed in my guest room, which doubles as my office. Whenever I felt stuck or disheartened, I would look through these artifacts of Anton's life. I could all but sense his presence, then—a feeling no doubt helped by Paul and the striking resemblance he bears to his astonishingly brave grandfather.

I was moved—so moved, I can't find the words to describe it—by Rita's gift of Anton's Wehrmacht workbook. I can't read the notes he wrote inside, but the blank spot on the cover, where he scratched away Hitler's swastika, speaks plainly across our language barrier. Just as touching are Anton's photos—the story they tell, if you look closely enough.

There is an image of a church spire in Riga, wreathed in flames—and a picture of his classroom at St. Josefsheim, empty of children. Anton kept a few photos of his life as a friar, but there are no pictures of any of the children he cared for while he was with the order. Clearly, their loss was a pain so great he couldn't bear to relive it in later years.

In the spring of 2017, when I was deep in the development phase of this book, Paul and I welcomed Rita and Angie to our home on San Juan Island. They had come to tell me more stories about *Opa* and the bells—and I was delighted by what they told me.

"You know," I said as they settled in, "this book I'm writing—it's fiction, not a biography. So I'm going to take some artistic license. I'll need to make a lot of things up, for the sake of telling an exciting story."

"Like what?" Rita asked.

"Well . . ." I paused, worried about how they would react. "I thought I might add some drama by involving your dad in a plot to assassinate Hitler."

Angie shrugged. "You don't have to make that up. He *was* involved in a plot to assassinate Hitler."

My eyes must have nearly popped out of my head. "What? Are you kidding me?"

"No," Rita said, "it's true. He told us a few times that he was wrapped up in something like that during the war."

"But he never went into much detail," Angie added. "He didn't like to talk about it."

I couldn't believe my good luck.

"He must have *told* you," Rita said, laughing. "Now do you believe?"

This is a perpetual joke my mother-in-law and I share: her ribbing me for being an atheist, promising me in ominous tones that I'll believe in God . . . *someday*. Meanwhile, I play along by pretending to hiss and cringe whenever she shows me a crucifix or a rosary.

That visit from Rita and Angie yielded more material for the novel. Angie, the first child of Anton and Elisabeth's marriage, was actually born near the end of the war. Some of her earliest memories are of wartime life, and it's from her that I learned of Unterboihingen's heavy curtains, its penchant for trading, and—I will be honest—a few colorful German curses. Though she was very young at the time, she had vivid recollections of British and American bombing runs. It was she, not her older half sister, Maria, who hid beneath the altar in a pitch-black St. Kolumban during a bombing raid on Stuttgart, near Christmas Eve.

In fact, Angie had so many memorable childhood adventures that I included the best of them in this novel, attributed to Maria instead. (Angie, of course, doesn't make her appearance until the final lines of the book.) The incident of the First Communion dress and the *Misthaufen* really happened to Angie—though it occurred at a neighbor's house, not the family's residence, as Anton and Elisabeth actually lived in a second-story apartment above a shop in town—and by the time Angie had her First Communion, the war was over. Angie was also the one who maintained a rivalry with her teacher—she is still bitter about it to this day—and would sneak away from school on a regular basis to make paper dolls in empty vacation cottages. It should be noted here, just in case my in-laws do watch me from some mysterious Beyond, that the real Maria Herter was an exceptionally well-behaved child. Angie was the naughty one of the family, and prone to amusing mishaps, besides, which has led Paul to dub his aunt the Anne of Green Gables of Germany.

It was Angie, too, who had a special bond with St. Kolumban's priest—whose name was not Father Emil. The priest's adoration of mischievous little Angie might have been what drew him to the Starzmann family in the first place, but it was surely Anton's and Elisabeth's essential goodness that kept him a firm friend of the Starzmanns. When Unterboihingen took in the refugees from Egerland, the Starzmanns took the priest into their home along with the family they hosted—and the father slept on the floor near Anton and Elisabeth, having given up his bed to those less fortunate. St. Kolumban's father was also complicit with Anton's resistance against the Nazis, though I have no way of knowing whether it was he who brought Anton into the work. It may have been Unterboihingen's mayor—a man who did not appear in this novel, for simplicity's sake, but who was nonetheless heavily involved in both of Anton's dangerous schemes—the Hitler Youth–thwarting marching band and the removal and burial of St. Kolumban's bells.

It may also have been the mayor who sealed the door in the ancient wall—or perhaps that was done well before the war. But the door is real, and you can see it if you travel to Wendlingen, the Württemberg town that has absorbed old Unterboihingen. Paul's family traveled to Rita's hometown several times throughout his childhood, and the cemented door remains as one of his most vivid memories of Germany. When, as a boy, he asked someone in the town what was behind the door, the only answer he got was "Nazi ghosts." Neither Paul nor I have been able to verify the claim that Nazi soldiers were sealed up in that terrible passage, but it's such a chilling image, I couldn't resist using it in this novel.

Whether anyone else in the town joined Anton in his quiet acts of rebellion, we will probably never know. But we do know that the mayor and the priest were involved. Their names were listed alongside Anton's in a certain letter, found on the abandoned desk of Unterboihingen's gauleiter the day after Hitler's death was announced. The letter read—as Rita paraphrased for me: "This town's mayor, priest, and music teacher, Anton Starzmann, are traitors who have betrayed the Party. Come and arrest them."

Yes, tiny, insignificant Unterboihingen had a gauleiter—unusual, for such a small town—and although his name was not Bruno Franke, the children did call him Möbelbauer. Rita and Angie also swear that he had a habit of propositioning the town's women, many of whom reluctantly gave in, fearful of what he might do to their families if they resisted. Like most other gauleiters, Möbelbauer fled when the Nazi Party fell, certain of a trial at the hands of the Allies.

If Möbelbauer had remained in Unterboihingen only a day or two longer—if he had sent that letter—the SS almost certainly would have taken Anton and his friends, for the SS still operated for some time after

Hitler's death. Anton would undoubtedly have died at the hands of the defeated Nazis, and my husband—and his wonderful family—wouldn't exist today. It's frightening—and somehow, strangely beautiful—to think how the best and most important parts of our lives can depend on a quirk of history, a sudden bend in the road. How different my life would be but for the passage of a few days, a few moments, in a tiny German town thirty-five years before my birth.

But history is never very far behind us. It's the familiar ghost we trail in our wake.

On the night I finished writing this book, there was a march at the University of Virginia, a show of power by a faction of white supremacists, newly emboldened by the sudden bend in America's road. The people carried torches, a snake of fire through a black summer night. They chanted "White lives matter" and "Jews will not replace us." They chanted "Blood and soil," the same words Nazis spoke in Anton Starzmann's time. A cowardly man, threatened by the strength of those who stood in protest against evil, drove his car into the crowd, killing one woman and injuring nearly twenty other people.

The same evil *Opa* fought—he and countless others—still lives. It thrives now on American soil.

We are fools to think the past remains in the past. History is our guilty conscience; it will not let us rest. Perhaps we will never learn the origin of this sickness, but we understand its cure. We are the White Rose, and the Edelweiss Pirates. We are *Widerstand*—resistance—you and I. No force can silence us, unless we permit silence. I prefer to roar.

I have seen the power of human goodness; I know how courageous the most ordinary person can be. The history of my own family bears testament to the power of resistance. Because I have seen, I believe—I know—that darkness cannot last forever. And beyond night's edge, there is light.

Olivia Hawker
August 2017

ACKNOWLEDGMENTS

There are many people who deserve my thanks—and have my deepest gratitude—for their assistance and support as I worked on this book.

Jodi Warshaw, my first editor at Lake Union, was instrumental in bringing this book forward. Partway through the writing of *The Ragged Edge of Night*, a twist of corporate fate landed me on the list of Chris Werner, a new editor to Lake Union, who took on this project with enthusiasm and helped create a smooth transition for me. I feel extremely fortunate to have worked with two exceptional editors, and I also must thank Danielle Marshall, editorial director at the press, who continues to believe in me. Her support is both humbling and energizing.

I have worked with developmental editor Dorothy Zemach before, but her attention, thoroughness, and expertise (not to mention her sense of humor) were especially welcome with this book. I look forward to working with her again in the future; I think we make a great team.

Michelle Hope provided an excellent, thorough copy edit; I am grateful for her sharp eye and thoughtful suggestions.

My warmest gratitude to my family, especially Rita Starzmann and Angela Cullers, who have so generously shared their time, memories, and priceless family heirlooms. I hope I've done justice to our family's history. *Danke und ich liebe dich.*

Thank you to my readers for their support and enthusiasm. As I write, I am always conscious that someone will be at the other end of my stories, reading and absorbing—and, I hope, enjoying what I create. It's my sincere wish that you find comfort and strength in Anton's story. I know he would feel honored if his actions inspired another person to shine their light against whatever shadows threaten them.

And, as always, thanks to my husband, Paul Harnden, who is everything to me.

ABOUT THE AUTHOR

Photo © 2018 Paul Harnden

Through unexpected characters and vivid prose, Olivia Hawker explores the varied landscape of the human spirit. Olivia's interest in genealogy often informs her writing. Her first two novels from Lake Union Publishing, *The Ragged Edge of Night* and *One for the Blackbird, One for the Crow* (2019), are based on true stories found within the author's family tree. She lives in the San Juan Islands of Washington State, where she homesteads at Longlight, a one-acre microfarm dedicated to sustainable permaculture practices.